Cl(

First published on Amazon in 2017

This is a work of fiction. Names, characters, businesses, places, events and incidents are either the products of the author's imagination or used in a fictitious manner. Any resemblance to actual persons, living or dead, or actual events is purely coincidental.

1

Chapter 1

It was barely six o'clock in the morning and still dark. The full moon shone high overhead boasting two small halos, dimly lighting the chilly air which felt too wintry for late September. Ralf stood just outside the front door, listening for the first signs of life in his scanty neighbourhood. The rattle of a chain inside a door a short distance away started things off, and the young couple whose name he couldn't remember emerged from their home. They acknowledged him as they always did and started up their car. Ralf chuckled to himself as their white Morris Minor choked into life and slowly moved off, jerking as it went around the corner.

Ralf loved where he lived. It was quiet and pretty, with very pleasant neighbours, especially the ones on either side of him. His favourites lived at number fourteen; Mr and Mrs Child. He was a keen gardener with a perennial smile upon his face, while his wife excelled in baking cakes and knitting, her Victoria Sponge her absolute favourite. At number ten lived George and Evelyn, they were lovely but ever so quiet. Ralf would knock on their door every now and again just to make sure they were okay. They had a TV and a record player, but nothing was ever heard coming out of their walls.

Ralf went back inside and into the kitchen to make some coffee and toast. He'd barely sat in the armchair in the lounge, when he heard the familiar sound of a diesel engine followed by the thud of a van door. He sprang up and reached the front door just before Ben the postman could ring the bell.

'Allo mate, up early ain't ya?' Intoned Ben, as he handed Ralf a parcel.

'Yeah, couldn't sleep. How's things? Gemma okay?'

'Yes mate, she's great. That fall didn't break 'er spirit. Tough as old boots, that one!'

'Glad to hear it Ben. Take care mate, thanks for the parcel. Catch you soon.'

Ralf unboxed his parcel and examined its contents. He held the big hardback book in his hands and read the title aloud with a nostalgic smile. 'Il Tesoro Di

Metamauco.' A tear ran down his face as he thumbed through the book briefly, before relegating it to the bookcase, making sure it sat behind the row of encyclopaedias. He often felt a smidgen of guilt about keeping his dark secret away from his friends, but it was better that way.

Another night of constant waking meant before long, Ralf was dozing in the comfort of his favourite chair. The trill of the telephone in the hallway startled him, and as he sprang up to answer it the doorbell rang as well. He swung the front door open and apologized as he darted back toward the trimphone.

'Hello, sorry can you hold the line just a second please, thanks...I got someone at the door.'

Ralf's face morphed into a pronounced frown when he realized who it was. A lady and a gentleman of middle age stood before him, the female holding up a pamphlet with the title *WATCHTOWER,* prominent as its heading. 'Have you heard the news, brother? Have you...'

'Oh look it's barely nine in the morning, why do you people insist on knocking on doors and annoying everyone with this crap? Why don't you just fuck right off!'

Ralf slammed the door on the two and ran back to the phone. A loud cackle could be heard coming from the handset. 'Jehovah's Witnesses I presume?' said the voice on the phone.

'Ah, fuckers! Can't stand them bastards. Especially when they... oh don't get me started on that one, because it'll just piss me off!'

'You make me roll, you do. So, you coming to the pool this morning? It'll be me and Debbie, Ozzie's coming and he might bring Julia along.'

'Who's Julia?'

'You know, Julia, Nicky's older sister. By the way, you know Nicky's got a soft spot for you; fuck knows why.'

'Cheeky sod. You know I scrub up pretty well for forty-eight.'

'Yeah, not bad baldy. Pick me up at ten?'

3

Ralf just made it to Pete's house for ten o'clock, and he emerged from his front door with his token Adidas bag, which he squeezed into the back seat of Ralf's Ford Capri. The two had been best friends for many years and their love for music was usually at the forefront of many of their conversations. Pete popped a cassette into the radio upon the dashboard. 'Just listen to this album mate. I got it yesterday from Tower Records!'

The song *Girls On Film,* came forth from the six-speaker system and Pete mentioned to Ralf that it was a group called Duran Duran. Ralf was enjoying its catchy melody and they managed to get through about six songs before they pulled into Gurnell Pool's car park, where Ozzie, Julia, and Pete's girlfriend Debbie, were waiting. Pete ran into Debbie's arms and lifted her off the ground while kissing her face and neck. Ozzie grinned and grabbed one of Julia's breasts as Ralf got out of the car, laughing.

'You're impossible, Ozzie!' He chuckled.

Ozzie was a rocker, pure and simple. He had long brown, shoulder length hair that often remained unwashed for a few weeks, a black leather jacket studded with badges and logos featuring his favourite rock bands such as Motorhead and ACDC, and stonewashed jeans that had slight rips at the knee area.

'Ah ya doin' mate... awright?' Ozzie had a strong handshake and a big heart. Julia was his latest in a long line of girlfriends and they'd been with each other for around two months, which was Ozzie's longest relationship so far, and he was clearly besotted with her. She had long dark hair, freckles that dotted her nose and cheeks and a smile that lit up her face. Julia apologized to Ralf, letting him know that her sister was unable to make it, and then the group of friends headed for the pool.

Gurnell centre boasted two pools, one for children and general chilling out and another which was a deeper and larger affair. Both pools were richly adorned with numerous house plants. They were artificial, but very attractive and lent the pools a rather soothing and organic appearance.

The group of friends went nearly every Sunday morning when it wasn't so busy. Both Ralf and Pete were strong swimmers, but their trips to Gurnell mostly involved huddling together in and around the water and just chatting away for a couple of hours, followed by another hour or so in the café that overlooked both pools through its large windows. Ozzie wasn't a bad swimmer either, but his mind was on other things that morning; he couldn't keep his eyes and hands off Julia, which resulted in a slight admonishment for too much petting, from one of the lifeguards. Ozzie responded remarkably well to the telling off, as Ralf and Pete waited for the possible ensuing barrage of colourful language to fill the air, but the rocker was amazingly sedate, considering.

Ozzie hated any kind of rules and regulations and often looked for ways to break them, usually resulting in heated exchanges and occasionally, a round of fisticuffs in which Ozzie usually came out on top. Pete and Ralf would often need to step in and hold back their rocker friend, sometimes catching the odd flailing blow from him as he got his point across of hating being told what to do.

'I don't believe it...he actually said *alright mate* instead of *fuck you, arsehole.'*

'He must be really besotted with Julia,' replied Ralf. 'Ozzie doesn't hold back when someone has even the slightest go at him. Wedding bells soon then.'

Ozzie strutted over to Pete and Ralf while mimicking the gestures of a drummer. He always wore his favourite swimming trunks with a Union Jack theme, and the words; *Hold Tightly Please* etched across the front. Everyone was surprised that none of the lifeguards spotted it. Ozzie sat between them as they made room for him just near the spectator seats.

'Well she's a good one, ya know. Dunno what she sees in me besides ma fasseek!'

'Your what?' Asked Ralf and Pete, in unison.

'Ma fasseek...ya know, ma luvverly body, ahahahahahah!'

Ozzie let out his trademark laugh, which sounded rather like a child imitating a machine gun.

'Ah you mean your physique.' replied Ralf.

'Yeah, yeah, jus' what I said, ahahahahahaha!'

5

After the session around the pool, the gang settled down for a few beverages in the café while people-watching from its large windows. Debbie and Pete were in deep discussion about where to go and eat out that same evening, while taking turns to listen to some music through Debbie's large headphones that plugged into her portable stereo cassette player. Julie and Ozzie were canoodling, with the rocker blowing in his girlfriend's ear. She was giggling and biting his nose. Ralf sat back sipping his coffee while grimacing at every taste, at how watery and flavourless it was. He smiled approvingly at his good friends and how happy they seemed. The thought of having some female company of his own didn't always occur to him. At times he thought it would be nice, but he wasn't usually bothered. Too much hassle was his first thought, and having to remember birthdays, Christmas, Valentine's Day, and so forth, ugh. He thought of Julia's sister, Nicky. He'd seen her a few times and they'd exchanged glances and fleeting smiles, but nothing more than that. She was attractive though, and apparently a good kisser. Ralf felt a slight stirring in his loins, but nullified the thought; at least for now.

'Oh Ralf,' exclaimed Julia, as she interrupted his train of thought. 'My sister wants to meet you. She says you have nice eyes and a nice mouth.'

Ralf smiled blushingly as the thought of Nicky's reputation of being a great kisser flashed through his mind. They all turned to look at Pete and Debbie as they burst into song while sharing a headphone each, as they stretched the headpiece as far as it would go. Pete was quite in tune, while Debbie was clearly a bathtub singer, but everyone recognized the Ultravox melody, *Vienna.*

After dropping Debbie off at her house in Acton, Ralf and Pete continued driving around for a while, as they discussed their usual plans for a project they'd both had for some time – a pipe dream of forming a band, a duo. Pete finally got the name he wanted after months of deliberating with Ralf as to which would be the best one from a long list of possibilities. 'Electroartz' – Pete even designed a stylized silver logo of the band name, with a capital Z at the end. All that was missing were musical instruments. Pete had a passion for synthesisers, and his bedroom wall was richly adorned with posters of different types; all very possible candidates.

The two friends often practiced at Pete's house mainly, as he had a few cassette decks and his latest pride and joy – besides Debbie – a reel-to-reel recorder. Ralf had a directional microphone and an unusual echo and reverb unit, about the size of a box of Matchmakers. Ralf also had his eyes on a keyboard he spotted in a shop, and was very serious about buying it.

'I actually tried it the other day in Dixons in West Ealing. There's a guy in there called Des; a really nice bloke who knows his stuff. It's a Casio keyboard; it's an MT68 or something. It's got loads of pre-set sounds and tons of rhythms, mate. It's bloody good.'

'Are you sure you want something like that, Ralf? I mean something that has auto-rhythm and stuff...I was thinking more along the lines of a drum machine and a mono synth for baselines, and a larger machine that would act as the main synth for melodies and stuff. A proper polyphonic synth. Fuck I'd love a Jupiter 6 or a JX-3P!'

'If only mate, if only!' chuckled Ralf. 'The thing is, I can't play the keyboard properly like you. You can play with two hands, but I need to play the automatic base with my left hand while plinking the melody with my right. I guess we could do some mixing with your reel-to-reel, what do you think?'

'Talk about plinking. My mum knows I want to get a synthesiser, and she keeps calling it a *plink-a-plonk*. A bloody *plink-a-plonk*. I tell you, that really fucks me off something chronic!'

Ralf let out a bellowing laugh that made Pete wince from its loudness. He loved the expression his mum used, but Pete wasn't quite as amused. He actually laughed at the way Ralf laughed so loudly, but after much deliberating about whether Ralf should buy the keyboard from Dixons, the two decided to go to Pete's house for a coffee and thumb through one of Pete's many magazines about synthesisers. As they drove toward his house in Northfields, Pete turned the car radio on. The song *Poison Arrow* had just come on Capitol Radio, and its andante beat and haunting, echoing saxophone melodies had the two friends pretty much entranced.

'I really like that,' exclaimed Ralf, 'That is one bloody good song. What did he say the band's called... ABC isn't it?'

'Yes mate, it *was* ABC. You're right, it *is* a good song.'

Ralf put his foot down as they drove down a straight road into Northfield Avenue. He loved it when music empowered him like that; he felt electrified, inspired, and ready for his musical mind to begin coming out with countless melodies for new songs to write with Pete.

Chapter 2

Ralf bashed on his alarm clock radio so hard he cracked the plastic front. It was seven in the morning and he'd had a bad night. The often recurring dream that plagued his sleep, usually made him wake up in the middle of the night with a jolt, then he would resume a normal slumber. This time it had stayed with him until a couple of hours before the rasping of the badly tuned clock radio. Ralf never told anyone about those dreams.

After a shower and a couple slices of toast, he left the house and crossed the road to go to work. Ralf was a school teacher and taught English and art to high school students at Hawk's High School, and it was a good thing that it stood just across the street from his house. He kind of liked that idea, as it wasn't very often that your workplace was just opposite your house.

Ralf liked his job and the satisfaction and rewards that came with it. His method of teaching was somewhat unconventional, but his class was full of loyal students who eventually came to understand what he was about. He was their form teacher since their first year at the school, and after more than two years, he'd gotten to know them all really well. He had a few favourites, some that showed great potential in their best and favourite subjects; a young lady named Anne, for example, was particularly gifted with words and poetry was her forte. She also excelled in art and cookery, but when Ralf took them for English and the subject featured creative writing, spelling, or poems, Anne usually came out on top with either an outstanding story or an enchanting poem.

Zack was a little clown but the life and soul of the party. His rude jokes, that often sailed close to the mark, were the highlight of many a lesson and Ralf was quite happy to listen to them, but only after checking that no other teachers were in close proximity. Ralf remembered Zack's Italian lorry driver joke, complete with fake Italian accent, as being a top contender. Lawrence, a blond haired chubby kid was rather fond of chemistry, but toward the end of the lesson, the fruit of his labours often consisted of stink bombs, which he'd save for the lesson after physics, which was maths. He, along with most of the other classmates, nurtured a particular discomfort for, and around the maths teacher, Mr Campion. 'He's queer, ya know, sir,' he would often tell Ralf. 'I worry 'bout me bollocks around 'im!'

Ralf had to keep a straight face, but ultimately admonished him for coming out with such things. Even if they were true, Ralf told Lawrence that it was wrong to judge people and if that were the case, Mr Campion couldn't help it. He added that Lawrence tell him first, if anything untoward ever occurred. Ralf knew deep inside that Daniel Campion was indeed homosexual, and more than once, noticed him glancing toward certain pupils in a particular way. He didn't confront Daniel until he was certain there was any danger. Ralf believed that everyone deserved a chance at being part of society and having a good job. He tried his level best never to drop anyone in it unless it was absolutely necessary.

Then there was Russell. He was the slightly more difficult one to tame, as he was always the bully in his year, and if he could get away with it, also of the years above and below him. Bullies were probably Ralf's biggest pet-hate, and he was determined to put an end to Russ's antics, but fortunately one of the pupils in the year above happened to be a close friend of one of Russell's latest victims, and ultimately gave him a good beating after school. Ralf watched the events unfold from around the corner while he was in a phone box. He didn't need to intervene, as it was over after just a few punches to Russell's face. After a lengthy chat with Ralf, the boy understood that karma always bites you on the arse sooner or later. Russell channelled his energies in his love for football. Despite his size, he was fast on the pitch and naturally skilful.

Michelle was an enigma. She was at times brilliant and other times she just fell flat on her face when it came to concentrating during lessons. Unfortunately, she hung around with tomboyish Karen, a fiery redhead with an attitude, and a stunning mixed race girl named Tanya, who had a mouth like the foulest of sewers. Ralf secretly nicknamed her *toilet mouth* and often had her stay behind after school, along with the other two, much to her disappointment, and although the colourful language would flow very freely, there was still a kind of mutual respect between them. Ralf knew of her problems at home with her alcoholic and unfaithful father who often beat upon his wife during moments of drunken stupor.

The rest of the class was a mixed bag of clowns, lazybones experts, and masters of Space Invaders during lunchtime and after school, and Ralf was fascinated by them. He was great at communicating with them at their own level, and no subject matter was ever too shocking, too wrong, or too bizarre. That's why they all liked him.

As he pushed his way through the entrance double doors, the head mistress, Miss Clare, marched rapidly in his direction. Ralf nervously looked behind him, hoping that she was perhaps gunning for someone else, but it wasn't the case. She was soon upon him like a lioness to a gazelle. She brought her lips so close to his ear, he could smell her breath – a mix of coffee and a peanut butter sandwich – he could feel another nickname coming on; *Death Breath Clare.*

'It's one of your students,' she hissed. 'That Lawrence Brady. He's in my office in tears...he won't talk to me. The lad seems terrified.'

'I understand. Give me two secs and I'll come have a word with him.'

'I insist you go see him now, Ralf. I'll take your class while you're gone. He says he'll only talk to you. '

'Okay, thanks Miss Clare. I'll be as quick as I can.'

Miss Clare grabbed his arm as he turned to go; 'Make sure you tell me what's going on, won't you Mr Avalon. I won't have students keeping things from me!'

Ralf hurried to the headmistress' office. He hated when Miss Clare had any type of conversation with him – especially when she started off calling him by his first name, and then finished off by calling him Mr Avalon – it always made him feel uneasy. In fact, of all his colleagues, Miss Clare was the one he had any dislike for. He never really took to anyone who was reliant on overconfidence, officiousness, or who liked the sound of their own voice. He entered the office and Lawrence, who was sat huddled with his head in his hands, looked up startled. His eyes were red from bitter-weeping and his shirt was hanging out of his trousers. Ralf pulled up a chair and sat opposite him and smiled reassuringly.

'Okay Lawrence, what's up mate?'

The frightened child shook his head and looked down at his shoes, sniffling. Ralf had never seen him like this before, not in over two years of being his teacher. The kid was shivering as though he felt cold, but the room was warm. He was clearly scared and unsure, and Ralf was worried. He asked him once again, what was wrong. Lawrence was silent and continued to bury his face in his hands.

'Take your time mate, no one's rushing you. When you're ready, you can tell me. You know you can. You want some water?'

At that point, Lawrence's head came up to face his teacher, and he nodded. Ralf took a small bottle of water from Miss Clare's desk and after checking that it hadn't already been opened, he handed it to the boy, who proceeded to down at least half of it. He paused for a few more minutes before finally talking to Ralf.

'He touched me...I knew he would. I told ya so.'

'Who touched you, Lawrence?'

'It was...Campion, sir...I went to the gym to get my new kit. He was there and....'

'And what mate?'

Lawrence burst into tears once again, and this time Ralf placed a hand on each shoulder. He waited until he was able to compose himself a little and speak once more.

'He said he had to fix my trousers...he put his 'ands up 'em, sir... then he tried to undo the zip.'

Ralf's blood began to boil. He knew the boy was telling the truth as he was one of the lads that Daniel Campion had particular eyes for. He thought back to when he caught his colleague gawping at Lawrence while he took a shower after a double games lesson. Mr Campion took the latter half of the lesson and therefore, was in charge of the boys getting showered and changed. Ralf went back to the pavilion to reclaim his watch, which he often forgot to pick up from his locker. Campion didn't see him as he stayed in the shadows to start with, but Ralf watched as he kept a particularly keen eye on Lawrence. He didn't want to believe it at first; his usual habit of giving the benefit of the doubt.

'I know this is bloody hard for you, Lawrence. I'm on your side, but just try and tell me if he did anything else, mate. Take your time, but I need to know everything so I can help you.'

The boy sniffed upwards to stop his nose running, and Ralf reached into Miss Clare's desk drawer for a tissue. Lawrence wiped his eyes and continued through his tears.

'He kept kissing my neck, he said I smelt nice. Then he…. he put his… hand down….' Lawrence could contain himself no longer, as he broke down and threw himself into his teacher's arms. At that moment, the headmistress walked in, a stern look was upon her face. She rolled her eyes and walked over to Ralf and Lawrence.

'Hey, pull yourself together lad. We won't have any of that in here. You're a little old for blubbing. Come now, enough of that!' Miss Clare continued to poke the boy on his shoulder, as she grew frustrated with his continued weeping.

'Miss Clare, I think that's quite enough!' Snapped Ralf, as he brushed her prodding finger away from the back of Lawrence's neck. 'Might I suggest calling Lawrence's mother… now!'

The headmistress stepped away and sat behind her desk and with a rather sheepish look on her face. Never had she been put in her place by any member of staff that happened to be below her in rank. She hated it. She began to thumb through a bundle of printed paper that had been stapled together. Lawrence could barely speak from crying and panicking and so Ralf proceeded to lead him out of the office and toward the school gates. Miss Clare was already on the phone to the boy's mother, Brenda.

Lawrence's parents divorced some ten years ago, and they lived in the town of Acton, not too far away from Chiswick, where the school was. His father passed away a couple of years ago, leaving his son devastated and Brenda, penniless. After finding a job as a hairdresser thanks to her college course and qualification, life became a little more affordable and bearable. Ralf had met Brenda on a couple of occasions during parent evenings at the school.

Teacher and student sat upon a bench in the school's forecourt and playground for around fifteen minutes and neither had uttered a single word. Brenda pulled up in her car and Ralf walked over to her with Lawrence, who immediately dove into his mother's arms. The boy was too exhausted for any more tears, and went to wait in the car while his mother and his teacher went over to a climbing frame nearby, for a chat.

'What's going on?' asked a worried Brenda. 'Miss Clare said I needed to come here urgently, but didn't say why. Is Lawrence okay?'

'Well, this is a first, definitely,' said Ralf, as he passed his hand over his head.

'What is it?'

'Lawrence has told me one of the teachers touched him inappropriately.'

'Who touched him *inappropriately*?' asked Brenda, on the verge of losing control. 'Which teacher would do something like that?'

'I can't say for sure until I can prove something, but he's pretty messed up. I've never seen him in that state before. The teacher in question *is* homosexual, but I must ask you not to panic or be anxious around Lawrence. It'll only make things worse. I know you're very upset, but in order to get to the bottom of it, I need a little time.'

'It's his bloody maths teacher isn't it?'

'Brenda...'

'He always said he hated him, he always hated the way that dirty bastard kept looking at him, and now he's... TOUCHED him as well, I can't fucking believe it, I...'

Ralf took Brenda in his arms and held her tight until she was able to calm herself a little. He felt his jumper becoming soaked from two sets of tears, and couldn't wait to get rid of it as soon as he got the chance to nip across the street to his house; but first and foremost, there was something he needed to do.

'Okay?' He smiled, while brushing wet hair from her eyes. 'Just take Lawrence home and I promise I'll keep you posted.'

Ralf went back inside and resumed his class. The crowd fell silent as he entered the classroom and one of the boys asked if Lawrence was okay and what had happened to him.

'Oh, he's just a little under the weather, Eric. Nothing drastic, touch of the flu. Okay young people,' he announced in his usual cheerful manner, to which the class always responded with escalating enthusiasm. It usually meant he was going to give them either one of his spelling tests where they had to think of a word that corresponded with a definition and then spell it correctly, or announce the next topic for creative writing. 'Pens at the ready – I'm going to give you some definitions – this time of a particular theme. Once you have the correct word, I want you to spell it. From these results, we're going to write the best story you've ever written. Got it?'

By the end of the mini spelling bee, it was clear that the theme was horror and the supernatural. Ralf knew the class loved that sort of thing and their heads were down before he could bat an eyelid. The remaining forty five minutes of the lesson flew by, not just for the class but for Ralf as well. He was sat at his desk in such deep thought, that he almost drifted off a couple of times. The pips chirped loud and distorted through the loudspeaker, and the class began packing their books away in time for the next lesson; maths.

As the kids tussled out of the room and dispersed into the dark corridor, Ralf's blood began to boil once again, as he made his way to the maths room, where Campion was lying in wait. It was unfortunate, but that was the only image he could picture; a filthy predator with a tenebrous dark side, just waiting for the next youngster to befriend and make his own. He thought of Lawrence and how he wept so bitterly while clinging to him, like the father figure the kid clearly missed having in his life.

Ralf knocked on the door to the maths room and popped his head inside, summoning Mr Campion. The teacher was curious and followed immediately as Ralf led him to the lecture theatre on the top floor. Ralf didn't answer when Mr Campion asked him where they were going. The two teachers entered the lecture theatre and Ralf switched the light on and stepped a little away from Campion and leaned upon the lectern.

The entire room was like a large semi-circle and adorned with dark brown wooden seats that went from the centre all the way up to the top edge, with just enough room to inch your way through, between each row of chairs. A huge white screen stood against the wall behind where Ralf was leaning against the dark wooden lectern, which had a menacing gargoyle on each side where your hands usually would rest while lecturing. There were three neon tubes that hung from the high ceiling, one of which was not functioning.

'Well, what is it Avalon, I haven't got all day, and why the bloody hell are we all the way up here?'

'I'm going to ask you something... I already know for a fact, that you're not going to tell me the truth, but I'm going to ask you anyway.'

'What?' asked Campion. 'This is actually quite weird!'

'Oh, weird is it. And you're a fine one to talk.'

'Look,' said Campion, as he unfolded his arms and began turning toward the door, 'If you won't tell me what's going on here, I'm just gonna go. I do have a class to teach!' Campion turned the handle but realized Ralf had locked the door. He turned toward him and snapped, demanding that he let him out.

'Okay, the boy in my class called Lawrence Brady,' continued Ralf. 'Apparently you were in the gym with him earlier on today, when he came to get his new kit from his locker. Tell me what happened.'

Ralf could see that Mr Campion was perspiring, as the light picked up the beads of sweat upon his forehead. There were dark patches forming under his armpits as well. Campion replied that he didn't know what Ralf was talking about and continued rattling the doorknob, demanding that he be let out. He cried for help a couple of times, but in vain.

'No one can hear you yell up here, Campion. No matter how loud you shout. Now tell me what happened with that kid, because I'm growing very impatient.'

'Look, I don't know what the fuck you mean, Ralf. He just came to get his football kit...like you said. What the bloody hell's he been saying?'

'What makes you think he's been *saying* anything?'

Ralf began slowly walking toward Daniel Campion, who was clearly frightened and guilt-ridden. All he needed to do was push a little more and he may get Campion to admit something or drop himself in it. Ralf moved closer still and clearly noticed that Mr Campion's perspiration had reached acute levels. His glasses were steamed up and his tatty mop of hair was sticking to his face.

'What did you do to him?' snarled Ralf, now just mere feet away from him.

'L..look, he was just, standing there in his underpants for ages and...'

'And what, Campion... thought you'd have a free fondle did you?'

Daniel's back was against the door, his hands shaking with fear and his face red and blotchy. He removed his glasses and put them in the inside pocket of his jacket.

'H...he was asking for it, you know...just standing there in his pants. You think it was just me...then why would he stand there for ages in front of me with just his PANTS, for fuck's sake!?'

Ralf's arms began to shake and he could feel a red mist descend in front of his eyes. He'd felt that same rage before, many years ago in similar circumstances; but that time, he'd lost control. He began to slowly step toward the sweaty and quivering Campion, his fists clenched so tightly, he could feel his fingernails piercing the palms of his hands. Daniel's bottom lip began to shake as though he was about to burst into tears at any second and he wiped his eyes and tried the doorknob once again. He turned to face Ralf once more. This time it was Ralf himself who began to well up inside, his eyes becoming watery and thus distorting the image of the pathetic Campion . Ralf wiped his right eye with the back of his hand and tried to calm himself down. He had two choices; one of them was to smash his fist into Campion's puffy face and keep pounding until he breathed no more – that would bring the inevitable result of murder if he killed him, or a very serious assault charge if he just beat him to within an inch of his life, which he was truly itching to do – or the second choice was to do the right thing. He mustn't do what he did all those years ago. Look what it brought him. Well, it wasn't so bad, but it could've been much worse. He took quick but deep breaths while focusing on Campion, his tatty clothes, stupid mop-like hairstyle, his ridiculous paunch under which you could barely see his belt, and his rather ill-fitting trousers which he wore day in, day out while he was at school.

'I'm going to open the door now,' Ralf said softly, 'and I'm going to stay here while you walk away and go back home. The kid told me everything; and I'm going to press charges.'

Ralf moved toward Campion and as he shuffled clumsily sideways away from the door, Ralf put the key in the lock and let Campion out. He edged out of the room while keeping his eyes on Ralf at all times, until he disappeared from view after pushing through a door at the end of the upper walkway that overlooked the assembly hall and stage. Ralf gave a deep and long sigh and stood in the doorway of the lecture theatre for what felt like hours. He didn't care. He was waiting for the raging ocean of anger that crashed around inside him to become the sea of stillness he had learned to control over the years.

He thought back to the book that arrived in the post and that he'd hidden on his bookcase. When he thought of that, it was his medicine; his only happy thought. His way of coping with the part of his mind that was often like an untameable beast with an insatiable appetite. It worked this time as well; it just took a little longer, but it worked its magic. He and his dark side would now return to his duties. He had a narrow escape; but so did Daniel Campion.

Chapter 3

Ralf left the school around an hour later than usual. He couldn't keep his mind focused on the latest batch of creative writing from his English class; the only thing he could think of was his earlier confrontation with the maths teacher, Mr Campion. One of Ralf's bad points was bearing grudges; and it was unfortunate that his grudges had very long legs. Years would pass from the day something or someone pissed him off and he wouldn't let it slide. Water under the bridge was alien to him; Ralf was all about retribution and revenge. Karma and comeuppances. He would more often stand up for someone else, rather than himself. That was how he was made, and was not prepared to change.

He rang Brenda as soon as he got home and mentioned everything that happened; the confrontation with Campion, the long discussion with Miss Clare, and phone call to the police. Brenda agreed to remain in the house until the police paid her a visit to take statements and proceed from there. Ralf politely declined an invitation for dinner afterwards; he did like Brenda, but the usual rules on professional distances, fraternizing with pupils' parents, and so on. He detested such rules usually, rebelling against them wherever he found himself. He believed that friendships and alliances were made regardless; you couldn't stop humans from being human. The more these stupid rules were enforced, the more people with a passion for life and fire in their bellies would break them.

Ralf worked at Heathrow Airport some years before becoming a school teacher. He was a sales consultant in a Duty Free shop and struck a close friendship with plenty of colleagues; in particular, with a man named Damien and a lovely lady named Lucy. Many of his line managers were around half his age and were adamant that his relationship with Lucy in particular, was hampering his ability to perform his job role properly, which of course, was completely untrue. Ralf never took any crap from anyone and usually voiced his opinions literally and ruthlessly, uncaring of whose feelings he may hurt in the process. His outburst after the umpteenth accusation of fraternizing and underperforming yielded the Wrath of Ralf. You usually *never* fuck with the Wrath of Ralf.

'Fuck you and your bloody ridiculous rules and regulations. Lucy is a close friend of mine and when she's near me on the shop floor, it's because she helps me when the tills are busy during the Russian and Chinese flights. I do my job just fine, so don't invent shit that doesn't exist. Whether I'm shagging her after work hours or not is none of your fucking business; You don't bat an eyelid when Damien helps me on the tills, do you? How do you know I'm not raiding *his* rectum? That doesn't bother you does it? You call yourselves managers...you're barely fucking twenty and still smelling of milk...do you know how much experience I have compared to you foreskin faces that are just about half my age!? I was doing your jobs while you were all still in your grandad's bollocks! Stupid, bloody kids!'

Ralf loved theatrical monologues, and he felt wonderful after that latest one. Lucy kept in touch until she moved to Scotland with her elderly mother, and Damien returned to his native Sri Lanka to practice his trade as a lawyer, after saving enough funds to open up a law firm near where he lived. The managers who had the unfortunate stench of lactose that lingered about their person eventually hung up their Duty Free attire to pursue other careers away from the airport. Ralf bumped into two of them at a nearby Tesco, while another was working at a petrol station near the M4 motorway entrance.

As he sipped a cup of strong filter coffee in the lounge, he thumbed through his Italian book to calm his nerves. The latest grudge to bear was one of the stronger ones and hung over him like a potent curse from an angry shaman. The image of the sweaty and unfortunate Campion kept hanging around like an extremely irritating and unwanted guest. A bad smell. Like one of those annoying bastards that drift around at parties wearing tweed or big chequered jackets, with sneering and belittling smiles, and impossible comb-overs. To top it all off, they'd also think they were cool and big hits with the ladies. The last plonker of that ilk met a rather painful ending at one of Ozzie's parties – his little nephew's fifth birthday – Ralf was having a rather interesting conversation with a lady about ghosts and the paranormal, when the aforementioned plonker found it amusing to persist in butting in with derogatory remarks, that belittled every question and answer. Ralf knocked the idiot's drink onto his lap, and feigned a stumble apologetically, elbowing the fellow across the jaw, knocking him out cold. Others had had their feet stomped on, pushed over, he even farted on one guy; it was one of his *Ralf specials,* a loud, crackling one. Ralf always referred to those kinds of farts as *flattening a duck.*

The trimphone chirped like a sportsman's whistle, jolting Ralf out of his thoughts. It was best friend, Pete asking him if they were all still on for that evening at their favourite after work haunt; Mike's Music City. It was a large bar situated along the Chiswick high street, where drinks and food were served upstairs, but downstairs was where the action was. Every night there were different bands that offered their own versions of current chart classics, seventies hits, and some of them even played their own material, much of which was just as pleasing to the ear as many of the current songs on the charts.

'Yeah mate, I'll see you there; unless you want to go in my car, in that case I'll come get you around eight-ish.'

'I think I'd better come to you, you sound like you've just killed someone. Wasn't that old bat of the headmistress was it?'

'No, silly arse, chuckled Ralf, just had a rather...*eventful* day, that's all. I'll fill you in on it later.'

After picking up Debbie, Ozzie, and Julia, Pete passed by Hawkshead Road to collect Ralf. They drove down The Avenue and parked somewhere along Turnham Green Terrace, just outside a shop called Domat Design. The shop belonged to a friend of Ralf's, and it specialized in marionettes and puppets, which the owner, Chris, fashioned with his own hands. He also sold a variety of puppetry related odds and ends, such as mini theatres, Punch and Judy stands, Muppet Show characters, and so on. Ralf had bought a doggie puppet which he'd named Domino the dog; a large open-backed canine character with an orange mane of fur and a green top and burgundy, corduroy trousers. At one point Ralf thought himself a bit of a ventriloquist, but after a number of small shows in primary schools and the odd small pub, he decided to give up and stick to singing. The decision was made when someone made a video of him during his last act and showed it to him; he had a very unfortunate and maniacal grin upon his face whilst throwing his voice, and when he heard himself muttering phrases like *gottle of geer and fretty feofle,* Ralf realized it was time to hang Domino upon a hook under the staircase at home. As soon as he switched the light on under there earlier that evening, he felt haunted by Domino's presence, just hanging there like a lifeless corpse dressed up like a seventies David Bowie.

While Ozzie and Julia walked on ahead of them with Debbie following close behind snapping pictures with her camera, Pete had his hand upon Ralf's shoulder, quizzing him about his eventful day. Ralf felt like the weight that had been lifted off of him earlier in the day had just been dropped back onto his shoulders.

'Fuck; I probably didn't hear the phone ring while I was in the bath. Shortly after, I went out the front door to get in your car. Brenda probably tried to call me!'

'Who's Brenda?' Asked Pete, thinking his friend had a new love interest perhaps.

'Lawrence's mum,' replied Ralf, I gotta go back and ring her. Can I quickly use your car? You go on to the bar and I'll catch up ASAP; promise!'

'I'll go with you. Not that I don't trust you with my car, I'm just worried about you mate. You don't seem yourself.'

Ralf reluctantly agreed and they zoomed back up to Ralf's house at number twelve. Brenda answered after a couple of rings and Ralf could straight away tell that there was something wrong, by her croaky and exhausted sounding voice. The news she gave him was like a smack in the face, but Ralf should have seen it coming. Campion had done a runner; when the police arrived at his flat, he'd gone. There were clothes and an old flight bag strewn across the floor in the lounge and his wardrobe was practically empty, Brenda told him.

'He's buggered off...gone with the fucking wind. Bastard. He'll probably do it to somebody else now; some other poor little kid!'

'Brenda, it's fine, they'll get him before he does anything else. He won't get far. How's Lawrence?'

'Oh he seems fine at the minute. His friend Jonas is here, you know, the one from that school in Acton. They're watching that Alien movie in the sitting room.'

Ralf could just about make out a Yazoo song playing in the background in Brenda's house somewhere. He remembered it from last week when Pete was trying to replicate the bouncy synthesiser solo on his little Casio VL1. After feeling a little guilty for not answering the phone earlier when she undoubtedly called and being distracted by a piece of music playing in her house, he offered to go round there tomorrow night after work, to see if things are okay and have a chin-wag with her son.

'Can you tell me what the hell's going on?' Said an inquisitive Pete, in a higher pitched voice than usual.

'Sorry bro; I was just too...I dunno...shocked maybe, to be able to talk about it. But it stays between us, yeah?'

'Oh come on mate, you know I won't say anything...how long you known me?'

Ralf embraced his friend and they both sat in the lounge with the TV on low volume, while telling him the tale of the Campion. Pete was shocked and ultimately gutted that his friend had to go through that kind of an ordeal, but thoroughly admired Ralf for handling it without breaking any bones. After getting all of his chest, Ralf went and grabbed his flamboyant stereo cassette player at Pete's request. Pete went and got a tape from the car and enthusiastically slammed it into the receptacle and hit the play button. The Yazoo song that he caught during the phone call to Brenda blared and bounced out of the speakers, that unmistakable and poppy synth solo that preceded the part that was sung.

'Yeah, this is great, Ralf intoned, 'I heard this in Brenda's house while on the phone with her. I love the synth bits!'

'You listen to her voice; it surprisingly suits the music. Listen!'

Alison Moyet's warm, bluesy voice clung to the andante melody like beautiful ivy to a wall. She had a lovely, rapid, and surging vibrato that enriched every note she sung, and her timbre, diction, and inflection were crystal clear. The song was entitled *Don't Go.* Ralf wanted to hear the rest of the album and as time passed, through chat and the tape, the two pals realized it was ten o'clock and a bit too late to head to the bar. Pete let slip that he'd composed a couple of instrumental melodies with his little VL1 and was anxious to let Ralf hear them the next day. He also revealed he had a name for the band.

'Band...what band?'

'Our band,' Pete replied with a broad smile, 'the one I've been meaning to get going for ages with you, ya plant.'

Ralf smiled with sweet surprise, and the two close friends went on to chat well into the early hours, through numerous mugs of tea for Pete and strong filter coffee for Ralf.

'Won't that strong stuff stop you sleeping?' asked Pete, 'I've never been able to get beyond two sips of that bloody coffee you love so much.'

'Aha,' said Ralf, doing jazz-hands, 'I've been drinking this elixir since childhood mate; doesn't affect me at all now. It's bloody good after a big meal; helps you digest beautifully!'

Pete looked a little beyond Ralf's chair and spotted a large, hardback book on the small coffee table. He reached and took it in his hands and began studying the cover, most inquisitively.

'What's this book?' he asked with an interested expression. Pete had this unusual benevolent frown when he was curious about something. It usually made Ralf smile; but not this time. He felt the words *Oh shit* echo in his brain, as he tried to quickly figure out what answer to throw back at his friend.

'Oh that belonged to Enza and Raffaele; an old couple that used to live here before I did. I found it in the loft while rummaging. Fuck knows what it's about. I think it's in Italian or something. Couldn't make neither head nor tail of it.'

'Hmm, interesting. It's got pictures of Venice in it. Must be a history book or something.' Pete said while thumbing through it. Ralf frowned at him. But not benevolently.

Pete left at around half past four in the morning, leaving Ralf in a state of mind that made him so nervous, that it quickly affected his stomach. After a lengthy bathroom reading session in a tub full of hot water and enough bubbles to hide in, Ralf returned downstairs to the lounge and read a little more of his book. He hated lying, especially to his best friend. Ralf hated people who held back as well, and now, he had just practiced becoming one of them. He was always a very open and down-to-earth man, and to him, those types who kept everything inside and thrived on yes and no answers, were one of his pet-hates. One of a long list, but at that moment, he didn't wish to mull those over. Every time he thought of them, it just pissed him off. He placed the book upon the bookcase again; he didn't need to hide it from view now. He just hoped Pete had bought his little white lie. Yes, he truly detested bullshitting his closest friend. But he *had* to.

Chapter 4

Pete was up nice and early that Thursday morning. He called his work and told them he wasn't going in today; stomach cramps. It was true, he *did* have them that morning and it was down to Ralf's insistence that he try some real coffee as Ralf put it, instead of that instant granule crap that he called *a shitty coffee drink.* Pete began to really develop a taste for it, especially espresso. It did indeed help him to digest; just a little too much.

After phoning Ralf and complaining that his so-called *elixir*, made him pebble-dash the potty, he called him a plant, a pleb, a git, a penis, and a complete and utter knob. 'Oh by the way,' Pete said, 'Ozzie said the band we missed the other night was apparently bloody good. They're on again tonight and they play some rock music. He said they sound a bit like that group he likes, that new rock band' Asia. He played me some of their stuff Ralf...you'll love it mate...Asia, I mean.'

'Okay mate, it's a date,' replied Ralf, 'You coming here to me first?'

'Yeah why not. We could walk down this time, I fancy a few drinks.'

Pete's father, John called him from the kitchen, asking him if he fancied any toast with his tea. 'Yes please, dad. Oh mum wants to use the car to go to Sainsbury's. She wants to know if...'

'No!' Replied John, with a firmness in his voice that usually meant he couldn't be talked round to it this time.

Susan, Pete's mother was a very cheerful and smiley lady. She looked great for her age, with dark shoulder length hair, blue eyes, and a talent for painting and making the best mashed potato Pete had ever tasted. She worked as a traffic warden at Heathrow airport, often crossing paths with Ralf when he finished his shift, before going into teaching. She and John were always full of life and often teased Pete about many things; such as his walk – he kind of bounced along while slightly bent forwards; kangaroos had nothing on him – and his high forehead. Ralf took the piss out of that particular feature of Pete's, but put it down to his intelligence and methodical ways, coupled with infinite patience when undertaking any task. Ralf used to tell him that his brain needed more space, so it could process information more easily. Pete called him a shithead.

After breakfast and another bathroom break, Pete retreated to his bedroom to do some more composing on the VL1. Peter's room was large but methodically filled and furnished. His wardrobe stood at the foot of his bed and next to the window that overlooked the back garden. Next to the wardrobe stood a tall and wide unit that housed his stereo stack-system that was split into different areas, comprising of tape-deck, amplifier, and record player at the bottom, and a small Sony Trinitron television that was connected to a video player that sat in a neat space just beneath it. Next to that was his desk, atop which stood his computer and cassette rack that was filled with audio tapes that he usually mixed himself and used black letter-transfers to entitle them. Ralf always showed an interest in Pete's collection of tapes with the words PARTY MIX written on the sides of the cassette cases. He had great taste for picking songs and bunching them together in one compilation.

John came stomping upstairs and headed for the bathroom, but shuffled out again, stumbling, and almost falling down the stairs.

'Peteeeerrrr!' He exclaimed.

'Yes dad!'

'You didn't open the window and it smells like something's just crawled in here and died!'

'Sorry dad!'

'I can't go in there for at least half an hour!'

'Sorry dad!'

John shuffled down the stairs stopping every few seconds, making Pete wonder what was going on. He heard his dad mutter something as he rounded the corner at the bottom of the staircase and head toward the kitchen.

'...'Think I've shit myself...'

Pete sniggered and felt slightly guilty and shouted at the top of his voice, 'Sorry dad!'

He heard the garden door opening and his father's voice stating that it wasn't funny. As the wooden door to the outside toilet slammed shut, Pete burst into fits of uncontrolled laughter as he heard John's distant and muffled voice shouting his disdain for outside bogs and bloody cold toilet seats. Pete laughed until his eyes were streaming with tears; then his mother ascended the staircase and dared to enter the bathroom. She walked straight out and down the stairs, cursing her son under her breath, 'For Christ's sake, Peter...' The rest, Pete couldn't understand, but he felt they weren't going to be talking to him for the rest of the day; at least until dinner time. 'Shit happens.' He grinned, as he continued plinking and writing.

Ozzie was at home and in his bedroom listening to a new record he had bought earlier in the day. It was his third play-through of the album, and he called Julia up to his room, as she had come to his house to visit. He grew a little impatient, as she had been chatting to his parents for at least forty five minutes after she had arrived, and he was feeling rather fruity. He began rearranging the contents of his trousers as soon as he heard the floorboards on the stairs creak from footsteps, and quickly unzipped his jeans, whipped his erect penis out and put a bright purple ribbon around it that he'd tied into a bow. He lay back and closed his eyes as the bedroom door slowly opened.

'Oi, you fuckin' dirty bastard!' Ozzie jumped out of his skin and curled into a ball quicker than lightning, and let out a cry of pain as his mother entered the room. 'Fer fack's sake mum, I've just 'urt me cock. What the fackin' 'ell you doin' in 'ere!?'

'Put that disgustin' thing away – and why 'ave you got a stupid ribbon around it for!? – what're you like!?'

Ozzie's mum turned to exit the room while covering her eyes and bumped her nose on the edge of the door. She let out an ear-piercing cry, and within seconds, the whole house was thrown into a cacophony of cries, curses, and thumping and thudding, as Ozzie's world crumbled before his very eyes. This was too much. His mother had just seen his dick; the last time she laid eyes upon it, was the last time she changed his nappy. After that Ozzie was self-sufficient and his shaft was for his eyes only; and now Julia's, but she was killing herself laughing downstairs, while his manhood almost instantaneously quit standing to attention. Ozzie knew that today, the train wouldn't be entering the tunnel.

Debbie Graves was standing behind the counter in the shoe shop where she worked in Ealing Broadway. She'd been at Lily and Skinner for over a year now and the only thing she liked about it was the generous staff discount which enabled her to accumulate a pretty sizeable collection of footwear. She was the proud owner of thirty seven pairs of shoes. Debbie wasn't overly enamoured with her job, but customers took to her; in particular, a recent admirer who'd been loitering around outside the store at lunchtimes and after closing. Debbie hadn't told Pete about the stalker as she knew he would definitely give the guy a kicking; besides, she knew him from school and he'd always had quite a crush on her. And who could blame him; Debbie Graves was a stunner. She had short and flicked back, centre-parted auburn hair and her smooth skin was always tanned, making her look Maltese or Greek or Italian. She had deep ocean-blue eyes and every time she and Pete got together, along with Ozzie, Julia, and Ralf, she often wore mini-skirts, happily putting her superb legs on display.

Just a little before closing time, Pete decided to appear at the store and surprise his beautiful girlfriend, and her lovely eyes lit up as soon as she saw him, but almost immediately her happy expression faded as her admirer, Andrew Blaine, stepped into view. Pete hadn't noticed her discomfort or Andrew who sported an enormous grin as his eyes crossed hers. Pete was leaning against the metal barrier near the traffic light when Andrew accosted him and handed him a piece of paper.

'Excuse me mate, you going in there at all...'cause I was wondering like...could you give this note to that girl in there for us? I didn't want to go in there myself, as I don't want to seem too pushy like, you know...'

Pete did his inquisitive frown again, but it wasn't a happy inquisitive; more like who the fuck are you, inquisitive.

'That girl there, said Blaine, pointing at Debbie, 'the gorgeous one. I'd love to smash 'er back doors in.'

At that point, Pete grabbed the guy's right shoulder pad and punched him square in the face, knocking him back several feet, and as he rolled back along the ground his head hit the metal barrier.

'That's my girlfriend you're talking about, you daft little shit!'

An arm of steel twisted Pete's arm behind his back, as an on duty constable enforced the law upon him. Debbie ran out of the shop and desperately tried to convince the policeman that her boyfriend was acting in her defence from a slimy stalker, but her pleas were in vain, as Peter was led away by the huge officer of the law, who was eventually joined by a female partner. She in turn, tried to comfort an anguished Debbie. Andrew was still out cold, and Pete felt his stomach tie into knots as a siren could be heard in the distance just above the noise of the curious bystanders, and grew steadily louder.

Ralf had been trying to get through to Pete for over two hours and was just about to go to his house and se if all was okay, when the phone rang. It was Pete's father.

'Oh hello Mr Sheridan. Everything okay?'

'Yes Ralf, it is now. Peter's on his way to you so he asked me to give you a quick call. Unfortunately, I had to go and bail him out...'

'Bail him out!?' Interrupted Ralf and apologising immediately after for doing so.

'I'm afraid so...but I'll let him tell you the rest. Bye for now.'

Pete pulled up outside shortly after the phone call and Ralf was eager to hear the news.

'That cu....arsehole actually pressed charges...can you believe that? He actually pressed charges. Good thing his dad persuaded him to drop them. Apparently he knows my dad from the training seminars at his work so they're sort of mates. But what a wanker, eh?'

'I don't blame you bro; I'd have done the same thing. Can't have bloody stalkers after Debbie. Is she okay after all this?'

'Yeah she's fine. She can't make it tonight though; said she's going to her nan's for dinner with her parents. Shame; she'd have loved the band. And on that note…geddit…on that note?'

'Yeeesss,' groaned Ralf, 'I get it. Do you still fancy going down there? I *can* understand if you're not up to it. You've kind of had a helluva day.'

'Nah, I'm fine mate. Could do with taking my mind off it. Besides, this band is the works according to Ozzie.'

The two pals made their way down to the bar on foot and didn't realize how far it actually was; it took an hour to walk down there, and Ozzie and Julie were waiting at the entrance for them. Ozzie hurried them both inside and downstairs, as the band were only playing for another half hour. The atmosphere was sizzling and the crowd was thick. The sound system the band used was obviously a rather expensive one, as the guitar riffs, drum beats, vocals, and keyboards were clear and distinguished. The lead singer wasn't anything to write home about unfortunately, but the band played their own material and their melodies were safe and true to the rock formula, with steady baselines, powerful chords, the electric guitar player performed arpeggios and twangy flanged note-bending upon his instrument, that he shone through and won the audience over more so than the lead vocalist.

Within minutes, the gang were dancing and swaying while Ozzie contorted himself in the middle of the dance-floor, playing air guitar. The lighting over the audience was dimmed to a minimum, while white and blue spotlights highlighted the stage and its musical occupants, making them look like ethereal creatures of the night, as they twisted and spun around. The drummer remained in penumbra, while the other band members were struck by the rays of stage lighting, like an alien abduction, swirling dust particles visible in the blades of light, like a swarm of locusts. The band played beyond the thirty minutes they had left, stretching the total to fifty five. The crowd were sweating buckets and were rapturous. Cigarette smoke hung in the air, blending with the flashing and flickering lights. The band was called Nightwave. Ralf and friends felt that they were going to go far.

Chapter 5

Friday morning paved the way for a nasty headache as Ralf put his feet down from the bed. He went in to work but returned home after just one English class. Miss Clare wasn't too happy about it, but then again, neither was Ralf. He hated taking time off work unless it was absolutely necessary, but when one of his nasty but rare headaches gripped him, he was usually out for the count for most of the day. As he lay in bed, he remembered that he didn't go over to Brenda's house the previous night as he'd promised. He rang her and profusely apologised, and she sounded a little disappointed, but was okay with it; as long as he let her come round to his place and cook for him. And she didn't seem to want to take no for an answer. He reluctantly agreed.

Pete was sat in the lounge at around six o'clock with his parents, as they sat having dinner upon their laps. Susan had cooked one of Pete's favourite dishes; the *Sheridan Share Fry*. She cooked it in a large wok, and it consisted of sausages cut into small pieces, cubed Spam, sliced potatoes, onions, occasionally she would add thin strips of frying steak – she did that evening – and sprouts. Ralf had it a few times and loved it. He always used to hint to Pete to invite him round for the dish, but Susan didn't make it that often. All the better, as it tasted divine the times that she did.

John was an ex-policeman, respected and revered by his colleagues, and feared for his right hook. He knocked a man down once, almost twice his size, and in a single blow. Pete was there when it happened, and swore within himself, that he would do his utmost never to piss his dad off; ever. Apparently the unfortunate fellow had offended John's close friend, a female police officer who always used to look out for him, by mentioning that she sucked rhinoceros dicks.

John was a true gentleman; he never swore in front of ladies, held open doors for them, etcetera. Pete had always admired that trait in his dad; he always did his best to follow his lead in the gentlemanly ways coupled with wonderful manners and beautifully spoken English. He almost got there, when he started saying the 'C' word and acquired a gusto for saying it to people who got on his tits; particularly women drivers who were at the wheel of large off-road vehicles and who had disdain for the correct use of the highway code. The school run was the thing that induced the longer, louder, and more venomous barrage of naughty words. Otherwise, Pete was one of the nicest people you could ever meet. Oh and he disliked traffic wardens and police constables; even though his parents were officers of the law. If ever in conversation with one, Pete would often address the officer as *cunt*stable, and hope the fellow didn't catch on. He'd been lucky so far.

Ozzie was out with Julia at Sainsbury's for a spot of food shopping. She loved it, he hated it. He only accompanied her on the trip today, on the promise that the 'coin would see the slot' and after the ribbon fiasco, Ozzie needed to redeem himself. He wondered if he needed more time, as when he looked at Julia's firm breasts and lovely curved and pronounced bum, the purple-headed-womb-ferret would rise to peep out of the burrow; when he thought of his mum coming in, the poor little mammal would go into hibernation.

Pete had two sisters; Janice and Harriet. They were a couple of stupid cows and he hated their guts pretty much ninety nine percent of the time. Janice was the eldest of the three and had been married three times and had no children from either of her marriages. She didn't want any. She always teased Pete about how crap his keyboarding skills were and that he wrote shitty little songs and that he had a small penis. She swore to him that she had seen it once, but he knew it wasn't true, so he told her to go and fuck herself.

Harriet was the youngest child and had just turned eighteen. She was more affable toward her brother but still, ultimately a pain in the bum. She teased Pete about his Casio VL1 and the fact that it was the size of a box of matchmakers and sounded like a Fisher Price toy. She then asked him how his baldy boyfriend was – meaning Ralf – Pete told her to go fuck *her*self as well. All in all, he had a pretty good rapport with his sisters, and Sundays spent with them, sat at the table tucking in to a roast dinner was always fun.

Ozzie's boredom began to set in and he started losing interest in Julia's in depth shopping experience. He told her he was nipping to the little boy's room but instead, decided to set off on his own adventures. He began by grabbing a few boxes of condoms and randomly dropping them into the baskets and trolleys of elderly ladies. He then would sneak into the ladies' changing rooms – God only knew how he managed that one – and after waiting until an unsuspecting female customer used the fitting cubicle next to his he would softly ask; 'Excuse me, I'm really sorry, but you wouldn't have any toilet paper in there would you; it's just that I've run out in here.'

'Oh for fuck's sake,' would be the usual response he got, 'you dirty bastard...security!'

He ran like the wind and disappeared down an aisle somewhere far away and lingered there to watch the results of his handy-work. Other tricks involved standing on whoopee cushions when certain customers drifted by, throwing rubber creepy-crawlies over the aisles at people during the Halloween season, and hiding inside camping tents and jumping out at people when they hovered nearby. All in a day's work for the bored Ozzie. But today; he had the ultimate trick beautifully planned. It would definitely mean he would be banned from Sainsbury's but it was totally worth it.

Ozzie approached the customer service desk, looking as lost and as sheepish as possible, and addressed one of the two ladies behind the counter. He had to keep a straight face for this one; it was going to be hard.

'Scuse me love, anybody know French in 'ere?' If they did the trick would have to be postponed.

'I'm sorry, but there's no one. Everything okay?'

'Well, it's me mum see. She's French and she don't know any English and she's got lost. Thing is, she's a bit...you know...lost 'er marbles, and I was wonderin' if I can call her on yer loudspeaker thingy...the tannerloy.'

'You mean the Tannoy,' smiled the attendant.

'Oh yeah, that's right...that thing. Is it okay if I just tell 'er I'm 'ere at this desk?'

The attendant was only too happy to oblige and handed Ozzie the microphone after announcing that *this is a customer announcement,* over the system. Ozzie tried his level best to keep as straight a face as was humanly possible.

'Oi mum…ya fackin' old bat…I'm 'ere at the customer service desk. 'urry up and git your fackin' arse over before dad pisses 'is pants! Murky Buckets!'

Ozzie handed the microphone back to a red-faced attendant and ran off toward the exit to the shop, but slipped while trying to vault over one of the barriers between the tills. Three members of security were onto him before he could scramble back to his feet, and overpowered him, despite being able to land a blow to the face of one of the guards. The two ladies at the customer service desk continued, at a complete loss for words, to follow with their gaze, as a cackling Ozzie was led out of the supermarket. Ozzie didn't see Julia again after that day for two weeks. He didn't call her; he hated rejection from any woman, and he somehow knew that he would receive a rather strong one if he dared attempt to contact her. He lived in hope. He hadn't got his leg over yet.

Ralf was eating his lunch in the school staff room while gazing out of the window that looked out onto The Avenue. Many thoughts always rushed through him. His mind felt like a busy train station, where many of his thoughts were fleeting and just rushed through, and others pulled in and lingered there for longer spells. The window seat was his favourite place and he would often make an effort to get there a little earlier, so he was the first; Miss Clare like to plant herself in that same seat as well. Ralf felt sure she did it just to wind him up. The day was a strange one; Lawrence had been back at school a few days now, after his unpleasant ordeal at the hands of Mr Campion – who incidentally was still missing – and was settling back in to his old routine again, but he was a little shaken by the welcome that was offered to him by the obnoxious Miss Clare. It involved the firm clasping of both of his hands and with her lips so close to his, that for an instant, he was convinced she was going to plant one on his mouth; the death-breath was in full strength, as the forces of peanut butter melded with a garrison of onion that fused itself with the sickly aroma of instant coffee. The senses were indeed stirred and disturbed.

The pips chirped loud and true as they echoed throughout the building, signalling the end of the school day and every corridor and classroom burst with hurried hullabaloo. The pupils spilled out from the edifice like ants from their underground dwelling and anxiously made their way to their lives after school. Ralf remained alone in the empty classroom and decided to check through a few of his schoolkids' text books, his curiosity particularly piqued by Lawrence's work. It was largely unchanged and the themes of his creative writing were pretty much on par with his other work; he possessed dyslexia which the boy himself, admitted and accepted to having and his spelling wasn't always up to scratch, but all seemed okay judging by his work. Ralf read through his creative writing piece which was not quite finished, but there were no signs of any trauma-related issues or changes in his work; in fact there was even the odd dash of humour in his story about a vampire who stalked the streets of his version of Victorian London.

The doorknob rattled and seemed remarkably loud, as its clatter echoed through the deserted classroom, that particular room being devoid of windows; it was built as an extension, along with three others with the intention of accommodating extra music classes. The sudden noise startled Ralf while he was absorbed in Lawrence's vampire tale, and his irritated glare unnerved Miss Clare, who stopped in her tracks just half way in the doorway.

'I thought I'd drop by as you were staying behind. Wondered if you fancied a coffee and a biscuit.' Said Miss Clare.

'I'm fine thanks, but it's very kind of you to offer. I won't be too long actually, I was...'

'Well I have a nice big mug of the strong stuff just here,' she said, producing a sizeable tankard-like mug of steaming filter brew; her hand was on the other side of the door, and resting upon the handle of a wheeled trolley. Ralf sighed irritatingly and turned to look at the wall and away from the glance of the insistent headmistress; he mouthed several curses and feigned a cough, then turned to face her again.

'Well how could I possibly refuse, Miss Clare; when you arrive complete with portable trolley...and biscuits too.' That was Ralf's nice way of saying something like, *Why the fuck are you here, I was just enjoying some peace and quiet, then you come along with your fucking biscuits and bloody coffee. I wish you'd just bugger off home!* Ralf was one to always try and see the positive in any slightly less than pleasant situation; the silver lining here, was chocolate digestives. He loved them to the point of easily finishing off more than half a pack. Actually the positive just slipped; she'd only put four biscuits on a small plate, along with some Rich Teas which he couldn't stand, and a few strawberry finger-wafers, and she'll undoubtedly want a couple herself. Fuck positivity sometimes, he thought.

She inched her way in, grinning with childlike glee and closed the door behind her, turning the key to lock it. Ralf wasn't liking the look of this. The headmistress went toward him almost swaggering, or trying to, as though she were modelling a new trend of fashion on a catwalk for double-plus sizes. She placed the tray of biscuits and drinks upon the desk after shoving Ralf's paperwork to one side, then proceeded to move a chair near to her and place one leg upon it. Ralf dared to glance down ward and notice she had slightly hairy legs and the nail varnish on her big toes was flaking off. She also wore the most atrociously oversized sandals; they looked like she'd made them herself, out of a pair of wooden planks, and then stuck some old straps with rusted buckles on afterwards. He didn't want to eat the biscuit anymore.

'I just wanted to say,' she said as she caressed his hand, 'that you handled the situation with Mr Campion beautifully. In fact, I will go as far as to say; you're my hero.'

Ralf hated being hailed as a hero, an angel, anything of the sort. He believed he handled it like any decent person would. Campion was still missing in action though, so being called anything heroic was truly un-called for. He didn't know what to say to Miss Clare either. He knew what he *wanted* to say; it would likely cost him his job. He smiled, forcibly, and looked toward her with the corner of his eye.

'It was nothing anybody else wouldn't have done, Miss Clare.' Ralf said, continuing his marking and ticking, as he pulled the paperwork back toward himself.

'Oh please,' replied Miss Clare, 'Call me Edwina.'

She moved the chair closer to him and sat a little too close for comfort. Ralf could smell her perfume as she gradually brought her cheek up to his shoulder.

'I've always had a soft spot for you, Ralf,' she continued, 'I find you a...very interesting man...like you've got some dark secret. I find that most...exciting.'

Ralf jolted out of his chair, startling Edwina and causing her to spill her coffee onto the desk. Ralf snatched away the paperwork just in time, scattering a few across the classroom floor. He glared at the headmistress then proceeded to pick up what was dropped and slammed them back onto the desk, startling her again.

'Miss Clare!' He snapped.

'Edwina?' She grinned.

'I think this is a little inappropriate, don't you think?' Continued Ralf, in a softer tone this time. It was probably best if he rejected her advances in a less pissed off manner.

'I'm sorry I snapped at you, but...I really need to get on. I don't view you...like that...I'm sorry. Please don't feel offended.'

Edwina pouted slightly, like a sulking child who'd just been scolded. 'Is it because I'm a little porky?' She added in an infantile little voice.

Of course it's because you're fucking porky...and not just a little either, you stupid, deluded old cow. Do you not have mirrors in your house? Have you not noticed the two hairy carbuncles growing out of your face, your peanut butter and onion breath, your bloody stupid, ridiculous giant sandals, and your hairy legs? A little porky? Woman, you are the size of two fucking armchairs!

Ralf wanted to voice that incredibly honest thought; and he usually always said what he thought, but after coming out with a rather tame, *Of course not, you're a very nice lady; it's not you, it's me,* reply instead, he figured that was the best way to handle *this* situation. Heroically.

Edwina left the classroom red-faced and decidedly embarrassed, and Ralf hoped that the following days, weeks, and months were not going to be hellish for him. He went home shortly afterwards and had a nice long chat with Pete about what had happened. Pete was unable to talk properly after Ralf had told him; his sides were splitting from almost incessant laughter, that the two friends gave up on the phone call and agreed to chat the next day, after work, at Mike's Music City.

Chapter 6

The following day, Ozzie had just come off the phone to Ralf who was asking if he was okay and if he was up for an evening at the bar. Ozzie agreed. He'd been lurking in depression-ville, as he called it, since Julia had left him and after having a long chat with her sister, Nicky, he finally laid his hopes to rest; Julia wasn't having any more to do with him; and all for a few little pranks.

The doorbell rang at the Blake's family home and Ozzie's mother, Jackie, called up to her son telling him to get the door as she had something on the stove. Ozzie stomped down the stairs and opened the front door, to reveal his sister, Kim and her three year old son clutching her hand with a cheeky grin on his face. He ran into his uncle's arms while a tutting and cursing Kim pushed her way past him and marched into the kitchen to her mother.

'Hello to you, too!' Exclaimed Ozzie.

Kim ignored him and continued to moan to her mum about the latest turn of events. Kim had moved in with a fellow named Tarquin about eight months ago, but for the past five months, she'd been on the phone to her mother almost every night after eleven because of various problems with her boyfriend and his rather obsessive problem with jealousy and possessiveness. Kim had, as of late, begun telling her mum that Tarquin had started beating her. That also explained why she hadn't visited her mother for a long time; she didn't want to upset her, and especially her brother by turning up with bruises and shiners, and after hearing that news, Jackie didn't mention anything to Ozzie; she seldom hid anything from her son, but if he ever found out his sister was being physically abused, he would undoubtedly do time for serious assault or murder.

Ozzie took his little nephew upstairs to his room and held him above his shoulders, while flying him around the bedroom, lobby, and back to the bedroom again. He switched on his record player and put on his favourite album of the moment. It was by a new rock group called Asia, and after the first song entitled *Heat of The Moment,* little Jacob was enthralled by the surging and melodic guitar riffs and solos. Ozzie's favourite track on the album was the second one on side one, entitled, *Sole Survivor*. The powerful electric guitar hits between each verse were forceful and so skilfully played, they were rousing and empowering, with their surging arpeggio that clung to every note with symphonic perfection. The lead vocalist, John Wetton, had a voice that was powerful and expressive and its tone and timbre suited the band's sound perfectly. His tenor seemed largely unschooled, and he sang using mainly straight notes with occasional modulation during and on the endings of words. The rest of the band sang also, but only providing backing vocals and harmonies when singing in unison.

Little Jacob lay upon his uncle's unmade bed and eventually fell asleep after the album had finished its play-through. Ozzie covered him with his dressing gown and went slowly downstairs, and as he reached the bottom, he caught the tail end of his sister's deep conversation with her mother. By then, she was in floods of tears and neither of the two ladies had noticed that Ozzie was standing near the kitchen door, which was slightly ajar. He didn't realise just how much suffering Kim was going through, but her last few sentences were enough for him to put two and two together. He burst into the kitchen and demanded to know where Tarquin lived and worked.

'Why didn't you tell me? You only ever told us you lived in Brentford, but you never gave us your address. Why mum…Kim, why?'

'Oh leave it Ozzie, said Kim, turning her face from him and wiping her eyes, 'just leave it…I'm leaving him anyway.'

'I couldn't tell ya, lovie. I know you'd kick 'is 'ead in.' Said Jackie.

'Damn Fackin' right I will; where's the prick live!?' Yelled Ozzie.

'Leave it love,' said his mum, taking his hands in hers, 'I wanna rip 'is 'ead off as well, but let the cops 'andle it. It'll be you in the wrong if ya touch 'im,'

A tear ran down Ozzie's face and he clenched his fists tightly. He tensed his arms and kept them by his sides. He stood on the spot for a few seconds, like a scolded child in a school classroom, while he cooled off. It was his way of coping when he was angry and when things were beyond his control or out of his reach; like Tarquin. Kim touched his arm and whispered that she was sorry, but she didn't want him to do anything silly. Ozzie usually locked horns with his sister, but that didn't mean he had no love for her. She was family and the thought of anyone laying their hands upon her was a big NO in his rule book. Jackie and Kim remained in the kitchen while Ozzie stormed out of the house, slamming the front door behind him. He lived just a five minute walk from Pete's house, and he stopped at a phone box along the way to ring him.

'I need to talk to ya, Pete,' Ozzie said on the phone, shakily. 'It's Kim...that facker of 'er boyfriend's been beltin' 'er.'

There was a pause on Pete's end of the line, probably surprise and shock on his part, but he told Ozzie to go right over to his house. The two sat and had coffee upstairs in Pete's room as Ozzie poured his heart out. Pete hated seeing his friend in such a state; Ozzie never usually cried unless he was truly angry. When he shed tears of rage, anyone unfortunate enough to be on the receiving end of Ozzie's wrath, was sure to meet a sticky end. He had a big heart but an even bigger temper, especially if any harm befell those close to him; both family and friends.

'We need to keep this between us mate,' Pete said with a frown of concern upon his forehead, 'my old man's an ex-copper and he *does* abide by the rulebook.'

'I know...it's fine, mate. I just can't 'elp wantin' to fackin' kill 'im. Mum and Kim won't tell me where the bastard lives.'

Pete had an idea; Ralf knew Kim when he worked at the airport. She worked in the landside staff canteen and he'd helped her write the odd job application letter here and there. Perhaps he could find out where Kim lived with Tarquin during casual conversation. Ozzie agreed, and they drove to his house after calling him first.

Pete drove through Northfields and along Pope's Lane, and turned right into Lionel Road, which eventually led out onto the Chiswick Roundabout and onto the high street. Pete clicked on the car radio as they came upon some congestion a little way into the high street; the voice of DJ, Tony Blackburn announced with his radio-voice enthusiasm, that he was going to play the latest single from ABC's forthcoming album, The Lexicon of Love. As the track bounced through the speakers, its funky baseline fused perfectly with orchestral embellishments, culminating in the lead singer exploding with joyous expression and yippeeyayea's, while powerful string arrangements rose in the background like a huge tidal wave, racing along the sea and engulfing all in its path. It was truly rousing and had even Ozzie bouncing along, and culling the rage that was eating away at him. The song was, The Look of Love.

'Fackin' brilliant!' He exclaimed, clapping his hands once, and startling Pete.

'Yes mate, that *is* a great track. Ralph would love that; he's got a thing with harmonic choruses and strings.' Pete said.

As the traffic inched slowly forward, Pete revealed his near-hatred for his car. Not just because of its slowness due to a small engine, but also because of the way his best friend, Ralph often poked perpetual fun at it. Pete had a Citroen Visa; red in colour, and with a top speed of just beyond seventy miles per hour. It felt like it did zero to sixty in fifteen minutes, and that was when you could hear every creak and groan from its bodywork. He used to quite like his little runabout, but not since Ralf's endless quips about how crap it was; especially compared to his Ford Capri; a clearly faster and superior car. Pete particularly detested when his friend would exclaim out loud, when they all went out together for an evening or day out; *Okay guys and girls; would you like to ride in the amazing Ralf-Runner, or the abysmal Peter-potty?* Pete tried smiling, but that became increasingly difficult every time. He really wanted to smack Ralf.

Pete turned left into Turnham Green Terrace and after accelerating a little after becoming exasperated by the crawling traffic jam, he was forced to slam on his brakes as three orthodox Jews stepped out in front of the car and proceeded to cross the road; and take their sweet time about it. Ozzie was propelled forward, hitting his head on the hand-rail just above him. The rocker rolled down his window and thrust half of his body out and over the car's roof to shout abuse at the fellows.

'Hey, you fackin' dick lickers! Whaddya think yer doin, steppin' in front of the car like that...got eyes in yer arseholes 'ave ya? Tossers!'

'Ozzie, Pete hissed, 'you can't go saying things like that, mate. I know they didn't look where they were going, but they're orthodox Jews. I don't think they use or even know language like that.'

'I know they're awful cock Jews, and I just 'urt me 'ead., 'cause they crossed the fackin' road without lookin!'

'ORTHODOX!' Chuckled Pete, 'not awful cocks; you plonker.'

'Why 'ave they got that stupid hair danglin' from their ears?'

'Not sure mate; think that's part of their religion.'

'Looks fackin' stupid!'

Pete pulled up outside Ralf's house, just as he was turning the key in the front door after going to get some sliced bread for toast. Ralf got some instant coffees on the go, and a filter coffee for himself, and the friends sat in the back section of the lounge around the dining table. Ozzie was always fascinated by the antelope horns hanging above the wall, just above where Ralf was sitting. He smiled when he noticed Ozzie gazing up at them, and turned to look up at them himself.

'I've not looked at them for ages,' Ralf said, 'they always used to freak me out when I first moved in here. They belonged to the old couple who lived here before me. They were a hand-me-down from *his* father. He used to tell his son they were the devil's horns, and of course, that freaked *him* out.'

'You never talk about them,' Pete added, 'you've not told us much about them at all; how come?'

'Don't know', Ralf replied, 'no particular reason, I guess...not much to tell. I didn't know the antelope they belonged to, unfortunately.'

'No, you plonker,' laughed Pete, 'I meant the old couple!'

'Ah, they were a nice elderly couple; my auntie and uncle. My heroes. The only thing I had in place of a mum and dad.'

'You ever thought of looking for your real parents?' Pete asked.

'No, I already told you that,' said Ralf, 'I'm not interested.'

'But surely...'

'Pete, leave it. You always press me with this and I give you the same answer every time. I'm NOT interested!'

'Okay mate, sorry; just asking that's all. It's just that I would really *like* to know who my real parents were; I'd be really curious, that's all I'm saying.'

Ralf rose from the table and went to the kitchen. Ozzie was still gazing at the horns hanging above him.

'I think I've pissed him off,' Pete said, 'but I *am* so curious about why he never wants to talk about it.'

Once Ralf returned to the table – undoubtedly after cooling off and letting the pissed off-ness with Pete slide away – the three friends talked about the latest problem that plagued Ozzie; and ultimately them. They were close. They always felt each other's pain. They were like a close family.

The following day, Ralf took the day off work and drove to West Ealing. After talking about Ozzie's situation – or rather, Kim's situation – the plans were set in motion; Ralf was going to try to get Kim to reveal where she lived, before she'd decided to move out and leave the lovely Tarquin. Ralf knew that on the same day, every week, Kim shopped at Sainsbury's with little Jacob in tow, and so decided to try his luck. He parked his car in the only parking space he managed to find; the town was bustling that day, more than usual. Perhaps there was something going on, but Ralf found a space down a side street just behind the supermarket's rear-side entrance.

He'd waited almost an hour before Kim eventually appeared among a congregation of red-capped and screaming school children, captained by a portly teacher who resembled the wonderful Miss Clare. Ralf scrambled out of his car before he lost sight of her; he wasn't sure if she had already finished her shopping or not. He shuffled past the army of kiddies and the frumpy teacher – she donned white plimsoles, and knee length skirt, and a blue polo-neck sweater. She had flesh-coloured, laddered tights and a slight odour of unwashed, and she probably heard his muttered remark of, *sex on fucking legs,* as he brushed past her. He caught up with Kim; she had indeed finished her weekly shop and was found at the side of the building, packing the many carrier bags into the boot of her Ford Fiesta.

'Hello stranger,' he said cheerfully as he feigned just having glimpsed her, 'long time no see!'

'Oh 'ello,' she said, 'yeah, not seen you in ages. How's you?' She leaned in for the usual peck on the cheek.

'Not bad; usual shit, different day; and how are you, big guy?' He said to Jacob, high-fiving him as he sat in the shopping trolley. 'You've grown so big. Too big to be riding in that trolley. Haven't you got a car yet? You got a girlfriend?'

The little boy giggled gleefully as Ralf picked him up and held him high above his head, then brought him down, back into his arms again. Kim looked on approvingly. Secretly, she always had a soft spot for Ralf, but never dared make it known to him, as she always thought he was kind of out of her league, with his well-spoken and cultured manner and gentlemanly ways. Ralf probably knew, but didn't want to risk taking it any further; not just because she was Ozzie's sister, but also because he didn't want to get involved with anyone with children. Although he loved kids, Ralf never saw himself as father material. He always claimed he would be too selfish as a dad.

'Come on, I'll buy you a coffee; unless you're in a rush to get home or something.'

'No, that'll be nice,' she replied, 'but I haven't got Jacob's buggy with me, so we'll have to hold his hand. You okay with that?'

'Of course,' chuckled Ralf, 'come on you, let's have your hand.'

After coffee and a bun at a café where Ralf retreated sometimes when he wanted time alone, they crossed the high street and went into the park, which was bustling with mums, dads, and children, as they flocked around the playground area. Jacob loved the slide and the roundabout and joined forces with a few other toddlers and a friend of Kim's from the nursery. Ralf tried executing the plan.

'So, where you living now?'

'Oh it's this flat in Chiswick. Really nice, it is; two floors. Tarquin's been living there ages. He loves it. Well, he loves it round there 'cause it's posh like…you know.'

'Yeah, I guess it *is* kind of…posh,' replied Ralf with a smile, 'I've been living there for years now; I love Chiswick.' My house is in Hawkshead Road, where's yours?' He finally got round to asking her, it was the only time he could possibly get an honest answer. Please, please, he thought.

'Oh bloody 'ell!' She exclaimed, 'You're just up the road from me then, I'm down at the end of The Avenue, just before you get to Turnham Green station. You go left at the roundabout and it's round there; Rupert Road. I'm number sixty-six, what number are you then?'

'I'm at number twelve. Well I'll be damned; all this time and I never imagined you were just down the road from me. Mind you, The Avenue's a long bloody road, but we're neighbours!'

Ralf jumped for joy – silently and inside – now he knew, and so would Ozzie. He'd call him that same evening, so he could have words with Tarquin the tosser once and for all.

'Oh by the way, before I forget; you still see Ozzie and Pete don't ya?'

'Erm, yeah of course; all the time. We're inseparable, us.' Ralf's heart sank as he knew exactly what Kim was going to ask him.

'Look, there's been some problems. I saw my brother and mum yesterday…I revealed something I've been hidin' for a while…'

'What, sweetheart?' Said Ralf taking her hand in his.

'Tarquin's been beatin' me….more often than usual now. He's really possessive like…I mean…I can't talk to no one else, male I mean, 'cause if he finds out, he'll just go mental. He does it in front of Jacob as well sometimes. I wanna move out and go back to my mum's, but it's just findin' the right moment to tell him.'

Kim was struggling to hold back her tears, but was doing well. She didn't want to draw any attention to herself, and she especially didn't want her little boy to see her suffering. Kim continued explaining to Ralf about the various occurrences in which her boyfriend assaulted her and the last time, he punched and kicked her in the stomach. Kim raised her blouse slightly to reveal some of her blackened and bruised skin upon her abdomen. Ralf was shocked and his blood began to boil. She touched his face, bringing him out of his chain of thoughts. Violent thoughts. He was already debating whether to tell Ozzie where she lived or keep his word, as she continued to beg him to.

'Please, whatever you do, don't tell me brother or me mum where I live. Ozzie'll kill him. He'll tear him to pieces, I know he will; then it'll be Ozzie who'll end up in jail for assault…or even murder. Please don't say anything, Ralf…promise me!'

'When are you going to leave him?'

'I'd do it tonight if I could, but it's just findin' the right moment.'

'You have to get out of there now, Kim, before it's too late. He could really hurt you. Look, I can help you. Just let me come with you so you can pack a few things, just a few…enough to get you by for a week or so, then we'll go back and get the rest.'

Ralf took Kim's arms firmly in his hands and gazed intensely into her eyes. She could see that Ralf himself was becoming emotional, as his deep, hazel eyes were glazing over. She caressed his cheek and agreed. They left the park, parked Kim's car down the same street as where Ralf had left his, and then made their way to Rupert Road, in Ralf's car.

The time was near four in the afternoon, and it was already dark, like the night had already fallen thick and hard, as the sky clouded over with the promise of a hefty rainfall. Ralf pulled into Rupert Road and drove slowly through its sharp bends. It was a lovely street with tall and imposing dark brick townhouses and the pavements were lined with many trees, the tops of which were washed with the neon light of the streetlamps. They parked just outside Kim's flat and proceeded to go through the front door. Kim began to tremble as she turned the key; she gave it to Ralf who let them in. The TV was on in the lounge and the smell of bacon wafted out from the kitchen, which lay straight ahead of them.

'Where the fuck have you been?' Tarquin's voice boomed out from the sitting room, making Kim gasp and stop in her tracks. She clung to Ralf, who was already shaking with a steadily rising rage. The ruffling of newspaper was heard and a thud, as Kim's boyfriend got up from the sofa and marched out toward the hallway. As soon as he saw Ralf, he stopped dead where he stood, cutting his sentence short.

'I asked you a fucking question, you stupid bi…!'

Ralf glared at the man, in his mid-thirties with his white shirt hanging out of his trousers, and with his tie unknotted and dangling just below his beltline, like a scruffy teenager who'd just got home from school.

'Go upstairs and get a few things together,' said Ralf, softly but firmly, and with a hand upon her back, ushering her toward the staircase just to their left. 'Tarquin and I need to chat.'

Ralf walked toward the clearly worried boyfriend, who backed up into the lounge. Ralf motioned him toward the sofa. Tarquin obeyed the gesture without delay.

'I'm taking Kim out of here. She won't be coming back. You will not call her, you will not write to her, you will not look for her. You won't make any contact of any kind. You are a filthy, low-life scumbag. You're a coward. If you ever go near her again, if you so much as touch a hair on her head…I'm gonna rip your guts out and make you eat them. Do you understand what I'm saying to you, you piece of fucking shit?'

Ralf's stern words of warning ended with a snarl and his face contorting into a menacing promise of much bloodshed, should Tarquin even dream about Kim ever again. The sorry excuse for a boyfriend, and a man of any sort, nodded in agreement, his whole body shaking with pure fear of disastrous consequences, as he sank further back into the depths of the black leather sofa, a vengeful Ralf, towering over him and looking down with an expression on his face that meant, *you're so fucking dead if I ever see you again.*

Kim came clumping down the stairs, and the two drove away into the night. Ralf took her to his house for the evening. They talked at length. Kim opened herself up about many things, some of which she didn't even tell her mother or brother. Ralf felt honoured that she was telling him all these things about herself, her feelings, and her plans for the future. She even told him she always had a little crush on him, to which he smiled broadly. Ralf wanted to tell her *his* secret. He really wanted to. He knew he could trust her, but it was too dangerous; far too dangerous. At that moment, she trusted him implicitly. He was her hero. If he dared tell her of what he was living with, she may not react like he would expect. What if she freaked out? What if she ran out of the house, into the night, and told the police? Told the others? It wasn't worth the risk. He couldn't risk losing all he had. It wasn't time yet.

Chapter 7

Ralf slept on his sofa while Kim and Jacob used his bed for the night. He drove them to West Ealing the following morning so Kim could retrieve her car and drive to Ozzie's house. They agreed to collect the rest of her things from Tarquin's house the Monday of the following week. Ralf spent the rest of the day at home pondering and referring to his book so he could relax a little. He turned on his record player with radio incorporated; the song, *The Voice,* by Ultravox was playing.

As Ralf sat pensively and in a stupor-like state, he wondered what to do regarding what Kim asked him to promise her. Should he tell Ozzie? He knew he could mention it to Pete, as he always kept a secret, but if he were to tell Ozzie, things would certainly take a turn for the worse. Ozzie would literally kill Tarquin. He'd seen Ozzie lose his cool before and on numerous occasions; and he was not someone to be trifled with, underestimated, or taken lightly. Push him too far, and he could tear a man to pieces.

Ralf was very fond of the funny rocker. He loved his sense of humour and totally carefree approach to life and he had a positivity about him that was infectious and enviable. Ralf was always impressed at how Ozzie could have practically any woman he wanted to, and having a chat-up line for every occasion. The female companions may not have stuck with him for that long, but he always appeared with absolute belters on his arm. Julia seemed more of a stayer than a passer-through; a shame she didn't have a little more patience with Ozzie's mad humour and love for life. One could get used to his antics; he didn't have a bad bone in his body. With that thought, Ralf made an on-the-spot decision, and sped to Ozzie's house.

He drove out of Hawkshead Road and turned right to go through Acton. He hated Acton, mainly because it was too chaotic at the best of times, and he could never find a place to park. He was offered to move in with an early girlfriend who had a studio flat there once. He turned it down immediately when he saw that it was a rather small room disguised as a studio flat; one of several within an Edwardian house. The bathroom and toilet were in the same room, with a tiny kitchen area in the corner. The bathroom door wouldn't even close properly, so having a poo poo while your girlfriend was watching television was a thought Ralf dreaded to think about. He certainly didn't want to experience things the other way around; *and* the fact that she really enjoyed hot curries; enough said.

Ralf drove through Northfields and was just about to pass his favourite café, when he braked hard and immediately pulled into a parking space just on the corner by the local family butcher. He remained in the car, while looking behind him and across the road, at a man wearing a green rain-jacket. He was walking along the pavement with an air of fear and mystery, while acting suspiciously and a little anxious as with every two or three steps, he kept looking behind him. Ralf waited until he drew a little closer; it was Campion.

Ralf got out of his car and kept his steely gaze fixed upon him as he shuffled along the pavement, looking in every shop window, clearly feigning window shopping. Campion raised his collar and stopped at the edge of a side street and pondered for a few moments, whether to turn down there or continue along Northfield Avenue. Ralf began sweating coldly as his blood began to boil once again. He feared his anger sometimes, as it often clouded his judgement. That always led to things going decidedly pear-shaped, as going in all guns blazing was his usual end result. All he wanted was to grab hold of Campion and beat the hell out of him, but he couldn't do it if Campion were to choose to continue along the main street.

 Ralf watched as he nervously peered all around him, turning on the spot. One minute crawled by and the maths teacher began taking a few steps forward; but he turned into the side street. Ralf waited for him to walk a few steps down, then he crossed the busy street, impatiently inching forward, first to the middle of the road ,then brushing past a car that honked its horn as he made slight contact with the back end. Campion turned around and noticed someone that appeared to be coming after him. Ralf rapidly darted to his right and behind a pillar that stood at the corner of a baker's shop. He didn't peek around the corner in case Campion spotted him. He waited a few seconds then, covering his face with his forearm, stepped out from cover and proceeded down the side street with his head down. He looked up slightly; there was no sign of Campion. Shit! He thought; maybe he saw him and legged it during those few crucial seconds that Ralf hid behind the pillar and lost sight of him. Ralf increased his pace whilst looking around him, scouring every front garden and every alleyway between the houses. He crouched down and at times went prone in an attempt to catch him possibly hiding behind vehicles. Campion was gone. Vanished into thin air. Slippery bastard.

Ralf let out a roaring cry of anger and frustration. Campion had surely seen him and in some unknown and sneaky or clever way, given him the slip. How did he do it? Where did he go? Surely a man of his size and poor physical fitness couldn't break into an almighty sprint and totally disappear from view. It wasn't feasible; Ralf was a big guy, but he was pretty fit for his age. Fitter than Campion for sure. But somehow, that slimy bastard had managed to outsmart him. 'For now fucker, for now.' Muttered Ralf as he turned and went back to his car.

Pete was in his bedroom in the company of his Casio VL1 and a catalogue with a folded page bookmarking the keyboards and synthesisers. A knock on the door that usually announced the entry of his curious mother induced a sigh of frustration; 'Yes mum, come in.' He said.

'What are you plinking?' Susan asked.

'Well nothing you'd know. I'm just trying to make up a melody for a new song I'm working on.'

'Oh,' smiled his mother, 'Thing is though...that thing just sounds too much like a kid's toy. It's hardly professional sounding.'

'I know mum, thanks for that. I *have* told you before, numerous times, that I *am* trying to save up for a synthesiser.'

'Are they expensive then?'

'Yes, they are. That's why it's taking a while to actually save up enough. Anything else?'

'Alright, no need to get stroppy. Just showing an interest that's all.'

'No, you're just bored, so you thought you'd come and wind me up about the whole idea; I'm surprised you've not called it the usual.'

'Oh, you mean plink-a-plonk!'

'Yes mum, precisely that!' Snapped Peter.

Susan closed the door and went downstairs, leaving an exasperated Peter seething. The doorbell rang and shook him out of it, as he listened to who was at the door. He heard a muffled male voice and realized who it was when his mother went into high-pitch-surprise mode; 'Oh hello Ralf, come in. Pete's upstairs in his room,' wait for it, 'with his plink-a-plonk!'

'Fucking typical!' Yelled Pete.

'I beg your pardon!?' Whined his mother in almost musical fashion.

'Nothing mother! Can you make a couple of coffees please!?'

Ralf entered the bedroom with a big grin upon his face, and apologised to his friend for being unable to keep a straight face.

'Fucking pisses me off when she does that. Just seconds before you came, she was in here winding me up about the same bloody thing. Same questions, same subject, then once she's done her job of annoying me, she just buggers off, closing the door behind her. I swear I feel like slinging the fucking VL1 against the wall. She just loves rubbishing everything I do, just because *she* doesn't believe in it!'

'So what *did* you compose on your plink-a-plonk then?'

Pete glared at his friend as though his face was about to open up and produce a cluster of firearms ready to let loose a barrage of deadly gunfire. Ralf reared his head back and let out a loud and flamboyant laugh, that echoed throughout his room and caused a slight reverberation in the nearby desktop ventilator. Pete smiled as he shook his head. Ralf always ended up making him smile in one way or another, when he was at a low.

'So what brings you round these here parts then?' Asked Pete in a more cheerful fashion.

'I got a result regarding the Kim and Tarquin thing.'

'Really? How? Spill the beans!'

'Nothing special. It was during casual conversation really; as planned. I drove her there after a bit of deliberating; I threatened the arsehole. He shit his pants. I doubt he'll bother her anymore.'

'You told Ozzie yet?'

'No,' sighed Ralf, 'that's the problem; I haven't yet. He'll only want to rip his head off if I do tell him. I'm just trying to think of the right words to use.'

'Ozzie'll be fine about it. As long as he knows stuff has been dealt with, he won't get pissed off if Kim told you where she lived first. We both knew you were the only one who had a good chance of getting her to tell you. He knew that.'

'Yeah, I guess. I just hate hiding stuff from my friends.' A chill ran up Ralf's spine; if they ever found out what he'd been hiding for real all these years. At that precise moment, he felt like a hypocrite. A deceiver. A lying hound. But it had to be done. Ralf loved his friends dearly. He would most likely lose every one of them if they ever knew.

'You alright mate?' Pete asked, placing a hand upon Ralf's shoulder, 'Thought I'd lost you there, for a minute.'

'Yeah I'm fine mate,' Ralf replied, 'just a little pensive. You're right; I'm sure everything'll be just fine.'

Ralf thought back to earlier that afternoon, back in Northfields, when he caught a glimpse of Campion. If only he had some idea of where he was hiding; it was eating away at him and he needed to find that slimy scumbag and teach him a lesson, once and for all. Ralf really wanted to believe in Karma. For the most part he did; but most of the time he really wanted to verify for himself and see the results, which was why he always liked to set out and dispense his own brand of Karma. He needed to see justice being done with his own eyes and preferably by his own hand. Ralf did not consider himself to be a vigilante; more like an equalizer. He hated the law at the best of times and detested the way the law was usually, 'soft' on those that crossed the line. Campion crossed that line. Ralf knew that when the police would eventually catch up with him, all he would face was a jail sentence, if that. Ralf wanted to make sure that before the law got their hands on him, he would lay *his* on him first. He was determined.

Pete showed Ralf the keyboard section in the catalogue he was thumbing through earlier, and remarkably, he'd reached a decision on a purchase. Pete had had his eye on a few synthesisers, but the ones that really tickled his musical senses were at the time, a little beyond budget, but he showed a particular interest in a Casio MT40, which had recently come down in price a little.

'What do you think mate? I can't get the JX3P or the JUNO 60 at the moment, but if you plug this thing into an amplifier, it's actually not that bad. I was thinking about going down to Dixons in West Ealing tomorrow and try it out. '

'Yeah, why not. I'll go with you if you like, I'm curious to hear what it sounds like, myself.'

The following day, Pete was up very early and he made sure Ralf was too, as he phoned him at seven in the morning. Both men were excited about being possible owners of new Casio keyboards; it was about time their plans for starting up a band got underway. By just before nine, Pete pulled up outside Ralf's and honked his horn. Ralf emerged shortly after and they drove toward West Ealing, to the Dixons store. Pete had a friend – more of an acquaintance – called Des, who worked at Dixons and he usually let Pete try out all the latest gadgets, when giving his manager the illusion that Pete was a potential customer.

Des was a big and smiley black fellow with a penchant for wearing a string of pearl beads around his neck. It was decidedly bizarre but if his manager eventually got used to it, then the rest of the world would have to. Ralf couldn't take his eyes off it to begin with, but once he heard what Des had to say about the keyboards and then demo them, he became used to it.

'Thing is Pete, the MT40 has been superseded by the MT41 – which unfortunately, we don't have – but we *have* got this one,' Des proceeded to pull out a large white keyboard from beneath the counter and plug it in just behind him, 'it's the MT 45. It's actually a better keyboard, and it sounds…well, listen for yourself; try it out.'

Pete and Ralf took turns in trying the little box of tricks out. While Pete was pretty good at playing the keyboard properly and with both hands, Ralf was more of a single finger key tickler. He used his left hand to play the automatic bass, which incorporated single-finger and chord bass-lines. The machine had eight preset rythms and eight preset sounds, such as piano, flute, harpsichord, etc. Pete didn't hesitate as he usually did; this was a done deal. Ralf was rather fascinated by this whole idea of automatic bass keyboards and wanted to know a little bit more, but Des unfortunately had no further information for the two pals. They both drove home, with Pete champing at the bit. Ralf found his childlike enthusiasm rather charming.

'Looks like you're gonna wank for joy any second now; you wanna pull over?'

Pete roared with laughter, his cackle sounding almost like Ozzie's machine-gun impersonation. The two drove over to Pete's house and spent the rest of the day making music. They had plenty to inspire them, and an evening at Mike's Music City seemed like a grand idea; a fine way to seal the day.

Chapter 8

The following Monday morning, Miss Clare knocked upon the door during Ralf's English class and asked to see him in private. Whilst reluctantly agreeing and excusing himself, the odd fleeting snigger from his pupils reminded him of what he could be up against. His heart sank. She led him to her office and after declining a hot beverage, he sat opposite her at her desk. She smelt nice and her face was lightly embellished with make-up; the full works, eye shadow, lipstick, the rest of it Ralf couldn't put a name to, but she clearly made an effort that morning, even with the clothes she chose. She wore a dark blue top with lace for the collar, a white skirt with floral patterns, and closed, dark shoes with a significant heel. Ralf just hoped it wasn't for him.

'I'm sorry I interrupted your class. I just felt that I should apologise.' She said, as she clasped her hands without making any eye contact with him.

'Apologise for what?' Ralf asked with an inquisitive tone; he was playing dumb but so as not to make her feel any more uncomfortable that she already probably was.

'Well…for my behaviour the other day. I was clearly…delusional…to think that you could have absolutely any interest in me whatsoever.'

'Miss Cl…Edwina, I…'

'Please…let me finish, Ralf.'

'Sorry, go ahead…please.'

'You see…I'm very lonely. I've never been married and I've not had that many boyfriends either. When my mother died, around ten years ago, I just spiralled downwards. I put on weight from comfort eating, I gave up swimming and walking, I never really had any friends either. My mum was my only friend. My dad used to treat me like dirt really. He used to beat me as well; then he died. I shed no tears for him you know, none at all. Anyway, I'm sorry if I'm boring you, but I really felt I had to tell you these things. And of course, why on earth would you fancy a fat, bitter old woman like me? When you came along, I was

so charmed…your gentlemanly ways, your calming voice, your smile. I just
wished I could be…with you…or even your friend. I'd be happy with that. I
know I've been a bit of a bitch sometimes…well…pretty much all of the time.
But I do like you and I think you're a very good teacher. There you have it; my
last scrap of dignity.'

Ralf listened intently to Edwina and felt a little flutter inside of him. He knew
she was being entirely truthful with him; he was even flattered that she felt
she could open her heart to him like that. In those few meaningful minutes,
Edwina Clare had gained his respect. He actually *liked* the woman now. She
poured herself a coffee from a silver flask she kept on the window sill behind
her desk. At that moment, the sun slowly emerged from a throng of grey
clouds, and the sunlight highlighted her hair, which now appeared a dark
auburn. Her frame became silhouetted in the large window, causing her
features to become veiled in shadow; but Ralf could still make out her eyes.
She was smiling, but shyly. She was probably blushing, but she stayed in
shadow as though trying to adopt a stealthy approach to the situation. When
she sniffled slightly, Ralf knew she wasn't blushing.

'I'm very touched, Edwina, ' he said reassuringly, 'I'm very honoured actually;
and I certainly *don't* think that you're a fat, old woman. You shouldn't be so
hard on yourself. After what you've been through it's quite understandable
that you were rocked a little. And don't feel at all embarrassed about last
week; you're human aren't you? We all like a bit of love and attention; and
why shouldn't *you* have it?

'You know, I should apologise as well; for snapping at you like that,' continued
Ralf, as he took Edwina's hand in his, 'I just felt a little unusual that someone
was taking an interest in me. It's just that…'

'I know,' she said, squeezing his hand, 'I know you're carrying with you,
something very heavy, and very obscure.'

Ralf looked up at her, both bewildered and incredulous. How did she know that
he had something to hide? Would this mean the end of his career as a teacher?
Had she been secretly gathering information because of her infatuation with
him? That was impossible; there was nothing to find, unless – his book – no,
she'd not ever seen that; she hadn't been to his home before and he never

took the book anywhere out of the house. It resided safely upon the shelf of the bookcase, behind other books. Only Pete had seen it, and he didn't know Miss Clare. Ralf's mind went into overdrive and over-thinking modes. It suddenly became too much for him to handle. He was on the verge of cracking. Edwina spoke, and the increasingly dark and stormy cloud dispersed quickly.

'I have no idea what it is that troubles you; and you don't ever have to tell me. Your eyes speak for themselves, Ralf. They tell stories. There's clearly a devil sitting on your shoulder; but if you ever feel like talking…I'm here for you.'

Edwina rose from her seat and stepped round the desk and to Ralf's side. She took his hand and brought it to her lips and kissed it gently and smiled warmly at him. She really *was* a nice person. For the first time in his life, Ralf accepted that he could be wrong about someone. He never usually was; he always hit the nail right on the head when it came to sizing people up and knowing what they're about. He had to, with what he was carrying with him. She got that one right – a devil on his shoulder – and it was there to stay. Just like a combination of an old friend and a bad smell.

'Do you fancy going for a coffee after school?' asked Ralf with a chuckle, 'Seems like a date as teenagers, doesn't it?'

'Well, I'd be delighted!' She replied, with a bright smile upon her face, her rather pretty face, today.

'Just as friends, like…you know.'

'Of course, absolutely.'

The two drove a little of the way into Chiswick High Street and parked just across the road from Music City, and went in and took a seat in one of its booths. The bar was a fantastically atmospheric affair; a mixed bag. The owner, Mike, had a vision of something Art Deco in its theme, but ended up making the place resemble something of a cross between an abandoned tube station and the Orient Express. The bar area was sectioned off by a huge, semi-circular counter in dark wood with patterns etched into its front panels. Several spotlights washed the bar area, making working behind there an extremely heated affair; Mike could often be seen sweating like a horse despite always wearing T-shirts, even in the dead of winter, as he juggled beverages and nibbles when the evenings were at crowded peak, and the live music raged and thudded from the downstairs area. Edwina kept gazing all around her and taking it in. Ralf could tell she was impressed with the place. He also couldn't believe that he was actually out with her and sharing some time over a drink. If only the others could see him now; they would undoubtedly be puzzled. Ralf himself was hearing the little echoing voice swirling around in his head shouting, *What the bloody hell are you doing, you idiot?* The voice of his physical persona was just replying with a less urgent manner; kind of like saying, *Talk to the hand!*

Mike acknowledged him from behind the bar, while he was both serving and making the usual preparations for the evening. The poster that Mike was in the process of putting up on the nearby walls and the front of the bar and on the front windows, announced the latest band that would be playing on that coming Friday. A band known as ELEKTROKINETIK was to be the star of the night, and immediately Ralf's mind began grinding; it reminded him of the name Pete had picked for their musical duo, ELECTROARTZ. Ralf was beginning to think that perhaps Mike would let him and Pete play there, once they had some good material down. It would be great.

Ralf and Edwina remained at the bar for over two hours, just chatting and reminiscing about various subjects; pupils, politics – of which Ralf had no idea and detested – and music. He revealed a bit of what he and Pete had planned in terms of their musical interests and she seemed very keen to know more. Although tempted, Ralf was not yet ready to reveal anything about what plagued him every day of his life and that he'd learned to live with it. He was not yet ready, and was very glad and grateful that Edwina didn't push him into telling her. Once again, his heart expressed its surprise at having possibly found a friend; in someone who was unlikely to have ever breached his defences, gently as she had.

Pete was in his bedroom and trying out another purchase he'd found on the local newspaper. He found a five watt practice amplifier and lead, with which he plugged his keyboard into. The usual knock on his bedroom door was the signal for yet another Mother-Peter showdown; over the plink-a-plonk.

'What the bloody hell is that thumping sound?' Enquired a bewildered Susan.

'Hello mum, yes…it's my new pli…keyboard. I've plugged into this amp that I found advertised on the Leader. Someone was selling it in Greenford, so I thought I'd give it a try. What do you think?'

'Hmm, well, said Susan, 'it certainly sounds more…professional than that other bleepy thing you were using before…'

'Yes…' Intoned Pete, smirking as though he were expecting one of his mum's usual armour-piercing statements.

'I think it sounds very nice…what you were just playing now. That melody, it was good. Is it one of yours?'

'Actually yes, it *is* one of mine. I wrote it on the other…bleepy thing. I think it sounds much better on this keyboard because of the auto-bass thingy.'

'Yes, and it sounds good through your little amp as well.'

When asked to play it again, all the way through, Pete was overwhelmed at his mum's reaction. She was actually smiling. Broadly. Like she hadn't smiled in a long time. She even had a little go at 'plinking' herself while Pete went downstairs to make a celebratory pot of tea to mark the occasion; his personal little achievement of making his mum smile with enthusiasm, and over something he believed in. Great! Peter and Susan, One; crappy, stupid and pointless argument, nil.

Ozzie was in Chiswick and in search of a phone box so he could ring Ralf. He had some great news of his own. Julia had contacted him, saying that she missed him and even his antics. The rocker was once again, on a high. An Ozzie style high, and that could only mean a trip down to Music City involving him buying almost every round of drinks. Ralf and Pete would never allow him to buy more than two rounds usually, despite the fact that he would only be too happy to do so, but they always took turns in buying a couple of rounds each.

There was no answer at Ralf's end, he was still out with Edwina, as Ozzie discovered for himself as the phone box was just across the street from the bar. Ozzie spotted both of them as they came out of Music City and walked toward the car. Ozzie observed as his friend strolled along the high street with a portly lady attached to his arm. Ozzie returned to the phone box and rang Pete.

'You alright mate,' Ozzie intoned with his usual cheerful twang, 'I just seen Ralf comin' outta Music City wiv' a fat bird. Either she's his mum or his new girlfriend. I didn't know he like fackin' 'ippo's!'

Pete laughed but was very curious about who the lady in question was. Ralf would have told them if he'd found someone special for sure. Ozzie proceeded to tell Pete the other news he had and Pete was very much made up for him. Ozzie was the life and soul of the party ninety-nine per cent of the time, so seeing him down in the dumps was unusual and disturbing. Pete said he'd call Ralf later and arrange times for picking everyone up, now that Julia was back on the scene.

Debbie Graves finished her shift at the shoe-shop and began making her way up to Ealing Broadway station, to take the bus home. She lived in Brentford, in the Green Dragon Estate, at the top floor of one of six tower blocks that dominated the skyline in the area. Each tower block was twenty four storeys high, and offered breath-taking panoramas of the surrounding urban sprawl. Debbie lived in the Maudsley House tower with her mother and younger sister, Melanie. She met Pete thanks to Ralf, who decided to introduce them after he got chatting to her, one night when she came across him loitering in the corridors of the top floor. He had quickly nipped inside as someone was exiting the building, so he could take the lift to the top floor and enjoy the view. After an initially tense conversation about why he was up there, Debbie's third degree acquired the answers that satisfied her enough to feel comfortable with Ralf inviting himself in. It was a couple of nights after, that Debbie agreed to meet them at the Music City, to meet Peter. The two clicked immediately, and they even shared a first kiss by the end of the evening.

Debbie left the bus just a short walk away from a long pathway that cut through a couple of housing areas leading up to the Green Dragon Estate. As she turned a corner into a narrow alley that cut a significant corner on the way home, she felt her arm being grabbed by a hooded figure that emerged from behind a lamppost. Its intense orange light made it hard to discern who it was, until he spoke. It was Andrew, the stalker that loitered outside the shoe-shop the other day.

'I don't appreciate being ignored,' he said, lowering the hood of his sweatshirt and revealing a sulky scowl; and a shiner that was undoubtedly the result of the Peter-punch.

'What do you want!?' Snapped a frightened Debbie, as she whipped her arm away from Andrew's tightening clutch.

'Relax baby, I just wanna get to know you better, that's all. Why are you being so hostile?'

'Look, just leave me alone okay...I just want to get home...I'm really tired, I've been at work all day. We'll chat another time okay?'

As Debbie turned to try and walk away, Andrew grabbed her arm again, but with both hands this time. She screamed at the top of her voice and managed to let out a couple of loud *help me's* before Andrew grabbed her in a hold from behind, covering her mouth with his hand. Debbie struggled as hard as she could, almost managing to break free from her assailant's grip and succeeding in letting out another ear-shattering cry for help, before Andrew grabbed her again, this time by the hair. He pulled her violently toward him and smacked her across the face, hard. Debbie staggered back against the lamppost, tripping over a large chunk of concrete and falling back against the wooden fence that separated the alley from someone's back garden. Debbie screamed once again, as she fell sideways and hit the ground, banging her head against the lamppost. Andrew kicked her violently, striking the legs, making her scream again.

'Shut the fuck up, you stupid bitch!' Andrew shouted, 'No one's gonna help you now...the lovely Peter's not here, is he...the fucking hero!'

The stalker kicked her once again, in the stomach this time, making her gasp desperately for breath, as the fierce blow winded her. Debbie coiled up into a ball and covered her face and abdomen, ready for the next onslaught. It was almost pitch black in that alley, except for the point where the lamppost was ablaze. Unfortunately, the one where Debbie and Andrew were 'liaising,' was the only street lamp in working order. There were two others that lined that stretch of pathway, and they had been out for a couple of months, leaving most of the alley in pitch black when night fell. At that moment, Debbie hated herself. She hated herself for taking that alleyway as a shortcut home, and all it truncated was a few minutes of walking time. She'd always used it when going home from the bus stop and there were never any problems. In fact, it was never heard of, that anyone had ever been attacked or mugged there. She lay on the ground in a ball, screaming, crying, and begging for Andrew to leave her alone, and her cries and pleas for help were muffled as her face and mouth were concealed behind her forearms, in desperate defence.

Andrew bent over her, screaming abuse and never-ending threats that he would be her 'fucking shadow' if she wasn't nice to him. He had stopped kicking her so hard now, but kept prodding and shoving her body with his leg, as though she were nothing but refuse in the gutter. He fell silent for a few seconds, and for an instant, Debbie thought he'd perhaps gotten fed up and left her, but as soon as she lowered her forearm and peeked from cover, a thundering punch came hurtling toward her like a train from a tunnel, hitting her square in the face. She screamed like she'd never screamed before. The ear-piercing screech sent Andrew into a squint and caused him to take a couple of steps back. It was her chance. A few precious seconds to spring up and run away. Debbie scrambled almost to her feet, when Andrew shuffled up to her and pushed her down onto the ground once more.

'Where the fuck do you think you're going, you fucking little bitch!?'

A splash of spittle burst forth from his lips and onto her face, as she covered up once again. Debbie wept loudly, bitterly, uncaring of any loss of pride or dignity. She just wanted to go home. Home to her mother and her sister, and sit down for tea. Scrambled eggs and beans on toast, with a cup of coffee, then some crap TV. She cried so hard, as though she would never see her family again; or in one piece. Why wasn't anyone around? Why did nobody ever come to her aid during such a drastic time? Debbie prayed to something or some higher power, that maybe, just maybe, someone would pass by. Someone that had enough gall and power to fight off this beast that relentlessly stood over her, like a wild animal toying with its prey before devouring it. At that precise moment, a bellowing voice came from further up the alleyway, just a few feet from where they were. For a split-second, Debbie thought the surreal clamour was her imagination desperately trying to conjure a hero or an escape route.

'Oi, what the fack do ya think yer doin, ya bloody scumbag!?'

Andrew shuffled backwards, almost losing his footing and stumbling back onto the fence that stood on the other side of the alley.

'Leave her the fack alone!'

'I'm not doing anything to her, she just fell. I was just helping her. Mind your own business. Fuck off!'

All was silent for a few seconds. Debbie began to shake and cry again. *Please don't get scared off and walk away...please, please, save me, she thought.* All she wanted was her saviour to carry through what he'd started. Debbie tried to get up once again, but was too exhausted to do so. She was utterly petrified and her legs felt weak and numb. The fear had got to them, besides Andrew's repeated kicks. Debbie looked toward where she thought the voice came from. The orange glow of the street lamp that bathed her felt like an unbearable spotlight from hell, and she was the tortured soul, the victim of the demonic force that was about to rip her to pieces. The disturbing lucence impaired her vision as she tried to stare into the dark of the alley. The source of her saviour's voice emerged. A figure upon a bicycle slowly materialised from the darkness, clad in a black leather jacket and ripped jeans at the knee. The young male had long dark hair and the badges hat adorned his jacket glinted in the light of the hellish streetlamp. It was Ozzie. He was on his way to Julia, who lived in one of the six tower blocks in the same estate where Debbie lived.

He dismounted from the bike and let it drop against the wooden fence. The clatter of the bicycle falling to the ground made a loud and imposing noise as it rose above the silence of the alleyway. Debbie recognized him and burst into tears of relief and joy, as he rushed toward Andrew, snarling with rage. He landed a thundering punch to the side of Andrew's face, knocking him sideways and back against the fence. Andrew attempted to hide his face from any further blows, but Ozzie grabbed him and effortlessly flung him toward the fence on the opposite side, not far from where Debbie now sat with her back to it. The shock from where Andrew smashed against the fence, sent Debbie forward, and she scrambled to her feet and moved away from the ensuing scuffle. Ozzie smashed his fists into Andrew's face, despite him putting them up in a desperate attempt to cover himself, like a tired boxer. Andrew even tried to fight back but his efforts were in vain, as Ozzie kept coming at him with punch after punch, kick after kick, every one of his blows connecting with unstoppable force. Andrew fell to the ground while Ozzie kept pounding on him incessantly. The stalker didn't cry out once during his punishment from the rocker. Ozzie was now straddling his foe as he lay on the ground. He grabbed both of Andrew's forearms, moved them aside, and proceeded to rain his fists down onto the man's face. Debbie cried out his name, and the rocker stayed his arm and bloodied knuckles before any further damage could be done. He got off of the now unconscious Andrew, his face unrecognizable from having being kneaded like a clump of dough. Ozzie's grey T-shirt beneath his leather jacket was splattered with blood, the knuckles of his right hand, more so than his left, were dark red and dripping with claret. Debbie ran toward him and threw herself into his arms, sobbing loudly and shaking violently. They two stood there for what seemed like hours, like two theatrical protagonists swathed in the spotlight of the dreaded streetlamp that would haunt Debbie for the rest of her life. In that time, not a soul passed through the alleyway.

Chapter 9

Pete was driving Debbie home after leaving her GP surgery. The two were silent for most of the journey, but Debbie spoke up as they approached the street where she usually got off the bus to cut into the alley where the events of two days before took place. She asked him to speed up and then take the long way round to where the tower blocks were. He accompanied his girlfriend up into her flat where her mum waited with some hot beverages and biscuits. As Pete entered Debbie's home, her mother invited him to sit and have some tea with them, which Pete was about to gratefully accept, when Debbie spoke up.

'He isn't staying, mum!' Debbie said.

Both her mum and sister, Melanie, stood in surprise as Debbie passed through the lounge and disappeared into the corridor and into her room, slamming the door. Pete remained where he stood and stared into the shadowy entrance to the hallway, his heart sinking as he felt like on the verge of tears. Debbie's mum gestured for him to sit down, but he refused.

'It's okay, Mrs Graves. Thank you anyway, but I think she needs time alone. She's just been to hell and back. I'd better go. I'll call her tomorrow if that's okay.'

'Of course it is, my love. You take care; love to your mum and dad.'

Pete left the flat and rode the elevator down in the company of an elderly lady and her poodle. Pete could see her smiling at him with the corner of his eye, but kept his head down. He wasn't in the mood for smiling or polite conversation and the lift seemed to take forever to reach the ground floor. The ride was interrupted as the lift stopped at the twelfth floor, allowing a young couple to step in and continue the journey. Pete's morale sank even lower as the couple of youngsters were locked in an embrace, kissing and gazing into each other's eyes. He knew deep inside, even as his mind attempted to grasp at positive thoughts that all would pass and heal, that his relationship with Debbie was pretty much over.

'Are you alright dear?' The old woman asked, touching his arm.

Pete replied that all was okay, as he valiantly held back a tear or two. The lift reached its destination and he rushed out into the cold air after nodding a polite goodbye to the kindly old lady and her pooch. He broke into a trot as his car came into view and once inside it, he burst into tears. He was scared of losing Debbie. He didn't deserve it. He'd done nothing wrong, but couldn't bring his mind into that pattern of thought. Debbie was badly scarred – not just physically – but her spirit was badly broken. Pete felt he was being possibly selfish in worrying about whether or not his relationship with her would end. All he believed he should be thinking was that Debbie needed all the love and support she could get from those around her; for some reason that seemed beyond his comprehension, just not him.

Pete was a grounded, intelligently methodical, but sensitive soul. His gut feelings were seldom wrong about anything or anyone, which was why this situation kept chipping away at him. He thought that maybe Debbie was angry at him for not being the one that was there instead of Ozzie. Maybe it should have been *him* that gave Andrew Blaine the hiding he deserved, but no. It wasn't that. It couldn't be that, surely. Pete happened to be on the scene when he'd punched Andrew the first time round, the day he was hanging around outside Debbie's workplace, so surely he would have done the same thing, had he happened to be in the neighbourhood that evening, in the alleyway.

Debbie wouldn't tell Pete what her GP had said to her earlier on. She didn't even want him to go in with her. He was completely in the dark about what the doctor had said to her, although he imagined what could have been said. Lots of rest, a couple of weeks off work, keep taking the meds, and so on. Perhaps the doctor told her to dump her boyfriend if she had one. No. Why would he say something like that? Pete sat in his car for over an hour before driving off and head for home. He turned the radio on. The song, Instinction, by Spandau Ballet, was being played on Capital Radio.

 On entering his house, Pete felt a tightening in his stomach and he ran upstairs and threw his face into the toilet bowl, throwing up immediately. He could hear his mother shout up the stairs, asking him if he was okay. He couldn't answer just yet. Susan cried to him again, but he retched once more and let loose what he hoped was the end of it. The phone rang, and Susan answered it after two rings; it hung just on the wall beside the door to the lounge. Pete could hear every word his mother was saying. He knew it was Ozzie by the answers she was giving.

'Yes, he's here. I don't think he's feeling too well. He's in the bathroom…he's feeling sick. No, Ralf's not with him. No, Debbie isn't here either. I'll get him to call you as soon as he's feeling better. I'd better go and see how he's doing. Okay, bye.

'Peter!'

He didn't reply. He'd finished throwing up, but he didn't want to talk to anyone. Not now.

'Peter, are you alright love!?'

Susan began thudding up the stairs and before she could get any further, Pete replied.

'I'm okay mum…can I talk to you later?'

A pause.

'Yes…okay. Shall I bring you some tea and cake?'

'Just tea…thanks mum.'

Pete remained knelt down in front of the green ceramic potty while he allowed a bit of life to creep back into him.

Ozzie had Phoned Ralf shortly after speaking to Pete's mum and asked if he could pop over. Ralf agreed and put the kettle on. Ozzie declined a lift and preferred to cycle to Ralf's instead. He had a driving licence, but couldn't as of yet, afford a car of his own. His motorbike had broken down and given up the ghost due to its age and so now relied upon his legs, both for walking and pedalling. He reached Hawkshead Road about forty five minutes later and the two friends settled down with some hot coffee and jam tarts; a favourite of Ralf's, besides Mrs Child's Victoria Sponge.

'Pete wasn't feelin' too good. He couldn't come to the phone so I'll call him later. You heard anything yet?'

'Not yet. Not since the cops found him. He's still in a coma. You must've battered him pretty good, Ozzie.'

'He fackin' deserved it…he was…!'

'I know, I know…you silly sod, I'm not blaming you. I'd have done the same thing; Pete would've done the same thing. The guy was a piece of shit. Anyone who beats up on a girl is a piece of shit!'

Ozzie quickly put his mug of coffee on the floor beside him; he'd scalded it while gesticulating to Ralf, who immediately handed him a wet-wipe that he kept beside his armchair.

'Do you think they'll find out it was me?' Asked a preoccupied Ozzie.

'There are no cameras that scour that area. If he wakes up and decides to squeal, then we've got problems.'

'Fackin' hell. I know what'll 'appen ya know. The little facker'll squeal to the cops and I'll be the one who'll end up in a cell. He beats the crap out of a girl…I get the blame, you'll see!'

'We don't know that, Ozzie. You just have to lay low for a while. You can crash out here for a bit if you want.'

'Cheers mate, I appreciate it.'

'Look, I've got a friend in the police force. He doesn't live here though, he's in Sussex. I'll call him tomorrow. He owes me a favour. I'm not promising anything, but I'll talk to him and see what he says. For now, we'll wait.'

Ozzie's eyes lit up for a brief moment but sank back into gloom seconds after. He wasn't confident he could get out of this one. Not only that, but he'd only just realised he'd stood Julia up. He was on his way to see her when he stumbled upon Andrew and Debbie. He'd forgotten to call her during all the ensuing stress and commotion. He was too messed up inside to even consider calling her now. He wondered if he could ask Ralf to call her and explain. He didn't think he could handle a rejection or a scolding at this time.

'Oh by the way, what did you mention to Julia?'

Ozzie's eyes lit up again, and he told Ralf that it went completely out of his mind. He was scared of mentioning any of it to her in case she freaked out at what he'd done to Andrew.

'You want me to call her and explain?'

'I dunno, what do you think?'

'I think she'll understand, Ozzie. She doesn't strike me as unreasonable. She'll probably think that it was a good thing you happened to be there. We can, but try.'

Ralf rang Julia and explained the situation and mentioned that Ozzie was with him. He hung up immediately after. Ozzie felt like crying his eyes out.

'Hey big guy...chin up, she's on her way.'

Ozzie managed a rather enthusiastic smile, and guzzled three jam tarts all at once, much to Ralf's amusement. Within fifteen minutes, Julia pulled up outside and Ozzie raced to the front door. He almost fell on his face as he stumbled over the doorstep. Ralf observed from the window, smiling, as the two lovers embraced tightly, while Ozzie planted countless kisses upon Julia's person, from the neck downwards. She laughed out loud when the rocker fell upon his knees, kissing her stomach; and a little further down. Ralf gave a hearty cackle.

Pete was in his bedroom, lying on his bed. Susan had brought him the tea, as promised, and left him to his thoughts after offering to be there if he needed to chat about it. He was going to tell both his parents. He felt he'd bonded with his mum even more that day she went up to admire the new plink-a-plonk. The only slight hiccup that held him back a little was talking to his dad, John. He was sure he would understand and undoubtedly spew forth the usual words of wisdom, based upon his countless experiences. The problem lay in the fact that John was extremely matter-of-fact, with brutal and ruthless opinions about the tapestry of life and the beautiful and colourful people that dwelt within it.

Once he heard his father's bellowing and cultured voice express one of said opinions, probably at what was on the television, he smiled slightly and rose from the bed.

'What an absolute tosser!' cried his father. 'How the bloody hell can you possibly miss such a simple shot!?'

Pete skipped down the stairs, looking at his footwork, which strangely, reminded him of Riverdance. He entered the lounge and dropped himself on one of the two armchairs, the one closest to the door; just in case a swift exit was required, should John come out with something Pete didn't want to hear. John exclaimed his disdain of a football player's shoddy tactic during a football match that was being played at Brentford football club. Pete sat back and enjoyed a few more of his dad's rants and raves about the beautiful game. Pete hated football as a whole, but would sit down and watch a match during the world cup. As soon as England was eliminated from it, he'd stop watching. That was the extent of his interest in football; every four years was the most he could withstand.

'So, what's up with you then?' asked John, sipping a glass of red wine, 'I sense you've got problems with your love life.'

Pete sat forward and on his elbows. He really wanted to talk about it, badly, but he just couldn't withstand any of his dad's possible negative comments. If he dared say anything untoward about Debbie, Pete wouldn't be sure to keep his mouth shut. John seldom took to any of Pete's girlfriends. It wasn't just Pete's impression either; his dad didn't like someone if he kept completely quiet about what he thought of them. Unless he asked his dad what he actually thought; then he would have a long string of reasons why she wasn't girlfriend material. Sod it, he thought; Go for it, Pete. If you don't like what you hear, just bugger off back upstairs.

Pete started from the beginning; the Peter-punch day, subsequent phone calls with his girlfriend being a little on the cold side, and lastly, the main event. John listened, miraculously, without interrupting his son once. Susan left the room during the conversation but returned shortly afterwards with a pot of tea and ginger cake. The little family helped themselves to a slice of cake each upon a small paper plate and got halfway through the mugs of tea until John voiced his opinion on the matter.

'I think you've been very patient and gentlemanly about the whole situation,' John said, 'She *does* indeed need bags of time to recover from such an ordeal.'

'Bags of time?' Asked Pete.

'Yes, I'm afraid so. I also think she's going off you, though.'

'Why would you say that?'

'You said that she's been a little off with you since the first encounter with this Andrew person. I think she kind of likes the attention of other men fancying her. Now don't get me wrong...neither she, nor anybody else knew that *this* would happen...I do like her, I think she's a lovely girl, and lovely looking. Best one you've gone out with so far. It's just that this incident has hit her particularly hard; so hard in fact, that she's not even thinking of you at all. An she won't for a long while.'

'Fuck me, dad,' exclaimed Peter, baffled, 'Do you *really* actually think that?'

'Yes, son, I do; much as it pains me to say it, but I do.'

'I really want to talk to her. Her mum said it was okay if I rang her tomorrow.'

'I'd advise you just speak to her mum. Try to get her by herself and ask how Debbie is. I assure you her mother will really appreciate that you're truly worried and concerned, but want to give her daughter all the space she needs. Debbie will contact you when she's ready. I know you've got to play a very painful waiting game, but it's the thing *I'd* choose to do if I were you.'

Pete sipped his tea and finished off his ginger cake. The room was silent for the rest of the evening, with the exception of John's opinions about the outcome of the match, and subsequently, some of the absolutely crap songs on Top of The Pops. He hated Hayzee Fantayzee and Jean Michel Jarre, and when Soft Cell appeared singing the song, *Say Hello, Wave Goodbye,* that was when the roof was raised.

'Bloody shirt-lifters! Just ludicrous! Look at him, bloody makeup covering his face and...bloody good voice, though!'

Pete sank back into the armchair and smiled. It wasn't a forced smile either. At that moment, he really loved the fact that his parents were in his life, and he, in theirs.

Chapter 10

Ozzie and his girlfriend had crashed out on Ralf's bed, but with the promise that he and Julia wouldn't do any boinking. Ralf stayed up for most of the night with his ears pricked up and didn't hear anything. He was pretty sure they didn't, as he knew Ozzie was a noisy lover; his words. He phoned his friend in the force, a certain Jeff Mallory. He was a trusted friend of Ralf's who in the not so distant past, gave his word that he would someday repay a favour. The day had come and so Ralf explained the entire situation to him.

'Leave it with me. When he talks, and I'm sure a bastard like that will, I'll take it from there. Just keep me posted as things happen, bro. I've got your back.'

'Thanks Jeff, I really appreciate it my friend. Things okay at your end?'

'Things are a little up and down at this neck of the woods. Liz is seeing her boss on the side. I'm just waiting for my moment to nail the greasy bastard.'

'Shit, I'm sorry bro. I had no idea. Has it been going on for long?'

'Only found out last week. Don't know how long they've been at it for. It's been a few days now, that she's been getting home late because of last minute conference calls. She sounded really convincing when she phoned me up to warn me she'd be late. Daft cow. She thinks I'm stupid.'

'Damn, you should have called me.'

'I did, but you were out, both times. You should get yourself one of those answering machines. Actually, I've got one here you can have. I'll bring it over, or you come here, whichever.'

'Hey, sounds good. Okay, they're waking up. They slept over last night. Ozzie couldn't handle going home. You know, all the never ending questions.'

'Okay Ralf, great talking with you, bro. Listen, keep me updated, yeah?'

'Will do, take care brother. Later.'

Ozzie and Julia came down some twenty minutes later and they had breakfast, comprising of one of Ralf's gigantic bacon sandwiches; around six rashers each person. Ralf told Ozzie and Julia he'd spoken to his friend, Jeff and he would be willing to help out as and when. For now, Ozzie was a permanent guest at the Hotel Chez Ralf.

Later that day, Pete waited downstairs near the entrance to Debbie's tower block until her mum emerged to go to work. He offered her a lift in his car and he drove her all the way to Islington, where she worked in a care home. Debbie's mum, Stella, greatly appreciated Pete's approach to asking about her daughter and she tried to shed light on how Debbie was feeling as best she could. What she couldn't understand was why Debbie wanted to hear nothing about Pete; but of course, she couldn't tell him in those precise words.

Pete drove back home feeling empty and downtrodden. He got caught in a traffic jam, commonplace in Islington on a weekday morning, but ultimately frustrating nevertheless. He switched the radio on to find the news blasting from the speakers. He had the volume up high the night before, and was just about to tune into another station, when he heard an announcement that sent ice-cold shivers up his spine, so much so, he shivered hard, as though someone had walked over his grave.

...police are still trying to piece together the last movements of the young man found badly beaten in an alleyway in Brentford last night. The man, who has been identified as Andrew Blaine, twenty two years old, died earlier this morning from his injuries...

Pete switched the radio off immediately and pulled over as soon as he could. He felt suddenly light-headed and on the brink of vomiting. He covered his mouth and tensed his muscles as much as he could, willing himself not to surrender to another throwing up fest. It was close to the mark; Pete felt the foul fluids rising up into his gullet, and trickle down from his lips. He activated his hazard lights and sat there with his head resting against the head restraint. Throngs of people continued to walk past him, some of them peering into his car; with curiosity rather than concern, and continued on with their lives.

Debbie emerged from her bedroom and went into the kitchen area for something to drink. Her sister rushed to the rescue when she heard the crashing of the drainer as it hit the floor, spilling its contents everywhere, but fortunately, only a bunch of utensils and cutlery were in it. The dishes had already been wiped dry and put away.

'Here, let me sort it.' said Melanie, 'you go and sit down. I'll fix you a drink. Tea or coffee?'

Debbie and her sister were very close and seldom quarrelled over anything. There were a few years between them, Debbie being thirty one and Mel being twenty seven, and the only serious argument they'd ever had was over Michael Jackson and Luther Vandross, over who was the better singer. The argument still remained unresolved to that very day. Debbie curled up on the sofa and wrapped herself with a warm blanket with flying pigs as its design. Mel brought her a mug of tea and a pack of her favourite biscuits; Malted Milk.

'Did you get any sleep at all?' Asked Mel, 'Or is it a silly question?'

'Not really. I *was* dozy...when I *did* drift off, all I could see was him.'

'I know,' said Mel, rubbing her sister's shoulder, 'It'll stay with you for a while, but time *is* a definite healer and you're strong. What about Pete, you heard from him since he brought you back from Doctor Stone?'

'Oh don't talk to me about him.' Debbie appeared to recoil in horror when Mel mentioned it. Mel had never known her sister to react in such a fashion any time Pete's name was mentioned. Usually, Debbie's eyes would sparkle like diamonds and she would simply jump at the chance to talk about her amazing boyfriend. Her gentleman of a boyfriend who even wrote a song for her. Pete was the perfect subject and topic of conversation. He was like the Cadbury among all chocolate, as she would so delightfully put it.

'What's wrong with him? I thought you loved him. Weren't you actually planning on telling him that at Christmas time? Remember?'

'Yeah...no, I don't know...'

'Debbie, what's wrong?' asked Mel as she held her sister's hand.

'I don't know anymore...he hit that bloke just because he was outside the shop. I didn't know he...that Andrew... was going to do...that...what he did, you know, beat me up. I had no idea he was going to get me. It's just that Pete punched him. I don't want someone who's jealous like that. What if I talk to any bloke, even nice blokes about anything...the weather, the TV, washing-up, anything...is he going to just go up and punch them too?'

Debbie burst into bitter tears and Mel held her in her arms, rocking her gently, like a child. The phone rang; they ignored it. The doorbell rang; they ignored that too. Mel was worried about Debbie, and Debbie needed her. That was all that mattered at that moment.

That evening, Mel drove over to Pete's house after ringing him to make sure he was in. As soon as she arrived, Pete went out to her and they both agreed to have a coffee somewhere quiet. Pete told her about a small café just down the road from him, in Northfield Avenue. The café was very quiet as it usually was late evening, and on a weekday, and they sat down nearest to the window that faced onto the street.

'I thought I'd come and tell you how things are. I think you have a right to know. As far as I'm concerned, you've always been good to her, treated her right and she usually never stops talking about you.'

'So what's the problem now?' asked Pete, 'why won't she talk to me? I just can't understand what it is I've done wrong. I've even agreed to give her all the space she needs; I know what she's just been through. It was fucking terrible for her. I don't know what else to do.'

'I spoke to her earlier this morning. She was...'

'Go on, Mel, please. I really need to know.' Pete pleaded with her.

'She said she was worried that you're too jealous.'

'What?' shrieked Pete, banging his fist on the table, and startling Mel and the two customers that sat in the café, 'Jealous? Me?'

'Sshh, keep your voice down. Listen, she said you just hit that guy just for standing outside the shop. She reckons that if you hadn't reacted that way, none of this would have happened.'

'I just don't believe this, so it's my bloody fault, is it?' said Pete, sighing heavily, 'I should have told her.'

'Told her what?'

'Look, it's simple. I went to pick her up from work and I notice this bloke standing there, right? Okay, he then gives me this piece of paper with his phone number on and asks me to take it in to Debbie, if I was going in there on my travels. I would've just left at that. I *was* just planning on going in there, give her the bit of paper, and then come out of the shop with her on my arm, just to see the look of horror and embarrassment on his stupid face, that's all.'

'So why did you punch him? I know that's not your style. You're too nice for that sort of thing…or am I wrong.'

'No, you're not wrong,' snapped Pete, once again, startling Mel, 'I'm sorry…no, you're not wrong. It was what he said that made my blood boil. I just saw red, then…well, that was it.'

'What did he say?'

'He said, *I'd love to smash her back doors in.* Now you tell me that wouldn't have pissed you off!'

Mel pondered for a moment and sipped her coffee.

'You could have just warned him, Pete. You didn't have to actually hit him.'

'Right, great, so now *you* think I'm some kind of violent, jealous psycho as well! That's great, just fucking great!' Pete banged his fist on the table so hard, it spilt both his coffee and Mel's, who at that point, rose from her seat and stormed out of the café. Pete watched as she crossed the road and marched toward where Pete lived and to where she had parked her car. Pete couldn't control himself and despite his efforts to hold them back, inevitable tears began streaming down his face. With the corner of his eye, he saw that the gazes of the other customers in the café, were upon him. He turned toward them with a scowl that would make an army of armed soldiers turn and flee.

'What the fuck are you looking at? Show's over, you nosey cunts!'

After dishonouring himself, Pete left the café and walked back home. He went straight upstairs into his room and locked the door. His parents were both bantering and laughing heartily, probably at something on the television, and the sound of joy and laughter was not something he wanted to listen to at that moment. He threw himself face down onto his bed and remained there until he fell asleep.

Mel went into her flat and sat next to Debbie, who hadn't moved from the sofa since before her sister went out that evening. She put her arm around Debbie and the two of them sat there in silence for the duration of a noisy reality TV show, followed by the evening local news, and the main headline caused the two sisters to sit up simultaneously in shock-horror.

Good evening, the local community of the Green Dragon Estate in Brentford is now in a state of alert after the body of a young man, identified as twenty two year old Andrew Blaine, of Ealing Common, was found badly battered in the main alley which runs from the Red Lion Road and through the various estates in the area. He was found by an anonymous caller who reported that they'd come across Mr Blaine, who was apparently barely alive, but later died from his injuries before the ambulance could reach the hospital. After speaking with many of the residents around the nearby homes, police have come to the conclusion that the incident was in no way gang related or personal, but rather that Mr Blaine had fallen victim to a mugging, as no cash was found in his pockets and Mr Blaine never had any history of drugs or alcohol abuse of any kind. The victim was an only child and lived with his mother on the edge of Ealing Common. Andrew's mother, Sheila Blaine, told the police that she is absolutely devastated. Andrew was a kind and friendly young man, and would never hurt a fly, as she put it. She has absolutely no idea who could have done such a terrible thing, as her son had hardly any friends, and never mixed with anyone. Police have appealed that anyone with any information at all, regarding the incident, should please come forward.

Mel hugged her sister tightly as she buried her head in Mel's embrace, bitterly sobbing and shaking like a petrified animal. Debbie repeatedly expressed her total disbelief that Pete could have had anything to do with this, and continued to say it for the next ten minutes. Mel tried to uncouple herself from her sister's desperate clinch and reason with her.

'Debbie…Deb…sshh…just listen to me.'

Debbie dabbed her eyes with the cover that enveloped her and paused for breath while looking at her sister.

'Are you sure it wasn't Pete?'

Debbie nodded, her face damp and blotchy from the endless lachrymal river that flowed from those blue eyes, now squinting and flooded with fear.

'Don't protect him, don't you dare…you're well shot of somebody like that. He could do it to you!'

Debbie began hiccupping from the overwhelming sorrow, as she desperately tried to speak.

'What is it…just take deep breaths…just tell me.'

'It…it w…wasn't him…wasn't Pete…,' whispered Debbie, still shaking as though bitten by cold, 'Ozzie…it was Ozzie…'

'Ozzie?' Cried Mel.

'Yes…yes, it was Ozzie, said Debbie, now steadily regaining her timbre, 'if he hadn't been there, Andrew would have probably killed me…you mustn't say anything…no police.'

'But, Deb…,'

'No police, Mel. Ozzie didn't mean to actually kill him. He just saw what state I was in; I was curled up on the ground all busted up and I had a nosebleed. Ozzie just wanted to…punish him…to just teach him a lesson for beating up a girl. He's not a killer. He's just someone with a bit of a temper, but he's a good friend. Please, Mel…you mustn't say anything, not even to mum! Promise me!'

Debbie slipped off of the sofa and fell onto her knees in front of her sister, clutching at her skirt.

'Promise me, promise me, promise me…please!' Debbie buried her face into Mel's lap and entered into fits of sobbing and crying. Mel slid onto the floor beside her and held her tightly. She didn't let go until Debbie cried herself to sleep in her arms.

Chapter 11

Ralf was in the kitchen loading the washing machine with his and Ozzie's clothes. Mrs Child had been round earlier to bring over her usual weekly Victoria Sponge cake that Ralf had fallen in love with when he'd first moved in there many years back. Maggie and Horace Child had lived in Hawkshead Road since the early sixties and were the first neighbours that welcomed Ralf when he first went to live there, and were good friends with Enza and Raffaele, the elderly Italian couple that had been there for roughly the same time. Ozzie asked Ralf about his auntie and uncle, but as usual, he was very reserved and withdrawn on the subject. He always had been, for as long as both Pete and Ozzie had known him and after numerous attempts at prising the information from him, they realised it was time to give up; even if it *did* seem ridiculous that he never wanted to talk about it. The other strange thing was that Ralf never kept any photographs on display anywhere in the house.

Ozzie turned the spare key in the front door and hauled several shopping bags through, with Julia close behind with a couple of her own. They mentioned they had just been to the supermarket – not the one where Ozzie last made an idiot of himself – and bought some provisions. Ralf had agreed that they both remain with him until the Andrew Blaine situation blow over, and Julia, like Ozzie, had a rather invasive family and at this particular time, she could do without endless questions. Ozzie's mum had phoned Ralf to ask him if she'd seen her son. Ralf hated lying, but when the need arose…

The three friends sat down to some dinner, a little late, but it was a light and healthy meal. Ozzie could never get used to the way Ralf ate, but each time he was invited to his place for food, he found it very pleasurable. Ozzie was a junk-foodie and chippies, Chinese and Indian takeaways, Mcdonalds, and KFC, were all part of his dietary rituals on an almost daily basis. Ralf had managed to convert Pete to his way of eating and he has never looked back since, but Ozzie had been a tough nut to crack so far.

'So who was the…erm…big bird you were out with the other day then?' Ozzie enquired with a mouthful of lemon drenched broccoli.

'If you saw me coming out of Mike's bar, that would have been my colleague at the school; well, by colleague, I mean the headmistress. Her name's Edwina; *and* she's a really nice woman and a good friend, so no bloody wisecracks!'

'Wisecracks? Me? Come on Ralf, now would I be rude about 'er. Ah mean, she did look like yer mum an'all, but…fackin hell mate!'

'Ozzie!' Snapped Julia; Ralf chuckled with his mouth full of food, almost coughing.

'Beauty is only skin deep!' Continued Julia.

'Yeah, and ugly goes straight through!' Replied Ozzie, bursting into his machine-gun laugh.

'We're not an item, you silly sod, she really is just a friend. You know I don't have many of those besides you guys and my mate the cop. Edwina always got on my tits, it's true, but a few days ago I saw a different side to her.'

'That's really lovely,' said Julia, touching Ralf's hand, 'sometimes it's…'

'Sometimes when you're an old fart like Ralf, you get to only pull the fat ones, ahahahahahahahahaha!' Interrupted Ozzie, and burst into an endless train of laughter. Both Julia and Ralf eventually joined him as it became all a little too infectious to resist. The phone rang, bringing the moment of funny times to an abrupt halt. Ralf thought he knew who it was.

'Pete, where the bloody hell are you? Are you okay?'

Ozzie and his girlfriend looked at each other, concerned and he rose from the table and went over to Ralf.

'Stay there, I'll come and get you. Can you move the car, or are you dizzy or anything?'

Ozzie went to get his jacket from the coat stand near the bottom of the stairs.

'Okay, we'll park it somewhere when I get there; Islington has tons of side streets. I'll be as quick as I can. Ozzie and Julia are here with me, so we'll have some company. Fuck knows where I'm going to sleep…'

Ralf slammed the handset down and went to the coat stand. He told Ozzie to stay put, as he had an apple pie in the oven and interrupting it half way through cooking would ruin it. He would be back soon. Ozzie agreed and offered to wait up with Julia until he and Pete returned.

Ralf jumped into the Ford Capri and pulled away with such urgency, his tyres screeched a little. As he rounded the corner of Hawkshead Road and turned left onto The Avenue, he slammed on his brakes, hard, as a man dressed in dark clothing appeared before him in the middle of the road. The driver in the car behind honked his horn at length after narrowly avoiding ramming into the back of him. Ralf got out of his car and the man behind him began yelling obscenities from his window. Ralf walked up to the car and apologised for the emergency stop, but told him that if he ever called him a bald-headed wank stain again, he'd rip off his bollocks and shove them up his arse. The driver sheepishly agreed and drove off gently.

Ralf began walking back to his own car when he noticed the dark-clothed man still standing in the middle of the road looking at him. He slowed his pace a little whilst briefly scrutinizing the fellow, around six feet tall and with dark hair, probably in his forties. Ralf walked toward him and asked him if there was some kind of problem.

'I see your English is perfect, now,' said the stranger, 'You seem to have a good life here. Nice car, nice house, nice job...'

The stranger had a good command of the English language, but Ralf detected an accent, a heavy Mediterranean inflection. He was proved correct when the fellow began speaking to Ralf in Italian.

'I don't understand a word you're saying. You must have me confused with someone else.' Replied Ralf, gently but assertively.

'You understand me very well,' replied the man, in Italian once again, 'Do you not remember who I am?'

Ralf looked him up and down and continued to speak back to him in English, still insisting, he knew nothing of what he was talking about, and proceeded to enter his car.

'Mio fratello, Bartolomeo!' Said the stranger, 'Ti ricordi adesso?'

Ralf slowly got back out of the car and affixed a scowling gaze upon the man in the middle of the road, who began slowly walking toward him.

'It seems I have jogged your memory; Raffaele!'

'What do you want?' Hissed Ralf, his eyes becoming filled with a familiar red mist.

'God forgives…I do not.' Said the man.

'I would seriously leave me alone if I were you.'

'I'm afraid I cannot do that. You see…I loved my brother very much…'

Ralf rushed the stranger with almost cat-like speed and grabbed his throat. The man tried to bring his right arm up immediately in an attempt to strike Ralf on the side of the face, but he repelled his punch and brought the man down on the ground, while tightening his grip, making him gasp for breath. The man attempts at escaping Ralf's arm of steel were futile, as he slowly began to pass out, at which point, Ralf loosened his grip on the stranger's throat, letting his head thud to the ground.

'If you try and come for me again, if you follow me, if you so much as try to fuck anything up for me here…in this life…I will fucking kill you!'

Ralf marched back to his car and drove off, tyres screeching, into the night and toward Islington where Pete waited anxiously.

Chapter 12

Ralf found Pete in a café just around the corner from where he'd felt a little fragile. He'd found a parking space just outside and after sharing a quick coffee, tea for Pete, they returned to Pete's car where they remained for the duration of peak hour traffic.

'You okay?' Ralf asked.

'Better than I was. I guess I look shit. People kept staring at me in that café.'

'Actually you've regained some colour. You look more grief-stricken than ill.'

'Debbie won't have anything to do with me anymore. Thinks I'm too jealous. Can you believe it?'

'That's too bad, mate. Maybe she just needs time. You know she's just been through the worst time of her life.'

'Yep, she has indeed.' Pete lit a cigarette and Ralf rolled down the window.

'Can you drive back or shall we find a safe place to park and come get the car tomorrow?'

'Nah, I'll be okay to drive,' replied Pete, exhaling a billow of smoke into the windscreen. 'Sorry I got you out here, mate; I bet you had better things to do.'

'Don't say that even for a joke, dick. You know I'm here for you, no matter what.'

'Cheers mate, I really appreciate it.' Smiled Pete.

'Don't mention it.'

'I guess you've not caught the local news yet.' Pete continued.

'No, not today's, why?'

'Andrew Blaine's dead, died from his injuries, before the ambulance even reached the hospital.'

'Fuck!' Exclaimed Ralf.

'Yeah, fuck indeed. Now Ozzie needs to seriously lay low. Is he still at yours?'

'Yeah, he's still there. This makes things delicate and dangerous. Look, we'd better get back, now you're sure you can drive yourself back okay...'

'Yes mate, fine. I'll see you back at yours.'

As Ralf and Pete entered number twelve, Hawkshead Road, they were treated to the sight of Ozzie and Julia upon the stairs, shagging like rabbits, with Julia close to climaxing, judging by the increasing shrieks and howls she was emitting, sounding more like a dog expressing its joy upon seeing its owner return home.

'Oh, for fuck's sake, you two!' Ralf cried at the top of his voice, 'We could hear you from outside, you sound like a pair of coyotes. Couldn't you manage to get up the stairs and to the bed!?'

Embarrassed, the two lovers, totally naked, scrambled up the stairs and disappeared into Ralf's bedroom, a joyous *SORRY!* Was cried in unison, as a thud and a creak where heard as they launched themselves onto the bed, like two boisterous children. Ralf and Pete went into the kitchen, Pete was grinning broadly.

'What's making you grin like a Cheshire cat then?' Asked Ralf, with a smile.

'Did you see Julia's arse? That is one wicked arse if I ever saw one, and those tits...fuck me...and the size of Ozzie's dick!'

'Pete...well I'm glad you're back to your old self, it seems...and no, I *didn't* look at Ozzie's dick...I was too busy noticing Julia's arse, as you say. I hope her sister's got an arse like hers. I might get stuck in then...'

The two pals laughed their socks off, especially after Ralf cocked his leg and let out a rip-roaring monster of a fart, that sounded like a huge sheet of wrapping paper being ripped in two. If there was something that Ralf did with real gusto, that was breaking wind. He would cut his back teeth with such alarming regularity, that Pete often wondered if his best friend was a petomane. It wouldn't matter where Ralf found himself, be it a supermarket – he loved letting them off there – a church, shops, trains, anywhere at all, he would just let rip with a very satisfied grin upon his face, as though he'd done a great thing; the louder, the better. Pete recalled with great amusement, a time when Ralf had accompanied him to the dentist. Pete was just having a filling applied to a tooth, when Ralf expelled the king of all duck flatteners, making the dentist turn around suddenly with surprise, and causing him to slip with the drill, doing a little unwanted damage to Pete's gum. Ralf heard the almighty scream, and thinking his friend was in danger, he burst into the room wondering what had happened.

'You thucking thrick!' Shouted Pete, with a mouth full of cotton wool sticks, 'You tharted and made the dentsssttt thucking muss my thucking tuth, you thuck!'

Ralf burst into incessant and bellowing laughter, making him fart a few more times; in fact, he was in fits of laughter, with little mini farts expelling from his arse, like a car exhaust in cold weather. He felt a little guilty laughing at his friend's misfortune, but this one was dead funny; and Pete was utterly hilarious when he got pissed off.

At around eleven o'clock, Ralf's phone rang; it was Brenda.

'Calm down, just tell me what's wrong.'

'He's here, said a near-hysterical Brenda, 'he's just across the road from us...I can't bloody believe it...just a few feet away from us. I'm following him. I'll find out where he goes, and I'll call you back...'

'Brenda, wait,' cried Ralf, 'don't hang up, are you at home?'

'Yes, I'm in the front room, but I want to follow the bastard. I'll phone right back, I promise.'

Brenda hung up and Ralf and Pete stood by the phone, anxiously waiting for it to ring once again; it did after around ten minutes or so, and after Brenda told Ralf where Campion was hiding out, the two pals decided it was time to take action. Ralf called upstairs to the shaggers, telling them they'd be back later. Ralf started the Capri up and drove to Brenda's house with Pete in tow.

'Ralf, are you sure you really want to do this?'

'Are you nuts, of course I bloody want to do this,' replied Ralf abruptly, 'the guy's a scumbag, Pete. He interfered with Lawrence, who's as innocent as they come. He's not like the other kids, who smoke behind the bike sheds and all the rest; he's a good boy. Fuck that, Campion's going to pay.'

'Look, what if he presses charges? He'll have every right to do so, you know. It'll be you in the wrong. You've already done the right thing by pressing charges on him. Don't bugger it all up by putting your hands on him.'

'I know you mean well, Pete, but I took my eye off the ball and the guy did a runner and now he's hiding from the police. Brenda knows where to find him, so the prick's going to pay dearly. Don't worry, by the time I finish with him, he won't have a mouth left to tell anyone anything. I hate low-life scum like that. He's finished!'

Pete said nothing more. He knew that when his friend's stubbornness kicked in and he dug his heels in, there was no stopping him. Ralf drove at more elevated speeds than normal, unnerving Peter a little and once they got to the long back street where Brenda lived, his felt his heart-rate beating at more miles-per-hour than the car. Ralf slammed the door of the Ford, making it rock and marched up to Brenda's front door, banging on it several times until she opened it.

'Okay, where is he?' demanded Ralf.

Brenda reached in and took her coat and joined the two as they walked up toward the top of her road. Ralf introduced her to Pete, as they made their way to the end of Burlington Gardens, a long road lined with Edwardian houses on both sides. Only a few of the streetlamps were aglow except the part of the street where Campion was staying. Brenda pointed to the house where he took refuge, and without hesitation, Ralf walked toward the entrance door like an enraged vigilante on a hell bent mission of destruction. Pete and Brenda watched in silence, like sentinels as his dark-clothed outline blended into the darkness as he headed for the large and imposing portal-like door.

'Hey…you're shaking.' said Brenda, touching Pete's arm, 'you're not cold are you?'

'No, Brenda. I'm not cold. I'm shaking because I know what's to come. He's such a stubborn git. I tried to reason with him earlier, but he wouldn't listen. He's really taken this personally.'

'I know,' replied Brenda, 'you may not think too highly of me either, but...I hope Ralph makes him spend the rest of his life sucking out of a straw. You know wha...'

'Yes, Brenda I know what he di...I know, okay?'

Brenda and Pete remained silent, as Ralf climbed the stone steps leading up the front door.

Debbie and Mel were in the lounge and actually dancing, while the bending basslines of the song; *Just an Illusion* by the group, Imagination bounced from the speakers of the family stereo system. Their mother, Stella, was in the kitchen area whilst doing the washing up and finding it difficult to tear her eyes away from her daughters and their decidedly average performance. Julia had convinced her sister that life did indeed go on, and that their secret must forever remain unveiled.

Stella pulled up a stool and sat upon it while pondering her life. She often did, and Mel had to often pinch her to bring her back into the world of the living. Stella had experienced physical abuse for several years during her married life and almost every two or three days, the mood swings led to shouting matches, which ultimately led to the exchange of blows, from which Stella always came off worse. It was more tolerable once she gained the courage to begin defending herself and attempting to fight back, but the bigger and stronger husband naturally emerged the victor. He had a problem with his wife being the independent woman she was, preferring to go to work, have fun, and have a total disdain of living in the shadows.

Her husband, Derek, would usually start his conflicts when his daughters were either at school, work, or somewhere out of the house, as Debbie and Mel would always make a point of leaping to their mother's defences, and they didn't care if he lashed out at them, but for some reason he never laid a hand on Mel. As Stella drifted through a movie-like chain of thoughts as she played out her life's lows, she remembered the reaction of her daughters when she broke the news one evening, that their father had unfortunately passed; an accident, just a freak accident. He fell down several flights of stairs after returning home from the pub, totally inebriated. The two girls looked at their mother and each other, and continued with their homework. Never a tear was shed from that day. They visited his grave only once a year, on the day of their wedding. That was all they felt he deserved.

Ozzie and Julia were lying in Ralf's bed after round three of 'Shagfest at the Hawkshead Corral,' They were finally exhausted and lay atop the bed covers, facing each other in a tender exchange of approving glances and smiles. They spoke of the Andrew Blaine situation and what the next step would be for them as a couple. Julia declared her love for Ozzie and the rocker sat up with a start. Julia remained in the lying position, while gazing up at him and smiling warmly. Ozzie on the other hand, wasn't too sure whether to feel over the moon about it all. He smiled back and lay back down again, pulling his girlfriend closer to him. Ozzie had always been an enigma as far as his love life was concerned. He loved having girlfriends and everything that came with them, but only in very short bursts. On entering a new relationship, he was filled with the usual enthusiasm of a new romance, having many things in common. The going out for dinner, parties, day trips, and the like were all present and correct; it was just that Ozzie lost interest rather quickly, thus ending the union once and for all, which often left him with a infernal reputation.

As he lay next to Julia, his mind was beginning to conjure up the usual images of how he was going to handle this latest inevitable breakup. It was stronger than he could handle, when the women that drifted into his life grew more and more attached to him, eventually leading to most of them declaring their love for the rocker. It was quite understandable; aside from his bestial temper, he was charming, funny, positive, and bursting with a love for life that was infectious and like an endlessly spreading forest fire. Pete and Ralf were his greatest fans, with Ralf often quoting his Ozzie-loving motto; *If I was a woman, I'd let you shag me!*

Ozzie thought long and hard, as Julia fell asleep with her head upon his chest, about why he found it so hard to handle the love of a woman. He could never put it down to ever having being hurt before; the rocker had never been unlucky in love. He just couldn't commit. That was that. He turned to look at his sleeping girlfriend. She was very beautiful, with lightly freckled skin and the way her long, soft hair fell about her face, tenderised the rocker, calming the raging spirit that lurked within him. He looked her up and down, her naked curves, perfect like a sculpture or painting that came from either the heart or the imagination. Ozzie kind of disliked himself for being that way. Why couldn't he fall in love like anyone else? Why could he not feel any kind of sentiment that was more than just casual affection? He got up slowly, so not to wake her, and crept downstairs to get himself a drink. He wondered where Ralf and Pete had got to.

Chapter 13

Ralf waited at the large door of the house at the top of Burlington Gardens. Several of the streetlamps were out, plunging him and the ominous edifice into almost complete darkness, save for the glow of light pollution in the sky just over the rooftops overlooking the main street a couple of blocks away. The swish of the traffic flow was the only sound that could be heard besides Ralf's own breathing and his footsteps. The *dang dong* of the doorbell sounded as he pressed the antique brass button beside the door, and the shuffling around of someone inside was heard at length before the chain was removed and the door was slowly pulled inwards. Ralf took two steps back as a female hand took hold of the door's edge whilst hauling it open. It wasn't Campion's hand, but that of a middle aged woman with a kindly face; so much so, that her welcoming smile and softly spoken manner wrenched the sword from Ralf's hand.

'I'm sorry to disturb, I'm looking for Daniel Campion. I believe he lives here…I'm sorry, I'm an old friend of his. I thought I'd surprise him. I've come from abroad.'

'Well that's a lovely surprise and I'm sure he'll be thrilled. His mother came to visit him last night; won't you come in?'

The lady spoke with a very cultured voice and gave the impression that she was the owner of the huge Edwardian house, rather than a tenant. She switched on the light in the hallway, and a huge chandelier boasting twelve candle lamps flooded the hall, its fulgent glow revealing the hallway's flamboyance. The staircase spiralled upwards just to the left, the wall was adorned with huge paintings; Ralf recognised one of them as *La Gioconda,* a large print of which, hung in the lounge of his house. It belonged to his auntie and uncle, and had always fascinated him since he moved there. The other paintings were singularly beautiful, but not being an art expert and only knowing what he liked, they meant nothing to Ralf.

'I'll just get him for you, he's at the top floor, in his bedroom.' Said the smiling lady. She was elegantly dressed, with a navy blue overcoat and beige coloured pantaloons, and black shoes with rather scintillant buckles, that collected the light from the amazing chandelier.

'Actually, if you wouldn't mind, is it okay if I just nip up there and *really* surprise him. I think he'll *love* that.'

'Oh I think that's a lovely idea; I tell you what, I'll make a lovely pot of tea, so by the time you've said your hello's and come back down here, it'll be ready and with a ton of my homemade biscuits to go with it. How's that sound?' Said the jolly woman, with one of the hugest toothy grins Ralf had ever seen since Tom Baker's Doctor Who.

'You're a very kind lady, and I think that sounds delightful. I'll be right back. I'm sure old Daniel will be…very surprised. You'll see, it'll be a meeting with plenty of punch.' Ralf grinned too, not quite like Doctor Who, but damned close. The lady disappeared through a sliding door while Ralf began climbing the huge staircase as quietly as he could.

Ozzie was downstairs in the lounge of Ralf's house, while enjoying a huge mug of coffee. Julia was still asleep, giving Ozzie a little time to juggle his thoughts. He was frustrated, angry, and a little confused. He was certain he didn't want Julia for long term; he hated her for daring to fall in love with him, and after such a short time. What was wrong with the woman, she'd only known him five minutes. Was she that desperate?

Ozzie hunched forward and let out a lengthy brooding sound. It truly felt as though his whole world had come crumbling down on him, and that a gloomy depression would likely set in very soon. He got up and began pacing the lounge and the adjoining dining area, the one with the antlers hanging up. He went through the nearby door into the hall and into the kitchen. He searched the various cabinets and cupboards to see what nibbles Ralf had in the house, and found a pack of Orange Dimples of which he ate three, from a six-pack.

Just outside the door to the back garden, a bulkhead light on the wall above shone a warm-white light over the some of the patio area, picking up a large picnic table and parasol. Ozzie ventured outside for some fresh air. It was cold, too cold for just a T-shirt which was all Ozzie was wearing besides his underpants. The sky was clear and filled with stars. Ozzie craned his neck toward the heavens and sighed out a wisp of breath and watched with childlike fascination as it rapidly billowed upwards and dispersed. He went to the shed that stood at the corner of the garden and pulled the door open. He brushed away at first, but then pulled at a length of string that dangled from the ceiling, switching on a naked lamp that hung in the middle of the shed's awnings. It was very small, but very tidy, and had a little corner table which appeared too small for a work top. There was a shelf just beneath the three windows that looked over the garden, atop which there was a small transistor radio. There were a few cabinets made from the same wood as the shed itself and just as old, and they stood on the floor nearest to the door, and a small cabinet upon the wall at either end. Ozzie saw no tools or garden utensils; clearly the shed was more of a little retreat for Ralf's uncle, rather than a gardener's storage shack. A light came on upstairs, behind a frosted window; undoubtedly the bathroom. Julia would come downstairs soon. Ozzie felt like remaining hidden in the shed forever. Until everything just went away.

Ralf had reached the top of the staircase and was slightly short of breath. There were four doors on the upper landing; two at either side and two just in front of him. He waited until he felt ready to confront Campion, who was without a doubt, behind the door to his left, where the muffled sound of swirling violins from a classical piece of music drifted from the small gap at the bottom of the door. Ralf pushed the door open very slowly and peered inside once it was sufficiently ajar. The dim light came from a small table lamp upon a bedside just ahead of where he was standing. To the left and hidden by the wall, two legs could be seen and wearing a pair of cloth slippers. The music grew steadily louder as Ralf quietly slipped inside and clung to the wall on his left, while stealthily sliding along, until he was certain that it was Campion sat upon the bed. It wasn't, and the young fellow that became startled by Ralf's presence curled up upon the bed and cried aloud, his displeasure in Ralf being there.

'Who the bloody hell are you!?' Get out, get out! Daniel, who's this man in here!? Daniel!?'

The bathroom opened suddenly behind Ralf; it was Campion and he moved with the speed of an alley cat as he pushed Ralf back and made a move toward the bedroom door. Ralf went to pursue him, but a desperate arm wrapped itself around his neck and left arm, as he was pulled backwards and onto the bed. Ralf roared with intense frustration and his old red-mist rage, as he wriggled free from the young man on the bed. He turned around, grabbed the man by the shirt and repeatedly punched him in the face until he was out cold. He then leapt from the bed and hurled himself through the doorway and down the huge staircase. He could hear Campion scuttling down a bit further along, and a loud cry as he probably lost his footing.

Ralf hurtled around the final curving on the staircase and just caught sight of Campion as he disappeared though the front door, leaving it open behind him as he continued his desperate escape. Ralf leapt off of the bottom stair propelling himself forwards like a tiger. He gained a little too much momentum and he smacked his body and the side of his face against the huge front door, scratching his ear against the sharp lock handle. Crying out in pain, he attracted the attention of the jolly lady, who burst forth from the sliding door to the kitchen. Ralf ignored the demand for what was going on, and ran outside, jumping and clearing the four steps that led up from the path to the front door.

Campion ran to the right as soon as he heard Pete and Brenda exclaiming after him, but Ralf was in hot pursuit. He was getting out of breath once again and was conscious about not having exercised enough lately, but his immense frustration and rapidly rising rage propelled him forward like an express train. Campion was filled with fear and adrenalin, and for a man of his size and fairly poor fitness levels, he was able to keep up a certain speed and pace, which frustrated Ralf even more. Determined not to lose his target, Ralf attempted to inhale more deeply the second they approached a straight section of pavement, and he roared like a lion as he exploded into a significantly quick burst of speed. He stretched his arms forward and managed to grasp hold of Campion's thick denim shirt, but the man struggled free, leaving his garment behind like a souvenir in his pursuer's hands. Ralf cast it aside and continued a relentless pursuit. Now he was really pissed off.

Pete and Brenda were hot on their heels and caught up about a minute after, to where Ralf had discarded Campion's shirt. Pete picked it up and examined it briefly, unable to make it out properly in the dark but the smell of the garment told him it definitely wasn't his friend's.

'Are you okay?' Asked Brenda, as Pete took hold of the nearby non-functioning lamppost.

'Yeah, I think so. Unfortunately, I'm not a good one for running or any extreme physical feats; I've got a back injury which I did to myself at work, and now I've got a slipped disc. Because of all this crap tonight, I've not taken my tablets yet.'

Ralf felt himself slowing down and he felt his prey slipping away again. He stopped briefly while bent over and tried to get as much breath back as possible, then resumed pursuit. The road with faulty streetlamps opened up into a side-alley leading to the high street. Now if Ralf *did* catch hold of Campion, the severe punishment he wanted to dispense would be public. Not good. Campion was still in view and now in a stagger. He kept looking behind him every few seconds, but he *had* slowed down. He was tired. The crowds of strollers were a good thing in Ralf's eyes as they would provide sufficient cover in which to stay on Campion's tail, and he would try and blend in with them each time Campion turned to look behind him. Ralf pressed on, using the slower and more strategic pace to regain valuable energy.

Pete and Brenda moved along slowly as soon as Pete's pain and discomfort subsided a little. Once they reached the high street, they weren't sure which direction to take. Pete looked to his left and noticed a police vehicle parked just outside a small amusement arcade. He gestured to Brenda that their friend lay in that direction. They entered the arcade that was filled with clusters of slot machines and Space Invader machines that were hogged by teenagers that somehow managed to wangle their way in, if they were fortunate enough to look a little older than their true age. The slot machines were guarded by older customers in deep concentration. The police were at the main counter and kiosk, and judging by the conversation they were having with the staff, Ralf wasn't the reason for there being at the scene. The two friends rapidly slipped back outside.

Ralf continued flitting in and out of groups of folk that roamed the high street until he felt he was sufficiently close enough to pounce upon his constantly moving prey. Ralf quickly shifted to a small cluster of Asian fellows on the left corner of the street and watched as Campion as he shuffled across the road to the other side and immediately turned right, as though knowing exactly where he was going. He disappeared into a narrow alley next to a laundrette, after glancing behind him one final time. Ralf recognised that alley as soon as he saw the laundrette's name. An old flame of Ozzie's worked there in the evenings and he remembered her mentioning its strange name during conversation. He also knew of the dark alley that ran alongside it and the small and mostly unknown wooden gate that led back onto one of the streets that connected to Burlington Gardens. Ralf ran across the road and peeked around the wall into the alley. Campion was half way down and standing still, bent forwards to catch his breath. He then proceeded to sit down with his back to the wall and light a cigarette. Ralf continued watching him until he got close to ending his smoke. He entered the alley. Campion turned to look at him and gasped so deeply, he unwittingly emitted a frightened whine. Ralf glared at him as the rage inside began bubbling like a cauldron.

'Get up!' said Ralf, quietly. 'Get up.'

Campion got up slowly, his back scraping against the wall behind him. He gazed at Ralf while his bottom lip began to tremble and tears began running down his face.

'Please...I beg you...don't hurt me. I'll get some help, I promise. Just...don't hurt me.'

'Didn't Lawrence say please? Didn't he beg you? I bet you ignored *his* pleas. I bet you got what you wanted.'

Campion began to weep and slowly sink back down to the ground, but Ralf yelled at him, ordering him to get back up and face him like a man.

'Who's the other guy in your room? Your boyfriend?'

Campion didn't answer, but continued to quiver and hide his face behind his forearm.

'I SAID WHO!' Screamed Ralf, moving closer to him.

'Yes, he is...my...boyfriend...please don't hurt him...'

A voice came from the entrance to the alley, and the silhouette of a young woman appeared peering toward Ralf and Campion. 'Hoi, what's goin' on down there?'

The woman's head bobbed side to side as her searchlight eyes scoured the dark of the alleyway. Campion sprang up and pushed Ralf violently away causing him to trip over a trash cam and tumble backwards onto the ground. He broke into a frantic run, heading toward the wooden gate that opened up onto the streets that were familiar to him. Ralf staggered back to his feet and sprinted after him, catching hold of his T-shirt just as he managed to take hold of the wooden gate.

'Hoi, what's happenin' down there? I'll call the cops!'

As the woman's voice continued shouting from the corner of the laundrette, Campion made one final attempt at freedom, by yelling for help, that someone was trying to rob him. He tried to swing for Ralf, but his blow was avoided by Ralf swaying backwards. He tried to kick out, one of his blows connecting with Ralf's hip. The woman's voice seemed closer, as she threatened to call the police once again. Campion tried to cry out once more, but Ralf's fist smashed into his face with immense force, silencing him instantly. Campion tried one last time, to land a punch of his own, but Ralf parried his attack and continued to rain down flurries of punches and kicks to the man's face and body, until Campion was completely still. Ralf couldn't see the extent of the damage he was doing, as it was near pitch-black, aside from a distant streetlamp in the street beyond the gate, and a window high above them, but he knew *what* he was doing; and at that moment, he regretted none of it. He beat Campion to within an inch of his life, until he was nothing but a pile of quivering flesh at his feet.

'Right, I'm comin' in there. You hear? I'm comin' down to see what's goin' on. I'm gonna call the cops!'

Ralf went through the gate and ran into the network of side streets. He couldn't find where Pete and Brenda had got to and didn't want to yell out any names, and so he returned to Brenda's house and waited for them there. He sat upon the doorstep and noticed a few spatters of Campion's blood on his jeans, sweatshirt, and right sneaker. The rushing traffic noise was broken by the sound of a police siren, followed by another and then that of an ambulance also. Ralf couldn't be sure if it was on its way to clear up his handy work; sirens were a pretty common thing as they howled through night-time Acton. Ralf never liked the place. He always referred to it as the shithole of suburban London. It felt strange to think that Chiswick was virtually around the corner and was a completely different kettle of fish; less multi-cultural, cleaner, definitely classier, and unfortunately more expensive. Ralf felt lucky to live there.

The only other place he liked was where Pete lived. Northfields was only a few blocks in size, but Ralf found it charming. He enjoyed roaming around there and strolling along its main street just looking at the many different shops; and of course, his favourite little café, the one with nautical themes as its interior design. The owner was an ex-sailor from Cornwall and every day, he would receive a hefty order of fresh fish caught that very morning at twilight. Ralf enjoyed a mixed grill of fish every Friday, usually without fail, as his old friend, Cecil, would always charge him a very reasonable price. That café was where Ralf met one of his girlfriends; a Polish girl named Basia. They were only together for three months, when she left to go back to Poland. She left without warning and left a note with Cecil, saying that she hated goodbyes, but felt that she was falling for him and couldn't handle it.

Ralf had had his fair share of female companions, but none were as of yet, marriage material. He lasted several months with them but his mind was always a little busy; too busy to keep up with their quirks and demands. Birthdays got forgotten, as did special occasions like Valentine's day, Easter, and Christmas. It was then that Ralf realized that he was better off on his own. He often preferred his own company, but he was a ladies' man; he enjoyed the company of women, mainly older ones, and sitting around a table having a drink or a meal with a group of them always brought him not only pleasure, but enlightenment as well. He loved women not for what he could get out of them, but for what they were. He felt that much could be learned from these beautiful creatures.

Pete and Debbie emerged from the dark at the end of the street and Ralf jumped up when he realized Pete had difficulty walking properly. His friend refused an ambulance, preferring to rely on his painkillers back at home. After a vague explanation to Brenda about what happened, Ralf drove Pete back home. He stayed with him until the tablets set in, and as soon as Pete began dozing off, he quietly slipped away.

Chapter 14

Ozzie gazed out from the shed windows and across the garden. The sky was overcast and the gloom that loomed overhead felt oppressive and frightening, plunging the whole garden into a dark grey shadow, with the only light coming from the glass panes in the kitchen door. He could see Julia moving about in the kitchen as she opened various cupboards and cabinets in search of where things were kept, and eventually found tea and coffee and Ralf's significant assortment of biscuits and cakes. Ozzie observed her as she went from task to task; he liked the way her hair moved around as she bent and swayed and looked up or down. He enjoyed seeing the perpetual smile she wore at all times, even as she walked along the streets. There were more positives in Julia than in the other conquests he'd made over time.

Ozzie continued observing, safely concealed by the shadows, like a silent guard in a sentry box. Julia began looking bewildered as she moved from the kitchen to the dining room and to the lounge. Ozzie watched as her figure passed across from the lounge door, through the hall and up the stairs. The bathroom light flicked on and then off again, and she returned downstairs to the kitchen. She pressed her nose against the window pane of the garden door and scoured the night garden as best she could. She opened the door and called Ozzie's name whilst leaning outwards. He didn't answer. He liked the shed. It was his safety, his little temporary escape from what life outside was throwing at him. As long as he was in there, nothing could touch him.

Julia continued pottering about in the kitchen, but Ozzie wasn't sure what exactly she was up to. Perhaps she was rustling up something to eat; maybe for both of them. Ozzie noticed her opening the fridge and take out a pack of bacon and a box of eggs from one of the cupboards. After turning on the stove he noticed four eggs being cracked. There was no way Julia would eat four eggs; it meant that she was doing something for the both of them. If there was one snack that the rocker really liked, that was bacon and eggs, fried bread, and baked beans, all washed down with a lovely mug of strong coffee. He emerged from the shed and made his way back into the warmth of the house. Julia was surprised to see him come in from the garden, and after asking him what on earth he was doing out there and why he didn't reply when she'd called out to him, he just desperately kissed her. She gave him her beautiful pouty lips as though she was giving him all she had. It was a most precious and heartfelt kiss which filled the rocker with all the fuzziness and stomach butterflies any man could wish for. Ozzie felt good. He felt proud, and most of all, he felt like the man he'd always wanted to be. What was it his mother always told him? *Behind every man, there's a fuckin' great woman, like me.*

Ralf pulled into Hawkshead Road and parked his car just outside the house, but didn't go inside yet; he decided he'd go for a stroll to unwind. It had been too much of an eventful night for him, and a breath of fresh night air would certainly do him the world of good. He noticed the lights were still on in the school where he worked; it was probably the cleaners and the caretaker still on the prowl, haunting the corridors like old phantoms waiting to cross over. Ralf liked the old caretaker. He was Ronald Kaye and despite being in his sixties, he was agile and sprightly, *and,* he had a thing for Miss Clare. God only knew why, but he did. There were two cleaners on patrol with him; Marva, a Jamaican lady with the happiest personality ever and a beautiful bright smile that could warm the hearts of anyone. Then there was Irene, a Filppino lady who would always manage to make Ralf absolutely kill himself laughing; she had the foulest mouth in England, but inside, she was one of the kindest people you could ever meet.

Ralf recalled when she absolutely ripped into poor old Ronald just for suggesting she wear some safer footwear rather than flip-flops. He'd pooped in to give Ronald an old Vera Lynn record he was after, and the ensuing barrage of juicy language that was hurled at the old caretaker was cringeworthy.

'I like to wearr what I blaady ewell peleeese, you undastand? Don't annoy me, you seellee stuped man! I am a fackeen Filippino laydeee you knooow! Don't annoy me...you deeckhead! Fackeen youself, bastard stuped man! You no like my shoes? You buy dem forr mee, bastaaard!'

It was a great variety of curses and naughty words and poor Ronald didn't seem phased by them; a little taken aback, yes, but ralf was sure he found it funny. Ralf himself found it extremely hard to keep a straight face.

Ralf walked slowly up toward the top end of the short road that was Hawkshead, where it bore a sharp left and became Greenend Road. The top of Hawkshead Road led into the alleyway that ran around the back of Greenend, and led down to a halfway point that passed through the street and into the back of a factory and the sewage plant that thankfully, diffused no nasty odours into the air. Right in the centre of the sewage plant was a large grey building which had fire escape ladders clinging to all of its facades. He remembered that a few years before his auntie had died, a few times, he had caught her climbing the ladders and reaching the roof of the edifice. Unfortunately, auntie Enza had been showing the initial symptoms of vascular dementia for the past year or so. She was still very able to engage in conversation – whilst sometimes repeating what she had said ten minutes earlier – but the condition often drove her to seek evasion from daily life, and poor uncle Raffaele, who was simply beside himself. He passed before she did, and although the shock was like a fierce blow to the soul, auntie Enza miraculously grasped hold of unforeseen lucidity that carried her through until her death, two years later.

Ralf never spoke about them when they had passed, much to the bewilderment of his friends, especially Pete, who was closest to him. He would never shed tears or mourn them in front of anyone, but would sometimes give in to the sorrow when he was alone, and it would come for him like a thief in the night. Ralf loved them dearly, as though they were his own parents; whom he never knew. They gave him everything and without condition or the need to explain. They loved him like he was their own son, not just because they were unable to have children, but because they had always been a solitary couple, and only after Ralf went to live with them, did they acquire purpose to embrace more of what life had up its sleeves.

Ralf loved his night strolls. Sometimes they would be lengthy and other times, shorter, but he truly preferred the mysterious and obscure shroud of night. He liked its merging of both haunting sounds and deathly silence; during the day there were sparrows, crows, blackbirds, pigeons, countless birds that sang their distinctive operas beneath the fire of the sun. At night, there was the ghostly and ethereal echo of the owl; the night bird that proclaimed its rightful place in the dark and phantasmal world of the night, with its haunting soprano.

The many streets around the area were, in Ralf's opinion, like little nocturnal postcards. He also had a thing about lighting, in particular, street lights. When he first came here, he became fascinated by the way that every region or borough in suburban London had its own different kind of streetlight. The borough of Ealing, for example, was home to those that resembled scimitars atop their posts with triangular glass that concealed the long, cigar-shaped sodium lamp within. Chiswick had Ralf's favourite ones. He always referred to them as big glasses of milk with overturned saucers on top. The neighbouring streets around Hawkshead Road were some of the most picturesque and quiet roads that Ralf enjoyed strolling along, under the cover of night. The combination of townhouses of several storeys and Edwardian buildings were a sight to behold, especially when night fell and the streetlights painted houses and trees in their vicinity with lunar whiteness.

Pete woke up at around three in the morning, and with a headache that felt like a pneumatic drill. After freshening up, he went downstairs and after a coffee boost and a sandwich, he got into his car and went for a drive. Destination; Debbie's house. As he drove through Northfields and turned into Lionel Road that bordered Gunnersbury Park, Pete switched the car radio on. The song *Heartbreaker,* sung by Dionne Warwick was being played on a local station. The huge structure of the M4 motorway flyover dwarfed the Citroen Visa, as Pete drove alongside it and toward the Chiswick roundabout. He put his foot down to escape the imposing and looming shadow of the flyover, as it passed over the vehicle, making the lights from the dashboard seem brighter than usual. The choice of song didn't help matters but Pete liked the tune, but when it was followed by the Phil Collins track entitled, *If Leaving Me Is Easy,* he hit the off button.

Pete took the meandering red tarmac road that led up to the Brentford tower blocks and parked his car in the parking area a little way from the tower's entrance. He switched the radio back on and waited. The windows steamed up, hiding him from the view of outsiders and he rubbed a little peep hole on the window of the driver side. He leant his head back onto the head restraint and wondered if he was doing the right thing. Pete had had a few girlfriends over the years, and besides the last one a few years back who broke his heart, Debbie was, as he always thought, the love of his life. He was particularly proud of how he had met her, and the fact that unlike other female friends he'd had, she was not introduced to him; he actually went up to her in a pub called the Mawson Arms, whilst at another girl's birthday party. Debbie was alone at the bar ordering a drink when Pete noticed that she was by herself for pretty much the whole evening. He overcame his shyness and reserved nature and sidled up to her. The rest was history.

Ozzie and Julia were still up and sat in the dining area – the one with the antlers – and engaged in deep conversation; Ozzie had decided to empty his heart and place all his cards upon the table. He'd told Julia all that he felt inside. He told her about his reluctance to commit, his incredibly short-legged relationships, and his inability to comprehend why. Julia was strong; her eyes showed signs of lacrymal activity, but she was strong. She listened without interrupting him and without asking why.

'Look,' she swallowed but continued to "pitch through her tears," 'if you need time, that's okay...I know this is a...unique situation...it will be hard to let you go, but...if that's what you need...'

Julia rose from the table and ran upstairs, and closed the door to the bedroom behind her. Ozzie didn't hear a sound from her and remained at the table.

Pete was drifting in and out of sleep and repeatedly bumped his head on the window as he dozed off. The radio was still playing and the radio station was transmitting,*All Night Soothers,* and when the beautiful Roxy Music ballad called, *Avalon* was played, Pete was enchanted for a few minutes as the haunting melody filled the misted up Citroen Visa. Bryan Ferry's warm, sexy, and passionate vocals blended with and became one with the soothing melody, and Ferry's voice was coloured by the tone and style of an Art Deco era. Pete looked at the time; it was nearly six in the morning, and Debbie's mother would soon be leaving for work.

At around seven, both Stella and Mel emerged from the entrance to the tower block and cut across the grassy communal area and made their way to the bus stop, avoiding the car park altogether and thus not noticing Pete's car. Pete seized the opportunity and jumped out of his vehicle and headed for the doorway to the tower; it was locked. Pete forgot, in his anxiety to go and talk to Debbie, that the door would shut itself and non-residents could not enter.

After cursing, Pete leaned against the door and pushed several times, but it wouldn't budge without making a racket. After about the fifth attempt, a resident came out of the lift and toward the entrance.

'Erm, excuse me, but do you live here?' Asked a middle-aged woman with an unfortunate bottom lip that protruded a little.

'No, I don't live here, bu…'

'Well if you don't live here,' she interrupted, without making any eye contact, which always irritated Pete about anyone, 'you shouldn't be trying to get in, should you?'

'Er, if you kindly let me finish, I know someone who lives on the top floor. She's my girlfriend and she's expecting me, okay?'

'Oh really, what's her name then?' Continued the woman. She was clearly in the mood for picking a fight, and Pete was definitely not in the mood for any of this; not now. The woman was obviously some kind of control freak; she had dark, shoulder-length hair and glasses and a perpetual scowl upon her face. The instances she *did* happen to make eye contact, she looked like she wanted to cut out Pete's heart and throw it at him. There was one pet-hate that really gnawed at him, and that was a 'bitch-for-no-reason,' and here before him, was one of the best examples.

'It's actually none of your bloody business what her name is, now if you don't mind, I'd like to pass. I don't believe I need to justify myself to you!'

The woman made a point of moving in front of the doorway and remaining steadfast, barring Pete's way. His patience was thinning with each second that passed. Pete was usually never discourteous with anybody, in particular to ladies, it was something his father always swore by from a very young age, and always made a point of drumming it into his son.

'Look, WHAT is your problem, I'm just trying to go up to my girlfriend's house, for fuck's sake, why are you stopping me?'

'Don't you swear at me…I'll call…'

'Get out of the bloody way then. Yu have NO right to do this, who the hell do you think you are!?'

Pete tried to push his way past while at the same time, being as gentle as he could, without hurting the stupid cow, but she just wasn't having any of it, and began pushing Pete back out of the doorway and tussling with him.

'Excuse me, but you are *not* going in there, so just go away or I'm calling the police!'

At that point, Pete lost patience and his usually unflinching self-control and forcefully pushed the woman back hard, causing her to stagger backwards and into the building. She fell on her arse and displayed the most horrified look of disbelief at having being manhandled in such a way. Pete marched straight past her and pressed the "Lift-call button. The woman sprang up from the floor and rushed over to him, ready for round two. Pete turned around suddenly and without either thought or hesitation, just screamed at her, like he'd never done to anyone before.

'WILL YOU JUST FUCK OOOOFFFFF!!!!'

The woman was still standing still, in the same place, aghast, and just staring at him as the lift doors closed. Pete felt good, he felt very good, even though he'd just been extremely bad. Totally unlike him. But some people just brought out the worst in him sometimes. He stepped out onto the top floor landing as the elevator pinged and jerked, making his stomach flutter profusely, as he realized what he could be in for. He walked up to Debbie's front door and pressed the buzzer. The steadily increasing sound of bare feet on lino approached the door and it opened. Debbie stood there with a look of surprise, but didn't smile back when Pete smiled at her.

Chapter 15

Debbie stood in the doorway with a serious look upon her face. Clearly unhappy with Pete's presence there that morning, she asked him what he wanted, to which he responded that he just wanted to talk.

'Talk about what?' Debbie asked.

'Come on, Debs...what's going on? One minute you're all over me, and the next...'

'Okay come in, but just for a bit. I'm a little tired.'

Debbie made some coffees and the two shared the sofa while both attempted to lay their cards upon the table. Pete went first.

'Okay, I'm just confused. Look...I know that what you've been through is just...unspeakable...and you're undoubtedly feeling demeaned and violated...'

'Look, Pete, I don't need you to tell me what I've been through or how I'm feeling; I already know that. You're here because of you and me, right?'

Pete paused for thought. In fact, he wasn't actually sure he knew *what* to think. Debbie had changed, for sure, but she *had* just been beaten up by a madman and it could have been worse. Pete felt bad for trying to think that he could press Debbie into moving forward, but he loved her and wanted the old Debbie back as soon as possible, but he wanted to *be* there for her too. That was one of the things Debbie found attractive about Pete; his unwavering loyalty.

'Look, why are you being like this? You're just really harsh, I just want to...'

'HARSH!?' she yelled, HARSH!? YOU THINK *I'M* HARSH!?'

'Debbie, keep your voice down sweetheart, all I'm doing is...'

'I've just been on the receiving end of a severe beating, and if Ozzie hadn't been there, I don't know what could have happened. Actually, I'd have been dead for sure, because that fucking weirdo would've carried on quite happily...and you dare to say I'm harsh. Look, just go. Go away, Pete because I don't need you here!'

'Okay, now that's enough!'

Pete rose abruptly from the sofa and slammed his mug of coffee on a side table nearby. Debbie jolted and looked up at him, almost cowering; as if he himself were about to strike her, but even *she* knew very well, that that was definitely *not* in Pete's nature. He would never hit a woman even if his life depended on it, and he felt sad that she would even remotely think that he would ever touch her.

'There's no need to cower, Debbie. I'm not Andrew Blaine; but I *am* Peter Sheridan! Remember me, the man you supposedly fell for? Now what the bloody hell's happened to you, YES, I KNOW YOU'VE BEEN THROUGH SHIT...but why do you keep throwing the fact that Ozzie was there and not me, back in my face? I'm not a mind reader or a psychic, I can't guess when you're in danger. Ozzie just happened to just be passing by, that's all. Think about it...if it had been me who passed by, do you honestly think I wouldn't have done what Ozzie did? You think I'd have just stood there and watched you get beaten up?'

'I know you'd have done the same thing...'

'Well then...what's the bloody problem? Why are you punishing me?'

'I hold you responsible for this, because if you hadn't played the bloody hero that day outside the shop, and punched that bloke, none of this would have happened. He wouldn't have followed me home, and I wouldn't be battered to a pulp. You should've just kept your stupid hands to yourself...but no, you had to go and hit him...the fucking hero, Pete. Conan, the bloody barbarian!'

'So...Mel was right.' Sighed Pete.

'Mel was right about what?'

'Didn't she tell you? She came to see me the other night, at my house. We went for a drink just down the road from me. She told me everything...the fact that you blame me for all this. I punched him that day because he insulted you...*I'd love to smash her back doors in*...I don't know about you, but I found that bloody offensive. It was just a punch, Debbie. If you're so worried about that, then let's talk about Ozzie...he killed the bloke!'

Debbie glared at Pete as though she hated him at that precise moment. Pete felt it. He could feel all of the venom coming forth from that look of daggers. All he could not understand was...why? He'd defended his girlfriend's honour as far as he was concerned. It was just a little punch, just something that would sting a bit, so the idiot wouldn't dare say anything like that again; to anyone.

'Mel told me she came to see you. She's my sister, she just cares...'

'I know, sweetheart,' Pete said, as he sat back down next to her, 'but so do I...'

Pete put his arm around Debbie and pulled her gently to him. She leant her head upon his shoulder, and a lone tear, probably one of sheer relief, trickled down his cheek. Debbie felt it, as it fell upon her hair. She looked up and immediately threw her arms around Pete. They both remained there, for as long as Debbie needed.

Earlier that evening, Ralph had walked as far as Turnham Green station, not too far from Mike's Music City, but he ended up inside a diner-like café that was further up from there. He ordered a refillable filter coffee and some cherry pie, a delightful slice of heaven that was homemade by the owner's wife. He was about three quarters of the way through it and tempted for a second piece, when a young lady, probably in her thirties, walked into the café and made her way to the bar. Ralf was, for some reason, quite fascinated by her and he observed as she went about ordering the same as what he was having, but with a little difficulty due to a language barrier. He detected an accent that was pretty familiar to him, and they exchanged fleeting smiles when their eyes met. Ralf beckoned her over, gesturing an invitation.

'Oh Thank you, thank you very much. My eenglish ees no good. Sorry.'

The young woman revealed herself to be called, Loredana, and she came from Venice, in Italy. She was in England for work experience and teaching Italian to foreign students in the evenings. Ralf had great difficulty taking his eyes off her and was rather enchanted by her warm and friendly brown eyes and long, dark curly hair. The two remained seated in the café for around two hours, up until near closing time, when the manager informed them of the time. They left the café and wondered up and down Chiswick high street for a while, then up Turnham Green Terrace, where Ralf accompanied Loredana to the tube station there. The conversation and things in common kept on flowing beautifully, and Ralf sat on a bench with her on the platform. The last train was due at just after midnight, and so the two friends continued their incessant but pleasant chatter, only pausing for breath each time the Piccadilly Line trains careened through the station, with their almost rhythmic clatter.

For the first time in a very long while, Ralf felt electric. His mistrust of people, especially those of the opposite sex, was beginning to wane. Loredana never seemed to ever stop smiling; in fact every time she did so, her eyes smiled with her, and that was when Ralf became slave to her charms, her natural charms and not just her boobs, which he realized he'd looked upon a little too frequently during their chance meeting. She undoubtedly noticed, but she too, seemed taken with Ralf. He thought he noticed her blush a couple of times when their eyes met, he could have been wrong, but he didn't think so. Ralf was usually never wrong about people, and this lovely woman appeared to wear her heart upon her sleeve.

Ralf began to wonder, if he should reveal the truth to her. There were a couple of instances where he wanted to, really wanted to, but something held him back. Her English was certainly not the worst he'd heard uttered by foreign students, but the frequent pauses as she thought about how to say something, were beginning to try his patience a little; definitely not in a bad way, but it seemed that the longer she tried to keep her head above water with the language, the more frequently she made grammatical errors. It was certainly not her fault, and undoubtedly, she would soon grasp a good command of the English language given time; she had a damn good head start.

'Why you look at me like dat?' She asked with a smile and a twinkle in her eyes that could easily have been stars or jewels; Ralf was *that* besotted with her, that all he could see was his romantic imagination running away with him. He actually *wanted* to see stars and jewels. In fact, every time she opened her mouth, he wanted to both desperately kiss her *and* climb up to the sky and get the moon and stars and bring them down to her, and no, he certainly did *not* wish to snap out of it.

'I'm sorry…Loredana…it's just that…that I actually *can't* stop looking at you. You are so beautiful…'

Loredana clearly blushed this time round, and Ralf saw her and chuckled. She smacked him benevolently upon the arm and gave a little chuckle herself, knowing that they would definitely see each other again. When the penultimate train rattled and creaked into the station, they arose from the bench they were seated upon, and with the numbest of buttocks and the raciest of heartbeats, they shared a lengthy kiss upon the lips. Loredana just managed to jump aboard the train as its doors were closing, seconds after the loudspeaker voiced the familiar, *Stand clear of the doors please, mind the doors.* They kept their eyes fixed upon each other until the District Line left the platform behind and disappeared into the darkness, its lights rapidly vanishing around a bend as it picked up speed. Ralf remained near the edge of the platform, listening to the distant *clackety clack,* as the train raced away from him. He didn't move from there until he could no longer hear the rocking and swaying carriages in the distance. A little voice inside his head emerged from a shadowy place it was hiding in all this time. *Soppy bastard,* were its words.

Chapter 16

Over the weekend, Ralf tried to busy himself with as many things as possible. Firstly, because he couldn't for a second, get Loredana out of his head and secondly, guests. They were like fish; after three days they stink, and Ozzie and Julia had become very stinky people indeed. The stench was constantly there, right under his nose. Not the smell of unwashed, not at all, but with the colliding of the tongues complete with sucking and slurping, the shagging in the middle of the night with the two of them being evidently noisy lovers, and between his and her orgasms, the alternating ugh's and agh's sounded like there was a donkey upstairs. Ralf had many nights of broken sleep and the sofa was beginning to become uncomfortable. He refused to use any of the two spare bedrooms, otherwise the live pornographic movie would become simply intolerable. Every time Ralf was abruptly woken up by the two lovers, the first thing he saw in the penumbra of the dining area as he faced it, were the antlers. For years they had never been taken down; Ralf thought they could finally get some use. He thought of seriously inserting them into Ozzie.

At around eight in the morning on Sunday, Ralf received the umpteenth phone call from Ozzie's mother, asking the whereabouts of her son. Ralf finally revealed that he was with him and that he couldn't take it anymore. She shrieked at him down the phone, so ear-piercingly loud, that Ralf had to continue speaking to her whilst holding the earpiece to his lips, like a walkie-talkie.

'Look, he's fine, seriously though, you need to convince him that it's perfectly safe to come home and that you won't give him a hard time by asking too many questions…why? I'll tell you why…I'm getting next to no sleep at all…the continuous shagging and moaning and bumping the walls…please tell him that you'll be happy to see him…PLEASE!'

On the Monday morning, just as Ralf was going out of the front door, his two friends were packing their bags and ready to move in with Ozzie's mum, Julia included. Apparently she was convinced that as a couple, they were for life. Ozzie had quickly briefed Ralf about his thoughts on his relationship, but was told that they'd speak about it another time. Ralf went into work and straight into his English class, and was looking forward to the change of scenery.

Edwina Clare greeted him with a smile and a wink as they passed each other in the corridor. She couldn't stop to chat as she was accompanied by a young couple, probably wanting to find out about their child starting school there.

As he entered his classroom, Ralf received the usual pleasant welcome from his pupils. Lawrence in particular, was in fine form and complete with a sense of humour.

'Sir, can I tell you a joke?'

'Yes of course, Lawrence, 'said Ralf with a smile, 'go for it!'

'Did you know they've found Dracula's boat?'

'Yeeess,'

'It's a blood vessel!'

A combination of groans and chortles began to rise and fill the classroom and Ralf wasn't quite sure what to say. He had a slight smile upon his face, but that joke was rather a lame one, for Lawrence's standards.

'Lawrence,' Ralf intoned, 'do you think that joke you just told is actually funny?'

'Yes sir,' Lawrence replied in almost musical fashion, 'I thought it was brilliant!'

'Lawrence.'

'Yes sir.'

'Would you like an hour's detention after school today?'

'Um…nah, think not sir…that'd really suck!'

'Okay, then promise me you'll *never, ever* tell such dreadful jokes like that again!'

'Okay sir, I'll tell you another one after the lesson!'

'I shudder to think what it'll be like…' muttered Ralf.

Later that morning, Ralf had just finished taking his music class, when his heart jumped into his throat, leaving him feeling sick and afraid. A cold sweat took over his body and his heart raced like a wild horse. Two police officers, one male, one female, entered the school premises and approached Edwina, who was pinning up a poster on the message board in one of the corridors near her office. Ralf waited and watched from the doors of the classroom, and sure enough, they began making their way to where he was. He dashed back to his desk, took out a tissue from the drawer and wiped away the sweat from his forehead as best he could. There was a tap at the door, and the two officers of the law let themselves in.

'Good morning, Mr Ralf Avalon?'

'Um, yes that's me,' Ralf smiled, 'how can I help?'

'I'm PC Trevor Hawkins, this is my colleague, PC Sally Cryer. We have a few questions regarding an incident involving a teacher from this school, a Mr Daniel Campion. A colleague of yours, I believe.'

'Um, yes, he's a colleague; a maths teacher. Something wrong?'

'Yes,' said the female officer, 'as a matter of fact there is. He was brutally beaten last week and has just today, been discharged from the hospital. His housekeeper called us after an incident at her home, where he apparently lodges. Do you know of this, or did you hear about it...it's just that the lady gave us a rather detailed description that matches your own.'

Ralf could feel himself shaking all over and his legs were beginning to feel like jelly. His abdomen became wracked with cramps that he was barely able to tolerate, and was unable to stifle a wince from the sharp pain that cut through him.

'Are you alright sir? You appear to be in some sort of pain.' Asked PC Hawkins.

'I'm sorry. I'll be fine in a second. I suffer from Crohn's Disease and I get these cramps occasionally. I'm afraid I can't help you unfortunately. I was the one who pressed charges following an incident that involved one of my pupils, and then he just disappeared. I've not seen or heard from him since.'

'We spoke to him regarding his attacker,' continued PC Cryer, 'but he told us that it took place down a dark alley, and he couldn't see who it was.'

In that instant, Ralf stood up and walked over to the blackboard and began to erase what was written upon it, while still facing the two police officers.

'I'm sorry, I wish I could help further, but...I don't really know what else to say. I don't know where he lives, so it definitely wasn't me the...housekeeper described. I'm sure I'm not the only bald man in Chiswick.'

Edwina rushed over to the classroom after the two officers left the building and asked if everything was okay, to which Ralf replied that it was. He had no information for them except that Campion was indeed a teacher there. Ralf couldn't bring himself round to telling Edwina the truth; his trust in her *was* growing and he'd undoubtedly found an unlikely friend in her, but if she ever knew that *he* was Campion's attacker, things may not be so easy.

'Did they just want to talk to you about the Lawrence incident?' Edwina asked.

'Oh…yeah, they just wanted to ask the same questions. Usual police habits, you know.'

'Had you heard about Daniel?'

'Yes, sometime last week. He was attacked or something.'

'Did the police question you in relation to that?' She insisted.

Ralf continued to erase the blackboard and tidy away some paperwork, as he tried his utmost to not make eye contact with Edwina, who wouldn't cease with questioning him.

'Why would they think that you'd know something about it?'

'I've no idea, Edwina. Maybe they're just conducting enquiries and so I guess…everyone's a suspect. I don't know…maybe.'

'Why aren't you looking at me when I'm talking to you, Ralf?'

Ralf *did* look at her this time. He was trying his best not to panic or seem remotely pissed off in any way, but Edwina wasn't having any of it. She was no fool. She glared at Ralf expectantly, keeping her eyes upon him all the time, whilst he made every attempt to keep from looking at her. He could feel her staring at him, even with his back to her, while he filed away his classroom notes and tidied his desk. Once it was done and there was nothing left for him to do, he sighed and turned to face her. She turned and exited the room. Ralf dashed after her.

'Edwina wait!'

She turned around and waited while he went towards her. Ralf took her hand after checking that they weren't being watched by any stray pupils between lessons.

'Look, I'm sorry. It's just…shit, I'm crap at explaining things…look, let's have dinner somewhere and I'll explain everything. How's that sound?'

'That would be very nice,' Edwina said softly and touching Ralf's hand, 'I'd like to think you can trust me. I know I trust you…'

Pete remained with Debbie for most of the morning, and after a late breakfast of croissants and coffee, she began to open up regarding how she had planned to tell him about where they stood with their relationship. Pete was a little surprised at how willingly she was speaking about the subject, considering what had happened to her, and as she continued to enlighten him about all sorts of future plans involving the pair of them, Pete's heart felt as though it was performing cartwheels and jumps for joy, whilst his soul was basking in the sun.

Debbie told Pete she loved him as he was near the front door and ready to go back home for some rest, in readiness for the weekly shopping trip with his parents that evening. Debbie thanked him for not pressing her into becoming intimate whilst they were canoodling on her bed; she wasn't ready and certainly wouldn't be for a while, but Pete knew that. He understood, and that was just fine by him. He left and enjoyed a slow drive back home with the radio turned up high. The song *Rosanna,* by the band, Toto, was being played and this time, despite not having a passion for singing, Pete enjoyed singing along.

Ralf decided to invite Edwina into his home and cook her dinner that evening, and she was most enthusiastic about the idea when he put it to her on the telephone. He thought that it wasn't always worth eating out as it cost money, and he was rather a dab hand in the kitchen anyway. He set about preparing everything after he went out to buy a few ingredients that he was short of, and once Edwina had arrived, he began to cook his speciality – well, one of them anyway – after leaving her in the lounge with a glass of red wine and a soothing musical choice of Burt Bacharach in the background.

Edwina wasn't a nosey type usually; curious about whom she was having the pleasure of dealing with, but definitely not invasive. What she didn't appreciate was being around someone who always held back, especially if it was noticeable. With wine in hand, she rose from the armchair near the window and began drifting around the lounge and dining room exploring her surroundings. Ralf's lounge merged into the dining area and was separated by a wide archway. On each side of the arch, there a couple of woollen petal-shaped fabrics with ceramic roses upon them, that hung above each other on the narrow part of the wall. Edwina was fascinated by them, probably because they seemed quite old. She was intrigued also, just like the others, at the absence of any family photographs dotted around anywhere. There were paintings – reprints of course – of famous works of art from times past; Edwina recognised the image of two boys eating grapes; she muttered the name *Murillo* as passed before it, and in the dining area, near the antlers, she came across *La Gioconda,* along with a few more obscure ones that were staggered as they hung near the patio doors.

Just as she turned to return to the armchair, Edwina noticed something on the floor, next to a wooden display unit that stood just below the antlers. It was a light wooden box similar to those where one would store cotton reels, needles, and suchlike, but she caught sight of part of a photograph that protruded from the little container's storage flaps. She bent down to open it, and it revealed its contents as indeed being of the sewing variety. The photograph was half buried in a handful of thimbles and cotton reels and on close inspection, Edwina noticed that it was the image of what seemed like a younger version of Ralf himself, and dressed in a monk's habit. He was smiling broadly and next to him, was a more elderly man, also in a monk's habit.

'What are you doing?'

Edwina jumped, letting the picture drop to the floor, but she noticed that Ralf followed it with his gaze as it fluttered onto the sewing box and onto the carpet.

'I'm so sorry, but...I just love these old sewing boxes. My mum used to have one, and I can't for the life of me find where it is.' She nervously twitched and fumbled with the photograph as she picked it up from the floor and placed it back where she found it.

'Give me that photo,' said Ralf coldly, 'I've been looking for that!'

Edwina handed the picture to him, and he attempted a cheerful smile as he took it from her. Edwina could see clearly through him, that she'd touched a nerve. She could see the skin upon his cheeks rippling as he gritted his teeth and the way he took a prolonged look at the image; the look upon his face certainly told a story or two.

'I'm sorry, Ralf...I didn't mean to pry. It wasn't very correct of me, and it's the first time I've been invited into your home.'

Ralf paused for a few seconds then looked up and smiled at her. 'This was taken years ago, you know…fancy dress evening. '

'Who's the gentleman next to you?'

'Ah, just a friend…a very dear friend. Anyway, ready for dinner?'

'Oh I can't wait, I'm starving. It smells delicious, by the way.'

They sat down at the table once Ralf had brought in the starters. It was a mixed Italian cured meat platter, with slices of mozzarella and southern Italian olives from the Puglia region. It was followed by pasta e fagioli, pasta shells with borlotti beans and celery in a beautifully juicy garlic and stock sauce. The dessert was a homemade tiramisu.

'Oh you sure can cook,' said Edwina with a mouthful of food, just about to be swallowed, 'did your mother teach you?'

Ralf felt his immediate vicinity become filled with what felt like a cold void. He had no idea how to answer that question; not without giving away some of the truth at least. Even as he kept his head down, feigning a profound interest in his delicious tiramisu,' he could still feel Edwina's eyes fixed upon him, as she awaited an answer.

'I'm an orphan.' He said blatantly, as he took a sip of white wine. He looked up at Edwina, who was clearly displaying an expression of sympathy. Ralf hated sympathy. He much preferred empathy in its place, and was a little pissed off by her expression. Edwina was better than that. She was a very intelligent woman, and that pissed Ralf off as well, at the moment. He usually liked such a trait in any woman, but not when he had something to hide. Edwina's scholar-like inquisitiveness was a little too much for him to accept but he didn't want to offend her by seeming too abrupt. Besides, that was just the headmistress in her coming out.

'It's fine,' he said, 'I've not even tried finding out who they were. Hurts if you know too much.'

'The place in that photo,' continued Edwina, 'it looks like somewhere abroad, maybe Greece or Italy or something…'

'Do you want some more tiramisu'?' asked Ralf, before she could ask anything else.

'Um…yes, actually…' Replied Edwina, as she passed her bowl to him. Ralf went into the kitchen to fetch the rest of the dessert that sat in a glass dish and rich with mascarpone cream that seeped from all sides. There were two generous portions left, and he and Edwina finished off all of it, and in total silence; until she resumed with the questions once again.

'So, tell me about the place on the picture then. Do you travel a lot, or…'

'Bloody hell, do you ever shut up!?' Snapped Ralf, slapping the surface of the table with the palm of his hand, 'it's like the third bloody degree, for Christ's sake!'

Edwina rose slowly from the table and asked where the bathroom was, to which Ralf replied that it was upstairs in front of her on the landing. Once she returned downstairs, Ralf could hear rustling in the hall as she began putting on her coat.

'Thanks for a lovely dinner!' She said, as she put her head around the doorway.

'Look, I'm sorry…I don't know what came over me…please don't go.' Pleaded Ralf as he dashed out into the hallway just as she was about to open the front door. She paused for a few seconds and closed it, then turned to face Ralf, who took her by the hand and led her back into the lounge.

'Look, I don't mean to pry…but it's just that…I find it a little hard knowing what to say to you sometimes. You're always ready to jump down my throat. I thought we were friends, Ralf.'

'We are, we are…look, I'm not good at opening myself up with just anyone. I need time, I'm a bit…private. Don't take it personally.'

'The thing is Ralf,' she said as she unbuttoned her coat and then sat down with it upon her lap, 'when you snap at me like that, I *do* take it personally. Please don't think that I'm pressing you into telling me your deepest, darkest secrets, but I like you and I'm just interested in knowing you better. That's all and nothing more, okay?'

'It was Italy,' replied Ralf, 'the picture was taken in Italy. I was in my late teens then, when that photo was snapped. Fuck…I can't believe I'm actually telling you this…I haven't even told my closest friends.'

'What, that you lived abroad? Why's that such a secret?'

'Edwina, listen to me,' continued Ralf, looking at her a little tearfully, 'In time, I will tell you everything…just not now. It's too dangerous for anyone to know. Please understand…'

'I do,' she replied, reaching across and touching his hand, 'when you're ready.'

'Look, perhaps we can meet up again another evening. I really enjoyed your company *and* your incredible food. Your culinary skills are truly second to none, but next time, you come round to mine and I'll cook *you* something special.; deal?'

'Deal, it's a date!'

Ralf walked Edwina to her car parked just outside the school gate and gave her a hug and kiss on the cheek.

'You're a special person, Ralf.'

'I wish that were true.'

Ralf returned to the armchair after washing up and making the kitchen look pristine, just the way he always liked it to. He stared at the antlers, whilst the ticking of the clock on the mantelpiece grew steadily louder as he began to drift into a mild sleep. He was awoken by a scraping sound coming from the kitchen. He sat and listened carefully as it started and stopped, a few seconds in between each sound. A few more seconds passed and the scraping became a slow, metallic creaking sound, like a door handle being slowly pressed down. Ralf rose from his chair and moved through the lounge, crouching all the way to the patio windows. The curtains were drawn fully aside, revealing the pitch-black outside. Ralf went prone and gently pressed his forehead against the bottom of the patio doors and looked to the right, toward where the garden door was. He was unable to see anything at all; it was too dark, but the door handle was definitely being tried; that he was sure of.

Ralf rapped his knuckle upon the glass once, and a fugacious shadow turned and fled toward the back of the garden and to the right of the shed. He heard whoever it was, climbing over the wooden gate that led out to the alleyway that ran behind the row of houses on Hawkshead Road. Ralf sprang up and made for the front door, leapt over his front gate and sprinted to the left and toward the alleyway entrance, the only way the intruder could escape. As he ran around the corner, sure enough, a figure dressed in dark clothing emerged from the alley and began running toward the end of Southfield Road. Ralf gave chase without thought of having left the front door of his house open, or whether he would even catch up to the intruder. The man – Ralf was certain that it was a man – possessed a good level of fitness as he showed no apparent signs of slowing up anytime soon, and Ralf was no spring chicken. He continued giving chase for as long as his stamina would allow.

With his energy levels dwindling, Ralf's pace began to flag a little and his legs were beginning to feel as though he were running uphill rather than on the level ground on which they were, and the intruder was gaining distance on him. On the brink of giving up the pursuit, Ralf saw the man stumble as he looked back to see if he was still being followed, and he fell to the ground, turning over a couple of times. Ralf reached him just as he was about to get to his feet and threw himself upon the dark intruder, wrestling him to the ground. Before the man could react, Ralf smashed him upon the side of his face, dazing him, then removed the balaclava he was wearing to conceal his identity. It was the man from the other evening, the one standing in the middle of the road. Ralf placed a firm grip around the man's neck while gripping his arm with his right hand and pinning down the other arm with the weight of his leg.

'Allora, dimmi chi cazzo sei!' Ralf hissed.

'So…you are him…aren't you?' Replied the man, gasping for breath.

'I said who are you? Who sent you and what do you want from me?'

Ralf released the intruder from his grip of steel and got up from where the man lay, clutching his throat. After about a minute, the man was able to form a sentence without rasping. He sat up, leaning his back against a parked car.

'I told you…my brother…the man you killed…it's time to surrender to karma…Raffaele.'

'I told you, if I ever saw you again, I'd kill you. Why are you still here…and more importantly, why are you trying to break into my home?'

'Ha! You have a comfortable life now, don't you…the old couple…they left you the house after they went. Don't worry…you'll pay. Trust me.'

Before Ralf could say anything more, a sudden bludgeoning force fell upon the back of his neck, and then another as he fell to his knees. The intruder struggled up from the ground and stuck Ralf across the face with a sharp backhander, knocking him sideways and into near-unconsciousness. Ralf felt his ears being forcefully grabbed and the intruder's voice, like a distant echo, issuing a warning to him in Italian.

'Ti terremo d'occhio, figlio di puttana. Non dormire troppo tranquillamente. Ci vediamo…Raffaele. Quanto e'dolce la vendetta!'

Ralf was thrown back down onto the asphalt as the man walked away. He lacked any strength to even turn around to see who it was that attacked him from behind. The overwhelming pain that invaded the back of his neck was like a debilitating and powerful ache that paralyzed and disabled him. He could do nothing but surrender to impending sleep, and pray he would awaken to see the sunrise the next morning.

Chapter 16

Over the weekend, Ralf tried to busy himself with as many things as possible. Firstly, because he couldn't for a second, get Loredana out of his head and secondly, guests. They were like fish; after three days they stink, and Ozzie and Julia had become very stinky people indeed. The stench was constantly there, right under his nose. Not the smell of unwashed, not at all, but with the colliding of the tongues complete with sucking and slurping, the shagging in the middle of the night with the two of them being evidently noisy lovers, and between his and her orgasms, the alternating ugh's and agh's sounded like there was a donkey upstairs. Ralf had many nights of broken sleep and the sofa was beginning to become uncomfortable. He refused to use any of the two spare bedrooms, otherwise the live pornographic movie would become simply intolerable. Every time Ralf was abruptly woken up by the two lovers, the first thing he saw in the penumbra of the dining area as he faced it, were the antlers. For years they had never been taken down; Ralf thought they could finally get some use. He thought of seriously inserting them into Ozzie.

At around eight in the morning on Sunday, Ralf received the umpteenth phone call from Ozzie's mother, asking the whereabouts of her son. Ralf finally revealed that he was with him and that he couldn't take it anymore. She shrieked at him down the phone, so ear-piercingly loud, that Ralf had to continue speaking to her whilst holding the earpiece to his lips, like a walkie-talkie.

'Look, he's fine, seriously though, you need to convince him that it's perfectly safe to come home and that you won't give him a hard time by asking too many questions...why? I'll tell you why...I'm getting next to no sleep at all...the continuous shagging and moaning and bumping the walls...please tell him that you'll be happy to see him...PLEASE!'

On the Monday morning, just as Ralf was going out of the front door, his two friends were packing their bags and ready to move in with Ozzie's mum, Julia included. Apparently she was convinced that as a couple, they were for life. Ozzie had quickly briefed Ralf about his thoughts on his relationship, but was told that they'd speak about it another time. Ralf went into work and straight into his English class, and was looking forward to the change of scenery.

Edwina Clare greeted him with a smile and a wink as they passed each other in the corridor. She couldn't stop to chat as she was accompanied by a young couple, probably wanting to find out about their child starting school there.

As he entered his classroom, Ralf received the usual pleasant welcome from his pupils. Lawrence in particular, was in fine form and complete with a sense of humour.

'Sir, can I tell you a joke?'

'Yes of course, Lawrence, 'said Ralf with a smile, 'go for it!'

'Did you know they've found Dracula's boat?'

'Yeeess,'

'It's a blood vessel!'

A combination of groans and chortles began to rise and fill the classroom and Ralf wasn't quite sure what to say. He had a slight smile upon his face, but that joke was rather a lame one, for Lawrence's standards.

'Lawrence,' Ralf intoned, 'do you think that joke you just told is actually funny?'

'Yes sir,' Lawrence replied in almost musical fashion, 'I thought it was brilliant!'

'Lawrence.'

'Yes sir.'

'Would you like an hour's detention after school today?'

'Um...nah, think not sir...that'd really suck!'

'Okay, then promise me you'll *never, ever* tell such dreadful jokes like that again!'

'Okay sir, I'll tell you another one after the lesson!'

'I shudder to think what it'll be like...' muttered Ralf.

Later that morning, Ralf had just finished taking his music class, when his heart jumped into his throat, leaving him feeling sick and afraid. A cold sweat took over his body and his heart raced like a wild horse. Two police officers, one male, one female, entered the school premises and approached Edwina, who was pinning up a poster on the message board in one of the corridors near her office. Ralf waited and watched from the doors of the classroom, and sure enough, they began making their way to where he was. He dashed back to his desk, took out a tissue from the drawer and wiped away the sweat from his forehead as best he could. There was a tap at the door, and the two officers of the law let themselves in.

'Good morning, Mr Ralf Avalon?'

'Um, yes that's me,' Ralf smiled, 'how can I help?'

'I'm PC Trevor Hawkins, this is my colleague, PC Sally Cryer. We have a few questions regarding an incident involving a teacher from this school, a Mr Daniel Campion. A colleague of yours, I believe.'

'Um, yes, he's a colleague; a maths teacher. Something wrong?'

'Yes,' said the female officer, 'as a matter of fact there is. He was brutally beaten last week and has just today, been discharged from the hospital. His housekeeper called us after an incident at her home, where he apparently lodges. Do you know of this, or did you hear about it…it's just that the lady gave us a rather detailed description that matches your own.'

Ralf could feel himself shaking all over and his legs were beginning to feel like jelly. His abdomen became wracked with cramps that he was barely able to tolerate, and was unable to stifle a wince from the sharp pain that cut through him.

'Are you alright sir? You appear to be in some sort of pain.' Asked PC Hawkins.

'I'm sorry. I'll be fine in a second. I suffer from Crohn's Disease and I get these cramps occasionally. I'm afraid I can't help you unfortunately. I was the one who pressed charges following an incident that involved one of my pupils, and then he just disappeared. I've not seen or heard from him since.'

'We spoke to him regarding his attacker,' continued PC Cryer, 'but he told us that it took place down a dark alley, and he couldn't see who it was.'

In that instant, Ralf stood up and walked over to the blackboard and began to erase what was written upon it, while still facing the two police officers.

'I'm sorry, I wish I could help further, but…I don't really know what else to say. I don't know where he lives, so it definitely wasn't me the…housekeeper described. I'm sure I'm not the only bald man in Chiswick.'

Edwina rushed over to the classroom after the two officers left the building and asked if everything was okay, to which Ralf replied that it was. He had no information for them except that Campion was indeed a teacher there. Ralf couldn't bring himself round to telling Edwina the truth; his trust in her *was* growing and he'd undoubtedly found an unlikely friend in her, but if she ever knew that *he* was Campion's attacker, things may not be so easy.

'Did they just want to talk to you about the Lawrence incident?' Edwina asked.

'Oh…yeah, they just wanted to ask the same questions. Usual police habits, you know.'

'Had you heard about Daniel?'

'Yes, sometime last week. He was attacked or something.'

'Did the police question you in relation to that?' She insisted.

Ralf continued to erase the blackboard and tidy away some paperwork, as he tried his utmost to not make eye contact with Edwina, who wouldn't cease with questioning him.

'Why would they think that you'd know something about it?'

'I've no idea, Edwina. Maybe they're just conducting enquiries and so I guess…everyone's a suspect. I don't know…maybe.'

'Why aren't you looking at me when I'm talking to you, Ralf?'

Ralf *did* look at her this time. He was trying his best not to panic or seem remotely pissed off in any way, but Edwina wasn't having any of it. She was no fool. She glared at Ralf expectantly, keeping her eyes upon him all the time, whilst he made every attempt to keep from looking at her. He could feel her staring at him, even with his back to her, while he filed away his classroom notes and tidied his desk. Once it was done and there was nothing left for him to do, he sighed and turned to face her. She turned and exited the room. Ralf dashed after her.

'Edwina wait!'

She turned around and waited while he went towards her. Ralf took her hand after checking that they weren't being watched by any stray pupils between lessons.

'Look, I'm sorry. It's just…shit, I'm crap at explaining things…look, let's have dinner somewhere and I'll explain everything. How's that sound?'

'That would be very nice,' Edwina said softly and touching Ralf's hand, 'I'd like to think you can trust me. I know I trust you…'

Pete remained with Debbie for most of the morning, and after a late breakfast of croissants and coffee, she began to open up regarding how she had planned to tell him about where they stood with their relationship. Pete was a little surprised at how willingly she was speaking about the subject, considering what had happened to her, and as she continued to enlighten him about all sorts of future plans involving the pair of them, Pete's heart felt as though it was performing cartwheels and jumps for joy, whilst his soul was basking in the sun.

Debbie told Pete she loved him as he was near the front door and ready to go back home for some rest, in readiness for the weekly shopping trip with his parents that evening. Debbie thanked him for not pressing her into becoming intimate whilst they were canoodling on her bed; she wasn't ready and certainly wouldn't be for a while, but Pete knew that. He understood, and that was just fine by him. He left and enjoyed a slow drive back home with the radio turned up high. The song *Rosanna,* by the band, Toto, was being played and this time, despite not having a passion for singing, Pete enjoyed singing along.

Ralf decided to invite Edwina into his home and cook her dinner that evening, and she was most enthusiastic about the idea when he put it to her on the telephone. He thought that it wasn't always worth eating out as it cost money, and he was rather a dab hand in the kitchen anyway. He set about preparing everything after he went out to buy a few ingredients that he was short of, and once Edwina had arrived, he began to cook his speciality – well, one of them anyway – after leaving her in the lounge with a glass of red wine and a soothing musical choice of Burt Bacharach in the background.

Edwina wasn't a nosey type usually; curious about whom she was having the pleasure of dealing with, but definitely not invasive. What she didn't appreciate was being around someone who always held back, especially if it was noticeable. With wine in hand, she rose from the armchair near the window and began drifting around the lounge and dining room exploring her surroundings. Ralf's lounge merged into the dining area and was separated by a wide archway. On each side of the arch, there a couple of woollen petal-shaped fabrics with ceramic roses upon them, that hung above each other on the narrow part of the wall. Edwina was fascinated by them, probably because they seemed quite old. She was intrigued also, just like the others, at the absence of any family photographs dotted around anywhere. There were paintings – reprints of course – of famous works of art from times past; Edwina recognised the image of two boys eating grapes; she muttered the name *Murillo* as passed before it, and in the dining area, near the antlers, she came across *La Gioconda,* along with a few more obscure ones that were staggered as they hung near the patio doors.

Just as she turned to return to the armchair, Edwina noticed something on the floor, next to a wooden display unit that stood just below the antlers. It was a light wooden box similar to those where one would store cotton reels, needles, and suchlike, but she caught sight of part of a photograph that protruded from the little container's storage flaps. She bent down to open it, and it revealed its contents as indeed being of the sewing variety. The photograph was half buried in a handful of thimbles and cotton reels and on close inspection, Edwina noticed that it was the image of what seemed like a younger version of Ralf himself, and dressed in a monk's habit. He was smiling broadly and next to him, was a more elderly man, also in a monk's habit.

'What are you doing?'

Edwina jumped, letting the picture drop to the floor, but she noticed that Ralf followed it with his gaze as it fluttered onto the sewing box and onto the carpet.

'I'm so sorry, but...I just love these old sewing boxes. My mum used to have one, and I can't for the life of me find where it is.' She nervously twitched and fumbled with the photograph as she picked it up from the floor and placed it back where she found it.

'Give me that photo,' said Ralf coldly, 'I've been looking for that!'

Edwina handed the picture to him, and he attempted a cheerful smile as he took it from her. Edwina could see clearly through him, that she'd touched a nerve. She could see the skin upon his cheeks rippling as he gritted his teeth and the way he took a prolonged look at the image; the look upon his face certainly told a story or two.

'I'm sorry, Ralf...I didn't mean to pry. It wasn't very correct of me, and it's the first time I've been invited into your home.'

Ralf paused for a few seconds then looked up and smiled at her. 'This was taken years ago, you know...fancy dress evening. '

'Who's the gentleman next to you?'

'Ah, just a friend...a very dear friend. Anyway, ready for dinner?'

'Oh I can't wait, I'm starving. It smells delicious, by the way.'

They sat down at the table once Ralf had brought in the starters. It was a mixed Italian cured meat platter, with slices of mozzarella and southern Italian olives from the Puglia region. It was followed by pasta e fagioli, pasta shells with borlotti beans and celery in a beautifully juicy garlic and stock sauce. The dessert was a homemade tiramisu.

'Oh you sure can cook,' said Edwina with a mouthful of food, just about to be swallowed, 'did your mother teach you?'

Ralf felt his immediate vicinity become filled with what felt like a cold void. He had no idea how to answer that question; not without giving away some of the truth at least. Even as he kept his head down, feigning a profound interest in his delicious tiramisu,' he could still feel Edwina's eyes fixed upon him, as she awaited an answer.

'I'm an orphan.' He said blatantly, as he took a sip of white wine. He looked up at Edwina, who was clearly displaying an expression of sympathy. Ralf hated sympathy. He much preferred empathy in its place, and was a little pissed off by her expression. Edwina was better than that. She was a very intelligent woman, and that pissed Ralf off as well, at the moment. He usually liked such a trait in any woman, but not when he had something to hide. Edwina's scholar-like inquisitiveness was a little too much for him to accept but he didn't want to offend her by seeming too abrupt. Besides, that was just the headmistress in her coming out.

'It's fine,' he said, 'I've not even tried finding out who they were. Hurts if you know too much.'

'The place in that photo,' continued Edwina, 'it looks like somewhere abroad, maybe Greece or Italy or something...'

'Do you want some more tiramisu'?' asked Ralf, before she could ask anything else.

'Um...yes, actually...' Replied Edwina, as she passed her bowl to him. Ralf went into the kitchen to fetch the rest of the dessert that sat in a glass dish and rich with mascarpone cream that seeped from all sides. There were two generous portions left, and he and Edwina finished off all of it, and in total silence; until she resumed with the questions once again.

'So, tell me about the place on the picture then. Do you travel a lot, or...'

'Bloody hell, do you ever shut up!?' Snapped Ralf, slapping the surface of the table with the palm of his hand, 'it's like the third bloody degree, for Christ's sake!'

Edwina rose slowly from the table and asked where the bathroom was, to which Ralf replied that it was upstairs in front of her on the landing. Once she returned downstairs, Ralf could hear rustling in the hall as she began putting on her coat.

'Thanks for a lovely dinner!' She said, as she put her head around the doorway.

'Look, I'm sorry...I don't know what came over me...please don't go.' Pleaded Ralf as he dashed out into the hallway just as she was about to open the front door. She paused for a few seconds and closed it, then turned to face Ralf, who took her by the hand and led her back into the lounge.

'Look, I don't mean to pry...but it's just that...I find it a little hard knowing what to say to you sometimes. You're always ready to jump down my throat. I thought we were friends, Ralf.'

'We are, we are...look, I'm not good at opening myself up with just anyone. I need time, I'm a bit...private. Don't take it personally.'

'The thing is Ralf,' she said as she unbuttoned her coat and then sat down with it upon her lap, 'when you snap at me like that, I *do* take it personally. Please don't think that I'm pressing you into telling me your deepest, darkest secrets, but I like you and I'm just interested in knowing you better. That's all and nothing more, okay?'

'It was Italy,' replied Ralf, 'the picture was taken in Italy. I was in my late teens then, when that photo was snapped. Fuck...I can't believe I'm actually telling you this...I haven't even told my closest friends.'

'What, that you lived abroad? Why's that such a secret?'

'Edwina, listen to me,' continued Ralf, looking at her a little tearfully, 'In time, I will tell you everything...just not now. It's too dangerous for anyone to know. Please understand...'

'I do,' she replied, reaching across and touching his hand, 'when you're ready.

'Look, perhaps we can meet up again another evening. I really enjoyed your company *and* your incredible food. Your culinary skills are truly second to none, but next time, you come round to mine and I'll cook *you* something special.; deal?'

'Deal, it's a date!'

Ralf walked Edwina to her car parked just outside the school gate and gave her a hug and kiss on the cheek.

'You're a special person, Ralf.'

'I wish that were true.'

Ralf returned to the armchair after washing up and making the kitchen look pristine, just the way he always liked it to. He stared at the antlers, whilst the ticking of the clock on the mantelpiece grew steadily louder as he began to drift into a mild sleep. He was awoken by a scraping sound coming from the kitchen. He sat and listened carefully as it started and stopped, a few seconds in between each sound. A few more seconds passed and the scraping became a slow, metallic creaking sound, like a door handle being slowly pressed down. Ralf rose from his chair and moved through the lounge, crouching all the way to the patio windows. The curtains were drawn fully aside, revealing the pitch-black outside. Ralf went prone and gently pressed his forehead against the bottom of the patio doors and looked to the right, toward where the garden door was. He was unable to see anything at all; it was too dark, but the door handle was definitely being tried; that he was sure of.

Ralf rapped his knuckle upon the glass once, and a fugacious shadow turned and fled toward the back of the garden and to the right of the shed. He heard whoever it was, climbing over the wooden gate that led out to the alleyway that ran behind the row of houses on Hawkshead Road. Ralf sprang up and made for the front door, leapt over his front gate and sprinted to the left and toward the alleyway entrance, the only way the intruder could escape. As he ran around the corner, sure enough, a figure dressed in dark clothing emerged from the alley and began running toward the end of Southfield Road. Ralf gave chase without thought of having left the front door of his house open, or whether he would even catch up to the intruder. The man – Ralf was certain that it was a man – possessed a good level of fitness as he showed no apparent signs of slowing up anytime soon, and Ralf was no spring chicken. He continued giving chase for as long as his stamina would allow.

With his energy levels dwindling, Ralf's pace began to flag a little and his legs were beginning to feel as though he were running uphill rather than on the level ground on which they were, and the intruder was gaining distance on him. On the brink of giving up the pursuit, Ralf saw the man stumble as he looked back to see if he was still being followed, and he fell to the ground, turning over a couple of times. Ralf reached him just as he was about to get to his feet and threw himself upon the dark intruder, wrestling him to the ground.

135

Before the man could react, Ralf smashed him upon the side of his face, dazing him, then removed the balaclava he was wearing to conceal his identity. It was the man from the other evening, the one standing in the middle of the road. Ralf placed a firm grip around the man's neck while gripping his arm with his right hand and pinning down the other arm with the weight of his leg.

'Allora, dimmi chi cazzo sei!' Ralf hissed.

'So…you are him…aren't you?' Replied the man, gasping for breath.

'I said who are you? Who sent you and what do you want from me?'

Ralf released the intruder from his grip of steel and got up from where the man lay, clutching his throat. After about a minute, the man was able to form a sentence without rasping. He sat up, leaning his back against a parked car.

'I told you…my brother…the man you killed…it's time to surrender to karma…Raffaele.'

'I told you, if I ever saw you again, I'd kill you. Why are you still here…and more importantly, why are you trying to break into my home?'

'Ha! You have a comfortable life now, don't you…the old couple…they left you the house after they went. Don't worry…you'll pay. Trust me.'

Before Ralf could say anything more, a sudden bludgeoning force fell upon the back of his neck, and then another as he fell to his knees. The intruder struggled up from the ground and stuck Ralf across the face with a sharp backhander, knocking him sideways and into near-unconsciousness. Ralf felt his ears being forcefully grabbed and the intruder's voice, like a distant echo, issuing a warning to him in Italian.

'Ti terremo d'occhio, figlio di puttana. Non dormire troppo tranquillamente. Ci vediamo…Raffaele. Quanto e'dolce la vendetta!'

Ralf was thrown back down onto the asphalt as the man walked away. He lacked any strength to even turn around to see who it was that attacked him from behind. The overwhelming pain that invaded the back of his neck was like a debilitating and powerful ache that paralyzed and disabled him. He could do nothing but surrender to impending sleep, and pray he would awaken to see the sunrise the next morning.

Chapter 17

Ralf opened his eyes, and welcomed the sight of the black firmament and its congregation of stars that flickered, and a half moon that washed the world around him with its ghostly white essence. He was certain he'd heard a vehicle pass him by as he lay still upon the cold blacktop. It still amazed him, the thought of so many people that out of sheer caution and fear for themselves, would not stop to see if a victim lying in the middle of the road was at all genuine. The stories were all true, featuring those that would feign injury or distress, in order to lure potential good Samaritans to the scene, so that an accomplice may spring out of hiding; the rest was history. Yet, it astonished him all the same. He had been lying there for at least a couple of hours…

Ralf staggered home and pushed his way through the front door, which he'd mistakably left open earlier, when he was giving chase. Frustration turned to anger when his eyes focused upon the fridge in the kitchen straight ahead of him. It had been moved outwards, to the middle of the kitchen and the garden door was left wide open. He stepped forward and caught sight of the state of the lounge. He turned to face the clutter that lay before his eyes and squeezed past the display unit that had been hauled away from the wall it stood against and left plumb in the middle of the lounge. The armchairs were overturned, the drawers of the unit that stood beneath the antlers were hanging open, their contents spilled and scattered, and the bookcase was pulled forward and left leaning against the dining room table, its books no longer inhabiting the shelves, but were spilled over the table and floor. The antlers were still hanging, untouched and looking more ominous than usual, as they appeared to survey all the discombobulation that both rooms now displayed.

To his own surprise, Ralf was not at all consumed by anger; either because it was utterly pointless – whatever the sentiments within him, he would need to clear up the chaos – or simply because it was kind of inevitable; sooner or later karma catches up and bites you on the bum, no matter how hard you try to hide from it or ride with the waves. Ralf knew deep inside, that the secret he had always tried to keep locked away in a box would escape eventually. It was just a matter of time. He made one of his trademark coffees and began his mission of restoring order to his violated home.

Pete and Debbie were in Brent Cross shopping centre and on the hunt for a suitable engagement ring for her. After their initial conversation, the subsequent chats began steadily bordering on their future as a couple, where they would like to live and what type of house they wanted, and Debbie's particular dislike of Pete's car. She wanted a Ford Escort RS 2000 and he had preference for BMW's. There were many jewellery shops within the massive complex and thanks to Debbie's keen eye, they left none unturned. They finally agreed to a rather delightful ring with three precious stones set into eighteen carat gold, for around the five hundred pound mark. Pete was more than happy to oblige, as his job of working with computers provided him with a fine salary.

'I rather fancy something to eat,' said Debbie, swinging her arms and grinning gleefully, 'I'm getting…Chinese. What do you think?'

'I'm getting tired.' Replied Pete, but agreeing to the food stop. Brent Cross was immense and on that day, overwhelmingly crowded with what seemed like three quarters of the world's population, and getting back to the car was like an adventure in itself. All the restaurants that matched Debbie's culinary desires for the day, were packed to the extreme and with lengthy queues of waiting customers, complete with those looks of impatience and frustration that came with insatiable hunger during a long day out and away from home. Pete and Debbie agreed that hanging around that adventure playground from hell was not going to yield results, and so they decided to drive to somewhere closer to home. They ended up in Northfield Avenue, just down the road from Pete's house, and in the Chinese restaurant a couple of doors down from the café where Pete met up with Mel.

As they perused the extensive menu, Debbie set her heart on the Peking Feast for two, which consisted of a mixed starter seaweed, spring rolls, ribs, and shredded smoked chicken with various freshly prepared dipping sauces. The main was hearty and simply delicious and came with crispy duck and pancakes, Hoisin sauce, shredded spring onions and thinly sliced cucumber. There were various main dishes that accompanied the duck that were incredible; beef in black bean sauce, stir-fried chicken in satay sauce, special fried rice, and plain Chow Mein noodles with bamboo shoots. The couple spent around two hours in the small but palatial eatery, which was replete with a few small water features, clusters of artificial house plants, and content looking Buddha statues. The soft lighting didn't impair vision of what was upon the food table and a jingle of easy listening oriental music sailed around the hideaway, designed to soothe the soul and ease away the tensions of the day.

'Ooh…I'm pleasantly stuffed.' said Debbie, sighing with relief.

'Yep, I'm suitably stuffed as well.' replied Pete, and after settling up the bill, the couple left the restaurant and headed for Pete's house. As they pulled up outside, Pete noticed that his father's car was not there. The spaces along the entire street were not allocated, but the neighbours were more than just acquaintances and respectful of one another's desire to park outside their own house.

'Strange,' muttered Pete, 'it's not shopping day today…wonder where mum and dad could be.'

'Maybe they fancied a Chinese as well.' said Debbie.

'Nah, my parents hate Chinese food. They've not gone to visit any relatives, because they're too far away. My auntie's in Scotland and my uncle and other auntie on my dad's side are up in Yorkshire. They wouldn't go there without telling me they would; they'd want me to go with them anyway. They wouldn't just take off without a word.'

'Strange then,' said Debbie, 'so where could they have got to?'

'No idea.'

As Pete turned the key in the door, Debbie leaned in for a passionate kiss.

'I love you Mr Sheridan,' she said, as she kissed him a few times more, 'I really like my ring. Happy times.'

Pete found a hand written note on his mum's sewing table by the sofa, with the words, GONE TO WICKES, BACK SOON. CAN YOU PUT SOME POTATOES ON? BACK BY SEVEN. LOVE MUM. X

Just underneath his mum's writing, Pete saw that his dad had written, I LOVE YOU TOO, IF YOU PUT SOME POTATOES ON. TEE HEE.

'What's that?' asked Debbie as she walked into the lounge.

'Just a note from mum and dad. They're at Wickes...that means...we have a few hours to kill upstairs. Shit, sorry love; that was insensitive of me. I shouldn't have...'

'Oh hush now,' said Debbie, placing a finger to his lips, 'I think that sounds like a plan.'

The two went upstairs, while Pete began feeling like a teenager about to experience his first kiss.

'You'd better move that keyboard off your bed, else we'll be plinking and plonking!' said Debbie as she kissed Pete passionately.

'Har har. You know me...music is the *key* to everything...' replied Pete, with a chuckle.

Pete turned out the overhead light, leaving only his side-lamp on and dimmed to a faint glow. He lay next to his beautiful girlfriend and gazed into her eyes. They seemed crystalline and glinted warmly in the bedroom's suffused atmosphere.

'Will you write me a song?' asked Debbie, speaking softly and with her lips to Pete's ear.

'I'll write you the best song I've ever written,' replied Pete, 'but you know I'm no singer; I'll have to get Ralf to sing it.'

'Yeah...sounds like a plan,' said Debbie, a nice one.'

The wind outside rose slightly and began to moan and lament around the windows of the bedroom and the fireplace. The rustle of the trees outside in the garden whispered as the zephyr rambled through them, and continued to sigh through the night in a steady and mollifying thrum. Pete and Debbie both wished that the few hours they had to themselves would last forever, as they began to lose themselves in each other's eyes. After succumbing to a very special ecstasy, the couple fell asleep in each other's arms.

It was gone one in the morning, and Ralf dove for the armchair nearest to him. The arms of slumber were ready and waiting to embrace him, but after recent events, he was too afraid to sleep, even though his gut feeling told him his foes wouldn't return that night, possibly for a while. They were planning something else, he was sure of it. They would strike again soon. He only saw one of them since the other remained shrouded in mystery as they attacked him from behind, and the more Ralf dwelt upon that, the more he thought he should have seen it coming. After all, someone who had been looking for him for all this time would surely not come alone. He definitely should have seen it coming.

As he sat back and downed yet another coffee, Ralf thought about that day. That eventful day that would change his life forever. He was forced to leave the place he had always called home since he was eight years old, and all because of what he'd done. But that man deserved it. He really had it coming, especially after what he had done. The most despicable act any man could perform, and in Ralf's eyes, that was worse than murder. When you do *that* to a woman, you kill her soul, her self-esteem, her confidence, even her courage and love of life and people. The anguished screams and pleas for it to stop, then the gagging…that man definitely deserved what came to him; and Ralf felt only too happy to have been the dispenser of justice. He had no regrets for the life he took.

Pete woke up and gasped as he almost fell out of the bed. Debbie stirred, but continued sleeping as Pete got out of bed and switched on the overhead light. The alarm clock read Four thirty seven. His heart began beating a little more than usual and he suddenly felt very afraid. He peeked around the door to his parents' bedroom. They weren't there. This was incredibly odd in Pete's eyes. His parents would have never done such a thing, especially without mentioning anything to him. Pete always wanted to visit Scotland again since going there a few times to visit his uncle and auntie, and his mum and dad knew that well, so where the hell were they?

Pete called the local police and informed them that his parents had been missing all day, and that they had left him a note saying they'd gone to Wickes, and after a lengthy conversation it was concluded that there was something clearly amiss with the whole situation. Debbie came downstairs and into the lounge, where Pete was

Chapter 18

The next morning, Pete awoke with a start, his body drenched in sweat and his bed covers strewn around the bedroom floor. As he struggled to his feet, he realised he had spent the night upon the floor and in a foetal position, and he had been wrestling with an unwanted and hateful nightmare that featured his parents alive and well, but both calling out to him in supplication. A gunshot was heard and they faded into nothing, allowing Pete to break free from the clutches of the poisonous incubus that had taken hold of his tormented mind.

The two policewomen from the previous night had mentioned that Pete would need to go and identify the bodies of his parents, as unfortunately neither he nor the two officers were successful in getting hold of his sisters. He tried to ring them a couple more times before deciding to set off by himself; this was crap situation number two. Debbie was number three and Pete thought he'd leave it at that. It couldn't possibly get any worse than this.

Ralf had finished breakfast in a tidy lounge and dining area and a thought occurred to him; he hadn't contacted the lovely Loredana, the Italian girl he met in the café a few evenings ago. He searched for the piece of paper he'd scribbled the phone number on and enthusiastically dialled it, with a smile upon his lips.

'Hello, gorgeous!' he intoned as she answered.

'Ah, Raffaele!' she exclaimed, and Ralf could clearly discern the joy in her voice.

'How are you? I thought you werrr nat goeen to call!' she said, brightly, in her charming broken English.

'Well I had to pluck up a little bit of courage first, but I said I would call you, so here I am. I was wondering…do you fancy dinner tonight? My place? I am a very good cook and I think you'd be impressed!'

Loredana accepted pretty much without hesitation, and the date was set for the following evening. Ralf chose a record from a burgundy coloured carry-case he kept just behind the TV set and sat watching as the needle lowered itself automatically and touched the vinyl. After a few seconds of familiar introductory crackle, the music began to fill the room and Ralf's soul felt more uplifted than ever. The song, *The Meaning of Love* by Depeche Mode had Ralf sitting up and doing a bit of armchair dancing, as its fast and tuneful refrain galloped along and took hold of his non-rhythmic body. Ralf was gifted with a great voice, but he danced like a bookcase.

The following evening, Pete was in the lounge with a photo album in hand, reminiscing and rearranging photographs. Janice, his older sister, had got in touch with him earlier in the day, and after much disbelief at what had happened, she and her husband offered to go halves with the funeral.

Pete went into the kitchen and tidied up the remnants of that morning's breakfast. He stood there for a long time just looking around, in particular at the pan with water and the potatoes inside, the ones his parents had asked him to put on the boil for when they got back from Wickes. Pete reluctantly took hold of the saucepan's handle and proceeded to empty the water into the sink. The potatoes went into the dustbin, which he tied and put outside in the garden. The phone rang and Pete walked slowly over to it, answering on the eighth ring. His stomach began to churn when the voice at the other end identified itself.

'Hello Pete…it's Mel. I'm truly sorry for your loss…I know what my sister's done…I really had no idea. Look, if you need anything, anything at all…'

Pete hung up and walked away from the telephone and returned to the kitchen. After washing and drying up, he stood motionless in the middle of the room and looked out across the garden. The outside toilet hut stood at the right hand corner, just beside a topiary bush which his father had lovingly crafted into an archway, leading into the barbecue area and then further down to where the shed stood at the far left corner, next to the wooden gate that opened into an alleyway leading to the next street. The neighbour's black cat ambled across the lawn and clambered onto the fence and into the alley. Three sparrows descended into the garden as though they had been waiting for their colossal foe to skulk across the land, so they could continue hopping about and look for food.

Pete's dad used to enjoy standing at the garden door and watch the little feathered wonders going about their daily tasks of mingling with each other and scavenging for scraps, which John provided regularly and almost on a daily basis, in the form of birdseed, mealworms, and bits of bread. Pete watched as more sparrows flew in and gracefully pranced about, hoovering up the last remnants of seeds and bread. Two pigeons and a collar-dove attempted to join the fray, but were chased off by the smaller birds for daring to gate-crash their little gathering. Pete began slipping back into his well of sorrow after he looked upon the wooden bench just to his left, where his father used to sit on a Sunday morning. His parents weren't church-goers, as john never had time for mass. He always found it tedious and a waste of good home relaxation time, and he particularly disliked the part where the priest would invite the congregation to offer each other the sign of piece. Pete didn't like it either, especially if the person whose hand he shook happened to be on the sweaty side.

The telephone rang once again. This time Pete rushed toward it and raised the handset at the fourth ring. It wasn't Mel this time…it was Ozzie.

'Hallo, mate…how ya been? Long time, no hear…hello? Pete, you there, mate?'

'I'm sorry, Ozzie, but I can't talk right now. I'll call you back. Love to Julia.'

Pete hung up and went upstairs to his room. He drew the curtains and turned off the light, then let himself collapse onto the bed.

Loredana called at Ralf's house at around seven, and as he opened the front door, she stepped inside and planted a wet kiss upon his lips. His loins began stirring immediately, and as he scrutinized her from head to toe, noticing that she was wearing high heels and a mini-skirt, they went into overdrive. At that precise moment, all his disdain for relationships with the word, *committal* in it, were discarded forcefully, as all he could think about was when he could fall to his knees and bury his head up Loredana's mini-skirt and savour the surprise that lay beneath.

He watched her as she brushed past him and made her way into the lounge, her incredible eyes taking in everything and smiling in admiration whilst praising Ralf's beautiful home. Ralf was, in his mind, praising her beautiful behind as it swayed with infectious undulating fashion, each time she took a step. Her legs were perfectly shaped and her skin was delicately olive. Her hair was down and she wore little makeup. As she seated herself upon the sofa and beckoned Ralf to join her, she crossed her legs while looking seductively at him. Ralf didn't give her time to repeat herself, and immediately dropped down next to her and leant in for another of her moist kisses, to which she lent her lips with steaming hot pleasure and eyes crammed shut. Ralf could smell the fragrance on her skin and the shampoo in her hair. Loredana clasped her fingers behind his neck and began to gently massage his nape with her fingernails in a circular motion. Ralf began purring like a cat and rubbing his cheek against her own.

Much to his disbelief, as she was a southern Italian girl, Ralf found earning Loredana's trust was unbelievably easy; they weren't usually this keen to drop their panties until several weeks, sometimes months into a relationship. This was only the second time he had seen her, and she was already feeling for the zipper on his trousers. Ralf shivered with extreme pleasure and made a humming sound that he didn't even know he was able to do, sounding like a very deranged version of Scooby Doo. Loredana chuckled and kissed him once again, as she began lowering his zipper and foraging for the beast. After a fleeting *what the hell,* shot through his mind, Ralf helped her with her dress and panties, and the two made love on the sofa to start with and later ended up in the bedroom upstairs.

Ralf was finally in a place he loved to be. Loredana was on top of him and rocking rhythmically back and forth, her hair falling onto his face and chest as she moved. Ralf watched her as the white light from the streetlamps invaded the room, casting dancing shadows on the walls and Loredana's body. Her firm breasts jumped up and down with each back and forth movement, her neck craned up at the ceiling and her eyes were closed in ecstasy. Ralf was finding it all the more difficult to contain himself, and forced his mind to think of anything but the ecstatic Loredana, as she rode him like a fine stallion. That was exactly what he was feeling like at that very moment; a magnificent stallion being put through his paces. Loredana sighed heavily and squealed with delight, as she felt an orgasm surge through her like electricity; at that moment, Ralf finally brought his thoughts back to the wonderfully statuesque woman that danced upon him, and let himself go. His body convulsed with unmatched pleasure, as he pulled Loredana's face to his own and kissed her with all the passion that raged inside him. The two remained in an embrace for at least half an hour, as they discarded the sheets and bed covers.

Ozzie was out shopping with Julia in Ealing Broadway, and they were just about to enter the station, when a voice called his name enthusiastically. Ozzie turned around and to his surprise, his old school friend, Garry Scott emerged from behind a group of nuns and clutching a briefcase. He was dressed in a dark grey, pinstripe suit and black, pointed shoes that made a clickety-clackety sound from their steel heel-studs as he walked. The two old pals shook hands tightly and after introducing Garry to Julia, they continued down into Ealing Broadway station.

Garry ushered them into the now empty waiting room as they descended to the platforms. The speaker announcement cut through the air, complete with screeching microphone feedback, as the announcer informed the passengers that had spilled out of the waiting room, of the approaching train and its destination.

LADIES AND GENTLEMEN, PLEASE STAND BACK FROM THE PLATFORM EDGE, BACK FROM THE PLATFORM EDGE…TRAIN APPROACHING PLATFORM TWO…THE GREENFORD CAR, THE GREENFORD CAR…CALLING AT…WEST EALING…DRAYTON GREEN…CASTLEBAR PARK…SOUTH GREENFORD…AND GREENFORD. GREENFORD CAR…ALL STATIONS TO GREENFORD!

'Oh bloody 'ell mate…it's so good to see ya. I can't believe it…such a long time.'

'Time flies, Garry. So…whatcha been up to? Last time we talked, you'd been bunkin' off school and ditched yer exams!'

'Bloody hell, Ozzie…you remember all that…yeah, I know. I just hated school…mug's game…just like fuckin' work as well, mate!'

'Tell me about it,' replied Ozzie, 'I ain't worked in ages. Last job I had was on a building site. Foreman kept callin' me a tosser, so I wacked the bastard!'

'Good fer you!' exclaimed Garry.

'So what do you do for a living?' asked Ozzie.

'Well…' Garry began, as he popped a gum in his mouth, 'I make deals.'

'Deals?'

'Yep, deals. Big deals, and they pay a *load* of wonga!'

'Go on,' Ozzie urged him to continue, 'I'm curious now.'

'Not here,' said Garry, as a couple of passengers stepped into the waiting room. 'Let's wait till we get on the train.'

'I've just realised something,' said Julia, pouting slightly, 'We're on the wrong platform. We need to cross over to the other one for Paddington.'

The three of them hurried over the walkway and toward the correct platform, scuttling down the stairs and reaching it just in time as the train pulled in.

Pete's doorbell sounded multiple times until he finally could stand its wailing tremolo no longer. He stomped down the stairs and abruptly opened the door, startling Mel, who stood at the doorstep clutching a small plastic bag.

'Can...I come in, or is it a bad time?'

Pete frowned.

'I'm sorry, I didn't mean it that way...I have something for you. I think you should have them back.'

Mel handed the plastic bag to Pete and hesitantly began walking away, turning around just once, to see if he was still standing in the doorway. He was. He gestured to her to return to the house and once inside, he led her to the lounge.

'Tea or coffee?' asked Pete, dropping the crumpled bag onto the sofa, next to where Mel was sitting.

'Coffee...please, one sugar, no milk.' replied a bedevilled Mel.

Pete brought the beverages in within minutes and sat down beside Mel. He opened the plastic bag and took the items out and examined them. One was the small black gift box he recognized – it was the ring he bought Debbie just days ago – the others were a silk foulard with a Versace design, and a silver charm bracelet he'd bought her the year before.

'I believe you should have these.' said Mel. 'Just because she's my sister, doesn't mean I condone how she's treated you.'

Pete muttered a stifled thank you, and sipped his coffee whilst cupping both hands around his mug. Mel observed him as he gazed at the glass unit just in front of him, as though hypnotized by it and its crystalline contents. Mel followed his steely gaze and saw what it was that he was staring at. Surrounded by a set of crystal chalices, was a large decanter filled with a dark liquid - undoubtedly cognac – with a large label affixed to it, featuring a photo of Pete's parents. Beneath the picture were the words, SUSAN AND JOHN'S MAGIC ELIXIR. Mel touched Pete's hand as he slowly began to fall apart before her very eyes. He let his mug of coffee fall to the floor and spill onto the carpet, then he fell forward, barely missing the glass unit with his head, by mere centimetres. Mel threw herself toward Pete and cradled him in her arms as he wailed and wept for the loss of pretty much everything he'd held dear in his life.

Chapter 19

Ralf accompanied Loredana to the station after their night of passion unleashed, and after a lengthy kiss goodbye on the platform of Turnham Green station, he went on to ring Pete once again after trying numerous times earlier that morning. There was still no answer from Pete's end and Ralf was beginning to worry. He rang Ozzie, who mentioned that he also had tried to phone him, and that Pete seemed dismissive. Ralf decided to drive over to his house to make sure all was okay.

Ralf pressed hard on the doorbell, but couldn't hear the familiar shrill of its mad arpeggio. He banged on the front door a few times and even called through the letterbox, after attempting to scout around the hallway by peeking through it. Nothing. Ralf knocked upon his neighbour's front door, but she knew nothing; although Pete wasn't on overly friendly terms with either of his next door neighbours. Ralf ventured into the alleyway which separated the houses and clambered over the wooden gate to Pete's garden. He moved up to the kitchen door and peeked inside after trying the handle. There were no signs of life within. Now Ralf was worried. He didn't know Debbie's number either, so the only thing left to do was to drive to Debbie's home and see if she knew anything.

Ralf pressed the corresponding button on the intercom and Debbie herself answered with a crackled, 'Who is it?'

'Hey Debbie, sorry to bother you, it's Ralf. Is Pete with you by any chance?'

There was a few seconds' silence, then a click from the intercom. Debbie had replaced the receiver. Ralf waited around a minute or two just in case, but then pressed the button again. The intercom crackled and clicked and Debbie shouted for him to go away. Ralf was puzzled and a little pissed off as well. He pushed upon the entrance door with his shoulder, then moved back and shifted forward with his body weight, pushing the door open and almost falling flat on his face. He rode the elevator up to the top floor and pressed the buzzer several times. There was no answer, and so he proceeded to bang on the door. Finally, it opened and Mel stood there, a little abashed.

'Mel, what's going on?'

'You'd better come in', she replied quietly, standing to one side.

Ralf entered and waited until she closed the door and followed her to the lounge area, where they both sat down.

'Do you fancy a coffee or something?'

'No thanks, just some answers. I'm worried about Pete. Debbie answered the intercom, but signed off as soon as I asked her…'

'You don't know, do you…?'

'Don't know what?'

'Pete's parents are dead…they were shot when a robber tried burgling a jewellery store in Brent Cross shopping centre. It happened almost a week ago. Had you not heard?'

'No, of course I haven't heard…evidently. Shit…I had no bloody idea.'

Ralf buried his face in his hands, aporetic and shocked. Mel placed her arm around his shoulders, but he rose from the sofa and sighed deeply, and glared at her.

'What's up with your sister? Something tells me she's not with him anymore, for some reason. Am I right?'

Mel hesitated for a moment and then answered that it was true. Ralf didn't seem surprised and sat back down beside her.

'Where is she?' he asked, in a sullen but avaricious tone.

'My sister walked out on him…just when he needed her most. There's no other way to say it…I'm bloody fuming, but what can I do? I told her what a stupid, selfish bitch she was, but that won't make any difference with my sister!'

Ralf stood up once again, and demanded that he speak to her. Mel looked up at him and saw the anger and disappointment in his eyes. She was afraid of that look; she'd seen it in his eyes before, about a year and a half ago, to be precise, at Pete's birthday party which he celebrated at Ozzie's friend, Dave's flat which happened to be in one of the other towers in the same estate. Debbie had been flirting with Ralf for most of the evening, while Pete was having fun with Ozzie and Dave on an old Binatone video game machine, the one that had *Pong* n it. Mel had noticed that Debbie had persuaded Ralf to follow her into the kitchen, and after just a minute or so, Ralf emerged; with that same expression upon his face, glaring at Mel, as though it were partly her fault. He never explained why when Mel later questioned him about it. He just said to let it go.

'That's not the first time I've seen you look at me like that,' said Mel, timorously. 'I've seen those eyes before. You didn't tell me why, back then, either.'

'She's hiding in her bedroom and I'm not leaving here until she has the guts to come out and talk to me.'

Mel stood up abruptly and walked over to Ralf until she was just inches away from him. He could smell her perfume and even the deodorant upon her person. Little did she know that he'd actually found her rather attractive the first time he met her, at Dave's flat. He didn't speak to her at the time, the booming music in Dave's apartment was too loud to even hear yourself think…except in the kitchen, with the door closed.

'Look, it's no use talking to Debbie. She doesn't care…not at the moment anyway…she probably won't. It's not that I'm remotely agreeing with how she's behaved, but just leave it…please.'

'That time…in Dave's flat. You saw how she kept sticking to me like a limpet…you know she took me into the kitchen and tried it on, don't you…she tried to kiss me, and I had to physically restrain her. She was like junkie, desperate for a fix. I never told Pete. He's my best friend, and the last thing to do was ruin his birthday by telling him *that*. I'm sorry I looked at you in that way. It was just that…you're her sister…but I just kind of knew you weren't like her. Truth be told, I've never liked Debbie. Especially after what she did, but unfortunately when Pete sets his heart on something, or someone…you won't shift him. I just got used to the idea that perhaps with time, she'd forget the whole thing with me, and just get on with her relationship with Pete.'

Mel stepped back a little and sighed. She went over to the kitchen sink and poured herself a glass of water and downed three quarters of it.

'For what it's worth, I'm sorry…really. I was with Pete the other night, and before you jump to conclusions, it's not what you think. I went over to his house after trying to speak to him on the phone. I was so disgusted with how Debbie treated him, that I gathered up the gifts he'd bought her, including the ring he got from Brent Cross, and took them over to him. She didn't deserve any of it. Your best friend broke down in my arms. God knows he tried to hold it together, but after seeing the stuff he gave my sister and bearing all of the sorrow on his shoulders, he just cracked. I tried to ring you several times, but there was no answer…you don't have an answering machine either. And no, I'm not blaming you for not being around, I imagine you're busy, so please don't take it as me being accusatory.'

'I'm not,' said Ralf, with a sigh, 'I just wish I could have been there for him. I can imagine what he's going through, and this is a fucking tough one to have to endure. I'll try his house again…this time I'll leave a message on his answering machine…I should bloody get one of those.'

As he went towards the front door, he turned to Mel and looked at her for a few moments. He thanked her for the chat and just as he was about to close the front door behind him, he said, 'Please tell your sister she's *not* to contact him anymore…at all, okay?'

Mel nodded and Ralf left.

Ralf sat in his car for a few minutes before moving off. He tried to process his thoughts and at the moment the only thing that passed through his mind was how much he hated himself for being so wrapped up in his own shit. His phone *did* indeed ring several times over the course of his adventures with Loredana and other times when he was doing whatever he was doing. He felt horribly conscience-stricken and angry at the same time. He was remorseful for not being remotely available whilst dipping his wick, and his anger toward Debbie was starting to conjure up the 'Theatre of Hateful things' in his mind.

'Fucking, gold-digging bitch!' he shouted, as he banged his fists upon the steering wheel. He started up the Ford Capri and drove off, tyres screeching as the car sped out of the car park.

Two days later, Ralf's phone rang and he dashed down the stairs with a bath robe wrapped around his waist. It was Pete.

'Pete…hello mate. It's good to hear from you, bro. Fuck, it's good to hear from you.'

'You too, matey. I'm sorry if I've been maintaining radio-silence as of late, but…'

'Pete…don't even think of it, you've been through fucking hell and you *certainly do not* need to apologize at all…are you nuts?'

'I heard you banging on the door and shouting through the letterbox. I even heard you climbing over the back gate. It rattles when the cat clambers up it…oh, and I disabled that fucking doorbell too. Sorry mate, but I just couldn't face anyone that day.'

'That's fine, bro. No problems. Are you up for a visit now, or…'

'Sure thing,' said Pete, enthusiastically, 'come on over.'

When Ralf got there, the two pals embraced each other at length on the doorstep, then they headed for the lounge where two mugs of coffee and a tin of assorted biscuits were waiting atop a wooden trolley.

'Pete…I'm sorry mate.'

'For what, you plant?'

'For not being there when you needed me most…'

'Ralf, you're not a mind reader. You weren't to know what was happening. Admittedly, I should've let you know…I always call you when something's up, but I seriously had no idea just where to bloody turn. It just all happened at once. One minute I was shopping in Brent Cross with Debbie, we found a lovely engagement ring, we went home and made love and…mum and dad left a note saying they were at Wickes and they'd be back around six, and can I put the spuds on…we had some time on our hands, we went upstairs and shagged the living daylights out of each other, then fell asleep for hours. When I woke up, it was pitch black and I ran downstairs…they weren't back yet, so I panicked, called the cops, Debbie came downstairs, so I drove to Wickes to see if they were by chance, still there, then Sainsbury's...you know, I asked the stupid cow to stay at home and wait for the police to call back if they found out anything...and when I got back, after trying to call her for ages from a phone box...it was constantly bloody engaged by the way, she was actually chatting away to one of her mates, and she had been for nearly an hour. Then I heard the rest...she didn't give a shit...she thought I was being neurotic about the whole thing...'

Pete began to sound out of breath as the stress began to overcome him, and he became slightly tearful. Ralf found himself welling up inside, as he listened to his friend describe the words Debbie was saying while Pete looked on from the doorway.

'It's okay, mate,' said Ralf as he put his arm around Pete, 'don't think about it too much. I know it's hard and you're angry, but tomorrow's a big day. I'll be there by your side. I'll do that speech you asked me to do, then it'll be laid to rest. You'll be surprised at how much easier it'll be to think straight.'

'Cheers mate...I appreciate it... my dear, dear friend.'

'Always.' Ralf said, with a smile.

Chapter 20

It was around noon, when the large congregation of family and friends gathered in the main hall of Ruislip Crematorium. Ralf sat at the front row next to Pete and his two sisters, as the rest of the crowd took their seats. The preacher was standing behind his lectern while a classical piece of music that Pete's parents were particularly fond of, played in the background. It was *The Planets,* by Holst.

The preacher began speaking of John and Susan and their lives together as a very happy couple, and details such as John's love for spy stories and aircraft, and Susan's love for sewing, arts and crafts, and old black and white movies. He spoke of their jobs and the cruel fate that befell them, and that they were wrenched from this world much before their time. Ralf began welling up again, and when the moment came for the caskets to be put to the roaring blue flames of the furnace that was concealed behind a red curtain just beyond the preacher's lectern, Ralf took out a pair of sunglasses that he brought purposely with him and put them on. He wanted no one to notice him shedding tears, especially Pete, who seemed to be holding it together admirably. Ralf had always envied the British stiff upper lip; his own were beginning to quiver. Ralf covered his ears, as he attempted to block out the sound of the roaring flame jets that shot out from each side of the furnace. He produced a paper tissue from the pocket of his jacket to dry the tears that were now very evident, despite his face being behind dark glasses.

After a couple of prayers and hymns, that nobody even attempted to sing, and why would they even try when sorrow hung so heavy in the air, it was Ralf's turn to offer his speech to the weeping people around him. He took to the lectern and bent the flexible microphone handle toward his lips. Pete smiled approvingly as they made eye contact.

'Well…I haven't prepared any written speeches. I'm not usually good at that sort of thing, but…Susan and John were a special couple that anyone who knew them…would find it very easy to talk about them as great people. I remember when I first met my best friend, Pete's dad. I was scared shitless of him…sorry, excuse the French…I was riding a friend's motorcycle down Pete's road many years ago, when I saw John. I rode over to him and asked, *Excuse me, are you Peter's father, sir? I am indeed. Yes, Peter is in, but I must say that if you're riding a motorcycle on the road, I suggest you wear a crash helmet.*

Pete told me that his dad asked him, who was the very polite fellow outside. The rest, as they say, is history. They've always made me feel so welcome in their home over the years, and I've had some great roast dinners at their place. They were also an extremely funny couple. They always found a way to make me laugh my head off, not only because of their sense of humour, but because they had this incredible positivity and love for life. I'm sorry that it was cut short, and in such a terrible way. But today...I don't want to think about how they died...I just want to remember how they lived.'

Ralf blew a kiss toward the heavens and returned to his seat. There was more he wanted to say, but his soul couldn't handle it. Ralf had always been terrified of dying. He'd seen too many people he loved, leave this world and in different ways and his past was always there to bit him hard on the arse. Today was all about Pete and his final farewell to his beloved parents, and that was all there was to it.

Outside in the courtyard, Pete went over to Ralf and embraced him.

'Thanks for that, mate. You don't know what that meant to me.'

'Anytime, mate. I'm sorry...I miss them too, and I could barely hold it together, but...well, it's done now. They've crossed over.' Ralf started off again, but Pete placed an arm around him and the two walked toward the edge of the car park and into an adjoining woodland area where they remained until it was time to head back to Janice's house for the wake.

Pete and Ralf were leaning on the wall that surrounded the patio area, separating it from the landscaped garden that Janice's former husband lovingly cared for before he ran off with his secretary. He was present that day, both at the funeral and at the wake, as Janice had invited him. He thought very highly of John and Susan, despite them not thinking too much of him, but there was a grudging respect. He approached the two pals and placed his hand firmly on Pete's shoulder. Pete turned and looked down at Roger's hand, then at him. Roger took the hint and removed it.

'Well…they're in a better place now. Life goes on, chin up, you know, old chap!' intoned Roger. Pete hated him. He had a ridiculous comb-over, a large and round face, replete with pimples and an unkempt beard which was mostly in the stubble stage. Pete glared at him, clearly disgusted by his presence and told him to go away. Roger moved near to Ralf and placed his hand upon *his* shoulder also.

'You must be…Randy, am I correct?'

'The name's Ralf, and if you touch me again, that hand won't touch anything else!'

'Oh come now, we're all friends here. This is a time for…'

'This is a time for you to get the fuck out of my face, before I rearrange yours!' snapped Ralf, whipping Roger's arm away from his shoulder. The crowd went suddenly silent as they looked in their direction. Roger coughed embarrassingly and walked away from them, disappearing into the depths of the crowded lounge.

'Cheers mate…that's Janice's ex. He's such an annoying, arrogant twat.'

'That's why he's an ex,' said Ralf, chuckling.

The pals continued chatting whilst the wake resumed its course and the people present began helping themselves to the finger buffet laid on by Janice's friend and work colleague.

'When are you going back to work?' asked Ralf, taking a few sandwiches from the table and putting them onto a paper plate.

'Probably the week after next,' Pete replied. 'I've got all the computers linked in a network and ready for the lesson with the under 15's. It can wait, after all, it's me who's organising it.'

'Yeah, that's fair enough. I'm sure that kind of work requires all of your concentration, and you'll want to be of totally sound mind to get on with it. Look, I know it may be too soon and you can say no…do you fancy coming over to Music City one of these evenings? It may help you ease back into the swing of things.'

'Actually…I forgot to mention, glad you reminded me…Janice gave me some tickets for Yazoo…they're playing at the Dominion, in Hammersmith. What do you say to that?'

'I say, fuck me!' exclaimed Ralf, with a start, and causing the room to go quiet. 'I'm in…sorry everyone,' he said, looking apologetically toward the crowd.

Pete and Ralf filled their plates up with a mixture of the triangular cut sandwiches, sausage rolls, pizza slices, and various chicken nibbles, and crisps. Janice joined them outside on the patio and the three of them tucked in, whilst celebrating their parents' lives.

Chapter 21

The month of October finally arrived, bringing the cold weather with it, autumn leaves began to decorate the ground making little side streets and park areas seem like a prettier picture than the other seasons would allow. Pete was trying to steadily piece his life back together after finding some sort of balance and acceptance of recent events, Ralf was going steady with Loredana, and Ozzie had disappeared, leaving Julia with no idea of where he could have got to. He'd been missing for around two weeks now and his mum was at her wit's end.

'It was since he met his old school friend at the station last month,' Julia told Pete and Ralf, 'we were sat on the train and this... Garry Peters was telling him about this amazingly well paid job that he's got. Something to do with making these lucrative deals or something...'

She continued to tell them about how Ozzie started the job with Garry the following Monday, and after that, he never came home. Julia was in tears and Ralf and Pete's attempts at comforting her were in vain. Ralf suggested to Pete that they go to Ozzie's house and ask his mum if she'd be okay with them having a rummage around his bedroom for any clues. Pete agreed and they cancelled their planned trip to London to search for a new microphone for Ralf and set off.

Ozzie's distraught mother was happy to oblige and the two friends went upstairs and began rifling through Ozzie's personal belongings. They searched through drawers, his two wardrobes, his desk, and under his bed and from underneath it, Ralf hauled out a rather heavy metal box with a lock on it. Pete forced it open with a screwdriver and its contents told the tale on what Ozzie had been up to, but not his whereabouts.

'He's left this diary here, with all his..."appointments," which could mean that he'll be back,' said Pete, 'but we just don't know when. We certainly can't just camp across the road from here and wait...what if he comes back while his mum's at work?'

Ralf continued to ransack the metal box and came upon a few crumpled bits of paper with some addresses on them. They were from different parts of the country, and were dated from three weeks ago. Ozzie had apparently ticked them, giving the impression that they were jobs or assignments he'd completed. Now the mystery had become deeper, like an endless and twisting rabbit hole, and Ralf and Pete were far from seasoned detectives. Ozzie's mum called them both downstairs for a hot drink and some biscuits and after the snack, the two pals headed off to the only place they knew that Ozzie would possibly go; Dave's flat in Brentford.

While Pete drove, Ralf thumbed through a phone book he'd taken from a public phone box unbeknownst to Pete, who called him a tealeaf.

'There are loads of Garry Peters in this bloody directory, mainly spelt with one R; after trying Dave's place perhaps we should give these a ring.'

Pete parked the car just beneath Dave's tower block, but after several rings of the intercom buzzer and no reply, they set off again, stopping off at Ralf's house and ringing the twelve names in the book with two R's. Only one of them sounded the old alarm bells; it was the name at the bottom of the list, and the phone was answered by a woman, who told them that Garry was at work and that he'd be back around eight. When she asked who was calling, Pete replied that it was Ozzie.

'Ah, okay…yes, I'll tell him you called, but if you ring back around half past eight, you'll catch him then.'

'Can you remind me of your address, 'cause I forgot,' said Pete in his best imitation of Ozzie.

'Um, okay…it's number nine, Courtfield Gardens, Ealing…'

'Oh yeah, I remember, ta, love. See ya then!'

'That was the crappiest impression of Ozzie I've ever heard!' said Ralf, laughing.

'Well, it did the trick with her, didn't it?'

The two pals got back in the car and sped toward the address that Garry's wife gave them, parked the car halfway down Courtfield gardens, and walked through the nearby Drayton Park to kill a bit of time. They had four hours to waste until Garry got home, and they planned to catch him before he went inside, instead of waiting until half past eight. Darkness began falling at around twenty past four and the park was beginning to grow into a den of gloom and shadow, lit up only by one single floodlight which stood tall in the neighbouring railyard of Drayton Green station. It peeked over the tree-line that surrounded the park, shedding a subdued orange glow onto the little playground at the park's top end. Ralf and Pete were seated upon the two swings in the playground, pretty much in near silence. The hum of the traffic could be heard a little distance away just ahead of them, while the rasping of the Greenford car's diesel engine echoed from the railway somewhere behind.

'Aren't the autumn leaves beautiful,' said Pete, 'the way they just accumulate just around the bottom of the tree trunks, depending on how far out the boughs extend, and all those oranges and browns; I used to come to this park when I needed to get away from the home hubbub; I used to enjoy watching this group of old men playing bowls just near those trees over there. I think they were Italian or something. Sometimes there was this young boy with them…bloody good, he was. He used to come out with some great shots, often putting the older guys to shame. I think they taught him a little too well.'

Ralf smiled broadly to himself; he knew who they were. He couldn't tell Pete though – not yet. The sky grew darker still, and was becoming overcast. Pete and Ralf continued to sit on the swings, bathed in the railyard's floodlight that illuminated them like a couple of stage performers about to begin their number. The rest of the park that lay before them was now swallowed by total blackness, as their eyes had become accustomed to the radiance that swathed the playground.

'You know…I never told you this, but…I hate the dark,' said Ralf, popping a mint in his mouth and offering Pete one.

'Are you serious?' asked Pete, declining the mint.

'Yep… absolutely bloody terrified. My own stupid fault though…I keep watching those horror and ghost movies. Sometimes if I happen to wake up in the middle of the night, I usually don't have the courage to even stretch across and switch on my bedside lamp. I'm scared something…monstrous will grab me or something…'

'You bloody plonker,' said Pete, chuckling. 'You mean to tell me, after all this time, that you're scared of the dark…ah, the mind boggles!'

'Oh the mind boggles, eh? Listen, dickhead…none of your pranks; I can just tell what you're thinking about now…I'm gonna play tricks on him, to spook him out!'

'You just crack me up,' continued Pete, now chortling at a higher pitch.

'You know what I've got in my pocket…my little keyring torch. Do you want me to light the way for you when we get out of the park?'

Ralf laughed, and the two remained upon the swings for a while longer, as they reminisced about times past. To the right of where they were sat, a distant street passed along the side of the park, where few vehicles were parked and just a handful of streetlamps shone. It looked like the little piece of road was floating in the air, suspended in the blackness of the night. A car came in from the left and slowed down to park. Ralf watched it as its driver reversed into a space between a truck and a smaller mini. He continued to keep his attention on the driver's behaviour, but more for curiosity and an insatiable habit of people-watching, rather than suspicion.

The lights in the car's interior remained switched on, while the dark outline of the driver could be seen moving around inside. Pete asked what Ralf was observing so attentively. Ralf wasn't sure at first, and dismissed it as nothing at all, but he continued to focus upon the vehicle; Ralf wasn't terribly big on recognizing makes of cars, but this one seemed familiar. Ralf was pretty sure that it was Mercedes, a silvery grey one. The driver's lights were still on, and his shadow was still moving. Ralf began to worry a little; he was now ninety per cent sure that it was his stalker. He prayed for it not to be; Pete was with him, and he couldn't know the truth just yet. If it *was* the man from the other night, it would be too dangerous.

The inside lights went out and the driver began exiting his vehicle. He stood at the driver's side and continued to just stand there, motionless, and appeared to be looking in their direction. Now Pete was puzzled. He questioned Ralf as to who the guy was, but Ralf didn't reply. He wasn't sure what to say, but now he was certain that the man in question, the man standing by the Mercedes was indeed, his stalker.

'Ralf, what's wrong mate? You're shaking.'

'Pete, listen carefully…I want you to do something for me…'

'What, mate?'

'I'm going to start walking slowly towards *him.* I'm going to draw his attention away from you. You start walking to your left and out of the park's main entrance, but only when I click my fingers. Go back to the car and drive away.'

'What, are you out of your mind? What's come over you?'

'Just do it, please!'

'Ralf, what the fuck's wrong mate? Who *is* that guy?'

'I promise I'll explain later, just go!'

'No way, I'm not just going to leave you here with some weirdo…what if he's got a gun or something?'

'Pete, you *have* to go!'

'But…'

'Please!' Ralf hissed. 'This is something I have to do alone.'

Pete very reluctantly agreed, and Ralf began slowly walking toward the Mercedes. He gave Pete the signal when he was a few steps into the darkness. Pete could barely see him, but as soon as he heard the click, he began walking toward the main entrance. Pete heard the man call out to Ralf, something in a language he couldn't quite understand, but seemed familiar to him.

'Ti sono addosso, sacco di merda! Dovunque andrai, io ti seguiro'!'

Ralf replied to him in English, 'I warned you! You're done here!'

Pete had stopped in his tracks to listen, and began creeping toward a hedgerow that bordered one side of the park, clinging to a wooden fence that separated the houses that faced the small street, from the pathway that circumvented Drayton Park. He stuck to the shadows and fortunately, his dark clothing kept him from being seen. Ralf heard the rustling from the darkness at the edge of the park and noticed Pete's outline slowly moving toward the man by the Mercedes. Unfortunately, the stalker also noticed Pete trying to flank him and immediately reached into his pocket. Ralf began shaking at the legs; bad thing, as the man pulled out a firearm and pointed it in Pete's direction.

'Pete, get down now! He can't see you, get down!'

Pete immediately hit the ground and the stalker fired a shot. His weapon was fitted with a silencer. He fired another two shots.

'That's enough!' Ralf screamed, 'That's enough! What do you want? Leave him be, he's not part of this. It's me you want. I'll go with you, just let my friend be, okay!?'

The stalker kept the gun pointed at Ralf as he moved slowly forward with his hands in the air. The man grinned malevolently as Ralf inched closer to him. Pete watched with disbelief as his best friend stepped out of the darkness of the park, hands in the air, and washed by the orange lambency of the streetlamps. Pete was shaking from both fear and the cold. He wanted to do something, but his mind was numbed by the circumstances, and he was worried that anything he attempted to do would cause the man to pull the trigger on his friend. He tried to slither along the ground, in an attempt to get just a little closer to the scene, with the slightest hope that he could do something, anything to help Ralf.

As Pete dragged his body prone to the ground as silently as possible, his hand touched upon a reasonably sized stone. He grabbed it and turned slowly onto his side, aiming the stone toward a nearby vehicle parked on the illuminated piece of street. He tossed it as hard as he could, and it struck the side of the mini parked near the Mercedes. The stalker turned abruptly and fired a shot toward the source of the noise. Pete then witnessed the extraordinary; Ralf dashed forward with lightning speed, grabbed hold of the man's arm that held the gun and twisted the firearm from his grip, tossing it away. The man tried to strike Ralf, but he ducked under the blow and hit him hard at the side of the ribs, winding him. The stalker attempted to tackle Ralf to the ground by diving toward his waist and wrapping his arms around him. Ralf was staggered back slightly, but kept his stability and brought his elbow up and down hard onto the man's spine, forcing him to cry out in pain. He then proceeded to toss the stalker aside, like a sack of refuse. The man was relentless and scrambled to his feet, fists clenched, and ready to come at Ralf once again. He swung with his right hand, Ralf blocked the punch and pushed him back hard; the man stumbled backwards, almost falling over, but managed to just regain control and stay on his feet.

Pete got up quickly and began rushing over to help his friend, but was stopped in his tracks, as Ralf parried yet another blow from his assailant, and another, and another still, the last parry knocking the stalker sideways. Ralf walked toward him with an expression upon his face that spelled death. Pete had never seen that kind of expression on the face of any man, and he was certain he didn't know what a look of murder actually was. But Ralf had a look that Pete was able to interpret well, despite having never seen it before. It was like being a parent; you've never done it until you become one, and despite no training given, the job's yours. You just knew what it was. As he looked upon Ralf's face as he marched decisively toward the stalker, Pete knew that the man was already dead.

Ralf threw a right punch to the man's jaw, hard like a sledgehammer. The stalker was knocked backwards several feet and onto his back. He rolled onto his side but was dazed. Ralf grabbed him by the shoulders, turned him around and knelt down upon one knee, and continued to reign down punch after punch that hit like an express train. The sound of flesh upon flesh had Pete wincing and recoiling in shock horror, as he incredulously watched Ralf's fists pounding upon the man's face like knuckles upon dough; even the sound was very similar.

'I told you…if you came for me…I would kill you!' Ralf screamed as though he were possessed by a raging, evil spirit, his fists still hurtling toward a now motionless stalker.

'Fuck you…fuck your scumbag brother…and I'm going to find the bastard who hit me over the head the other night…!' - Ralf was still punching, ' - …and I'm going to kill him too…you piece of shit!'

At that moment, Pete scrambled up from the ground, still in shock, and dashed over to his enraged friend, staying his arm. He barely managed to contain Ralf's umpteenth blow; his strength was fearsome.

'That's enough, mate…I think he's…gone…'

Pete stepped toward the stalker's motionless body, after letting go of Ralf's arm, which flopped exhaustedly down by his side. He touched the man's neck and felt for a pulse, and then he raised his wrist. The man was dead, his face bruised and black with blood, and unrecognisable from Ralf's repeated blows. Pete was in total nihilism; he wished all of what had just happened to be just a fleeting nightmare. He looked at his fingers and saw that they had the stalker's blood on them. It wasn't a nightmare. He had really witnessed his best friend of many years transform from the mild-mannered gentleman he had always known him to be, into a raging and uncontrolled beast. The beast however, had just saved his life.

'You saved my life, Pete…' Ralf said, sounding out of breath.

'I think you'll find it was the other way round, mate!' Pete said, as he rose from kneeling beside the stalker's corpse. 'Now…we need to call the…'

'No!' snapped Ralf, getting up suddenly and moving quickly toward Pete. 'Drag the body into that hedgerow…where you were hiding. There's a phone box over there…I need to make a phone call!'

'Are you completely fucking nuts!? Actually, don't answer that!'

'What do you mean!?' shouted Ralf, grabbing Pete by the shoulders and shaking him, 'What the fuck do you mean, am I nuts?'

'You've just beaten someone to death, you fucking psycho!' Pete snapped back, knocking Ralf's hands away. 'Ralf…you've killed someone…' Pete brought his voice down to a desperate whisper, 'You want to make a phone call? Who are you going to call, the salvation fucking army? Believe me, there's not much salvation for us.'

'For me,' Ralf continued, 'there's no us. This is *my* problem.'

Ralf walked toward the phone box, leaving his friend with the cadaver, lying on the edge of the park. Pete desperately dragged the body toward the hedgerow as Ralf suggested, cursing as he moved him. He followed Ralf to the telephone box. Ralf inserted a couple of coins and spoke to the person at the other end.

'Hey Jeff, it's Ralf, mate. Listen…I need your help. Yeah…it's an, "I'm in deep shit," kind of help…others are involved and I need some advice. Okay, when can you come down? Yes, it's ultra-urgent. A man is dead…yeah…I killed him. I told you he'd come after me sooner or later. Thanks bro…I truly appreciate it.'

Ralf replaced the receiver and turned to face Pete, who was standing there as though he'd seen an army of ghosts. He was white as a sheet, his eyes, wet from the cold and probably tears of some kind or another.

'Are you going to stare at me like that all night?' Ralf asked him with slight sarcasm in his tone.

Pete's expression was no longer that of disbelief, but of dysphoria. Ralf pushed past him as he exited the phone box and walked back to the body in the hedgerow.

'Jeff's coming down. He'll be here in about three hours. We need to stay here…or rather, *I* need to stay here…keep the corpse hidden…you know, passers-by.'

'Quite.' Pete said, finally.

'You owe me one fucking hell of an explanation.'

'I'll explain in time, Pete. Bear with me, okay?'

'Bear WITH you?' Pete yelled.

'Keep your bloody voice down, will you?' Ralf hissed, like a venomous snake, spitting poison.

'Yeah, there's that look in your eyes again. Are you going to kill me too?'

'Don't be silly, Pete. You're overreacting now…'

'Oh really…*I'm* overreacting…'

'Pete, please stay with me on this one, mate...'

'Who the fuck are you?'

'You know who I am, Pete...whatever you may think, I'm still me.'

'Ralf...I'm going home now...please don't follow me, contact me, just stay the fuck away...'

'Oh, come on...'

'No! Just seriously...I need time to...process this whole thing. I don't know who the hell you are anymore.'

'Don't just leave me here with...this corpse!'

Pete turned and began walking away from Ralf and toward where he'd parked the car.

'Pete!'

'You made that corpse...now you can lie next to it!'

'Hey...are you going to tell the cops? I need to know. There's more to this, Pete...I need to know. Are you abandoning me completely?'

Pete stopped and turned to face Ralf; he wondered if it was for the last time.

'No, Ralf...I'm not going to drop you in it. But I *will* say one thing...I don't want to ever see you again. Sort it out...and stay out of my life. It was nice knowing you...whoever you are!'

Pete turned and walked slowly away from Ralf. He stood and watched as his best friend disappeared around the corner at the top of the little street and into Courtfield Gardens. Ralf turned to look down at the stalker's battered corpse, half buried under the hedgerow. Ralf fell to his knees and sank into an unwanted sorrow; a sorrow that felt like a bottomless abyss. Once again, he felt like he'd lost everything. His best friend had abandoned him. He was on his own now. In a couple of hours it would be eight o'clock, and he should be at Garry Peters' house, ready to find out where Ozzie was. One friend had gone; at least he could salvage the other.

Chapter 22

Ralf had pushed the stalker's corpse further beneath the hedgerow, astonished that despite the commotion, not one single passer-by was seen – or was it perhaps the same reason as the other night, when he lay in the middle of the road after being conked on the head - and as eight o'clock began approaching fast, Ralf set off toward number nine, Courtfield Gardens. He waited some ten minutes or so, and at around a quarter past eight, a dark blue Ford Cortina pulled up just across the street from number nine. A young-looking fellow with fair hair, gelled back and slightly spiky, and dressed in a dark burgundy pin-stripe suit emerged from the vehicle. He seemed a little perplexed at the sight of a stoney-faced Ralf leaning against the wall of his front garden.

The young man began warily walking across the road toward his house, increasingly diffident with each step. Ralf approached him and the fellow stopped dead.

'Garry Peters?' asked Ralf, frowning copiously.

'Who wants to know?' replied the man, avoiding eye contact and instead, reaching out to try and touch the safety of the front gate, as if it would deter the wrath of Ralf.

'I have a few questions for you,' said Ralf, as he placed his hand firmly upon Garry's while he tried pushing the gate open.

'Do I know you?' he insisted.

Ralf immediately grabbed Garry's scrawny neck and forced him back out onto the pavement, and slammed him against a parked car, keeping his grip on his throat. 'I said, I have a few questions for you. I think it's polite that you answer them...okay?'

'O...okay...' , replied Garry, choking as Ralf released his grip.

'Ozzie Blake, where is he?'

'Who? I don't know...'

Ralf slapped Garry hard across the face and grabbed his neck once again, but not squeezing quite as hard as before; he didn't need to, as Garry was suitably scared enough. 'Don't play fucking games with me. I'll ask you again, and this time I want the truth. Where is Ozzie Blake, the man who's been working for you for around three weeks now; he's not come home, and I'm worried about my friend. Now where *is* he?' Ralf squeezed harder when Garry gave no response.

'O...o...okay, okay...okay, he's been working for me...but I don't know where he is or why he hasn't gone home...I'm not his keeper.'

Ralf slapped him again and resumed his grip around his throat.

'Not good enough, arsehole...I'm really running out of patience, now WHERE IS HE?'

'M...my boss probably knows...you're stopping me...breathing.'

The sound of metallic clanking, followed instantaneously by a sharp and pressurizing pain wracked the back of Ralf's head, as he was struck by a blunt object, knocking him sideways and onto the pavement. As he felt himself passing into unconsciousness, Ralf heard Garry urging his wife to get back inside the house and lock the door and windows; he also caught something that sounded like; *Call Raymond, now!*

Ralf's willpower was teetering on the edge; he was succumbing to passing out, but he crammed his eyes shut, banged his fists upon the cold stone of the sidewalk and scrambled to his feet. He staggered into the gate of number nine, and as he dashed toward the front door, he heard the sound of it being bolted from the other side. He waited a few seconds more, as he bent over with hands on his knees, allowing those for few precious seconds to let life creep back into his body.

Ralf stood up straight and looked toward the front windows, leading supposedly into the lounge. At that precise moment, he saw an arm protrude from behind the net curtain and manipulate the lock on the upper window pane. A face appeared from the darkness behind the curtains; it was Garry Peters. He was pressing his head against the window whilst laughing, with his mouth wide open, and offering Ralf the middle finger. As Garry's maniacal grinning visage began disappearing back into the safety of the house, Ralf wasted no time. He looked down to his left and lying upon the neatly paved front garden, he noticed a stray paving stone, as large as a frying pan. He grabbed hold of it and immediately launched it against the windows of the lounge, rending asunder the glass with a deafening crash. Ralf leapt through the gaping hole and into Garry's lounge and caught the tail end of him escaping through the door. Before Garry could pull it shut, Ralf managed to grab the long handle and with greater strength compared to Garry Peters, wrenched it from his puny hands. As Garry stumbled back into the lounge, Ralf grabbed him by the shirt collar and picked him up like a suitcase and threw him across the room, making him fall against a wooden standard lamp, which fell to its side and into a nearby television, knocking the set over but not shattering its screen.

Ralf marched toward Garry, who was literally petrified at what was undoubtedly about to happen to him, but this time Ralf's awareness didn't let him down; he spun round just in time to stay the arm of Garry's wife, brandishing a huge saucepan, probably what she had used to strike him with when they were outside. Ralf wrenched it violently from her grip and threw it against the wall beside him, then hurled the woman toward the sofa. Garry scrambled up and dove onto the sofa to shield his wife.

'Don't you touch her!' he yelled, spitting saliva out in front of him.

'I don't hit women,' replied Ralf, 'but I *will* tear you to pieces if you don't tell me where my friend is; oh…and I don't appreciate being mocked and laughed at after some bitch hits me over the head with a saucepan. You think you're funny giving me the finger from behind your fucking window?'

Ralf delivered a stomping kick to Garry's ribs. He cried out in pain, cursing and spitting like an angry child, and rolled back onto the floor. His wife attempted to make for the door but Ralf caught hold of her arm, and pulled her back to the sofa. 'You stay there and don't move, or I'll forget that I don't hit ladies.'

Ralf looked toward Garry and came down to his level, just inches from his face, once again, demanding Ozzie's whereabouts.

'He…he's at Raymond's place…'

'Who the bloody hell is Raymond?'

'I…I told you…he's my boss. He runs the show, Ozzie's with *him*, at his home…'

'Why is he at his home? What's this amazing job you do?'

'I…I can't tell you that…he'll kill me!'

'*I'll* fucking kill you if you don't tell me what's going on. Talk!'

Ralf heard his name being called from just outside, it was a familiar voice that said it and an outline loomed close to the net curtain and brushed it aside. It was Pete.

'I thought you'd buggered off!' said Ralf.

'I had thought about it,' said Pete, 'but you can explain later. Right now, we need to find our friend.'

Pete clambered and stepped carefully through the glassless window and looked down at Garry and his wife.

'Have you gotten any useful information from these two?' he asked.

'I'm working on it,' Ralf replied, 'we're nearly there…aren't we, Garry?' Ralf said, kicking Garry's legs, like a football.

'Alright!' shouted Garry at the top of his voice, 'alright, you fucking psycho…I'll tell you…you won't find him easily…he'll find you!'

'You just let me worry about that. You just tell me everything you know…and I guarantee that you'll live longer.' Ralf said, crouching down near him.

'Raymond Franklin…that's his name, he's some kind of posh businessman. He sends me out to deliver these packages to…clients.'

'What's in the packages?'

'I don't know…'

Ralf knuckle-whipped Garry across the face, 'Wrong answer, shithead.'

'I really don't know what's in them for sure,' said Garry, 'I *imagine* what's in them…I just don't ask.'

'Where's Ozzie staying now?' asked Pete, stepping around from near the window and in front of Garry and wife.

'I think he's at Raymond's place. He stays there now. Most people do when they join the company.'

'Where is Raymond's place?' asked Ralf, 'and what's this company?'

'Look, it's probably drugs or something…'

'Garry…I think it's time to tell the truth.'

Garry looked at his wife disdainfully. She caressed his face and kissed him on the forehead. 'This could be our chance to get out of doing this.' She told him.

'Raymond will kill us, Lisa. He'll go ape -shit if we betray the group's trust. It's because of this good money that we can live like this.'

Pete sat upon an armchair that was near to the door and crossed his legs, folding his hands beneath his chin. Ralf always called it, *The Lawyer Look*. It also made him wonder what Pete was about to come out with next.

'Okay, this is how it is.' began Lisa, 'my husband has a criminal record; he went down for shoplifting and fraud so when he was released, he found it really difficult to find work. No one wanted to give him a chance. Raymond overheard us talking in a pub one evening. He approached us and made this offer and left his phone number. I totally disapproved of it…I really did, but after some thought Garry agreed to it. The money was good. Each delivery was the equivalent of several months' wages. It was hard but we were struggling…yes, it's wrong, but…at least we can eat and live in a decent house.'

Before Ralf could say anything else, Pete spoke up, still in his lawyer stance; his hands still remained folded under the chin and he also now sported a studious and quizzical frown. Ralf usually found Pete's frowns rather amusing, mainly due to the fact that his friend was gifted with that famous ample forehead.

'How many people work for this…company?' he said.

'Me, Ozzie, and another girl,' replied Garry, 'she only does it twice a week though.'

'And is Raymond your only boss, or are there other bosses?' asked Ralf.

'His wife...and his right hand man, some guy called Kamal, a tall, ugly guy with a crater-face. He kind of oversees stuff. He's a nasty piece of work, he never smiles, hardly says a word.'

'Okay...now tell us where to find him...please...' Ralf asked gently.

'It's a house in West Park Gardens, in Richmond. Number seventeen. Raymond's got a gun in his office...in the drawer. I saw it once when he pulled it out and pointed it at the other girl that works for him. Her name's Amanda. I don't know where *she* lives; she keeps herself to herself. I don't even think Raymond knows where she lives. That's all I know, and that's the truth...'

'Okay, Garry,' said Ralf, 'I believe you...for now, but just in case you get second thoughts and try and warn him that we're on our way there, my friend Pete here, will stay and keep an eye on you guys, okay?'

'Hang on mate,' said Pete rising from his chair, 'I'm going with you. This is suicide...Garry just said Raymond's got a firearm, don't be stupid, mate!'

'I don't trust these two; I need you to stay here. I'll be fine, just relax.'

'Don't worry about us,' Lisa said, 'I stick by him because he's my husband, but I didn't sign up for this.'

Garry turned to look at his wife in admiration, with an approving smile and an expression on his face that looked like his heart was melting. Pete gave a subdued smile but felt a little touched by it, whilst Ralf wasn't impressed. He turned and walked toward the broken window of the lounge and clambered out. Pete followed him.

'Hey, wait up! What's the matter with you?'

'The matter is, she means it, and he doesn't!' said Ralf, still scowling.

'Ralf...she's desperate to get out of this; and we need to get Ozzie out of it too, before it's too late. Let me come with you...'

'No, I need you to keep an eye on both of them, especially him. She's relying on us and he's dreaming of the next paycheque. He's doing it more for him that for the two of them; trust me...he doesn't give a shit about her!'

Pete grabbed Ralf's arm as he turned to go, Ralf tore it away from him and glowered at his friend.

'Now look, you can't know that.' Pete said, 'besides...you owe me an explanation.'

'When it's over,' Ralf replied coldly, 'when it's over.'

As Pete returned to the window and climbed through it once again, he noticed that Lisa had moved to the armchair that faced the lounge windows. She had a worried and unusually guilt-ridden look upon her face; a look that began speaking a thousand words and Pete was just beginning to understand what they were. Before he could turn round, a sharp and thundering jab to the side of his face sent him sprawling sideways and onto the TV set, which collapsed along with its wooden stand, as all four of its legs gave way from the bulk of Pete's weight. The ensuing crash and clatter alerted Ralf, who turned and began running back toward the house. He leapt through the open window and landed almost in the middle of the lounge. Garry stood near the door, with one arm around Lisa's neck in a hold, and the other was clutching a small pistol.

'I knew it,' Ralf said with a slowly rising growl, 'I knew it!'

'Stay where you are!' Garry said, panting with stressful breathlessness, 'I'll kill her...you make one move and she gets a bullet in her brain!'

'You piece of filth...you'd kill your own wife? You're fucking lost...'

'No, I'm not lost...I'm a businessman...and you're interfering with my business transactions!'

Ralf turned toward where Pete was lying, when he heard the rattling of debris as Pete stirred from unconsciousness, clutching his right temple. Garry moved the gun barrel toward Pete and yelled that he stay where he is. With the gun now once again pressed up against Lisa's temple, Garry reached for the door, pulling it open and guiding it the rest of the way with his foot. Lisa was crying and screaming with desperation, yelling at Ralf to stay back, fearful that her husband may accidentally pull the trigger if he becomes overly stressed. Garry continued to drag his wife out of the lounge. Ralf kept his eyes fixed upon them both, especially the hand that gripped the pistol; Garry's hands were beginning to shake and his finger was gradually slipping its hold from the gun's trigger. Ralf focused his steely look closely on Garry's right trigger-finger; it had passed from being pressed upon the front side of the trigger that faced the gun's barrel, to the back of it. Ralf needed to be lightning-quick if he was to attempt to rush Garry and disarm him, and all he needed was around two seconds for the finger to slip from one side of the trigger to the other and squeeze. Pete stirred again and attempted to get up but fell back into a sitting position, still clutching his face in pain.

Lisa began to struggle and her shaky legs gave way beneath her, causing her to stagger sideways, making Garry stumble and lose his grip on the pistol. The firearm fell to the floor and let off a shot that ricocheted off the edge of the open door and into the side of the sofa. Ralf dashed forwards and grabbed Lisa's arm, pulling her toward him. Garry sprang up from the floor and reached for the pistol, but Ralf got there first and quickly pushed it away with the side of his foot, making it slide underneath the sofa. He grabbed Garry's collar with both hands and hauled him upwards, and proceeded to slam his face against the door of the lounge, slamming it shut. Garry was dazed but still attempted to kick out at Ralf as he was thrown across the room and onto the floor, near to where Pete was now on all fours, his face like a mask of blood. Ralf glimpsed an ornamental fire-poker that was lying near to the debris of the ruptured TV set and figured that that was the weapon Garry had used to strike Pete with.

Garry scrambled to his feet and made for the window, but Ralf managed to grab his arm before he could make it through. He pulled Garry violently toward him and brought his knee up to his midriff, winding him. Garry crumpled to the ground and Ralf stepped backwards before offering him a hard backhander across the face, knocking him sideways. Garry was too dazed to react any longer and rolled onto his back, clutching his jaw and head. Ralf went over and helped Pete up from the floor as Lisa re-entered the room with a roll of kitchen paper and a first aid box.

'I'm so sorry,' she whimpered as she broke down. 'I didn't…know he would do this…and that gun!'

'It's fine,' Ralf said, helping her over to the sofa, 'thanks for the first aid stuff.'

After Pete had been successfully patched up, dusted down, and ready to go, the three of them, including Lisa, got in Pete's car and drove toward Ealing Broadway station, where they put her on a train to her mother's house in Brighton. Following that, Pete and Ralf drove toward West Park Gardens, to Raymond Franklin's abode.

West Park Gardens was a crescent shaped street that was just off the main road that passed by Kew Gardens. The houses that lined each side of the road were a mixture of Edwardian and modern constructions, with a small section of the crescent belonging to a row of bungalows with attic rooms. Raymond's house was the one in the middle, an Edwardian home with three storeys and a manse attached to one side that seemed like it was recently constructed. A large Bentley was parked in its large forecourt just beyond an automatic gate that fortunately, was low enough to easily climb over. Ralf surpassed it and crouched down when a light came on in the window of the manse. An outline could be seen drifting around inside and after a few minutes, the light was extinguished. Ralf scuttled toward the wall of the manse and hugged it as he shuffled toward the corner nearest to the innermost area of the courtyard.

Pete clambered over the gate after Ralf signalled the all clear and tiptoed over to him. The two friends peered into the windows and Ralf raised his hand when he thought he'd spotted what appeared to be Ozzie slumped over a table.

'I'm sure it's him,' whispered Ralf, 'the long hair…it has to be him. We have to get him out of there.'

Pete moved toward the other side of the manse and whispered to Ralf that he'd found a side-door that was open. Ralf went inside first and moving cautiously through the darkness and guided only by the faint residual glow of a nearby street lantern, found his way to where Ozzie was. Ralf shook him gently a few times and once Ozzie began to stir, Pete crept in as well. The two friends took an arm each and dragged him out of the door and into the forecourt.

'How are we going to get him over the gate?' whispered Pete.

'It's a smaller one than usual; I should be able to force-drag it to open a little, then you drag Ozzie out and to the car. Think you can manage that?'

Ralf took hold of one of the two sections of gate and dragged it along with all his might and although stubborn, the gate moved with him just enough for Pete to squeeze through with the sleeping Ozzie. The two of them managed to get Ozzie into the back seat of the Citroen Visa without attracting any unwanted attention, and they finally drove away from the house without being detected.

Back at Pete's house, Ozzie was safely asleep on the bed and the two pals were sat in the lounge with some coffee and fruit cake.

'Okay, you wanted an explanation...I guess I owe you that much.' said Ralf.

'You guess?'

'Look, I'm sorry mate,' Ralf said, placing a hand firmly upon Pete's shoulder, 'I really appreciated you coming back. I really thought I'd lost you.'

'You did...almost. I *am* fucking curious though...as to who you really are.'

'I'm me, you silly sod. But yes, there are some things you should know.'

'I appreciate it mate,' Pete said, 'and I promise I'll try not to judge you.'

'Many years ago...I lived in Italy, down in the south. When I was eight years old and after the umpteenth beating from my dad, I planned to run away. That didn't work out, as the bastard caught me and locked me in my room. Every time the alcohol and drugs took over, that was when the abuse came...not sexual, thank God, but nevertheless...it was nasty stuff. One evening, both my parents were not only pissed out of their heads...but they were fully dosed up too...and delusional. They wanted to take me with them...'

'Take you where?'

'Out of the bedroom window...seventeen floors up. I only just managed to get out of their grasp...they were both so high and so drunk...it was unbelievable. They jumped and landed on top of a parked car. I didn't even look out of the window...didn't need to. I heard the almighty crash and seconds after, the screams came as people below just freaked out. That was the last I ever saw of

179

my parents alive. I saw them when I went downstairs before disappearing into the night. They were almost on top of each other…blood and glass everywhere. I remember that since that day…I never shed one single tear for my parents. I still dream about them at night…still see their faces sneering at me…then they would leap out of the window and as soon as I hear the crash, I'd wake up.

I was living on the streets and sleeping under bridges and on the beach for months, surviving only on shoplifted bread and prosciutto. Then one day, I was loitering near an old monastery…I could smell cooking coming from somewhere inside. It was brodo, and I just needed to get in there somehow. One of the monks caught me snooping around and took me to the Abbott. They took me in and the Abbott raised me as his own son. The memories I had of my own parents weren't ones I wanted to carry with me and over time, I'd almost forgotten…almost…except for the nightmares.'

'What happened next?'

'When I was around twenty, I caught one of the other monks raping a young girl. She was barely fourteen; I knew her from the village market. She used to help her mother on the stall. I'd been noticing this particular monk's odd behaviour, you know…not paying attention to his work, sneaking off during chores, and touring around town in civilian clothing – I followed him once, I saw where he used to hang out. But it was that day…that day that I happened to be out in the allotment gathering herbs and vegetables for the minestrone…I heard these muffled whimpers coming from around the back of the old building…the place where they kept the old wooden furniture and firewood. When I went to see what was going on, that's when I found him. He was with another guy who ran off as soon as he saw me.'

It was horrible, Pete…she was bleeding…all down her legs, and he had this fucking filthy…maniacal grin on his face. I just ran toward him and grabbed him by the hair…he even had the audacity to try and fight back. I beat him like I'd never beaten anyone before in my life…I beat him until he bled like a stuck pig, and then some. The girl was taken to hospital by an ambulance, including the monk. He died later that day, from his wounds…I didn't care…I didn't even bat an eyelid when they told me…'

'But how come you came here?' Pete asked him, his face white as a sheet.

'The Abbott, Donaldo, told me that this guy's brother was some big-shot lawyer...he knew people, and so he would find out something for sure, and I had to stay out of site. I couldn't stay at the monastery anymore.

Donaldo sent me to the elderly couple who you've always known as my aunty and uncle. They were friends of his, and they agreed to keep me with them. He was funny and she was the loveliest lady you could ever meet. They left me the house and everything they owned; this house and a few pounds here and there.

My real name is Raffaele Avagliano. I chose an English sounding name that had some kind of familiar ring to the original...for me, for my own piece of mind, as I knew that I would never be known by my real name again. That's why I chose Ralf Avalon. You know, all these years that I've been here...I knew deep inside, that sooner or later, they'd find me. It was just a matter of time.

Well, there you have it, mate. The truth's finally out. And now you know it. You're the only one who knows, so let's keep it that way, okay?'

'Er, yes mate...sure...'

'Hey,' said Ralf, smiling and squeezing Pete's shoulder, 'I promise I'm the same guy you met all those years ago.'

'I just can't understand why you never told me anything from the beginning...'

'Look, I had to protect the ones I loved. Auntie Enza and uncle first of all, and when I met you and Ozzie, I realised I had an even greater responsibility.'

'Can you tell me about this Mallory guy...your friend, the cop.'

'A few years ago, I saved his life...twice. Since then, he owes me one, or several as the case may be...'

'Shit, Ralf...that body in the hedge...!'

'Relax... Jeff's taken care of it.'

'Does he know your secret?'

'Yes, he does. He needed to know. Jeff's had a few dodgy scrapes in the past, but I'll tell you more about that another time. It'll take too long to explain.

Right now, we'd better let Ozzie's mum and Julia know we've found him and that he's…okay…well, kind of…'

When Ralf and Pete dropped Ozzie home, he was a little disorientated. He barely recognised where he was and even who he was talking to, but as he sat at the table with his mother and Julia, he began to relax and ease himself back into the old routine of conversation in the Blake household.

'Ozzie, my son…you look fuckin' awful!' intoned his mother.

'You can fackin' talk, you old hag…how much ya been drinkin' while I was away?'

Amused and satisfied, as thought they'd done a good and hard day's work, Ralf and Pete left the Blake house and high-fived each other as they went back to the car. Pete felt a sense renewed vigour and a warm, fuzzy feeling inside. He'd got his friend back and felt happy about finally knowing who he really is. In his mind, onward and upward were the resounding thoughts. Not even the loss of Debbie's love bothered him any longer, and aside from a stinging headache and a temporary visual trauma of his best friend beating down on someone's face like a raging gorilla, all was okay.

Ralf felt contented that they had gotten Ozzie back from the clutches of the mysterious Raymond Franklin without involving the police, but that was only temporary. Jeff had taken care of the corpse under the hedgerow in Drayton Park and after all that, still felt that he was in Ralf's debt for having saved his skin twice. Yet, there was something else that was still plaguing Ralf's mind. The stalker was gone and Ralf was sure that he had no one else who had his back despite being such a big name lawyer back in Naples. Everything as far as Ralf was concerned, should have been just fine. As he sat back in Pete's car and watched the world scroll past, with Kraftwerk playing in the background, an uncomfortable feeling of unrest, anxiety, and wariness gnawed away at his mind like a thorn in his side. It wasn't over. Something or someone was still out there, hiding in the shadows, watching…waiting…and it was either from Raymond's neck of the woods (Garry Peters was still around and therefore still capable of causing annoying problems) or from Ralf's past. There was definitely something that was still decidedly unfinished.

Chapter 23

It was a mild evening in mid-October, and Ralf and Loredana were at a pub called The London Apprentice, a nice and friendly place just by the river. They were joined by a broadly grinning Pete and his new conquest, a voluptuous and curvy short-haired blonde lady named Sandy. Ralf couldn't take his eyes off of Sandy's arse, much to Pete's amusement, despite the fact that Sandy's main highlight was her flamboyant laugh. It sounded like a combination of a foghorn and a donkey's bray. As they climbed the few stone steps leading up to the front terraced area of the pub, Ralf was directly behind Sandy and he felt compelled to hang back and let Loredana walk in front of him.

'You alright, matey?' asked Pete, tapping him on his bald head.

'Yeah, fine mate...except for one tiny but important thing...' replied Ralf, with a mischievous smirk.

'What's that?'

'I really want your Sandy to sit on my face, do you think she'd be up for it?'

'You cheeky shit!' exclaimed Pete, smiling and slapping Ralf hard on the arm. Once inside, the foursome made for the rear terrace that overlooked the river; Pete had booked it with the pub landlord, who was a friend of his father.

'This part of the river,' said Ralf, 'with the lanterns and reflections in the water, reminds me of Venice.'

'I'd love to go *there*,' Pete said, 'always loved the look of that place...'

Ralf smiled and winked, badly. He wasn't good at winking; it always came across as either a nervous tic or looking like he'd just had an insect fly up his nose...but Pete knew what he meant.

'Hey, Frankie,' exclaimed Pete, as he shook the barman's hand. 'Long time no see!'

'Likewise!' replied Frankie, leaning across the bar and expertly projecting his voice above the hubbub.

'These are my friends…this is Ralf and his beautiful lady, Loredana, and this is *my* lady…Sandy!'

'Pleased to meet you all!' said Frankie, leaning over once again. They returned to the terrace after ordering food and drinks and once the pub grub arrived, they tucked in thankfully; even Loredana, who being Italian, was very fussy about what she ate. Ralf had become used to British food over the years and his lovely lady hadn't yet realised that he was really Italian. He wasn't ready to tell her either, not yet, perhaps not for a long while. Ralf loved burgers – freshly made and not those in packets – and he had a particular fondness for pies; the completely encased ones with shortcrust pastry. He also enjoyed steak and kidney puddings. Loredana chose a mixed grill of meat and surprisingly, devoured the lot. Sandy was a fish and chip girl, with a love for battered haddock and tartare sauce, while Pete went for the same dish as Loredana.

Julia was in the kitchen with Ozzie's mum, who was once again distraught after an altercation with her son. Apparently, Ozzie had taken some money from her purse, probably earlier that day, denied it, and stormed out of the house saying that he would never return again; that was at ten o'clock that morning. It was now gone eight o'clock and there was no sign of him. As much as Julia attempted to keep strong for Jackie, she eventually burst into tears herself and became anxious with worry. Since returning home thanks to the intervention of Ralf and Pete, Ozzie wasn't the man he used to be. Gone was his sense of humour for a start, and his love for life and spirit for mad adventures was nowhere to be seen; he'd prefer to spend entire days either in his bedroom sleeping or listening to music or sitting in front of the television and watching videos all day.

Julia rang Ralf's house again and also tried Pete's once more, but she had no idea they were out. They had rung Ozzie with the hope that he'd go out with them – he loved the London Apprentice – but he waved a hand of dismissal when his mum told him it was Ralf and Pete on the phone.

'This time we have to call the police,' said Jackie , God knows when those two are gonna get back.'

'I know, Jackie...but we can't really, not yet. He'll only get done himself, for drug dealing...or delivering...either way, we're stuffed. Ralf and Pete will be back soon, they're probably at that Music City place. They know where that scumbag lives...the one where Ozzie worked...'

'Okay...I suppose...but I'm so worried about my son...why's he such a dickhead?'

Ozzie's mother broke down in Julia's arms and wept bitterly. Julia's tears were those of fear and guilt. She felt guilty of what she thought she may be forced to do. She didn't really want to give up on Ozzie, not again. She'd already dumped him once, over the supermarket prank. She didn't want to do it again, but she didn't have that kind of patience, that kind of staying power. And certainly not for someone who was proving to be unstable and in the fashion that Ozzie was being. A further wave of guilt rushed over and overwhelmed her, like a raging river. Her tears were undoubtedly for that reason; she hated it but it was becoming stronger. She felt culpable, immoral, damned even. Perhaps she was selfish. What if he were her husband? Would she abandon him in such a moment of need, or would she stick around and fight her man's corner?

As Julia continued cradling Jackie's head upon her shoulder, those little voices began altercating again, echoing through her mind and tugging at the heartstrings. In truth she actually hated all of this. Why couldn't she ever have a healthy and happy relationship with plenty of intelligent conversation, witty banter, and passionate intimacy? All the other men in her life were decidedly colourful, easy-going, some were down to earth as well, but never perfect. One had a weakness for alcohol, another was overly obsessed with football and formula one, and the rest were forty somethings with the brains of adolescents with a penchant for serial cheating, low sex drives, and being emotional voids with the personality of a peanut.

Ozzie had a sense of humour – had, being the understatement of the year at present – he was gifted with a high sex drive, crap conversation, but he hated football and formula one, and he loved Julia very much. His heart was definitely in the right place and his sense of justice and courage to confront the wrongs and wrong-doers of society were second to none. Ozzie *was* kind of a catch. But, and there was still that underlying but, that bugged Julia like an annoying housefly that seemed to follow you from room to room…

I'm sorry, Jackie,' Julia said, as she abruptly lifted Jackie's head from upon her shoulder and stood up, 'I can't do this…I just *can't* do this. It's really too much for me.'

Jackie stared up at her as she took her overcoat from the back of the chair and began putting it on along with her scarf and beret. Julia looked down at her and her expression appeared to be that of sheer disdain, even if it wasn't what she was trying to display, but nevertheless, through red and squinted eyes and dark lachrymal trails upon her weathered face like trenches, Jackie gained an expression of her own. It was hate.

'Oh please don't look at me like that.' Julia cried in supplication, 'I've done my best to be patient with him…it's just…'

'Oh, it's just that you don't give two fuckin' shits.' Jackie said, in a hushed tone. She was too exhausted to raise her voice or lose her temper, but those words seemed to cut into Julia like a blade. A fresh tear ran down her cheek, as she fastened the last button on her overcoat, then she turned and left the house, closing the door gently behind her.

Julia drove home slowly and erratically as she listened to the little voices in her head again. Some of them were telling her that she did the right thing, while others were scolding her, calumniating her, castigating her…she lost control of her vehicle, but thankfully only for a second or two, as the blast of an oncoming car's klaxon shook her out of the moment of weakness and left her abashed. She pulled over for a few minutes and got out of the car and entered a newsagent that dominated the other small businesses along a parade of shops. A bottle of orangeade and a bar of chocolate later, and she felt fit enough to continue her journey. *So long as YOU'RE alright, nothing else matters, does it?* The little voice in her head exclaimed again. Julia furiously cast aside the empty plastic bottle. It bounced off of the steering wheel and hit her just above the eyebrow and fell down between the passenger seat and the handbrake. She pulled away from outside the shops and drove home.

Debbie and Mel were sat upon the sofa whilst watching a documentary about dating agencies. They were happily exchanging opinions and comparing notes about their boyfriends past and present, and Mel was enthusiastic about *her* new conquest; a student named Frederick, who was a year younger than she was. Debbie had her eyes on a very handsome young fellow named Ian, who lived not far from Pete's house. She'd met him in a pub in Northwood while she was working in the new shoe store that had just opened a couple of weeks earlier. Ian worked a few shops down, at a restaurant that served Lebanese food with some English dishes that were added to the menu with the idea of not alienating British customers.

'I've seen his cock, you know,' Debbie told her sister, with a wink.

'Er, too much information, girl,' said Mel, laughing.

'It's not a bad size either,' continued Debbie, chuckling, 'I'm just working on how I'm actually going to get it.'

'I'm glad you've found happiness again…'

'Yeah, so am I…that Pete was such a tosser!'

Mel looked down at her fingernails. She hated it when Debbie ill-spoke of Peter. Mel liked him, rather a lot in fact and unbeknownst to her sister, would often pass by where he worked after her early shift. Pete had no idea, and when Mel saw him with Sandy just the other week, she stopped her detours.

'I should've shagged Ozzie while I had the chance,' Debbie continued, 'now *that* is a man!'

'Pete was a good man, Debbie,' Mel said, looking up at her, 'and he always treated you nicely…too nicely, in fact…' Mel got up and went to put the kettle on. 'I don't like it when you bad-mouth him like that.'

'Ooh, listen to you,' Debbie whined, mockingly, 'fancy him do you?'

'As a matter of fact I do!'

'Bloody hell, keep your hair on…'

'I just hope you don't treat Ian like shit as well.' Said Mel as she left the lounge and went to her bedroom. Debbie got up and followed her, entering her quarters without knocking.

'What the fuck's wrong with *you*? Aren't you supposed to be my sister and always on my side?'

'It's not about picking sides, Debbie,' replied Mel as she lay upon her bed and grabbed her book from the bedside, 'it's about...'

'Go on...'

'You should be ashamed of how you treated Pete. It was downright wicked...you selfish bitch.'

'DON'T EVER call me a bitch...you little brat!'

'Go away, Debbie,' said Mel quietly, 'If you're out to pick a fight, I'm not in the mood.'

'Who the FUCK do you think you are!? You reckon you're SO SUPERIOR...well up your stupid spoilt little arse, bitch!'

'Stop calling me a bitch, you self-centred slut!' Mel sprang up from the bed and went bounding toward her sister like a gymnast from a crash-mat.

'Fuck off, you stupid cow! I thought you understood me!'

'What's there to understand, Debbie? You treat people like shit when you get bored with them; at least be honest with them and tell them you don't want to be with them anymore, and NOT try and take them for everything they've got. You know, for once...when you found Pete and your relationship lasted for more than just three months, I really thought you'd found someone who actually *gets* you. Instead, you got bored but you didn't tell him; you just thought you'd try and fleece him. You make me sick!'

'Oh listen to the high and mighty brat...you're bloody perfect, are you? Little Miss perfect. You make *me* sick, with your great morals and wonderful school reports...mummy's pet...teacher's pet, and all the boys love me and my hair, my nails, my shoes, my handbags...look at you. You're on the moral high ground now that you've found Frederick...more like Fred-the-prick!'

'Get out, Debbie...seriously, get the fuck out of my room before I really swing for you.'

'Going to cry are we? Blub, blub, blub...poor lickle Mel, poor little...'

Mel slapped her sister hard across the face, so hard in fact, that Debbie was knocked sideways and into the wall, narrowly missing the corner of the shelf that hung just above the dressing table. Debbie clung to her cheek with a look of sheer bedevilment. She turned and left Mel's room without a word. The front door slammed as their mother walked in from work.

'I could hear the pair of you yelling, from the lift. What on earth is going on?'

'Oh nothing, just your spoilt brat of a fucking daughter lecturing me on how to be a good girl.'

'I'll have none of that language in here, thank you very much, and why are you covering your face?'

'Because she slapped me, that's why!'

Stella looked at Mel disdainfully and asked her daughter why she would do such a thing, to which Mel replied that it was personal and that it would blow over; they'd sleep on it.

'Sleep on it my arse! Debbie yelled, 'It bloody hurt!'

'You deserved it.' said Mel.

'I won't tolerate my daughters slapping each other...'

'I was the one who swung at her, mother. I don't regret it either.'

'All this was just over how I treated Pete...for fuck's sake, leave it! I can't help how I feel...I just fancied Ozzie, but he was with that other slag, what's her name...Julia!'

'You fancied Ozzie for the wrong reasons, you stupid little bloodsucking slut!' hissed Mel, stepping forward once again, as though wanting to slap Debbie a second time.

'He rescued me from that rapist...I'm glad he killed Andr...'

'What?' interrupted Stella, 'what did Ozzie do to Andrew…I imagine we're talking about Andrew Blaine here, am I right?'

The two sisters went silent. Stella took both of them by the arm and led them into the lounge and on to the sofa, like mischievous children being led to the naughty step.

'Explain…please,' said Stella, 'what's this about…killing? Who killed Andrew?'

The sisters looked at each other, both of them as pale as moonlight. They clutched each other's hands and continued to look down at their laps. Stella pulled up a chair from the folding table in the kitchen area and sat in front of them, closer than before.

'Look at me, the pair of you. *Who* killed Andrew Blaine?'

'It was Ozzie, mum,' replied Mel, 'he just…happened to be passing by on his way to his girlfriend's house, when he disturbed Andrew beating up on Debbie. He only wanted to beat him up, to teach him a lesson. He went too far and…'

'I'm sorry mum,' said Debbie, as she threw herself into her mother's arms and cried desperately. Stella held her daughter tightly with one arm, while squeezing Mel's hand in the other.

'Okay,' said Stella, 'okay…there's something I have to tell you both. It's going to be hard for me to say it, and it's going to be a shock for you, but I think now's definitely a good time.'

'What is it, mum?' Debbie asked, as she looked quizzically at Stella.

'Mum…what is it?' asked Mel, with absolutely no idea what was about to come next. Stella looked at her daughters as a tear came down from her eye, but she kept it together. The few minutes that passed were the longest ever, as Mel and Debbie nervously awaited what their mother was about to tell them. The two sisters still had no idea what was coming, but they were pretty sure it was going to change their lives forever.

Chapter 24

Stella began breathing heavily, as though she'd run a marathon. Mel tried to calm her down while Debbie fetched a glass of water. Stella drank the whole tumbler and put it down onto the floor.

'Remember when I told you about your father...all the abuse, all the beatings he gave me...just bloody everything really...well, I told both of you that he'd died...shit, I don't believe I'm actually telling you this.'

'Come on, mum, spit it out!' exclaimed Mel, taking her mum's hands in hers.

'It was me who killed your dad. I did it...I just couldn't take it anymore. That black eye and cut lip you saw me with that evening...that was the final straw.'

Mel continued to look at her mother, while Debbie slipped down from the sofa and came to kneel at Stella's side as she revealed what she'd hoped would always remain sealed away, even though her two daughters had never mourned or felt the pain of his passing; she'd always had the impression that they were relieved when their abusive father finally gave up the ghost.

'Well,' she began, once she was able to form a sentence without breaking down, 'this...is something we really need to take with us to the grave. Fortunately it seemed like an accident...he had me by the hair one evening, as he dragged me out from the bathroom...pulled me out toward the top of the stairs and kicked me where it hurts most. That was my chance...I grabbed hold of his hair and pushed as hard as I could...he went down those stairs like the pissed old shit that he was...I called the ambulance...then it was over. It never went any further than one simple police statement you know...'

'Mum...,' said Mel, on the verge of yielding, 'dad touched me...I was in the bath, I must have been around ten or eleven. I never told anyone, especially you...you had enough on your plate...don't worry, mum. This is our family secret.'

Stella embraced both of her daughters and held them tightly. Debbie reached out and took her sister's hand and squeezed it. Mel reciprocated.

Ralf's phone rang at around midnight; Pete told him that Ozzie's mum had rung him to say that Ozzie still wasn't back. Pete had gone over to Garry Peters' house to see if there was anything to find out, but the house was empty. After checking with a couple of neighbours, he'd managed to find out that Lisa had been there that morning to pick up a few things but she was alone.

'What do you think? I reckon Peters is still working for Raymond Franklin and Ozzie's been roped in again. Both Jackie and Kim are beside themselves, and get this; Julia's walked off, couldn't take any more!'

'Bitch!'

'Exactly right,' said Pete, 'What is it with these bloody flaky women, eh?'

'Bear with me and I'll be right over to pick you up.'

Loredana stirred and asked what was going on. Ralf assured her that he would return before daybreak, although he knew that it would undoubtedly be a long night.

'Right, floor it!' said Pete, hurriedly, as he threw himself into the Ford Capri and fastened his seatbelt. 'Shame we can't get the cops involved.'

'Yeah, crying shame, but it would mean the end of Ozzie.'

'Ralf...'

'Yes, mate...'

'Has it been *just* two...or is it more?'

'How do you mean?' asked Ralf, glancing at Pete, fleetingly.

'Was it just the *two* lives that you took?'

'What kind of a question is that, you dick?'

'Answer me...honestly.'

'Pete...I told you the truth when I told you the story...and if you're worrying, and I can tell that you are, I can assure you that I don't intend to kill anybody else.'

'Okay,' said Pete, continuing to look ahead, 'Sorry mate…it's just a lot to take in, that's all. It just seems so…so…oh shit, I can't explain it…it just seemed so…'

'Easy!'

'Yeah…I guess that *is* what I meant…easy.' The guy in the park…you just took him without mercy or hesitation. And you were remorseless after the deed was done.'

'He would have killed us both, Pete. He had a gun, remember? He fired two shots on you. Had he seen you crawling along the ground, he'd have shot you without fail!'

'Yes, I know…you're right…you *did* save my life.'

'You saved mine…but let's not dwell on that now. Let's go find Ozzie – and when we do find him, we tie him up and keep him under 24 hour surveillance – we can't have him buggering off all the time…' Ralf chuckled.

As the two pals approached Raymond's home, Ralf instinctively pulled into a parking space just on his left. A large silver Jaguar emerged from the Franklin driveway and turned left. Both Pete and Ralf clearly saw that the driver was the only person inside the vehicle and from his semblance, they deduced that it was the infamous Raymond Franklin himself – a fifty-something gent with seemingly uncombed grey hair. He looked harmless enough but his henchman, the aforementioned Kamal, likely performed his dirty tasks for him and was more than likely on the premises.

'What do we do, follow him?'

'Here, take the wheel,' said Ralf as he exited the car, 'you follow him and see where he goes. I'll go in the house and see if Ozzie's in there…again!'

'Be careful, mate.'

'I will, now go, go after Franklin!'

As Pete drove away, Ralf watched as the Ford disappeared around the horseshoe's bend before beginning to clamber over the front gate of the house again. He sidled up to the windows of the manse, but it was pitch-black inside. He crept around the back but still no sign of life. Even the windows of the main house were devoid of the orange glow of electric light coming from within. Ralf rang the doorbell and waited just at the foot of the three steps that led up to the front door, convinced that there was nobody home, until the sound of a rather large and heavy key was heard clanking on the other side of the door. Ralf turned and dashed toward the far side of the manse and waited until whoever was inside the house descended the steps to investigate. There was silence for a good few seconds before the sound of padded footsteps could be heard as they carefully came down the stone steps, stopping dead as they crackled upon a clutter of pebbles on the driveway. Again, silence, as the occupant was probably scouring his surroundings.

Ralf's patience wore thin and he slowly inched his head around the corner of the manse, as he peeked round. A tall, Asian fellow with a sullen and frowned expression stood at the foot of the stone steps, glaring in the direction of the fraction of Ralf's bald head as it emerged from the corner of the manse. Ralf froze and kept his gaze fixed upon the man, who he imagined was Kamal; he remembered how Garry had described him – ugly and with a crater-face – as the man indeed, bore the skin marks that were like clusters of scars on his cheeks. Ralf remained as still as he could; the dark of night was undoubtedly enveloping him, along with the manse. The lantern that hung outside the doorway was aglow, and its lucent shaft illuminated the whole of the area where Kamal was standing. Ralf was sure that the man couldn't see him. Sure enough, the tall man's gaze became averted to a rustling sound coming from a large bush that ran from the pillar at the side of the front gate.

Kamal began stepping toward the source of the sound and on reaching the bush, proceeded to shine a narrow beam of light from a small torch that he produced from his pocket. Ralf moved around to the back of the manse whilst Kamal was engaged in searching the foliage and when he reached the rear side of the house, he took a large stone from the flowerbed that lay beneath a side window and hurled it toward the gate. Kamal marched toward the clatter and Ralf threw another one, aiming for parked cars beyond. Kamal clambered over the gate and toward where the second noise supposedly came from, giving Ralf the chance to slip through the open front door and inside the house.

The foyer was dimly lit by several wall lights that had probably been dimmed to a faint glow. The large, dark wood spiral staircase twisted upwards, barely discernible in the emulsified glow of the wall lights and appeared to disperse into the blackness above. The ticking of a grandfather clock could be heard coming from somewhere nearby, concealed in the murky shadows. Ralf could hear Kamal calling out to an invisible prowler outside and as soon as he realised that the tall man began clambering back over the gate, a surge of anxiety shot through him, and he silently darted up the darkened stairs, taking two at a time and slowing down as he reached the top. The upper landing was veiled in a tenebrous and creeping dark, which triggered Ralf's fear of it as his face felt like it was being brushed and enveloped by a malevolent Tenebrae.

He turned to look down below him and to the tall oblong shape in the darkness that was the doorway, as the faint orange glow from the streetlamps spilled inside. Kamal's figure appeared in the doorway and closed the large door behind him. He stepped forward and became concealed by the shadows as he walked toward the left side of the stairway. A shaft of yellow light briefly streaked across the wooden floor and just as quickly, disappeared as Kamal slammed shut a door behind him. He vanished into the depths of the house, leaving Ralf free reign to search upstairs.

Ralf inched his way along the top landing, fingers feeling the wall as he carefully made his way toward a corridor that lay to his left. He continued to hug the left wall as he fearfully tip-toed through total darkness. There was complete silence and that unnerved Ralf all the more, as he continued to move slowly toward a nothingness that his eyes could not get accustomed to. There was not a single sliver of light from any of the doorways his fingers discovered along the way, and he clumped his left foot against the wall that stood in front of him. Within seconds, the door downstairs that Kamal had supposedly walked through was flung open and the wall lights in the hallway were turned up to full glow. Ralf's skin began to crawl as heavy footsteps began climbing the stairs. He didn't usually fear people, only situations, such as the dreaded dark, heights, tight spaces, aeroplanes; but never people. For some strange reason, tonight, he was afraid…or perhaps excited.

As Kamal reached the top landing, his footsteps made their way toward the opposite end and down the other corridor. Ralf hadn't noticed the other one in the pitch-black and Kamal fortunately made for the other corridor first, giving Ralf a second window of opportunity to either search or escape. He chose the latter, despite all attempts to ignore this strange and sudden burst of newfound fear...he needed to get a grip, find Ozzie, and get out of there. Ralf tried the door at the end of the corridor and it clicked open, creaking slightly. Ralf shuffled inside, as silently as he could.

Ralf quickly and instinctively made his way toward an alcove in the far left corner of the bedroom, as Kamal's footsteps came thundering toward the door Ralf had just closed behind him. He dashed back to the door and gripped the doorknob as hard as he could and held on as Kamal tried to twist it open. Kamal made no sound or any attempt at communicating to whoever happened to be behind the door, as he continued to try and twist the handle open. A muffled and distant voice called unto him from what seemed to be the downstairs foyer, causing Kamal to release the doorknob and answer the call.

'Up here!' he cried, and Ralf immediately slipped toward another door to his left and into an on-suite bathroom as Kamal walked away from the door to the bedroom. There was another window in the bathroom, which Ralf opened immediately and looked out of. Below him was a black abyss that yawned up at him and just in front, was another wall. Ralf noticed a dark drainpipe and without hesitation, climbed through the window and stepped onto it. He could still hear muffled voices exchange indecipherable sentences with each other, increasing his anxiety to get away as quickly and as silently as possible. Ralf proceeded to painstakingly climb down the narrow but strong metal drainpipe and descend into the blackness below. Once he reached ground level, his skin began to crawl again as he crouched down and curled into a ball, as though something was about to attack him. Ralf's fear of the dark bestowed unto him an unfortunately vivid and shadowy imagination, featuring monsters and creepy beasties that would reach out and take him to some unimaginable and twisted place of nightmares.

He raised his head slightly and probed the darkness for any signs of something even slightly lucent, but nothing showed itself to him that was benevolent; only a dark void of nothingness, and the silence – the two things that when combined with one another, spelled only phantasmal incubus. What began as another search for Ozzie gradually transformed itself into a battle against Ralf's greatest fears. His hands began to feel their way along the cold brick wall once again, like a blind man desperately seeking safety. The sudden thud of a wooden door opening just a little way ahead of him, made him jump out of his skin and Kamal's imposing frame appeared and edged its way into the alley, torch in hand. The thin beam was raised and pointed in Ralf's direction, blinding him momentarily. Ralf thought of nothing else and with split-second timing, threw a left and a right punch into Kamal's face, knocking him backwards. Ralf pushed his way forwards and through the wooden door and immediately collided with the elderly man that was driving the car out of the driveway earlier. The man yelped as Ralf kicked him hard in the ribs, sending him into a stagger and hitting the wall as he fell against it, clutching his side. A hard and unexpected blow to his back sent Ralf flying forwards and he lost his footing as he hit the ground face first, just inches away from the elderly man, supposedly Raymond Franklin. As he tried to get up, a kick on his back side sent him back to the ground once again and into Raymond's embrace, as he attempted to take hold of Ralf's neck.

Kamal marched toward Ralf who was locked in Raymond's rear neck-hold and brought his right leg up and ready to strike downward in an attempt to stamp on Ralf's stomach. Kamal missed with his stomp as Ralf had managed to turn onto his side, releasing himself from Raymond's grip. The stamping blow made heavy contact with Ralf's ribs and he cried out in pain, as he felt as though he were being stabbed with a large blade. For a split-second, Ralf thought that his side *had* been pierced with a blade or spike, but the sensation dispersed rapidly as he now felt his arm being wrenched upwards by a grip of steel. A thundering blow came down upon his stomach, but didn't cause damage or pain; Ralf seized the opportunity to spring up to his feet just in time to see Kamal attempt to strike a blow to his face, as his fist was pulled back behind his head as though shooting an arrow. Ralf ducked underneath the blow, shuffled to Kamal's right side, and immediately smashed him to the side of the temple with a hard back-fist and immediately followed up with a hard, left straight across the chin.

An arm wrapped itself around Ralf's neck as Raymond Franklin attempted to lock him in a hold from behind once again. Ralf pushed himself backwards, causing Raymond's back to slam up against the wall of the house and causing him to release his grip. Ralf spun round and hit him hard with a snap-punch, breaking his nose. Ralf felt Raymond's blood splatter across his face as his blow connected, forcing him to spit out the few drops that reached his lips. Ralf felt Kamal's presence upon him as he felt his arm grabbed and pulled backwards. Ralf spun around and shoulder-barged Kamal away from him, immediately dashing forward and throwing his fist hard, into Kamal's face. The man hit the ground with a sickening thud and remained there, dazed and surprised. Raymond attempted one last onslaught but Ralf delivered a fierce, straight punch to his face, his knuckles slipping across his blood-soaked visage.

Raymond fell backwards like a collapsing tower and struck his head on the wall as he hit the ground. Kamal had gotten himself into a seated position and was about to attempt to rise up from the ground, but Ralf kicked him hard and fast in the face, knocking him unconscious. These seemingly insurmountable foes were now like worthless carcasses, as they lay upon the ground like rag dolls covered in blood. The bulkhead lantern that hung upon the wall nearby went out, startling Ralf; it was probably on a timed movement sensor, and the whole area was plunged into darkness once again, until Ralf waved his hand activating the sensor. He went over to Raymond and crouched down next to him and demanded to know where Ozzie was. Raymond was too dazed to talk and so fell back into his imposed slumber. Ralf turned his attention to Kamal, but after trying to shake him back into reality without any success, threw him back onto the stone pathway.

Ralf returned into the house, now that the foyer's wall lights were on full light he could search better. To the left of the huge stairway was the door that Kamal had gone through earlier. Ralf went through and found himself inside the first part of a large office room. He proceeded through a large archway and into the second section of the same room, complete with desktop computers and disorganised piles of paperwork atop every desk. The flashing red lights on telephone answering machines caught Ralf's eye as he quickly scoured the room before continuing on through a corridor lading to another doorway.

As he pushed open the door, Ralf realised that something was behind it. He pushed it harder, but the obstacle seemed stubborn and for an instant he thought that someone could have been hiding on the other side. He paused for a couple of seconds and in the silence he was certain he heard faint breathing. Someone was definitely behind the door and so Ralf pushed as hard as he could until the pressure induced a yelp and a gasp from the person behind it. Ralf passed through and look behind the door; it was Garry Peters.

'What the fuck are you doing here?' he cried, almost whimpering like a child.

'Where's my friend?' Ralf asked him, quietly.

'I don't know what you're on about…'

Ralf grabbed him by the collar and threw him onto a nearby table and the impact knocked a computer monitor off the table and crashed to the floor with a bang and the shatter of glass.

'You're seriously starting to irritate me,' Ralf growled, 'now quit arsing about and tell me where Ozzie is, or you'll be number three…'

'Eh, what the bloody hell are you on about?'

Ralf popped Garry hard just under the nose, cutting his upper lip. Garry yelped and thrust himself forward, in an attempt to rugby-tackle him. Ralf brought his right leg upwards and struck Garry's groin, causing him to release his grip around Ralf's waist.

'No more fucking games, where is Ozzie? Either you tell me, or I WILL take your life. WHERE!?'

'Okay…okay, you psycho…he's next door…next door, now please leave me alone!'

Ralf grabbed Garry's hair and pulled him up from the floor and continued to drag him along with him and through to the next room. He ordered Garry to open the door, and after he did so, Ralf pushed him inside the room first, before entering and rapidly scouring his surroundings for any other hidden enemies. There were three women in the room, two of them startled, the other was more curious than worried.

'Who are you?' Ralf asked her.

'Amanda,' the girl young woman replied. 'Are you a police officer?'

'Not a chance,' Ralf said, 'but I'd advise that you leave now if you want out of this crap for good. It's your only opportunity. I'd take it.'

Without hesitation, Amanda began collecting her things and smiled at Ralf before exiting the room. Garry tried to move towards the door in an attempt to slip out quickly, but Ralf's glare of disapproval convinced him otherwise.

'You said he's in this room. I don't see him.'

Garry pointed toward a side door at the far right of the room they were standing in. Ralf motioned to Garry to go ahead of him and open the door. The room beyond was like a dormitory where two bunk beds stood at each end and separated by a large window overlooking a floodlit garden. The beds were empty, but Ozzie was sat upon the bottom bunk of the left hand one, looking bewildered and exhausted. He recognised Ralf, as he called his name, but was unable to stand on his feet easily. Ralf went toward him and tried helping him up gently, giving Garry Peters yet another opportunity to make a getaway.

As Ralf heard the doorknob being rattled, he spun around and saw Garry try and rush through the open door. He gave chase and the two men began hurtling through the adjoining rooms, throwing up paperwork like high speed trains rushing through little stations. Garry was slim, nimble, and younger, making it a little harder for the older and bulkier Ralf to keep up. For every chair overturned, Garry leapt over it while Ralf had to go around, thus gradually increasing distance between them. Ralf began to grow angry again, red mist angry, and the bad thoughts of what he would do to Peters when he got hold of him, began to take over. His promise to Pete of not killing anyone else was fading rapidly. Garry Peters was an annoying and cowardly little weasel, and all Ralf wanted to do was beat him to a bloody pulp.

The two running men began nearing the front foyer of the huge house, and as Garry looked behind him to see if he was still being pursued, he unwittingly collided with Amanda and they both fell to the floor, the contents of Amanda's bag spilling everywhere. Ralf grabbed Garry's leg and dragged him to the middle of the foyer and began beating down on him. Garry attempted to hide his face from the fearsome blows of the raging Ralf, but it was ultimately useless; Ralf was strong, fast, and relentless. Garry was fading fast and his light would extinguish soon.

As Peters began passing into unconsciousness, Ralf felt himself being tackled from the side, and as he sprang up in readiness to strike, he realised that it was

Amanda who had just intervened. The expression upon her face was that of a tired and desperate young woman. Her eyes were soft and sincere and Ralf instantly felt the pain that they were hiding. Over the years, Ralf had learned to read people very well, and Amanda's face was full of the troubles and anguish that he'd seen many times before. He rose from the floor and put out his hand to the young woman. She took it and Ralf proceeded to help her to put her scattered belongings back into her bag. Ralf couldn't keep his eyes off her, and she appeared to feel the same way. They exchanged continuous looks and glances that wanted to speak many words, as Ralf helped her with her things, and as he handed the bag to her, they both remained standing by the doorway, their eyes getting lost in each other's.

'Thank you...' she said, gently.

'Thank *you*.' replied Ralf.

Amanda turned and left the house and effortlessly clambered over the gate, pulling and adjusting her skirt as she went. She gave one final and fleeting look at the entranced Ralf, and she was gone. Ralf hoped that he would see her again.

'I 'ate this fackin' place,' exclaimed Ozzie as he emerged through the doorway next to the stairs.

'Let's go home, rocker!' said Ralf as he placed his arm around his friend.

Chapter 25

Pete struggled to stay on his feet as he tried to pull himself up by clinging to a drainpipe. He wasn't sure where he was and he didn't take notice of his exact location whilst he was intent on tailing Raymond Franklin, and his concentration remained steadfast as he made every attempt to not lose him. Only twice, was he forced to allow a vehicle to pull in front of him, as they came out of side streets and Pete was too far away from Raymond's to impede them, but they didn't remain in his trajectory for too long, so he was able to resume following him without risk of him getting away.

Pete sat up with his back against the brick wall of the alleyway he happened to be in. Nearby, the sound of crockery colliding with cutlery and a dishwasher, and the smell of food, made it obvious that the alley ran at the rear of an eatery of some kind. On occasion, the door would open and a pair of burly forearms could be seen casting out refuse sacks as they filled up with foodstuffs or whatever else the kitchen staff discarded. It was dark, further down the alley and whoever was throwing out the trash hadn't yet noticed the battered and bruised Pete, who felt too mangled and exhausted to even whisper for help, let alone make any attempt to cry out. He remained in the sitting position for at least two hours before his energies slowly returned to him and he found himself able to shuffle up to a dumpster, where he remained for a few more minutes before pressing on.

Pete felt frustrated, embarrassed, and humiliated. Not necessarily because of the beating he'd just taken, but for taking his eye off the ball, perhaps even underestimating his opponent a little. Pete had always prided himself with being a thinking man – a methodical and strategic planner and someone very calm in his approach to even the smallest detail – but his tailing techniques were sorely lacking. There were times like these when he wished he'd done national service; at least people like Raymond Franklin wouldn't have pissed on his fire.

Raymond had momentarily pulled over to park just outside what appeared to be a kebab eatery that offered a take-away service as well, but when much time had gone by, Pete began growing impatient and so went to find out what was taking so long. He stood at the corner of the eatery's outside wall, that backed into the alley and began to peek into the building, when a rope or string suddenly wrapped itself around his neck, and he found himself being pulled into the dark alley behind him. As soon as his assailant loosened his grip, Pete turned to look behind him, fists at the ready, but instead, was met by the loud crash of a dustbin lid as it made hard contact with his face, toppling him. Before he had time to react, a fierce kick to the groin sent Pete back to meet the ground as he was forced to fall on one knee. The dustbin lid was used one more time, as the assailant clouted him across the face, hard and true. Pete fell back against the wall of the alley, as a fierce kick landed upon his face, dazing him. He fell sideways and cried out in pain as another kick struck his side, probably breaking at least one of his ribs. He managed to look upwards and recognise that it was indeed, Raymond Franklin, who'd taken him by surprise before another thundering blow sent him into cuckoo land.

Whilst Pete's mind was busy recounting the ordeal and playing it back like a recorded movie, he had managed to reach Ralf's car and he sat within it for quite a while before finally deeming himself able to drive away, and after navigating a labyrinthine network of back streets that were alien to him, he eventually came across a phone box just near a parade of shops. Pete hunted for a coin within the depths of the vehicle, eventually finding a few in the side pocket of the passenger door. He rang Ralf's number but there was no reply. He sat back in the car and waited a while longer before trying again. Pete continued on home, stopping by Ralf's house along the way, but after knocking at the door and making the doorbell go into overdrive, it was clear that Ralf was not home. Pete got back into the car and drove himself home.

Ralf and Ozzie phoned for a taxi from a phone box on the main road, after Ralf had gone through Kamal's and Raymond's pockets. He confiscated both of their wallets and felt over the moon at the amount of cash that he found inside them. He figured that after so much trouble he'd been put through because of their antics and their dodgy dealings, a generous remuneration package was definitely on the cards. The school stipend was adequate, but this bonus was just the ticket. Once the cab reached Ozzie's home, his mother appeared on the doorstep. Without hesitation she embraced her son and after staying with them for about a half hour, Ralf walked to Pete's house, which was only five minutes away.

'What in fuck's name happened to you?' exclaimed Ralf, as Pete opened the front door.

Pete motioned to Ralf hurriedly and the two went into the lounge.

'Pete, what happened, mate?'

'My own stupid fault...I was tailing Franklin, like you asked...'

'And...'

'Well, he pulled over to go into some kebab shop. I waited for half an hour and because he wasn't coming out of there, I got out and hid at the corner of the alleyway just next to it. He must have somehow crept behind me...next thing I knew, I felt this rope around my neck...it went on from there. The fucker took me by surprise...had me out of breath from the rope, then he beat the crap out of me with a fucking dustbin lid before I had the chance to react.'

Ralf's attempt at stifling a chuckle after holding back a slight grin were futile, and Pete glared at him as though he were about to kill him.

'Sorry mate,' said Ralf, chuckling, 'it's just the...thing about the dustbin lid...sorry.'

'Cheers, mate...really appreciate your sympathy. I'm fine...don't mention it.'

Ralf continued laughing.

'Ha...what if it was an old lady we were chasing...she'd have beaten you up with a rolling pin or a saucepan...'

'Ralf...you're not helping...'

'He beat the shit out of you with a...wait for it...drumroll...DUSTBIN LID!'

'Ralf!'

'Sorry, you're right. I'm being a dickhead.'

'Anyway, did you find Ozzie?'

'Yeah, he's fine. I called a cab and dropped him off at his house.'

'What about Raymond and gang?'

'I don't think Raymond or his henchman will be bothering with us again.'

'You didn't kill him did you?'

'No, I didn't kill him…Pete, listen mate…about that…'

'What?'

'Nah, forget it. It's fine.'

'Go on, tell me.'

'Another time. You need those bruises and cuts seeing to. You want me to drive you to A and E?'

'Don't be silly…I could've driven there myself if I wanted to. I'll be okay after a good rest. You go on home, get some sleep. We'll talk tomorrow, okay?'

Ralf returned home and found Loredana downstairs in the kitchen. She'd prepared some perfect boiled eggs and soldiers, which he devoured instantly. After making some more for herself, she asked Ralf what had happened and why he was gone for so long. Ralf began to feel uncomfortable as Loredana continued with the questions. He made attempts at being slightly more vague, but she found a way of wriggling around it all and persist, like a headstrong footballer battling his way through opposing defences with bewitching skills.

'Look, I just told you what happened. Pete had a few problems and he needed my help, that's all. Why do you keep on? Feels like the third bloody degree!'

'Sorree, I jast eenterested, dat is all. No get hangry weet me!'

Ralf finished his breakfast while Loredana finished getting dressed, and afterwards the two decided to go out for some food shopping at the Asda superstore, in Park Royal. On arriving there and parking the car, Loredana told Ralf she'd catch up with him, as she needed to make a phone call. Ralf took a trolley from the scattered throng that lay just outside the main entrance and made his way inside and toward the deli counter. Even her once amusing broken English pissed him off at that moment.

Ozzie had just prepared a pot of tea for himself and his mum, and as Jackie entered the kitchen and sat at the table, Ozzie placed the pot down along with two mugs, a plate of assorted biscuits, and a little jug of milk.

'I tried to phone Julia today,' Ozzie said, 'but she wouldn't pick up the phone.'

'Maybe she was out,' Jackie replied, 'you know what we women are like...always out shopping for bags and shoes!'

'Why aren't you looking at me, mum?'

'Leave her alone, son.' Jackie said, raising her head and looking up at him.

'What do ya mean?'

'She ain't for you, luvvey. She's not for the likes of us!'

'What did she do? I thought you liked her...'

'She just got up and walked out...couldn't take it anymore, she said. Yer better off without her, son!'

'I guess I'm too much for her. What with all the shit that's been goin' down...no wonder she facked off.'

'You're well out of it now...the other stuff I mean...not just Julia.'

The phone rang but they ignored it, along with the doorbell shortly after. Mother and son remained silent for most of the evening, until Jackie turned in for an early night, after giving Ozzie a kiss on the forehead. Ozzie later phoned Ralf, but there was no reply. He tried Pete as well, but he was unavailable also. The lounge entered into a melancholy silence, the only sound coming from the open fire. The Blakes enjoyed the warmth from its crackling flames and Ozzie enjoyed throwing potatoes into it and eating them with melted butter, salt, and pepper, and a glass of wine. It was his father's favourite thing, and with that thought, Ozzie felt loneliness overwhelm him. It took hold of his soul and remained attached there, draining him of his will to live. He thought of his mother and his sister, Kim. He thought of his dear friends, Ralf and Pete. He thought of Julia again. He was beginning to fall for her after all. He had reached a point where he was no longer scared of that awful word; commitment, but it was pointless now. Julia was gone and Ozzie knew that this time it was for good. He looked up at the mantelpiece and at his mum's heart medication tablets. There were three containers.

Pete phoned his girlfriend, Sandy. He hadn't seen her for a while and he felt that he could really use the company. She hadn't called him either, but she was always a busy girl, being a kindergarten teacher at her local school, which she herself attended when she was a toddler. After quite a few rings, she answered.

'Hey darling, it's me…Pete.' There was a pause at the other end.

'Oh…how *are* you?'

'Erm…I'm not too bad…I guess. I thought I'd give you a ring, you know…long time, no hear. Just wondered if you were up for an evening or a day out sometime…tomorrow maybe?'

'Oh…listen, Pete… I've been kind of…really busy…with the school and that. I'm not sure I'll be available sometime soon…can I call you back?'

'Sandy…why is it that nobody has the guts to just be sincere? Look, you don't need to make stupid excuses, just tell the truth as it is. You don't want to go out with me anymore. Is that so hard!?'

'Okay, I don't want to go out with you anymore.'

Pete was at a loss for words despite knowing full well what Sandy was about to say. He just hoped that out of all of the women he'd been out with, and they were few, at least *she* would make an effort to be less nasty to him. Pete often wondered if his face brought out the worst in people. Was it because he was too nice? Too laid back, perhaps? Or was it because he just wasn't reckless enough? Nevertheless, he could think of absolutely nothing that would explain why, and now Sandy was the next lady in his life to slip back out of his life, and in record time. At least Debbie lasted two years.

'Okay, any particular reason why?'

'I've found someone else.'

'Oh, and what does this someone else have that I don't? Does he have a better car, higher paid job, or a bigger dick perhaps!? Go on, tell me. I can handle it, you know. You didn't waste much time did you!?'

'Fuck off, Pete.'

Sandy hung up before Pete could utter another word. She was gone, like all the others. Pete went into the lounge and picked up his keyboard and took it upstairs into the bedroom, connected it to his little amplifier and began composing. At least he still had his beloved plink-a-plonk.

Ralf had almost finished the shopping by the time Loredana caught up with him at the meat aisle. 'Good phone call?' he asked, to which Loredana replied by nodding her head. Ralf continued picking food from the counters as he strolled along the aisles, whilst Loredana took hold of his arm. He was beginning to feel a certain empathy toward Ozzie's attitude with women; for some inexplicable reason, he was beginning to tire of his Italian girlfriend's company and perhaps starting to become fearful of her becoming too attached. He was also beginning to dislike her taking hold of his arm when they were out walking. He still liked the sex though...but only that. Maybe it was time to call it a day.

Ozzie stood at the mantelpiece clutching one of his mother's tablet pots and staring at the label. He focused upon the writing in bold print; TAKE TWO TABLETS TWICE DAILY. He twisted the lid off of the container and looked inside. It was full of oval shaped white pills and they emitted a slightly garlic-infused odour. The thought of downing the pot's contents entered his mind, and seriously so. All he needed was the whole lot and all would be over in an evening.

Ozzie thought of his mother who was upstairs, probably reading before dropping off, and completely unaware of what her son was thinking of doing. He could have done it by now and neither Jackie nor anybody else would be any the wiser. No one would miss him because he was just a burden to society, an annoyance to his friends and girlfriend, a pain in the arse to his sister, and a thorn in his mother's side. At least she wouldn't worry after he was gone. The thing that was swaying him toward the darker of two sides was the total absence of guilt or remorse on his part. Ozzie felt as though he couldn't care less and that, in his eyes, was the deciding factor.

A loud thud from somewhere upstairs startled Ozzie and his sudden jolt caused him to drop the pill container, spilling its contents on the carpet just shy of the fireplace. Without a second's hesitation, he darted up the stairs when he heard his mother cry for help. Without taking hold of the doorknob, Ozzie shoulder barged the door and fell into the bedroom, where his mother lay in a pool of blood. She had fallen asleep whilst reading and dropped out of her bed, hitting her head on the corner of the bedside table as she went down. Ozzie cradled her head in his arms, and her blood began soaking his sleeve. She was barely conscious and her legs were shaking. Ozzie reached for the phone's handset that had come off its cradle during the fall, pressed the button to obtain the dialling tone, and rang 999.

'Mum, mum stay with me. Mum!' Jackie began fading gradually, despite her son shaking her. 'I'm sorry mum. I'm really sorry. Please stay with me!'

The ambulance arrived within minutes of the phone call and Ozzie yelled at the top of his voice for them to smash down the door after they rang the bell. The paramedics were upstairs in mere seconds, but Ozzie's mum was fading ever farther away into the blackness that Ozzie himself, just minutes earlier, was planning to venture into.

'Please save her, please!' he cried, as he fell to his knees in bitter tears.

Chapter 26

As the night slid into the early hours, Pete and Ralf appeared at the doorway to the ward where Ozzie's mother was. Ozzie was sat on a chair near her bed and holding her hand, and she appeared to be asleep and breathing normally. Before they entered the room, a hasty and efficacious nurse brushed past them and headed to Jackie's side and proceeded to adjust her pillows. Jackie stirred and opened her eyes to a squint, smiling slightly when she appeared to recognise Pete and Ralf at the door. The smile became a more pronounced one as she turned toward her son, who smiled back with relief. Ozzie got up from the bedside and went toward his two dear friends, embracing them both.

'We came as soon as we heard the news,' Ralf said, 'we went to your house and the neighbour said she heard the ambulance and she saw the paramedics break down the door. Is your mum okay?'

'Yeah…she is now.' Ozzie replied.

'What happened?' Pete asked.

'It happened too fackin' quick. I was downstairs just…well, I heard this fackin' noise and I ran upstairs and mum had fallen out of fackin' bed, hadn't she…hit her head on the bedside table, so I rang the ambulance and they got there fackin' quick.'

'Ozzie,' Jackie murmured.

'Yeah mum, you okay?'

'Stop fuckin' swearing, you potty mouth little shit.'

The hasty nurse paused to laugh along with Ozzie, Ralf, and Pete. The laughter was a little on the flamboyant side, what with Ozzie's machine gun impression and Ralf's baritonal bellow, but the stony-faced nurse seemed to condone it at that moment. Jackie put her head back and smiled broadly.

Ralf and Pete left the hospital, leaving Ozzie with his mum until the evening. They decided to drive to Ealing Broadway for a spot of record shopping, as the two pals both felt that it was a buzzing positivity day.

'I fancy going to Our Price records today,' Pete said, 'If I heard correctly, Spandau Ballet's new album's out and apparently, it's brilliant.'

'Well, if the song True is anything to go by...and that other track, what's it called? Oh yeah, Communication...'

The two friends entered the shopping centre through a central walkway that was lined with brand new shops on either side, including Thornton's chocolate and an elaborate jewellery store. The new shopping centre was still being developed but the area was still open to the public to roam around in. Pete and Ralf headed toward Our Price which was at the opposite end of the courtyard, just past a large fountain. They walked through the entrance and were immediately blasted by the warm air of the air conditioning grille just above them. The familiar and comforting odour of the record store – of new carpet and wooden shelves - overwhelmed them as the excitement of a new album release drew them toward the pop section.

Pete snatched up the vinyl as soon as he caught sight of it. He had an almost maniacal grin upon his face as he read the song titles on the back of the sleeve. His smile faded a little as he exclaimed that the album had only eight tracks. 'I'll bet they'll be quality songs though.' he exclaimed.

Ralf began perusing the shelves and yelped when he spotted an album that peaked *his* interest. It was ABC's new record, entitled, The Lexicon of Love. Pete went over to read the back of the record sleeve with Ralf, and the two friends agreed that their afternoon would be rather filled up with music listening time.

The Spandau album took first spin on Pete's record player and each track was a great one. Ralf's favourite was *Heaven Is a Secret*, but every song was top quality and extremely tuneful. Compared to their previous records, the group had changed their sound by making it sharper, relaxing the tempo a little, and the lead singer, Tony Hadley, took on a more technical and elastic approach to his vocals. Both Ralf and Pete were true fans, and the album was played one more time, just to take in the group's new sound.

Next up was ABC's record, which Ralf had decided to purchase in cassette form. Ralf and Pete listened intently while the fascinating sound of the album graced Pete's speaker system.

'Bloody hell, this is brilliant,' Ralf exclaimed, gleefully, 'it's got orchestral bits in it; actually more than just bits. They've combined it with a pop sound, and the string arrangements are brilliant. I love the tune and the chorus is really catchy!'

The first song on the album was called *Show Me*, and it was a very upbeat track with a surging and bouncy bassline. *Poison Arrow* followed, and it was a song that Ralf and Pete had caught playing on the radio whilst they were in the car, about a month earlier. The two pals agreed that Martin Fry's voice was very distinctive and his tone and timbre were warm and perfectly suited to the music. His voice was rich and expressive without the need for him to push it. He had the right amount of power and mellowness, and like Spandau Ballet's album, True, every song was excellent and very tuneful. The two friends were hooked once again, and this album was also played twice, before they were both inspired to get the keyboards out and begin composing.

Pete and Ralf came up with three songs – one from Ralf and two from Pete who produced one number with lyrics and an instrumental song called Crystal Tears. Ralf's lyrics were usually less about love and more focused upon life and everyday feelings and emotions. Pete's words were more love orientated and sometimes bordered on tragic happenings and love loss, and of course Ralf never let the opportunity slip by to simply rip Pete to shreds about how dreary and dramatic his lyrics were compared to his own more jovial ones. But what mattered was that they both came up with some great melodies. Pete liked Ralf's often catchy tunes while his own earned equal praise for intelligent tunes as well as memorable ones. The two friends knew not just what they liked to hear, but also had a very good grasp on what the public wanted as well.

The following evening, all three good friends met up at Mike's Music City, with both Loredana and Edwina in tow. They entered the building and owner Mike, acknowledged them from behind his glittering bar. He wore a gold sequined shirt and matching trousers which were revealed when he stepped out from his flamboyant kiosk and led his friends downstairs to where the action was just about to start.

'You are in for a rare treat, guys!' exclaimed Mike, enthusiastically. 'This is a group that I've been trying to corner for months now, and I can't believe that just this morning, I actually managed to bag them at such short notice!'

'Bloody hell mike, don't keep us in suspense, mate...who *are* they?' asked Pete.

'THEY...are The Overtures, and get this...the saxophonist is the one from that amazing group, ABC. He left them to join another group, but that fell through so he joined these guys...ah fuck, yeah!'

Pete, Ralf, and company laughed at Mike's enthusiasm, and also his big tombstone grin, as he continued to express the joy at his latest booking.

'They've got this amazing, massive keyboard that they connect to a great big computer on stage...think it's called a...Fairfax, Fairlamp, Fair...'

'Fairlight!' intoned Ralf, 'a fucking Fairlight, bloody hell I *want* one of those!'

'You can get one if you've got twenty grand handy, mate!' said Pete with a chuckle.

The Fairlight CMI was a digital sound sampler that was used by a fair number of people and professional musicians that could afford it. Ralf had always been fascinated by the use of strings and orchestral accompaniment in songs and both he and Pete knew that the best string ensemble sounds came from the Fairlight. Their Casio keyboards' string sounds just weren't up to scratch and sounded nothing like the real thing, not even close, even when combined with other sounds such as Pipe Organ with Violin, and so on. In other words, the Fairlight was definitely a dream, unless Pete and Ralf's Elektroartz band ever became a reality.

As they descended the stairs to the secret underground hall, the smell, lights, and above all, that incredible atmosphere that hung in the air and was so palpable, just hit them with a rush that was overwhelming and that made them feel like children again, just like that feeling of awe and enthusiasm that struck you when you saw a deep snowfall for the first time; it was electric.

The large room was around thirty feet long and twenty wide. There was a small bar with a dumb waiter behind it and dimly lit, with just three recessed mains halogen lamps above, in an upper shelf where bottles were kept. The walls were decorated with beige and green coloured two-tone tiles, simulating an underground station and with two wall lights on each side, with glass teardrop shades over candle-lamps. There were round tables with three chairs each and they were scattered about erratically over the wooden floor, but leaving room enough for dancing just in front of the stage. An eight light chandelier in mock crystal hung from the ceiling and was dimmed to a minimum as were all the wall lights, while a light veil of smoke hung in the air – not cigarette smoke, but from a hidden machine tucked away somewhere by the side of the stage.

Hugging each wall, bar the one with the stage, were rows of patterned sofa seats tucked beneath oblong tables. Ralf noticed that the seats were taken from underground train carriages and that Mike had undoubtedly rescued them from disused rolling stock. He admired and soaked in the atmosphere even more as he saw that the lamps adorning the tables were old-fashioned kerosene lamps with tall funnelled glass over the wick. The menu leaflets were made to resemble train tickets and stood on their sides and lighted by the radiance of the old-style lamps.

Ralf's eyes were now drawn to another row of train carriage seating a little further along the far wall, but these were inside a section of an old underground train, the deep red colour and curved edges of its three-windowed front revealed it to be the rolling stock used on the Bakerloo Line. The doors were removed to favour entrance by customers and Ralf marched over there to observe, his face lit up in absolute awe like a child. He could hear his name being called, but at that moment he didn't care. He stepped into the half-carriage and sat upon one of the seats. There were small oblong tables between each row of seats with the same kerosene lamps as the main room, and the train ticket menus also. The windows that faced the walls reflected the flickering flame of the funnel-lamp that lit up the shimmering image of an art-deco symbol that adorned the tiles. Every last detail of the carriage was left untouched, from the grab-rails to the grabbing handles that hung from the ceiling. Ralf sat there in an awesome world of his own and wouldn't be anywhere else at that moment. Mike appeared at the doors, smiling approvingly and with the others behind him.

'It's alright, mate,' he said, 'the special train's yours for the evening. Enjoy!'

The hubbub of people chatter, clinking glasses, and chairs and tables being moved seemed to signal that the band was about to walk out onto the stage and burst into energy giving music, and as soon as the group of friends found where they wanted to sit, two band members appeared from behind the burgundy coloured curtain that hung at the back of the stage, concealing a back entrance to another room.

'That's him!' exclaimed Ozzie, pointing to the blond-haired saxophonist as he emerged from behind the curtain and clutching his polished golden instrument. 'He's a mate of mine – his name's Mark!'

Three more musicians appeared, one of them wheeling a trolley bearing something that made Ralf's heart thump and leap into his throat. It was the Fairlight, with double keyboard and computer monitor. He watched with utter fascination as the keyboard player manipulated his light-pen upon the screen like a fantastical mage's wand. Ralf set his mind into overdrive whilst attempting to calculate what he could sell in order to have one – the only thing he could think of that would definitely do the trick was his very soul, his musical soul, that was alight with fire.

Edwina looked at Ralf whist his gaze was affixed to the sight of the musician waiting for the cue – it came, from the click of the guitarist's fingers, and the band began to play. The first song opened with a synthetic drum roll which flew into a fast and rhythmic rock beat. The bass was bouncy and skilful, while the electric guitar chased it all with arpeggios that soared and clambered. It was like a combination of jazz-funk and pop, with elements of light rock. The vocalist was talented – an unschooled tenor who's tone and timbre resembled that of Sting, the lead singer of The Police. The song spoke of the love of all things music, and that even the patter of rain upon a rooftop was music to anyone's ears if they listened. The second part of the song featured the slowly rising orchestral melody of the Fairlight. The violins sounded like they were really present, and produced by actual violinists upon the stage. Ralf felt shivers rising up his spine, not just for the music that spilled from the stage and into his soul, but from the odd but not unpleasant way that Edwina Clare had taken hold of his hand from under the table.

She began to slowly caress his hand from fingertip to wrist and in a way that Ralf could feel her sweetness and her passion for him. He wasn't sure whether to pull his hand away or just let her continue. Loredana was none the wiser, as she was holding his other hand atop the table, but Edwina didn't let up. Her motion gathered speed and she increased the pressure a little as her delicate fingertips began to take hold of his entire wrist and move slowly upwards into his sleeve. Ralf began to feel an unbelievable stirring in his loins, as Edwina began to caress his leg, moving slowly upward with each stroke. Eventually, she reached his zipper area and when she realised that Ralf had a raging hard-on, she flinched with sweet surprise, stopping her movement for a few seconds. She began once again, this time feeling for the tab of his zipper.

Edwina took hold of the metal tab with her fingers and slowly pulled it downwards. She took hold of his shaft and eased it out of its hiding place and with thumb and forefinger, began to move up and down, slowly increasing in both speed and pressure. Ralf's eyes went into a squint and his palms were sweating. Loredana turned to him and asked him if anything was wrong, as she was still holding one of his hands. Ralf jolted as if snapping out of a trance as he turned toward her, completely bedevilled by it all.

'Ralf, you okay mate?' asked Pete, 'you look like you've either seen a ghost or you need a good sleep…'

At that precise moment, Ralf ejaculated and gave a shudder, startling Loredana who let go of his hand. Edwina quickly replaced Mr Dicky inside Ralf's jeans and proceeded to sip her wine, while everyone else continued to wonder what the hell was going on with Ralf's extremely odd behaviour – except Edwina, who signalled the waiter over to ask for a refill. The band continued to play and Ralf's attention was drawn once again, to the sound of the Fairlight's wonderful string arrangements. Loredana took hold of Ralf's hand once again and turned to look at the musicians upon the dimly lit stage. The hidden smoke machine continued to generate its atmospheric haze which veiled the faint glow of the wall lights in a welcome mist that filled the room, some of it drifting into the carriage. The tables out in the main room could now barely be discerned as the penumbra turned them into outlines, with all who sat around them looking like faceless shades, giving them an element of mystery and looking like shadows of their former selves. The flame inside the funnelled glass in the middle of the table began to flicker as though disturbed by a breeze. Its radiance warmed and illuminated each of their faces, making them feel as if their table was the only one shining brightly in the near- darkness that fell around them. Even the slightly frumpy Edwina looked that bit prettier in the half-light, while Loredana's slight frown made her resemble a gargoyle.

The latest song that filled the room had the Fairlight replicating strings and pipe organs that complemented each other beautifully. The drummer made his drum machine shine and sing as he percussed varieties of rolls and fill-ins as the melody rattled along like a train at full speed. The vocalist began to grow on Ralf, especially as he was more critical of vocals being a singer himself. He liked this guy – he could admirably hold a tune, despite his vocal simplicity with total absence of vibrato and poor attempt at an American accent. There was no doubt that the singer's voice suited the band's sound perfectly.

Some ten songs later, the band ceased playing after announcing to the audience that they'd be back in twenty minutes. Ralf got up from the table and excusing himself, headed upstairs and outside for a breath of air. Edwina followed him when Loredana went to the bathroom. She caught up with him as he was walking slowly toward the direction of Turnham Green. As he turned toward her, Edwina took a step back. Ralf had an expression on his face that resembled the anvil cloud, the one that imposed itself in the heavens, announcing the coming of a fierce tempest.

'WHAT were you thinking in there!?' Ralf hissed.

'I…I don't know…sorry.'

'You don't KNOW?' he whined.

'Keep your voice down…I said I'm sorry…that way your eyes lit up when you were listening to that band with that keyboard…it was just so sweet. I just wished *I* had the twenty grand to give you so you could buy it. I just loved that childlike enthusiasm that took hold of you…and when you were inside that underground carriage…I *am* sorry, Ralf…'

Ralf embraced Edwina and they stood at the corner of Turnham Green Terrace for a while, until Pete came out to call them, taken by surprise by the way they were locked together. Edwina went on downstairs while Ralf mentioned he was going to the bar for a quick word with Mike while Pete followed.

'What's going on with you two? Looks like you're an item...am I right?'

'I'm not sure,' replied Ralf, sighing with near exasperation, 'she fucking puzzles me...and I think I'm strangely attracted to her. And that's just weird, I know.'

'It's not just weird, it's mental!' Pete said with a harsh whisper into Ralf's ear, 'come on mate...she's got cankles and carbuncles!'

'Look, she's a bit on the dumpy side, but she's far from completely gross!'

Pete looked at him, smirking and raising his eyebrows, then altering them to morph his expression into his famous lawyer-look.

'Don't look at me like that, she's really making an effort...do you see? Nail varnish on her fingers and toes, a little makeup, lip gloss...'

'What about Loredana?' Pete asked.

'Ah she's starting to get on my tits. She asks too many questions, she follows me with her eyes, every move I make I feel those eyes upon me like scarab beetles. And she's sex mad...wants it practically every night *and* the next morning just before I go to work, I hear, *Poot one condom on eef yoo like a kweekee!* I mean, what the fuck, where did she learn that shit from?'

Pete laughed almost uncontrollably until his eyes were filled with tears.

'What if she realises?' he said.

'She'll go nuts. The woman has psychotic tendencies, trust me.'

'Was she wanking you off under the table?'

'Yes...it was bloody good too. That's what fucks with my head...she uses her hands better than Loredana does. In fact, every time she touches me, even if it's just patting my hand or a peck on the cheek...it moves me more than my hot Italian girlfriend does when *she* touches me. Can you believe that?'

'Actually, nothing you say surprises me anymore.' Pete said, placing an arm around his friend.

Chapter 27

Ralf awoke the next morning feeling as though he were wrenching himself free from the binding ropes of a familiar nightmare – the usual one he had, that depicted a hurried journey through a village in southern Italy, culminating in a showdown that played out like a hide-and-seek game between children, taking place within the gothic walls of a dark abbey. He rolled out of bed, leaving the discomforting reverie behind him, lurking beneath the sheets. Loredana stirred as he left the bedroom and went downstairs. She wrapped a gown around herself and followed.

'I thought you were asleep.' Ralf said, as he took a box of muesli from the cupboard and emptied some into a bowl.

'I was,' she said, 'but you wake me. Why you shout? You scared of sumteeng?'

Ralf shook his head slightly and proceeded to pour milk into his bowl and sat at the table, while Loredana continued to look at him from the doorway.

'Are you going to carry on eyeballing me, or do you want some breakfast?'

'I no hangry…I go beck to bed. See you letta!'

Ralf finished his bowl of muesli and hit the shower before going out to work. He saw Edwina crossing the school playground before entering the building and she was unaware that he was approaching.

'Hey, doll!' he called.

'Well hello, gorgeous,' Edwina replied with a wink and a smile. Ralf found that little gesture of hers rather charming, as it was something she'd only just started doing. 'You know, that group…that place…I love it. When are we going back?'

'They've got the Ultravox tribute band this Friday coming,' said Ralf, smiling, 'Pete heard them at the Red Lion in Brentford a couple of weeks ago and he was impressed, and usually when Pete says I'll like something, he's usually right.'

'Well it's a date then,' said Edwina, 'I can clearly see why you guys find that place so addictive.'

'Oh it's just the perfect tonic for a Friday evening. I just hope the council never gets to find out about downstairs – that's why he's kind of…selective of his clientele. He only reveals the downstairs music thing to a select few, and we follow suit. A careful filtering process then, but so far, so good. So remember – it's our *big* secret.'

'My lips are sealed.' replied Edwina, smiling broadly. She disappeared into her office after blowing Ralf a kiss.

Ralf entered his classroom and found his colourful pupils a little more animated than usual. Lawrence was twisting his head to look behind him at the squall at the back of the room, and it appeared that none of them had noticed that Ralf had entered the classroom. Four girls were huddled together to the left of the blackboard while a young boy named Lenny had another boy in a headlock, but their grins clearly stated that they were play-fighting.

'OKAY!' intoned Ralf, with his powerful baritone, 'that's quite enough, and Lenny, please don't kill Sanjiv just yet, not until the lesson's over. And you four young ladies, discussions about tonight's plans can wait a while.'

'But sir,' replied Tanya, of the four young ladies by the blackboard, 'Claudia's got a new fella, and she's telling us all about it!'

'Is she, now?'

'Yeah, apparently he's got a massive knob!'

'Tanya!' exclaimed Ralf, attempting to stifle a smile, and failing miserably, 'size isn't everything!'

'Yeah, sir…said the man with a *small* knob!'

Ralf dropped into the chair at his desk and laughed along with the rest of his class.

After walking around Ealing Broadway that afternoon, Pete found himself compelled to visit *Our Price* records again, this time in search of some jazz, mainly the old style. He was approached by a sales assistant who eventually introduced herself as Sally, and she had quite a passion for jazz and the music of the present day in general. Pete seemed happy to chat at first but Sally's enthusiasm and persistence in following him around the store began to unnerve him. Pete was never one to dislike a good chat to pretty much anyone, especially the subject was shared by both parties.

Sally was very attractive. She had shoulder length dark, brown hair and the only make-up she had was a little eyeshadow and a light lipstick. He was very taken by her and she was quite well-spoken and smiled perpetually, but with every minute that passed by, Pete found himself building a wall that was getting steadily higher and impregnable.

'I'm so sorry,' Sally said, 'I'm just waffling again aren't I...yeah, everybody tells me I waffle when I enjoy chatting to someone I have something in common with...'

'No, that's fine...sorry, I'm being a bit standoffish but I don't mean to be. It's just that I haven't chatted to a female for a while now...'

'Oh you've not been burnt have you...?' enquired Sally, putting a hand upon Pete's arm, and retracting it slowly, caressing his wrist. Pete's skin tingled a little and he was sure he felt himself blush.

'Well...yes, unfortunately I have...'

'Oh...you know I've just gotten myself out of a really dodgy relationship with this college student from Oxford...total knob-end...'

Pete laughed loudly.

'I was going out with him for two months, TWO whole months, then he started going on about introducing me to his mum and dad, and that they had a huge mansion in Surrey...and when he said he was bi-sexual and had a boyfriend who liked to watch while he had sex with a female...that was the last straw...I just told him to stick to his bum-chum and leave me alone. Can you believe it?'

'Have you heard of Mike's Music City?' asked Pete, once he felt able to contain his laughter.

'Yeah, isn't it a pub on Chiswick High Street?'

'Not just a pub…'

'Oh?'

'There's an Ultravox tribute band playing there this Friday…if you fancied coming along…'

'Oh I'd *luuurv* to…but, I don't drive…train to Turnham Green station, that's it. What time's the gig start then?'

'Would you like me to pick you up…doesn't have to be your home address as we've only just met, but perhaps we can meet here and we'll drive there…'

'Okay…it's a date…well, you know, not *a* date as such, but…well, yes…it's a date…oh my, like…yippee!'

Pete had bought only one jazz tape, it was the album, *Give Me the Night,* by George Benson, and he drove home with the title song playing in the car. He was certain that he had eyes upon him at every set of traffic lights he stopped at, as his head was continuously bobbing up and down, side to side, as the title song's addictive rhythm filled the car and flowed through him. The *ba ba ba's* of the backing vocalists fascinated him as they echoed and haunted the background of the song, complimenting George Benson's voice perfectly. Pete giggled at his rather poor attempt at singing along in tune with the music, but he felt he had something to actually sing about – something worth feeling joy for – he'd met the jovial and eccentric Sally, and she would be his date at Mike's Music City.

Edwina entered the staff room and joined Ralf in a spot of lunch. All Ralf could be bothered to come up with was a couple of rounds of peanut butter sandwiches and a little bag of taralli. Edwina offered to share some of her home-prepared crayfish and mango salad with rocket leaves.

'Too bloody healthy for me; at least today, anyway…'

'Oh I nearly forgot…I've got to interview a young lady for the role of maths teacher today. She's replacing Daniel Campion. Have you ever done any interviews?'

'Oh plenty…last one was here, in this school. You conducted it, remember?'

'No silly, I don't mean that. I meant, have you ever conducted an interview?'

'No never. Why?'

'Well…I just wondered…would you like to conduct your first interview today?'

'Why on earth would you want me to do that?' asked Ralf with a rather high pitched inquisitiveness.

'I think you'd be good at it. You have much charm, young man…'

'Thanks for the young.'

'…And I thought of nipping home early…'

'Oh I see…any particular reason?'

'You'll laugh if I tell you.'

'Try me.'

'I'm a Doctor Who fan, and this afternoon's the last time we'll see Tom Baker. He's regenerating into Peter Davison.'

'You sad cow!' said Ralf laughing loudly, 'no, you go for it, girl. I'll give the…conducting the interview a go. Who's the lucky lady?'

'Some lovely lass called Sandy Grice. Know her?'

'Is she blonde, voluptuous, short hair, lives in Acton?'

'That's her. How come you know her then?'

'She was Pete's ex, after Debbie. She seemed okay at the time, then she dumped him over the phone but he had to chase her up to get that response. Another one in a long line of women that take Pete's kindness as a weakness.'

'He's been through some fair old crap lately, hasn't he? I think it's time he found some happiness.'

Ralf walked Edwina to the school gates and gave her a hug and a kiss goodbye, then returned to his class for the last two lessons of the day, English and European Studies, a lesson he particularly enjoyed teaching.

Ozzie was sitting in the lounge with his mother as they enjoyed watching an old comedy re-run on one of the BBC channels. Jackie had her feet up upon a padded stool and they were cosily enveloped in a pair of oversized hairy slippers that resembled roadkill. The rectangular coffee table that stood between them was adorned with the last couple of pieces of fruit cake, empty mugs, and an ashtray containing about half a dozen cigarette ends amidst what looked like a silvery apocalyptic wasteland, with a straight billow of smoke rising from the most recent fag-end.

'I thought you were givin' up fackin' smokin' mum.'

'I will…just bear wiv me. It's me only vice at the moment, son…ain't got much else goin' on.'

'Remember what the doctor said…'

'I know what he said, Ozzie. I'm working on it, okay?' replied Jackie, turning to face her son and with a stern look on her face.

'Alright mum. I'm just sayin' that's all. It's only 'cause I care aboutcha.'

'Did you speak to Kim yesterday? Is she comin' down tomorrow or not?'

'I spoke to her but she ain't sure if she's gonna make it. She might come in the evening only.'

'I saw Julia in the high street today.'

Ozzie turned to look at his mum. He didn't care too much about his ex, but he was curious to know if Julia and his mum chatted and what they talked about.

'She tried to say she was sorry. She shed a couple of tears as well. We had coffee and a good old chat.'

'You had coffee with her?'

'Two actually…'

'What did you chat about then?' asked Ozzie sighing and putting his head back on the sofa.

'Oh, this and that…'

'A bit more info, mum…'

'She's sorry she abandoned you…us. She misses you…apparently.'

'You don't sound convinced.'

'I've been round the old block many a time, son. I listened, but I wouldn't trust her as far as I could throw her. She's fuckin' flaky as shit…she did it once, she'll do it again…first sign of more trouble, and she's off out the back door. Fuckin' cheek! Two coffees, I bought her!'

Ozzie closed his eyes and smiled.

Ralf turned the key in his front door and stepped inside a quiet house. There was no reply the first time he called out to Loredana, but he heard two feet thudding onto the floor upstairs and she came slowly down. Ralf felt slightly unnerved. He felt a storm brewing when he looked into her eyes and he wasn't wrong when he asked her what was the matter.

'Who wos dat woman you kees and caddol? Why you do dat? I em you girlfriend, not she!'

'Relax, Loredana. Edwina is just a good friend, that's all.'

'Stronzate!' yelled Loredana. Her eyes were wide and her skin had become pale with a rising anger inside of her. 'Stai dicendo stronzate!'

'I don't understand what you're saying…'

'YOU understand very well!' she hissed, as she came up and stood just centimetres away from his face. Loredana snatched her coat from the nearby wall hooks and pushed Ralf aside as she opened the front door to let herself out. She stormed off around the corner while a baffled Ralf remained at the door. He stood there until he could no longer hear her piercing footsteps on the pavement. Ralf closed the door behind him and sighed deeply; he wasn't certain if it was with relief, but at that moment he was glad she went. He thought about her words – *stai dicendo stronzate* – they whined loudly in his mind like a siren. *Stai dicendo stronzate. You're talking shit!* He was certain she knew. He was almost certain that she was probably a part of the revenge plot devised by Francesco, the stalker. A honey trap? Ralf had a strong feeling he hadn't seen the last of Loredana.

Chapter 28

Pete was at home in his bedroom. The silence of the house sank into his bones and always sent him upstairs eventually, even if he had the television on. Despite coming to terms with the loss of his parents and finding some sort of balance in his life, Pete still felt disquieted every time he came home. Once he'd fixed himself some dinner he knew that when he went into the lounge and sat down with the plate of food upon his lap, those unwanted feelings would take hold of him again. He sat in his usual place, the armchair that faced toward the window, with the sofa to his left and the television to his right. That was the problem; that was when he would miss his parents more than anything. If he focused on the window, he could still see the blurred outlines of his mum and dad on the sofa, with his peripheral vision. Pete always felt that after you lost a loved one, it was always that part of your eyes that would pick up on fugacious shadows and flickering lights. He drew the curtains from then on.

Pete had bought himself one of those folding trays that were used to have breakfast in bed and dinner times were now enjoyed in his bedroom. It felt warmer up there as well, and Pete felt safer. He hated that word. It was like an echoing, mischievous little spirit in his mind that would dart about only to remind him of the ghosts that he felt were still lurking around downstairs. As much as he hated to think that way, he did indeed feel safer upstairs in his bedroom. At night he slept with his stereo system playing gentle and soothing music so he wouldn't hear the rest of the house creak and groan from age and sometimes weather. The music would be turned up a little higher if it was windy outside, as every time a stronger breath of wind hit the wooden doors of the little shack just outside the kitchen door to the garden, it sounded as if there were footsteps in the kitchen. Susan often got up in the middle of the night to make a cup of tea, and the noises were almost the same.

Earlier that morning, Pete left the office to pop into the sandwich shop that was just across the road from where he worked. While he waited for a quick window of opportunity to dart to the traffic island in the middle of the busy main road, he saw Debbie coming out of the sandwich place cradling a large paper bag full of food and cups of hot beverages. She saw him too and the look of awkwardness and embarrassment upon her face angered Pete. He was aware of his own face morphing into a scowl as he watched her attempting to look for her own opportunity to avoid him. It came, as two buses approached from either side and as they crossed paths with each other, those few seconds were all it took for Debbie to hurry on further down the road and appear several feet away from him. She dashed to the traffic island, continuing to look ahead of her, avoiding all eye contact with Pete, who didn't take his eyes off of her for a single second. Pete watched her from the traffic island, as she reached the other side of the road and vanished through a pair of large wooden doors and into the old and grotty edifice of an estate agent's firm. Selling shoes didn't pay so well then, he thought.

Ralf greeted a rather confident but slightly bedevilled Sandy Grice as she stepped into Edwina's office for her interview.

'Don't I know you from somewhere?' she asked.

'For your sins, yes you do,' replied Ralf with a chuckle. 'You're my best friend's ex-girlfriend, but no matter. Please don't let that get in the way of our meeting, will you…'

'I guess you're right, it's old news now, totally forgotten.'

'So…I take it you have teaching experience right?'

'Oh yes, I taught at St. Anne's for three years, mainly English and geography, but they realised that maths was more my thing, so the remaining eighteen months were all for the mathematics group. After that I taught at Drayton Manor for four years, then moved on to teach at Cardinal Newman for three more years until just two weeks ago, when they announced that they were merging with Cardinal Wiseman. The old building is going to be used as a Japanese school now, from what I hear.'

'Okay…you've got the job, congratulations. Now bugger off, because I hate conducting interviews!'

Sandy remained in her seat with a gaping jaw while Ralf gathered up his paperwork, ready to flee the scene as fast as he could.

'Still here? Do you need any help picking your jaw up from the floor?'

'Is that it?'

'Yeah. Now tell me why you dumped Peter so brutally.'

'Do I get to keep the job for being brutally honest?'

'Go on…' said Ralf with a smile and his leg propped up on the chair.

'Bit of a schmuck, clingy as hell, and bloody pompous. Sorry, but that just doesn't do it for me.'

'Well you certainly are honest; and that's a very good thing here. Good quality for a teacher. When can you start?'

'Well…I don't really have a notice period as such…they sprang it on me rather quickly, that Newman was merging, so I'm pretty much available as and when.'

'Okay, how about in a week's time, let's say Monday week? That's just over ten days away, so take some time to gather your thoughts and I'll see you then. Welcome to the fray!'

Ralf went home shortly after the interview and barely got inside the front door when the phone rang. It was Pete.

'Hello mate, listen…I can't really keep it in any longer, but…I have a date for this Friday. She's agreed to come to Mike's to hear that Ultravox tribute group. I met her at Our Price while I was choosing some Jazz…yeah, I know. Jazz. I just wanted something to play on the stereo system at night time.'

'Hey that's great, bro. I'm made up for you. You sound a heck of a lot more cheerful when you meet a woman.'

'Yeah I do, don't I?'

'It's good to hear. I, on the other hand, have some other news but I'm sure it won't bother you as much…'

'Oh…okay, hit me.'

'I interviewed and gave the job to the new maths teacher today. It's none other than your ex that you had for a short time, that girl called Sandy.'

'You're kidding…really?'

'Yep, it's her. Apparently, she's got a lot of teaching experience, especially maths beside other subjects. I think she'd be ideal. Just thought I'd tell you. You *do* know that if it were Debbie being interviewed I wouldn't give her the job...you know that.'

'I know mate...speaking of which...I saw her today across the street from where I work. She was coming out of the sandwich shop that I was headed for. She saw me and the bitch had the nerve to ignore me *and* run off to cross the road further down, so she could avoid me. Cheek of the bitch. She treats me like shit, then she runs away!'

'Yeah...amazing how these people sleep at night. Still, you're better off without her. So what's this new one's name then?'

'Sally's her name, and she's bloody potty as hell, but really sweet. I'm officially enthusiastic!'

'Loredana stormed out the other evening. She saw me giving Edwina a hug and a kiss...friendly like, nothing like what she thought, but she was furious.'

'Oh, I'm sorry mate...there's me waffling on with my news...'

'Nah, don't sweat it. But I know she's onto me. She knows I'm Italian *and* I'm certain she was in on the Francesco thing. It's not just my burning gut-feeling. It's no hunch, she's coming back...and not to re-ignite old love either...'

'Shit...maybe you should stay at my place for a bit. She doesn't know where I live...'

'I won't drop you in any danger Pete, you know that...'

'Come on Ralf, she has no idea where I live, mate. If you're worried, it's a safer bet, don't you think?'

'I'll think about it...'

'You stubborn bastard!'

Ozzie was relaxing in his mum's armchair after she had turned in for the night. He was watching one of his favourite videos of all time, one of those classics that he would watch repeatedly when the mood took him. When he wasn't in a rock music kind of mood, he would often be in a movie mood, and tonight was the turn of the film, Alien. Ozzie was a real sci-fi fan at the best of times and it was something instilled in him by Pete who was also a fan of all things sci-fi. Even Ralf was hooked after watching that movie; so much so, that he got into the original Star Trek series which he now owned on video and would watch when he felt like being alone, which was quite often. Ozzie on the other hand, didn't like to be too alone. He had got used to Julia now and therefore in his eyes, being alone wasn't an option; until the day when she had decided she couldn't take any more of the crap that was going on in his life.

Ozzie was quite angry with Julia; not completely though, as it was his mother that was present when she apparently stormed out, but he knew that Jackie wouldn't lie or even exaggerate things. She would have shown support even if she had disliked Julia, but Jackie was overly disappointed in her flaky behaviour. Ozzie was beginning to lose concentration while watching his movie. Julia had come into his mind now, and each time he thought about her, he would get that combination of butterflies and disillusionment. He often thought of just going over to her house and having it out with her, but his pride and disappointment in her always got the better of him and he let it be. He was never one for the chase. For Ozzie you either had genuine and honest feelings or nothing; one slight sign of any mind game or playing hard to get, and you were finished. In other words, once Ozzie said *fuck off,* that was it.

He switched off the film around three quarters of the way through and remained on the armchair, hunched forward and with his chin resting in his hands. Ozzie sat in the same position until the early hours, when twilight was just starting to break and the birds began gossiping. At around nine o'clock he made some coffee and toast and rang Julia. She answered the phone with a croaky morning *hello.*

'It's me. Mum said you saw each other yesterday…'

'Yeah…we did. You okay?'

'As okay as I *can* be…why did you just walk off like that?'

'I'm sorry…'

'Sorry don't cut it, darlin'

'Look…I just felt that it was getting too much for me. What with the Andrew Blaine thing, you going missing for days, then once we'd got you home, you stormed off again. What was I meant to do? Try to see it from my point of view, Ozzie; what was I supposed to think? I do love you but I need someone more stable in my life…I got used to your funny ways of looking at stuff, and bloody hell, I actually found them hilarious and charming. It's just that when you went off the rails…then you went off the radar as well…sorry. I just couldn't cope with it.'

'I'm sorry I'm not the perfect man you're lookin' for.'

'Oh, I'm not perfect either, Ozzie…don't be silly. I'm not expecting that. Just some form of…normality…stability, that's all. I do miss you…I do, but…I'll admit that I'm a little scared of what'll happen next. Surely you can understand that.'

'I do…I do, and I'm sorry. You know…all my life all I ever dreamed about was havin' a really nice bird, a nice bird like you. I've had loadsa girlfriends, but none that really…got me, ya know…none that actually made me head spin…til you came along…this slightly posh bird who's a fackin' blow job queen and all…I was scared at first, and I was gonna end it with you too, just like all them other birds…but I thought about it…I just didn't wanna be alone anymore. I know I gotta nasty temper, but it only comes out when I need to protect people I love…friends, family, and all…sometimes I make stupid decisions as well. Like when we saw my mate, Garry Peters and he offered me that job. I just thought I could start working proper like, you know…full time and earn some good dosh. I didn't know that we had to deliver fackin' drug packages to these rich people…'

Julia began sobbing as she listened to her beloved Ozzie pen his heart to her. She was touched by his sincerity, his honesty, and his desire to do things right. A part of her really wanted to just say, *sod it, let's give it another go*…but the other part of her, the sensible part, kept telling her; *yeah, until the next time…*

'Mum nearly died one night…she fell and hit her head and I called 999 and they just managed to get here in time…they saved her because I used my head quickly. That's why I know I'm ready for you. I was thinkin' of toppin' meself, then this happened…mum needed me and I was there…all I'm askin' is you give me…us another chance. If I fuck up again, then go and never talk to me ever again…but I need you, Julia…I love ya…'

'Oh…dearest, dearest Ozzie…' Julia was in almost uncontrollable floods of tears now. Ozzie meant everything he was saying and she knew it. Her heart was melting by the second and her legs were buckling from feeling like jelly, so she sat upon the floor of the hallway and crossed her legs, like children in an assembly hall. 'Oh fuck it, let's give it another try…come here now and fuck my brains out!'

'I'm coming!'

'What already? You desperate and ravenous bastard, come over here now!'

Ozzie put on his trusted black leather jacket, slapped on some of his musky after shave and ran upstairs to check on his mother. She was snoring steadily, so he dashed down the stairs and ran out into the cold air of the morning. As the cold sting of the winter air lashed at his face and neck, Ozzie began feeling like a man again. That man he always wanted to be, and that the love of a good woman could bring out in him.

Ralf was dialling a number on his phone. He was feeling anxious like he'd never felt in a long time. It was time to air on the side of caution now. Loredana had gone, but Ralf knew that she was still out there, skulking in the shadows, watching and waiting. Ralf's anxieties were very much like weather pains; rather than have headaches or achy limbs when the weather was about to morph from serene to menacing, Ralf had waves of anxiety that would sweep over him every time he thought that something would happen, and in this case it was on a scale of around six out of ten; not a huge amount, but he had a pretty good hunch – and he relied on those as well – that Loredana was the only threat that was left to deal with…or eliminate.

Jeff Mallory answered the phone and his dulcet Yorkshire tones always soothed and amused Ralf.

'Hey mate, how you doing?'

'Not too bad Jeff. How's the situation with the lady?'

'Finally gone, but she still wouldn't admit it. Stupid cow only saw sense when I showed her film footage that I took with my cam. I hid it under a coat on the back of the chair in the bedroom.'

'I'm sorry to hear this mate. I know it hurts...'

'Nah, that's fine matey, really. Once she knew she was caught out, the split was quite amicable. I'm working on this other girl in forensics. Tits like melons and a figure like an hour glass...anyway, how's things your end?'

Ralf went into detail about Loredana, from the first meeting to when she stormed out, including the jealous tendencies. Jeff agreed that there was definitely something to be cautious about. She would definitely be back.

'I doubt she's got anything going on with Raymond Franklin, but I'm bloody sure that she and Francesco were in on getting back at me. I can surely tell you...she is fucked in the head. But I don't want any more blood on my hands. It's starting to wear me down now...I'm starting to find it a little too easy.'

'That's what happens when your life's in danger mate, but I can get you a piece if you want. I'll get it to you by internal courier. The girl in the postroom is a friend of mine and she won't ask questions. It'll be with you tomorrow afternoon. That okay?'

'Jeff, you're a true star as well as my good friend from the north, you Yorkshire scoundrel you...'

'No worries, mate...I'll be down to see you as soon as I can shake off a bit of work up here. Look after yourself, mate!'

'Will do. You too, bro!'

Ralf put the phone down and noticed a figure across the road standing by the school gates. He pulled back the translucent curtain and saw that it was Loredana. She was glaring at him in such a way that he became perturbed; and that took a lot of doing to someone like Ralf, but her eyes looked sullen and sunken in, as though she hadn't slept for days. Her skin was pale against her red overcoat and she looked like the walking dead. Ralf rushed to the front door but once he opened it, Loredana was gone, just like the phantasm she resembled. He crossed the street and walked up to the corner of Hawkshead

Road but there was no sign of her. He crouched down and looked beneath the parked cars but still no sign. Ralf decided to phone Edwina at home and warn her about his ex. Edwina told Ralf that she would take a few days off as they were owed to her, and she could even do it at short notice. Ralf was relieved and wondered if it was time to reveal his secret to another. He pondered before packing a few things and leaving the house. He thought he would take up Pete's offer.

Chapter 29

Friday morning was hectic for Ralf. He hadn't slept too well at Pete's house, as the folding bed was rather uncomfortable. It was wide, but felt like it had rift cutting it down the middle and he was rudely awoken every time he shifted toward it, feeling as though he were about to tumble into an abyss. He'd also forgotten how long the journey was from Pete's house to Hawkshead Road and the crawling commuter traffic didn't help either.

Ralf entered the school building with only a minute to spare and upon reaching his classroom, he found two of his pupils brawling over something trivial. After separating the two and putting them outside in the playground for the duration of the first lesson, he pretty much left his pupils to their own devices after giving them instruction on the task at hand. He dropped off at his desk, much to the amusement of the class, whose rising titters awoke him. He laughed it off himself, and proceeded to chat with his class about Mike's Music City, but not of what lies beneath at the weekend. He felt honoured to share his musical taste with the alumni as well, and quite a few of them showed some talent with either vocals or playing an instrument.

At that point, Alistair Evans pulled out a harmonica from his bag and gave a couple of tunes, and the whole classroom engaged in both clapping and singing along with the tunes Alistair produced. The classroom door opened abruptly and the music teacher entered with a scowl upon her face. The room went silent almost instantaneously as she directed her hot glare toward Ralf.

'Thank you, and I should like to remind you, Mr Avalon, that *I* am the music teacher in this school and if there is any melodious activity to be performed it will be in my classroom and mine alone. You boy, give me that harmonica. You shall have it back when I see fit!'

Mrs Mortimer was a fifty-something lady of slight frame and with tied up hair in a bun. She was extremely cultured and well-spoken and of the old-school ilk. The female pupils feared her while the male ones often ridiculed her Shakespearean inflection and decisive march when her back was turned. She knew they did. The woman wasn't daft, but she didn't care. They were on their best behaviour when she was present and that was enough for her.

'Excuse me, Mrs Mortimer, but this is my classroom and if there's any confiscating to be done, it will be me and me alone that will decide it. Are we clear?'

The stern lady stopped in her tracks and gave Ralf yet another death-stare, looked at the class, and left the room, closing the door gently behind her. Lawrence and Alistair both punched the air with a pronounced whisper of; *Yesss, that's what I'm talking about*!

Ralf pointed a finger at the pair of them in admonishment, but at the same time, approval. The class could read him well. They knew he couldn't stand the sight of Mrs Mortimer and they also knew that she would have had the extreme pleasure of being headmistress. She resented Edwina Clare ever since she was awarded the role, but the two ladies never really liked each other that much anyway, and the only words they ever exchanged were strictly work related.

On the corner of Altenburg Avenue, John Price stood in wait for his girlfriend of over a year, Marie Dunston. They had both been staying at John's parents' house in Wales, while John assisted his father with the family business he started a few months ago, selling used cars. The couple had been back in London for just over a week as John had a job interview for a part-time position at a new record shop that opened in Ealing Broadway. Marie was a friend of Debbie Graves and the two had known each other since high school, yet Marie was never introduced properly to Pete, and had only exchanged a few words with him at a party. They were, however, good friends with Ozzie.

Marie emerged from the dental practice just across the road and John examined her two white fillings. 'Yep, very good,' he said, 'you can hardly see them.'

They went for a coffee at the café with the nautical theme and Ozzie joined them shortly after, and with the lovely Julia in tow. Her sister Nicky was also with them.

'So what's been happening with you two then?' asked John. 'From what I heard, you've been in the wars...'

'Tell me about it,' replied Julia, 'I've been having to put up with this pain in the bum.'

'You dumped him and walked off...that was what *I* heard...' Marie interjected, 'so how is *he* a pain in the bum, then?'

Julia's freckled cheeks reddened slightly and she looked down at her coffee cup, unsure of how to answer. Nicky touched her leg reassuringly beneath the table.

'It's okay, Marie. We've sorted things now. We all make mistakes...' Ozzie said, trying not to get pissed off.

'On a more positive note,' John intoned, smiling, 'I'll be working part time at Roxeene records in Ealing Broadway as from a week Monday. Isn't that great? That means discounted records, yeah!'

'That's brilliant news, John,' Ozzie said, 'so you can get us the new Asia album.' Ozzie let out his machine gun laugh.

'Yeah, no probs, mate. Will do...I like 'em as well.'

'So what music are *you* into then, Nicky?' Marie asked.

'Oh, same as Ozzie. I like some of the electronic stuff as well, but rock is really my thing...ACDC, Motorhead, and I love Asia.'

'Are you coming to the Ultravox tribute band tonight, Nicky?' Ozzie asked her.

'Um, yeah, I guess...is Ralf coming?'

'Yeah,' replied Ozzie, with a chuckle, 'he'll be there...'

Ozzie explained to John and Marie about Mike's Music City and the very secret underground live music weekends and after swearing that they would never reveal what happens, they felt very enthusiastic about going along. Marie especially, a she was a huge Ultravox fan.

Nicky was a very pretty girl, with short blonde hair and blue eyes, and her skin was clear and not freckly like her sister's. She'd had a thing for Ralf for quite some time now and she was sure that he felt some kind of spark for her; he just never followed it through for some reason. They never chatted for long enough for Nicky to probe any deeper and so he remained a bit of a mystery to her, but she knew that she fancied him. Ralf always had this inner temptation to go out with Nicky, but when it got to nearer the time, he would back out at the last minute. He did find her incredibly attractive but despite her reputation for being an extremely good kisser, he remained elusive.

It was in his forties that Ralf was enjoying increased female attention, as when he was still a monk back when he was in his twenties, the clerical habit would quite often put off the opposite sex. Ralf was a sensitive soul at heart, but it seemed a long time ago now. He would often cry at tear-jerker movies and swoon when he encountered a charming and affectionate toddler or playful and adorable puppy or kitten. Now it appeared that he needed to don his cagey attire and raise up barriers to keep away those that should not get too close, like gargoyles on a church to ward off evil spirits. He disliked being this way, but over time he had gotten used to it. Only Pete ever saw his real self, but only recently began doubting it when he learned of Ralf's past.

Marie on the other hand, bore a powerful grudge against both Debbie and Julia; Debbie because she was disappointed in her and Julia because of her apparent lack of loyalty and staying power and Marie was someone who wouldn't mince her words. She had already marked Julia's card back at the café and she wasn't going to leave it there either, regardless of Ozzie's feelings. That was her bad point; when he had something to say, she didn't care what consequences would arise and who she would hurt in the process. What had to be said would be said.

John was a more mild mannered soul who always wore a big beaming smile upon his face. John was a man who saw positivity in every person and every situation; a storm would be followed by clear skies and sunshine, a bad day would always hide a bright side, and so on. Any day without laughter was a wasted day in his eyes, and it would sometimes irritate Marie, who classed herself as a realist; be positive, yes, but don't overdo it. Shit does happen.

'You smell nice, John, is that aftershave what I think it is?' Julia asked, perfectly innocently.

'It's called mind your own business aftershave!' replied Marie, deliberately not making any eye contact.

Ozzie looked up and at that moment, hated Marie. He knew her well and unless he or someone else would dilute the situation and edge out the dark clouds, the day would end up with no silver lining at all. He looked at John, who in turn looked at his girlfriend with a little disdain. He shushed her gently.

'Is there some kind of problem?' asked Julia.

'You're the problem, you flaky cow. I've seen your kind many times before; the slightest hint of trouble or little problems, and you're heading for the back door!'

'I don't need to justify myself to you, Ozzie and I have sorted things out. I made a mistake and chickened out, but now I'm back. Leave it, okay?'

Ozzie's gaze crossed Marie's scowl and the look of disappointment and slight sadness on his face did little to stay Marie's onslaught; it only fuelled her more and she continued.

'Hey,' said John calmly, 'do you have to start a fight wherever we go? We haven't seen Ozzie for ages, let's just enjoy each other's company for a while...'

'Oh shut up, Mr Positive...always trying to see the good in everyone...*ooh, look on the positive side, think positive, always look for the positive*...for fuck's sake, get a grip!'

'Not necessary, Marie,' John said, rising from his seat and heading outside for a cigarette, 'I'm positive yes, and I don't always pick fights either...'

John could still hear the two ladies bickering from outside the café, although he couldn't discern what they were saying. The raised voices were steadily becoming stronger and he knew that Marie wouldn't let up; not until she was satisfied that she had either truly hurt Julia's feelings or reduced her to tears. The door opened abruptly behind him, hitting him on the back and propelling him toward the edge of the pavement. It was Ozzie, and he was red-faced with anger.

'I'm fackin' fed up of this. I ain't seen you and Marie for ages, and I wish I hadn't seen *her*. Sorry mate, but your bird's out of order!'

Julia brushed past Ozzie and crossed the road without even looking, causing several vehicles to slam their brakes on and sound their horns almost in unison. Julia marched briskly onward, not looking back. Ozzie put out the cigarette he had just lit and set off after her. John felt drained and angry at the umpteenth outburst from Marie. He could feel his positivity rapidly dwindling, as his girlfriend was still yelling abuse across the street to Julia, while Ozzie broke into a run to catch up to her.

'Are you happy now?' John asked her, this time with slightly raised voice, 'are you totally happy now that you've finally proved your point *and* fucked up the whole afternoon not to mention the evening out? What's wrong with you, Marie, for fuck's sake, woman!?'

John seldom swore. He rarely even raised his voice unless it was to call Marie downstairs for dinner at his parents' house in Wales, or to summon the family beagle. Marie was gobsmacked at his outburst and she couldn't take her eyes off him either. John was red-faced, just like Ozzie, and for the first time since she'd known him, he was wearing a rather frightening scowl upon his face.

'Do me a favour,' john said, curtly, 'go home…just go home and pack your things, go to my mum and dad's for a bit. That place seems to relax you. Go and cool down and come back when you've finally learnt how to control that poisonous gob of yours!'

John walked away from her, after casting his cigarette stub at her feet. Marie stood there and watched in horror and disbelief, as her boyfriend, her once gentle and sweet boyfriend walked rapidly away from her. Nicky stood there and stared at her, emotionless. She wasn't sure what to say and how to feel; it was quite new to her, that someone could just explode like that relentlessly.

'What are *you* looking at, stupid!?'

'I'm not stupid…and I'm *looking*, at absolutely nothing at all.' replied Nicky, and walked away. Marie stood outside the café for a long while, until the elderly owner emerged from deep inside and touched her gently on the shoulder.

'Your beverages need paying for, darling.'

Marie went inside and settled the bill.

Ozzie finally caught up with Julia, who was just entering her car. Ozzie went quickly around to the passenger seat and launched himself inside before she could move off, and in the state she was in, she probably would have gone and left him there.

'Why are you stopping?' Ozzie asked, as she pulled over between a car and a bus.

'Look…just get out of the car, I want to go home…'

'You live with me and mum, Julia…which home do you mean?'

'I mean my own home, Ozzie. Marie's right. I'm no good for you. I am flaky, look at me now…someone yells at me and I just want to walk away from everything. That's hardly somebody with staying power, is it?'

'Look, you're just upset. I didn't expect her to come out with that crap…nobody did…'

'I just want a nice and easy life with no dramas and since I met you, it's just been one thing after another; and it's not going to end here…this is you all over, Ozzie. I do love you…really I do, but I'm not good at dealing with all this crappy stuff and confrontation…I just can't.'

'Julia, people argue all the time. You can't head for the hills every time the shit hits the fan, that's just life!'

'It's a life I don't want…sorry.'

'So you're saying that you don't want to be with me anymore, you're leaving…again.'

Julia nodded her head while searching for a tissue in the car. Ozzie took one from his jacket pocket and handed it to her. She dried her eyes and stuffed it in her sleeve. Ozzie waited until she calmed down before trying to take hold of her hand. Julia withdrew it from his gentle grasp and looked away from him, and out of the driver window.

'Please go…' she whispered. Ozzie got out of the vehicle and just before closing the door, whispered some words of his own; 'Please don't contact me anymore.' He shut the car door and slowly walked away.

John was at the top of the street where Julia parked her car and waited until Ozzie walked up to where he was standing.

'You alright, mate?'

'No, I'm not,' replied Ozzie, 'thanks to your girlfriend, *my* girlfriend's just dumped me. Listen mate...I need to be alone. As long as you're with that woman, just don't come anywhere near me, okay?'

Ozzie walked away as fast as he could, so as not to engage in any more conversation, *and* to possibly avoid hitting John very hard.

John went home to his flat. Marie was on the sofa with a hit drink and a video. She smiled as her boyfriend walked through the door and beckoned him over for a cuddle. John looked at her with a sneer on his lips that unnerved Marie.

'What's the matter with you? Come and sit down for a cuddle-up. I put a nice romantic film on.'

'What did I tell you just a little while ago?' John asked calmly.

'Oh come on, surely you didn't mean that...'

'I just saw Ozzie. Julia just dumped him...'

'Ha, told you...she's a stupid cow!'

'That's beside the point!'

'Don't shout, John...you even swore outside, where people could hear you. Since when do you yell and swear at me?'

'I'm fed up of your disgusting attitude toward people. Ozzie told me he doesn't want to see me anymore...because of you. He said as long as I'm with you, I've got to keep away from him. Thanks very much, your bloody big mouth has possibly lost me a good friend that I've known for years!'

'Well, I know him too!'

'He's never liked you. He's only ever tolerated you. I told you to get out of here and go to my mum's...now I'm telling you to get out and go wherever the bloody hell you want. Just get out of my sight.'

'You just go and calm down, I'll make you a nice cuppa and we'll just forget about the whole thing. Who needs them anyway? We've got each other, right?'

John took hold of Marie's wrist and squeezed a little more tightly than he intended to, making her wince.

'I'm not joking.' John said quietly, but with a snarling whisper.

'You're hurting me...'

'Get the hell out of here and stay away from me, you nasty, spiteful little bitch!'

John went into the bedroom and slammed the door behind him. Marie waited for around an hour for him to emerge and after tapping gently on the door and whispering his name, his forceful and foul-mouthed response made her understand once and for all, that her time with him was over.

Ralf answered his phone just before he was about to go out to Mike's place with Pete. It was Nicky.

'Well what a surprise...actually I can't really chat now, I'm on my way out...'

'I know, Ozzie and Julia told me...but I think Ozzie's not coming. I just saw him at the London Apprentice...he was rather drunk. Not totally inebriated, but...getting there.'

'What's happened?'

'Well we met up with some old friends of his and his mate's girlfriend started mouthing off to Julia about how she's flaky and that she's met her type before...before you knew it, they were screaming at each other in the café just down from where Pete lives. Now Julia's dumped Ozzie again and John's dumped Marie. Ozzie also told John that he doesn't want to see him anymore, as long as he's with Marie. So there you have it. We were supposed to come to this gig as well, but that's out the window now.'

'Oh, bloody great. Okay, I'll go get Ozzie. Pete's already at the pub, so he'll be wondering where I've got to...never mind. Thanks for telling me...nice to hear from you, despite circumstances...'

'Can I come with you? I actually like Ozzie and I'd like to help, if that's okay…'

'I don't see why not. Okay, where are you calling from?'

'I'm in a phone box across the road from the Red Lion in Brentford.'

'Okay, I'll come get you. It's on the way. See you in ten.'

Ozzie was sat at the bar in The Apprentice and was tipsy, but in control of his faculties and relieved to see Ralf but not so much to see that Nicky was with him. They led him out of the pub with each of his arms around their shoulders and to the Ford Capri. As they drove away, Ozzie fell asleep while slumped across the back seat.

'I hope he doesn't vomit.' murmured Ralf.

After dropping Ozzie at his home, Ralf and Nicky drove to Hawkshead Road. Ralf turned the key in his front door whilst looking around him carefully. Nicky asked why he was doing it, but he replied by telling her that there had been a burglary in the adjoining Greenend Road and he was wary. Nicky knew it was bullshit; that area was one of the quietest and nicest parts in Chiswick.

Nicky made herself comfortable on the sofa while Ralf made a couple of coffees. The room was warm thanks to the central heating and Nicky was intrigued by the imposing antlers. She asked about them as Ralf came into the room with two mugs of coffee and a biscuit tin.

'Everyone asks about those. They belonged to my auntie and uncle. I don't know where they got them from, but they always scared the crap out of me when I was younger. I know…that's funny and I'm a big, grown man, but they do freak me out still today. At night, especially, if I'm down here reading or listening to music with just the side lamp on. I turn around and they're up there, looking down on me.'

'Shame about today,' Nicky said, 'I was looking forward to the gig. I'm sure Pete will fill you in on how brilliant they were.'

'That, he certainly will.'

'Are you two still making music together?'

'Oh yeah, that always features in our lives.'

'Do you have anything I can listen to, then?'

'Pete has the tapes, but it's all mainly in the form of demos, so it's not complete. I'll get one of the cassettes off him and play you one, but remember, they're only demos.'

'You know… you really intrigue me…' Nicky said.

'Oh, why is that?'

'You just strike me as someone who has secrets that he won't share with anyone.'

'Like…'

'Oh, let me think now…I'd say you're a…mass murderer.'

Ralf turned his sudden glare quickly into a flamboyant laugh.

'Well, have you killed anyone?' Nicky said jokily.

'Well…if you can count the odd house spider, some ants, and the occasional housefly, then yes…I'm a mass murderer.'

Ralf sipped his coffee and leant his head back upon the sofa.

'You've been rather hard to pin down. I've been wanting to go for a drink with you for ages.'

'Well you're here now; and we're drinking, just not anything stiff.'

'Bloody hell Ralf, you don't half put those barriers up…'

'Don't take it personally, sweetheart. It's complicated.'

'Try me.'

'No.'

'Oh come on, you man of few words, you…'

'Nicky, leave it, sweetheart.'

Nicky placed her empty mug on the coffee table and knelt down in front of Ralf. She moved closer and kissed him several times upon the lips, the last kiss taking a more passionate turn, as their tongues briefly collided. Ralf moved away momentarily and took a long look at Nicky's features in the half-light of the side-lamp. She was certainly pretty and her hair was soft to the touch and felt silky smooth. Her blue eyes reflected the abat-jour's suffused light as she moved in for another kiss. This time Ralf responded with more warmth, taking her head in his hands and running his fingers through her hair. She murmured and sighed, as he touched her face and cheeks.

'That's better.' she said, and kissed him with more passion than before. Ralf agreed with the rumours; she was indeed a splendid kisser. They both made their way upstairs into the bedroom and closed the door to the world, for the rest of the night.

Chapter 30

Ralf woke up early and eased himself out of bed slowly, so to not wake Nicky who appeared to be sleeping most soundly. Ralf put his dressing gown on and stood at the side of the bed, scrutinizing every part of Nicky's naked body. She was laying on her right side and had her back toward where Ralf was standing. She was beautiful, almost statuesque. Her body curved perfectly in all the right places and she was not slim by any means, but not overweight either. She was more on the voluptuous side and her skin tone was perfect and smooth.

Ralf found the duvet at the other end of the bedroom, as though the previous night had given it a mind of its own, and covered Nicky with it. He went downstairs and put the kettle on while hunting for some of his favourite muesli. As soon as he heard Nicky moving around upstairs, Ralf took another mug from the wooden tree by the kettle and proceeded to make her an instant coffee. He placed both mugs upon the kitchen table and sat until Nicky came into the kitchen. She smiled at him as she stood in the doorway before shuffling in and straddling him. A slow and passionate kiss followed.

'Haven't you had enough, young lady?'

'Well…if you let me stay another night, I'll think about it…'

They kissed again and Ralf felt himself becoming aroused once more. Nicky felt it through his dressing gown and began feeling her way down there, but Ralf stopped her gently.

'How about we have a nice substantial breakfast and then do something with the day?' he said.

'I think that's a lovely idea. I fancy some eggs; after last night, I feel I could do with a protein buzz.'

Pete put the phone back on the receiver for the seventh time at least, and was now starting to worry about his best friend but at the same time he was feeling as though he were the cow from the famous nursery rhyme, the one that jumped over the moon. He couldn't wait to tell Ralf that he and Sally had a great time at the gig and that they both went back to her place for a nightcap. Pete had stayed there until around three in the morning and that he was sure that this time, he had found someone he really wanted to be with, a perfect match, even though she was a bit odd. Pete decided that he quite liked 'odd.' Life would certainly be les boring now that little Miss 'Odd,' had come into his life. *Nothing odd about those tits,* he thought, *if she hadn't shoved them in my face, I would never have grabbed them, and I would never have known that I'm a boob man.*

Nicky and Ralf had cooked, eaten, and washed up together and after a couple mugs each of great tasting filter coffee, they were relaxing in the lounge and finding out that they had more things in common than they could have imagined. They both liked horror films and of the same genre – Ralf had gone off the gory ones, as seeing gallons of blood flow on screen after a hapless fool had been eviscerated was now becoming stale – but both he and Nicky had a growing fondness and enthusiasm for a good and creepy ghost story and anything highly supernatural including demonic possession.

Nicky liked cooking and particularly liked Italian food. Ralf revealed that he was a keen chef when in the kitchen and rather good at producing Italian dishes, but obviously held back about his backstory. Nicky also shared Ralf's fascination with the night. Like him, she loved the drastic difference between the dark and the day, the palpable mystery and atmosphere, the haunting sounds of the urban nocturne – they both could have sworn that an owl could occasionally be heard somewhere out there, perched upon the branch of who knows what tree...

They agreed to go out for a night walk after midnight, when all was quiet. Ralf hadn't done it in a long while and the thought of planning it with someone who loved it as much as he did, made the butterflies in his stomach swirl in an insane frenzy.

'We've got a few hours yet, so I guess we could go out somewhere, perhaps grab some lunch and go somewhere nice; away from the suburbs. What do you say?'

'That sounds lovely.' Nicky said.

As they both stepped out the front door, Ralf felt disquieted and a little anxious. It felt like one of his gut feelings. The butterflies had fled and taken shelter and the euphoria was suddenly replaced with an inexplicable dread. He tried keeping it hidden from Nicky, but he could tell that she'd noticed something. Ralf could see with the corner of his eye that she kept looking at him. She knew something was wrong and as they entered Ralf's car, Nicky asked if there was anything wrong. Ralf replied in the negative, but Nicky was persistent.

'As long as you're sure of it; from where I'm sitting, it looks like you felt as if we're being watched. You don't have some psycho ex-girlfriend skulking in the shadows, do you?'

'As a matter of fact I do,' Ralf replied, 'and she's also stupidly jealous. But I don't care, and you shouldn't worry either. She's history.'

Nicky didn't say anything else for a while and the journey was a quiet one for some of the way, until Ralf began to feel jittery again. Nicky noticed that he was continually glancing at the rear view mirror and after around ten minutes, she turned around to see a red Fiat Mirafiori closely following. She knew that the driver was definitely tailing them as the vehicle was so close, the number plate could not be seen. She asked Ralf what was going on, and the worry in her voice was evident.

'Look, don't worry, it's fine, she's just being silly.'

'Who?'

'It's Loredana. She's southern Italian, they're all obsessed. She can't have me so she doesn't want anybody else to...'

Ralf seized an opportunity of a straightaway and quickly overtook the two cars that were in front of him. He knew where the road went and so, put his foot down, hoping that the law wasn't on patrol nearby. He pushed the Capri up to just over sixty miles per hour and as the long road curved slightly left, he braked hard and pulled into a side street on the right, then immediately left, and into a small crescent. He quickly parked between a car and a large caravan and waited. Fifteen minutes went by and he decided it was safe to continue. Nicky wasn't so convinced.

'She must think very highly of you, then...'

'Oh, she *is* devoted.' Ralf said.

'So what's *her* story?'

'Oh she's just some lost tourist I met in a café. She came in asking directions and it went from there. We went out for over a month, had some good times, but she was getting a bit too demanding and clingy. I was steadily losing interest and she was becoming increasingly frustrated. In one way it's a shame; she wasn't bad, just clingy. I couldn't so much as say thank you to a waitress, and she'd go ballistic...'

'You can't be doing with that crap...'

'No, definitely not. Thing is; if someone wants to cheat on you, no matter how much you're on their case, sooner or later, they're gonna do it.'

'Did you?'

'No, of course not. I'm just saying. I'm too long in the tooth to do stuff like that, anyway. At this age, one's enough. I'm not a womanizer, Nicky...well, not anymore.'

Nicky smiled and touched his hand while it rested upon the gear stick. They took to the Western Avenue and toward Ruislip, a favourite haunt of Ralf's when he felt the desire to evade suburbia. The Lido was a vast area of woodland with a large lake at its centre. The surrounding areas were a mix of forest, open fields, and a mini beach complete with sand where children could paddle, where a fence closed off any further wandering into deeper water that rose above a child's knee. A little further along, was a mini train station where children and adults could board the miniature train that circled a large part of the Lido, and upon which Ralf confessed to Nicky, he liked to ride.

'I suppose you think it's mad, don't you?'

'No, actually I think it's rather sweet. So there's a soppy old sod beneath the seemingly hard exterior...'

Ralf chuckled; and once aboard the train, which surprisingly still ran during that month, he laughed contentedly for the first time in a long while. He and Nicky held hands tightly each time the little train passed through a small tunnel, and kissed at the entrance to the last one before the train stopped at another little station to let another small crowd of adults and toddlers join the train's open carriages. The couple rode the kiddie express three times before continuing on toward Ralf's favourite trail, much of which ran near the lake.

'Strange, isn't it?' Nicky said, 'that in all the years I've lived here, I've never been to Ruislip Lido. It's actually really nice here.'

'Yeah, I love it too. Bang in the middle of Middlesex and once you're in here and trekking through the woods and riding on the train, it feels like you're miles away; as though you're somewhere in the vast countryside. They use this lake for water skiing in the warmer months. I've always been curious to see how I fair up, but never had the guts to follow it up. Have you ever tried?'

'Nope, but I have ridden on a jet-ski. It was a whole load of fun. I can't wait to try it again in the summer.'

'You know...I've often wondered about something...about you...' said Nicky, taking Ralf's arm and placing it around her shoulder.

'Oh...and what might that be, pray tell...'

'This is going to sound really weird...but you don't strike me as being...British.'

Ralf looked at her. He could feel himself almost scowling, but quickly looked away and around himself, feigning to flinch from the arrival of an insect around his face. Nicky didn't notice his disapproval of her comment, as she was still smiling, although inquisitively.

'Oh yeah...so where do you think I'm from then?' he said, smiling sardonically.

'I'd say you're probably Greek or Spanish or something...'

'What about Italian? I could be Italian...'

Nicky kissed Ralf's lips hard, and several times over until they reached a fork in the woods, marked by a large log that had been hollowed out. There was a bench nearby that bore a memorial plaque dedicated to someone called Warren Critchley. Ralf and Nicky inaugurated Warren's seat with a passionate kiss and Ralf's gesture of tipping his hat in acknowledgement. They sat down with Nicky laying down and resting her head upon Ralf's lap.

'So how come you've not come forward with all those chances you had, then?'

'To be honest with you, I didn't actually want to get tied down in a relationship. I just wasn't ready. I'm not ready with Loredana either, but she was so enthusiastic and keen, that I found it kind of...well, sweet, so I gave in. I regret it though...'

'Do you regret us?'

'No. Definitely not. I wouldn't have let myself give in to passion at my place when you came over, if I did.'

'That's good then...I'd hate to think that I've pushed you into anything.'

'Nah, you're okay. I've always had an attraction for you. I was just too scared to do anything about it.'

'Silly arse.'

'Yep.'

The red Fiat appeared in the rear view mirror once again. Before Ralf could think about saying or doing anything, the driver behind the wheel slammed down the accelerator and shot past the Ford Capri, almost taking the wing mirror with it. Fortunately the mirror remained undamaged and in place, and Ralf got a good enough look at the driver. The glowering glare was unmistakeable. It was Loredana, and Ralf recognised her even though she wore a head-scarf. Nicky looked at Ralf and gave an unsurprising smile.

'I've seen worse, you know,' she said, 'a friend of mine had this stupidly obsessed girlfriend who used to hide near his home and his workplace; in fact, pretty much everywhere he went. She enjoyed shooting his legs with an air rifle and those little pellets were bloody painful. At night she used to slash his tyres. Every week he needed new tyres, but he wouldn't shop her to the police; he loved her too much, so he said...but when she set fire to his cat, that was the final straw.'

Ralf let out one of his bellowing laughs, making Nicky jump out of her skin.

'Are you laughing at the fate of the cat!?' she demanded.

'Yeah…sorry, I don't like cats…well, not as much as I love dogs.'

Ralf continued to snigger like a mischievous child. Nicky slapped him on the arm causing him to jerk the car slightly. Tears began trickling down his cheeks as he continued laughing, but he urged Nicky to continue the story.

'That's it. End of story. He pressed charges and never heard from her again.'

After stopping for a pub lunch back in Chiswick, Ralf and Nicky decided to head back to Hawkshead Road. They retreated to the bedroom for some more indoor sports and a quick nap before the midnight stroll, but they both woke up after half past one in the morning. By the time they got themselves dressed, it was almost two.

'Okay, you ready?'

'Absolutely,' said Nicky, 'let's hit the night!'

Ozzie was in the kitchen and probably on his third cup of instant coffee. Jackie felt compelled to come downstairs and see what was going on and without saying anything, pulled up a chair and sat with her son.

'Done it again, has she?' she asked.

'Yeah, mum. She's gone, but for good this time. I told her not to bother contacting me anymore. I've had enough now.'

'I know it's late, but I fancy some toast. Shall I do a couple of bits for you as well?'

'Okay mum that sounds good, actually. I've had a few coffees, so I might as well add the toast.'

Jackie made six slices of toast, cut it into triangles and piled them onto a large plate and placed it on the table in front of them both, along with a jar of strawberry jam. Ozzie bit into a slice didn't realise he felt hungrier that he actually was. There was always something about the smell and taste of freshly toasted bread that never failed to awaken the taste buds.

'What is it, son?' asked Jackie, 'It's not just Julia now, is it?'

'I dunno, mum. I just dunno anymore…'

'I know. You gotta have something else in your life, mate. You got talents…there's stuff you're good at and you should put it to good use, instead of just drifting through life every day. I know I get my pension, but it ain't always enough to cover all the stuff we like. We both smoke and we could…*I* could, especially, do with cuttin' down on the buggers…or givin' up altogether.'

'I ain't had a fag for nearly four days, mum. To tell you the truth, I can't even be arsed with them anymore. People say they calm you down, but I just think it's a load of old bollocks.'

'I spoke to your sister today. She's not had one for six weeks. She's over the moon. Six weeks.'

'When's she comin' over again? I miss our Sunday roasts together. I miss the baby.'

'I'll mention it to her for next Sunday. I'm sure she'll be up for it. She even asked how you were today.'

'Nah, you're joking aren't you?'

'Nope. She really did, son. Don't always think she hates your guts, she's your sister. We're family and you can't change that.'

'I was a shit to her, mum. You and her…you always gave each other the good bits…'

'She always loves you, son. Look, why don't you talk to Malcolm tomorrow?'

'I doubt he'll want to talk to me, mum. I've not spoken to him in ages.'

'He always needs someone to help in his bike shop. It's only down the road, and you're good at fixin' them. Just give him a call, God knows we could do with a bit of extra money in the house.'

Ozzie sipped his coffee and washed down the piece of toast he just ate, and continued staring at the calendar that hung on the wall ahead of him. He couldn't explain it, but a warm feeling was beginning to materialise inside of him, and he slowly began to embrace the fact that despite being a stubborn pig, he loved his family. Malcolm was a friend of his father's, the closest friend his dad ever had, and after his passing, Malcolm began drifting away from the

Blakes. Ozzie had turned into this raging monster with a very short fuse and Kim began giving the impression of being a little on the 'easy' side, and appearing to throw herself into the arms of practically every man that came her way. One minute the fellow had bought her a drink, and the next day, after a night in the sack, they were engaged. A week later, he'd moved into her flat and was already an established member of her family unit, with his feet up, beer can in his hand, several fag-ends in a nearby ashtray, and the almost never-ending sound of cheering football fans blaring out of the TV.

This was happening every couple of months, and each time Kim appeared at her mum's house bearing a new fat lip or a shiner, Ozzie was on the case and donning the cape of the avenging angel, rushing over to his sister's flat and literally hospitalizing her boyfriends; the one who'd laid his hands on Kim when she was six months pregnant ended up never walking again. Malcolm was a good man, honest and hardworking. His wife passed away a couple of years before and he was left with a big hole in his life that could never be filled. He had no children but Ronald Blake and his family was all he needed. When the Blakes began crumbling, Malcolm tied to help by giving Jackie a sum of money he had saved, but she refused, twice. His visits to them became less frequent and after his numerous offers of work to Ozzie were always met with refusal, and so after a while, he kept himself to himself.

Ozzie hadn't thought of Malcolm in a long while and now that Jackie had mentioned his name, he thought it was time to rebuild at least two important bridges in their lives. Kim was the other. Ozzie had always thought she hated his guts for being such a bastard to her, but Jackie kept reassuring him that she never did. She was frustrated with him, yes, but there was never any hate. Kim knew that at the end of the day, her overprotective brother was only acting in her defence, and that his control freak attitude emerged often, only to keep her safe.

Ozzie kissed his mum on the cheek and turned in. The toast was all gone, mugs and plate washed up, and mother and son were determined to try something different in their lives. As he lay in bed staring at the ceiling, Ozzie scrutinized the faint remains and imprints of the countless newspaper cuttings that stared down at him. Whoever lived in that house before them had the idea of pasting fragments of newspaper on the ceiling, and since boyhood, Ozzie had always been fascinated by them. Never once had he ever felt compelled to examine them closely; they were just a part of his room. Many of the pages had faded so much, that they appeared to resemble faint sketches of people and shapes, as if someone had mounted a ladder and taken a pencil to the ceiling. But they were definitely fragments of newspapers, without a doubt; and now they were just ghosts on the ceiling. They often helped Ozzie to fall asleep when he was a child and his restless hyperactivity had surged through him during the day, and now as an adult, they were still his thinking and sleeping tonic. As the final good thought tumbled through his mind, Ozzie fell asleep.

Chapter 31

It always felt like a strange coincidence, that every time Ralf fancied one of his night walks, the heavens were always obliging with an absence of clouds, crisp and bright moon light, and a throng of stars, as long as he was far enough away from too much urban lighting. He and Nicky headed for the roof of the main building of the water purifying plant behind Greenend Road. He always accessed it from the alley way that ran behind Greenend Road's houses; he had loosened one of the stone panels from the wall in order to crouch through and climb atop the roof to enjoy the night sky. They took a couple of folding deck chairs with them along with some blankets and a flask of coffee.

'You know what I do sometimes,' Ralf said, 'you'll either find this funny, or ridiculous...'

'Go on,' said Nicky, smiling and taking his hand in hers.

'When it's a clear night and the moon's full...I do the same thing we're doing up here, but in my back garden. Just a deck chair, a warm duffle coat, flask of coffee or cuppa soup, and just enjoy the night garden lit up by just brilliant silvery moon light. Some say it's bloody odd, but I find it just magical. It's like...the plants, the shed's windows, the grass and the stone pathway...all silver. I can't explain it, but...it's surreal. Truly magical.'

Nicky couldn't - and in that moment - wouldn't take her eyes off Him. Ralf had adopted a sweet and almost childlike enthusiasm and his face was lit up with curiosity and a joy to just be alive and to be a part of when nature painted its most special pictures.

'There are so few people who know how to appreciate all this, Nicky. This is my safe haven. This rooftop. When I'm up here, in these moments that I've broken away from the world, nothing else matters. It's just me, the stars, and the moon. One happy family.'

'What's wrong with your eye...you got something in it?' Nicky asked, knowing what he was feeling, but not needing to mention it. Ralf discreetly wiped away the lone tear that rolled slowly down his cheek. It looked like a glistening gem as it captured the moonlight. It fell just as he mentioned the word; *Family.*

'I don't think it's odd at all. I kind of like your…oddness.'

'Well that's nice, sweetheart. I didn't know you cared…'

The two night owls dragged their deck chairs a little closer and continued gazing out across the rooftops of their sleeping neighbourhood. The light of the full moon generously bathed everything in an otherworldly glow that was as beautiful as it was eerie. The long row of houses that lined Greenend Road, slanted to the right, while the smaller row on Hawkshead Road went off to the left, making them look like a glistening chevron. The moon's distorted reflection played upon the upper windows of the school where Ralf taught. He kept his eye upon it whilst Nicky was beginning to doze off with her head on his shoulder. Ralf could smell her hair; it was like a combination of coconut and mango and the delicate fragrance made him feel unusually calm, yet a little fearful. He began to feel he could seriously get used to all of this.

Ralf had never thought he would ever share his grody, but to him, especial nocturnal activities with anyone, but Nicky possessed something magnetic about her. She didn't say much when mingling with a group of friends on an evening or day out, but this never made her come across as cagey or unfriendly. On the contrary; her content and blushingly smiley expression was very captivating and alluring. It made you feel like you really needed to talk to her. You just *had* to. Ralf had always wanted to get to know her better and he did indeed take the step toward striking a conversation. It was just the uncertainty about the whole relationship thing that prevented him for going any further than mentioning the weather and the latest songs to hit the charts.

'Have you ever stopped to take a long look at the stars?' he asked Nicky, as she began stirring from her light but comfortable slumber, 'there are just so many of them up there…'

'They're incredible aren't they?' whispered Nicky, snuggling closer to him.

'I always ignore the fact that they're arranged into constellations. I just gaze upward and there they are; distant, twinkling, and mysterious. It just makes me feel good when they're visible. They kind of keep me company when I'm on one of my solitary night walks.'

'I don't really know any constellations. Why don't you show me some?'

'Okay, look at those three stars in a row just over there. That's the constellation of Orion, the hunter. The three stars are meant to be his belt. Now look just to your left, follow my finger. That group of stars there, it's shaped like a huge ladle. That's known as the Big Dipper.'

Nicky smiled warmly at Ralf's childlike enthusiasm. His eyes were wide and his face, lit up with fascination. She felt like she was falling for him.

'It's actually Ursa Major, meaning the great bear in Latin. Now look over there, almost directly overhead. See that cluster of stars, that tiny group of stars that's shaped just like a small kite?'

'Uh huh...' Nicky gently kissed his hand. Ralf looked down at her. The pearl-white moonlight glinted in her beautiful, crystalline eyes, as though her soul had captured its very essence. At that precise moment, Ralf thought he loved her. He felt an unusually mort-like, but strangely pleasant shiver rise up his spine.

'Someone walk over your grave?' Nicky said.

They kissed.

'When I'm with you, it feels like I've risen from it.'

'Soppy sod.' Nicky said, smiling.

'That's my favourite constellation,' continued Ralf, 'It's called Pleiades.'

Ralf pressed his lips gently onto Nicky's mouth and passionately kissed her. Her tongue was warm and moist and her hands squeezed his body and pulled him closer to her. She gave him her lips like she was giving him the gift of life. Her eyes were closed and she trusted him. Despite the biting cold, Ralf's loins began calling out to him again; well it certainly felt that way. *Hoi, randy bastard, get in there!*

The eastern horizon caught their eye, as the rooftops in the distance began to glow like embers. The night's shoulders were catching fire and Ralf and Nicky hadn't realised just how quickly time races by when there is fun or relaxation to be had. They took a deck chair each and Ralf carried the small bag containing the thermos flask and the blankets. They carefully descended the stairs that wound around the building and Ralf's heart sank a little. He didn't want the night to end, and the packing up of the deck chairs and descending the stairs felt like a tortuous journey downward from a perfect dream world, and down into the murky cycle of reality. Up on the roof felt like another world; a world away from what goes on down below, where the streets buzzed with headlights and living souls that crossed each other, and where problems and hang-ups, and arseholes lurked around every corner.

After a long hug on the doorstep of number twelve and the promise of doing it again soon, Ralf drove Nicky home and managed to grasp a precious couple of hours sleep on his return, before getting up and crossing the road to go to work. Edwina wasn't in that day and didn't mention anything to Ralf either, which he found odd, because she usually did. Between lessons, he attempted to reach her on the phone but there was no reply all day. Once the pips chirped and every pupil in the school rapidly made his or her way to the exit, Ralf quickly walked toward the gate when a young lady approached him, shyly, and asked to speak to him. She must have been in her late twenties or early thirties and was very attractive, but she had a job making eye contact with Ralf.

'I'm sorry to stop you like this, but…my name's Alison. I'm Edwina's sister. She asked me to wait for you after school. There's no easy way to say this, but…she's been beaten up…'

'Beaten up?' asked Ralf, shocked and taking Alison gently by her arms, but in a gesture of comforting her. 'I'm sorry, so sorry…is she okay?'

'She's at home, she has been all day. She was taken to the hospital late last night, at around nine thirty. She went to get some bits from the deli just down the street from us, and was attacked from behind and beaten quite badly. She's okay, miraculously, just shaken.'

'Do we know who it was?'

'She told me she was sure it was a woman. She made grunting and yelping noises while she was hitting her. The strange thing was…she didn't try to steal my sister's bag or anything. It was unprovoked, but Edwina had this feeling that it was…something personal.'

Ralf's blood froze. He knew who it could have been, but why Edwina?

'Are you okay…?'

'Yes…sorry, I'm… just a little shocked, that's all. Can I go and visit her, or is she not up to it yet?'

'Actually, she wants to see you. She didn't want anyone else. I can drive you there if you like. I'm parked just over there.'

'That's very kind, but I'll just freshen up and make my own way there. Thanks for coming to tell me. It was nice to meet you, Alison.'

Ralf changed clothes into something more casual – jeans and a sweatshirt and a smile – it was something Pete used to say to describe his best friend in a few words. Ralf roared away from Hawkshead in the Ford Capri and made his way to Edwina's home. She lived on Lionel Road, just near the main entrance to Gunnersbury Park. Her home looked like a welcoming place and as soon as dusk fell, the lantern that hung on the wall next to the front door would turn itself on and light the small pathway that wound its way through a tree in the front garden and a large bush, in the flowerbed on the left.

Alison let Ralf in and he made his way to the lounge to where Edwina was sitting in an armchair, feet up, and wrapped in a pink blanket. She didn't look as bad as he expected, but sported a shiner in the right eye, a slightly swollen bottom lip, and some nasty redness on one side of her neck. Ralf went over to her and kissed her hand whilst kneeling in front of her.

'You look pretty shit,' he said jokingly, 'but still fanciable.'

Edwina smiled and squeezed his hand at length before saying that she was glad he was there. Alison emerged from the kitchen moments later with some tea for her sister and a mug of filter coffee for Ralf.

'I don't want to keep you,' Edwina said, 'I know you're looking forward to that Ultravox tribute band at Mike's Music City this evening.'

'Don't worry about that. I just want to know that you're okay before anything else. Have you eaten yet?'

'Alison was going to go and get a takeaway for us. You're more than welcome to join us, but I really don't want to tear you away from that concert. The others will be disappointed...'

'They'll understand, don't worry. What are you planning on having then, Indian or Chinese?'

'I love Chinese,' Alison said, 'but Edwina likes both. But we settled on Chinese tonight. Our local one does something called a Jade Garden Special; it's a kind of mixed vegetable Chow Mein. Are you joining us?'

'I think that would be great, I'd love to.' Ralf said with a broad smile, 'any excuse for a takeaway.'

The stereo was playing softly in the background. The song, *Sweet Dreams Are Made of This,* could be heard as its swinging rhythm flowed beautifully, lending itself perfectly to that precise moment.

'Park your bum.' Said Edwina, patting the seat of a chair she had pulled near to her own armchair. Ralf obliged and she took his hand in hers and held it for a while before releasing it to drink her coffee.

'As much as I hate remembering,' she continued after downing the mug of coffee, 'I'm pretty sure she had an accent...'

A shiver ran up Ralf's spine. He wasn't the type to ever feel in denial, but he was certain of what could well be hiding around the corner, like a troll under a bridge.

'It was like she was...punishing me. But for what? That's what keeps playing on my mind. As far as I know, I don't have any enemies...at least to my knowledge, anyway...'

Ralf was jolted out of his deep whirlpool of thoughts as Alison handed him a filter coffee.

'Are you alright, Ralf?'

'Oh yeah...fine. I'm just listening...'

'You've gone suddenly pale.'

Ralf acknowledged Alison with a smile and sipped his coffee, each taste resulting in a nod of approval to the mug. He always nodded and smiled at the mug he held if the coffee within it met his very particular tastes. He observed Alison's behind rather keenly as she went back into the kitchen. He noticed with the corner of his eye that Edwina was smiling and probably thinking, *dirty bastard.* At times, Ralf wasn't discreet enough when it came down to noticing attractive ladies that passed him by.

'I'm okay, just tired.' He said, trying to focus on another subject. 'Today just felt like a long day, and I didn't get much sleep last night either. Blame it on the stargazing.'

Ralf enjoyed Edwina and Alison's company until close to midnight, before heading home. The next morning, he awoke to the sound of the letterbox being rattled and the thud that followed meant that a rather heavy package had arrived. He struggled out of bed and carefully went down the stairs, taking one step at a time, like a child. He opened the parcel and a chill raced up his spine when he realised it was the firearm promised to him by his friend in the force, Jeff Mallory. It was a small pistol that undoubtedly packed a punch and judging by the box of bullets that lay in the package next to it, he suspected it was an automatic. Ralf hated guns of any kind, particularly when they were pointed in his direction. He had only ever handled a gun twice in his lifetime, both times were back in Italy and thankfully at a firing range. He wasn't a particularly great shot, but if the target was substantial enough in size and not moving too quickly, he was fine.

Ralf remained in the lounge for a long time, pondering and downing several coffees before putting on some smooth jazz to soothe his nerves. Loredana featured heavily in his thoughts, as did every consequence for his possible actions. The phone rang a few times but he ignored it. The doorbell too, twice that morning, went unanswered and Ralf couldn't bring himself round to caring who it was. He turned and sat facing the window and for a good few hours, watched as the ever peaceful neighbourhood went from quiet to quieter. He saw only two vehicles leave their parking spaces and return a while later, and Mr Child's voice was the only one he heard in all of the time he played sentinel.

'I know you're out there,' he exclaimed in his own language. 'I am waiting, and I know you are too. But I'm ready for you. You can hide in the shadows all you want, but you won't hurt anyone I care about anymore. When you come back, you'll die.'

Ralf spoke as though whoever was out there could hear him. It made him feel better. It made him feel as though he was prepared for what was coming. As a child he used to talk to himself a lot. His ill-fated parents told him that if he ever felt afraid that the 'bobo' would come for him, he should speak aloud to it and that it would scare it off. That was something that had been drummed into him when he was a toddler – and he remembered that part of his life well – when his parents insisted that he sleep with the light off and in pitch-blackness. It was from those moments on, that he developed his intense fear of the dark and of the invisible, child-snatching 'bobo.'

Ralf flinched as the first street lamp flickered to life and whitewashed the side of the tree that stood just outside the front gate, with its cold neon glow. 'Il bobo' was coming – maybe not on this night – but it was coming. But this time, it was going to be put to sleep.

Chapter 32

The phone rang but this time Ralf answered it after the fifth ring. He shivered when there was a pause of a good few seconds on the other end. He could hear passing traffic and muffled and distant voices that were muttering indecipherable gibberish.

'Che cosa vuoi?' he said, coldly.

'Eh? Ralf, is that you?'

Nicky's voice came through, bewildered and inquisitive, and Ralf sighed with slight relief.

'Hey, gorgeous…' he said, smiling, 'nice surprise. Where are you?'

'I'm just outside the chippy by the station, just down the road from you. I just wondered if you fancied some unhealthy dinner, consisting of battered sausage and large chips. What do you say to that? Shall I nip in and get it or have you eaten?'

'That sounds greasy and disgusting; just what I need. Go for it and I'll pick you up in five. It's a lengthy walk from down there and it'll go cold.'

Nicky jumped into the Capri as Ralf pulled up outside the chippy. She planted a wet kiss upon his lips and he pulled away, turning round at the nearby mini roundabout and going back on himself.

'What was that you said when you answered the phone? It sounded like a foreign language.'

'Oh, nothing…every time I get a weird phone call and people go quiet on the other end, I just pretend to be foreign, so they get discouraged and hang up.'

'Ah okay…' she said, chuckling. Ralf felt impressed at his quick thinking at what to respond. It was better that Nicky didn't know too much just yet. He felt pretty confident that she'd understand – well, perhaps the two lives he took may be a little too much to process – but she showed signs of being strong and grounded and non-judgemental. Or would he have to take his secret to the grave if he ever got more serious with her?

'Doesn't it smell amazing?' she said. 'I like being with you, you know...'

Ralf glanced at her briefly, smiled, and returned his eyes to the road. She caressed his hand as it rested upon the gear stick. Ralf's body and loins tingled every time she touched him, even if she did it softly like just now. Nicky had something about her that he couldn't explain. Words failed him. All he knew and wanted to know was that he wanted her with him; more and more. She had eyes like the sky and hair like the sun. When she kissed him, he died and went to Heaven. When she simply gazed at him, he rose again. Nicky just exploded inside Ralf like an incredible sunset and after just a few days together, she had managed to enchant him and now he was under her spell.

It was Nicky's spell that scared the crap out of Ralf. It was undoubtedly the fact that he had spent too many years enjoying his own company and staying pretty much a good distance away from anything too deep and meaningful. He had got used to having occasional casual relationships rather than serious and lengthy ones. And it wasn't that Ralf didn't get any female attention either. He wasn't short of charm and wit and despite having lost his hair and being a couple of stone overweight, he usually scrubbed up pretty well. Nicky and Loredana certainly had no complaints, and neither did any of his past conquests, and all of these women were certainly not spiders in appearance.

As they turned into Hawkshead Road, Ralf noticed the back end of what looked like a Bentley turning left into Greenend Road. At first he thought nothing of it, but once he and Nicky got inside and sat on the sofa, eating the takeaway from the greasy paper it was wrapped in, he clung to an uncomfortable thought, and unfortunately, Ralf had a tendency to always think the worst before thinking even remotely positively. He glanced over toward a small writing desk in the corner of the lounge near the window. The gun that Jeff sent him was safely concealed within and wrapped in a large jiffy bag, and already loaded.

'I really love that little antique writing desk in the corner there...' said Nicky. Ralf almost choked on a large chunk of battered sausage, and when she asked what was inside...

'My dad loves antique furniture,' she continued, 'he attends auctions every couple of weeks. Would you ever consider having it valued? You know, just for curiosity?'

'Never in a million years. Not that one, it belonged to my auntie and uncle, and I am a sentimental old bastard. It's kind of like they're still here in the room when I look at it.'

'Don't you have any photographs of them?'

'Yeah, I have quite a few, but I've put the photo albums in the loft, all boxed up. I'll eventually get them down at some point; for a bit of nostalgia...'

A vehicle passed by slowly outside and stopped outside the house. The idling engine made the windows vibrate and as Ralf sprang up and looked out of the window, the silver Bentley pulled away. Ralf saw the dark outlines of the driver and the passengers. His stomach began to churn again.

'You alright?' Nicky asked.

'Yeah, fine. Just a little jumpy in my old age.'

'Is it that ex of yours again, driving past to see if you're home?'

Nicky had hit the nail right on the head. If only it were that simple...he could handle a little lovesick ex, but the thought of things to come was eating away at him. Ralf now felt that it was time to warn the others and keep them as far away as possible. This was *his* battle.

'Oh, shit...sorry, but I left my purse in your car. Give us your keys and I'll fetch it...'

'No, stay here, I'll go!' said Ralf, rising quickly to his feet.

'My, we *are* a little jumpy aren't we?' said a bewildered Nicky, smiling. 'I am a big girl, you know...'

'Sorry, I'm just being protective...comes with being Italian, I guess...'

'I'm sorry...?' intoned Nicky, inquisitively.

Ralf's stomach tightened like a vice as soon he realised what he'd said. He'd taken his eye off the ball, now. That meant he was particularly stressed; and that meant being more prone to serious mistakes that could cost him his arse on a plate. He stepped outside the front door and went toward the Ford Capri. Once he'd retrieved Nicky's purse, Ralf was sure he could hear a car's engine idling just around the corner, on Greenend Road. He locked the Capri and began making his way to the corner of the street that led onto Greenend. He peeked around the corner and sure enough, it was the Bentley. It was stationary just a few feet ahead of him. Ralf crouched down and began creeping toward the car, taking care to keep out of sight.

As he drew closer to the Bentley, he was certain he recognised Loredana sat in the back. The front passenger turned to look to his left and Ralf recognised him as Kamal, which meant that the more elderly fellow in the driver's seat must be Raymond Franklin.

'Hoi, what the bloody hell do you think *you're* doing?'

Ralf sprang to his feet and whirled around to face the voice behind him. It was a middle-aged man, probably from one of the houses on the street. Ralf glared at the man, short of punching him, especially when he heard the car door of the Bentley swing open. He turned to see that it was Kamal, and with a most satisfied grin upon his face, as he began reaching into the inside pocket of his suit jacket. Ralf burst into action without the slightest inkling of thought or hesitation and dashed toward Kamal, grabbing his arm. Kamal swung a rapid left hook that caught Ralf on the side of his face, knocking him sideways and causing him to stumble onto the short wall of someone's front garden. Ralf quickly swayed back as Kamal came at him with a right backhander, now clutching the firearm that he'd taken from his pocket. Kamal missed and stumbled, hitting the same wall and Ralf took his chance, punching downwards and hard onto Kamal's temple.

A hard and unexpected rugby-like tackle brought Ralf to the ground with a thud. Raymond Franklin was upon him now, trying to pin him down whilst Loredana jumped out of the Bentley and began running toward the downed Ralf with her intentions clear as day. By her run, Ralf was certain of her next move; she was going to run up and kick him hard in the head and such a blow would be sure to do a serious amount of damage. Ralf gazed quickly upward and caught a quick glimpse of the middle-aged man fleeing the scene and returning to his home then his attention focused once again on Loredana who sure enough, was now mere feet away from him and rearing back her right leg ready for the devastating penalty kick. Ralf barely managed to grasp her ankle and twist it away, making her stumble and fall, hitting the back of the Bentley on her way down. He had bought himself a little more time to resume wrestling with Raymond in an attempt to free himself from the big man's mass besides his surprising strength for a man of his apparent age. Loredana got to her feet and resumed her run in Ralf's direction and with his energy now dwindling, he feared the worst. Kamal was coming to and helping himself up from the ground. A voice in Ralf's head exclaimed the words, *I'm fucked*!

Loredana attempted another kick but the adrenaline allowed Ralf to raise himself slightly off the ground, bringing his face up close and personal to Raymonds, almost kissing him, therefore making the point of her shoe miss the side of his head, with her calf brushing against the back of his neck instead. Loredana stumbled once again and fell backwards but managed to grab hold of a nearby lamppost, keeping herself upright. Ralf managed to free his right arm and bring it out from between himself and Raymond, and proceeded to push away on his face with his forearm, making Raymond fall sideways and onto the pavement. Ralf sprang up and shuffled away from him and faced Loredana, who was ready for her next onslaught. She rushed him, but Ralf grabbed her in an embrace and held her tightly, before throwing her to his left and onto Kamal, who was on his knees, still a little dazed.

Raymond Franklin had managed to get to his feet meanwhile, and tried to swing for Ralf, who ducked under his punch and countered with one of his own, to the side of Raymond's jaw, rocking him. Ralf followed up with a powerful right backhander across the face which knocked Raymond onto the Bentley. A third punch to the jaw knocked the big man down and out cold. Now it was back to the screaming Loredana who was already dashing toward him, teeth bared and fists clenched. Ralf dodged quickly sideways, making her sail past him and end up smacking her face into the side of the Bentley. The piercing sound of a police siren could be heard just around the corner in Hawkshead Road. Ralf broke into a sprint and headed for the alleyway that separated Greenend Road into two halves and leading into the footpath area that led around to the sewage plant. He could hear screaming and cursing as he ran away from the commotion and a sharp tug at his sweatshirt rapidly slowed his pace. He turned quickly to see that it was Kamal and before he could react, the big Asian fellow hurled himself toward him, knocking him to the ground and once again, Ralf found himself pinned down and this time by someone more agile and younger than Raymond. Ralf was beginning to tire and he could feel the strength in his arms waning as he tried desperately to push Kamal off of him. Kamal's forearm was pressing down onto Ralf's throat in an attempt to make him pass out but another opportunity reared its head and Ralf brought his knee up to make contact with Kamal's groin.

He pushed Kamal off him and staggered up, falling against the nearby wall and doubling forward to regain valuable breath. As Kamal lay upon the ground writhing in agony an anguished but angry look of sheer vengeance was upon his face. Ralf drew in as much breath as he could before Kamal would regain some sort of composure and get back up for round two. Sure enough, he was on his knees and clutching a nearby lamppost, fists clenched, teeth bared, and pissed off like an aggravated rhinoceros. He came at Ralf once again, sure that he would overwhelm him, but Ralf immediately dodged sideways, putting his leg out and tripping Kamal over, sending him crashing into the wall.

Kamal sprang up right away and dashed toward Ralf once again and immediately threw a right hander in his direction. Ralf ducked beneath it and Kamal launched a backhand which Ralf avoided by swaying backwards like a skilful pugilist. Kamal jabbed with his left hand but Ralf parried with his right and side-stepped, jabbing with his own right hand and catching Kamal on the left cheek twice. The big Asian roared with frustration and launched himself toward Ralf once again, wrapping his arms around his waist in an attempt to bring him down to the ground again. Ralf gathered a little momentum with his right leg and managed to loosen one of Kamal's arms from around him and making him stagger in the process, as he moved backward a couple of steps. Kamal fell forward and onto his hands, but quickly sprang to his feet once more.

Ralf marched toward him, clearly anticipating his next move and sure enough, Kamal threw a right cross which Ralf side-stepped and parried. He hit Kamal hard across the jaw with a thundering left hand and then immediately shoulder-barged him, making him topple. Kamal threw a straight left punch which was avoided by Ralf who immediately countered with a powerful right cross onto Kamal's jaw, followed by another and another still. Kamal went crashing to the ground and into unavoidable unconsciousness. The fight was over.

Ralf caught his breath for a few seconds and moved further down along the outer wall of the sewage plant, until he reached a point where a couple of empty paint cans and an old microwave oven could be used as stackable aids to assist in climbing over. After evading a couple of plant employees, he reached the hole in the wall that ran along the alleyway behind Greenend Road's houses. He made his way carefully toward the corner of the last house on Greenend and where it joined onto Hawkshead. The fracas was still audible as curious neighbours came out of their homes to see what was going on, and the now silent police car was parked in the centre of the street, near the Bentley. Ralf inched slowly along the pavement as soon as an officer had his back to him. He saw no sign of Loredana or Raymond; they had probably fled the scene. Once they found Kamal and took him into custody, he would likely not talk, anyway.

As Ralf approached the front door, he noticed that it was ajar. He didn't remember leaving it that way and now had a very sickening feeling he knew what would await him on the other side of the door. He pushed it open slowly and entered his home. There was total silence aside from the squall in the next street, but the sirens had now stopped. The kitchen that stood just down the hallway in front of him was empty, there was no sound coming from upstairs, and the garden door was closed. Ralf slowly and reluctantly entered the lounge, to his left. Loredana was standing by the dining room table, her hand pressing down upon a kneeling Nicky's head and a gun pointed at her temple. Ralf looked toward the writing desk by the window. It had been opened. Loredana had found his firearm and the look on her face was one of a woman who was not playing games.

'Let her go,' said Ralf quietly and in his own language, 'she has nothing to do with this. I'm the one you want.'

'Zitto, stronzo!' she replied, hissing like a venomous snake about to strike. Ralf was worried. Those eyes couldn't be trusted and that trigger finger was too dangerous to underestimate. Nicky was hiccupping and crying, fearing for her life.

'Shut up, you beetch!' shrieked Loredana, pressing down even harder upon Nicky's head, almost making her kiss the carpet. She looked back at Ralf with monstrous and unforgiving eyes. A woman scorned had just taken on a new meaning and it was frightful. Ralf had no plan B and the slightest move in Loredana's direction would surely result in Nicky's brain decorating the walls and floor. There was no way out. If Ralf moved, Loredana would pull the trigger and that would be the end of Nicky; he would get to Loredana in time to disarm her, but would have to sacrifice Nicky in the process, and hers was one life that was definitely not on the list of those to waste. Or perhaps she would raise the gun and shoot Ralf, himself and then Nicky. Either way, it would end badly if Ralf dared to move a muscle. He was scared now, terrified even. The way Loredana was feeling, she could pull the trigger anyway, and she wouldn't lose a moment's sleep over it. Ralf stood as still as a doornail. He closed his eyes briefly while letting out an exasperated sigh.

Chapter 33

Pete and Ozzie were scouring the deepest reaches of a huge playing field that played home to a large boot sale that lasted until late evening. Each had a large hessian bag full of knick-knacks and trinkets that would get some kind of use one way or another. Ozzie stumbled across a box full of rock music vinyl records while Pete found a few videos and stray computer parts that he was sure he could use. For the most part, the afternoon into evening was a rather cringe-worthy affair, mainly due to Ozzie in full form for criticizing, slating, and insulting people. The latest victim for his colourful barrage of choice words was a little dog, a French Bulldog strutting its thing alongside the elderly owner.

'Alright Missus…love yer scarf, but why did you buy that ugly facker of a dog? Looks like you picked him up and slung him against the wall. Fack me, that's one ugly doggie!'

'Ozzie!'

'Oh come on, Pete…'

'Ozzie, you can't say things like that to people,' the woman's jaw was agape and she appeared to be on the verge of tears, 'dogs are like children to people that have them, you idiot!'

The woman turned to leave quickly and went back the way she came, while a baffled and embarrassed Pete hooked Ozzie under the arm and dragged him away in the opposite direction.

'For fuck's sake, Ozzie,' hissed Pete, 'I think it's best if we make a move, before you end up getting us killed…'

'Whatcha mean?'

'The ugly doggie was the last straw. That poor girl…the large woman you told to get out of the way of the sun…then there was that mini-bus at the entrance when we just arrived…you can't go saying things like…retards and spasmos…for fuck's sake, Ozzie!'

Pete searched desperately for where he'd parked the car, among throngs of people and badly parked vehicles at the playing field's edges, and he noticed that Ozzie had slowed his pace and was pointing toward something.

'What is it now?'

'Look… there's Debbie…and Julia…I don't fackin' believe it…they carpet munchers now, or something?'

Pete followed Ozzie's finger and spotted what it was he was looking at. It was indeed Debbie and Julia walking toward the exit and holding hands.

'I don't know whether to be shocked, pissed off, or relieved…' Pete said, frowning.

'I'm not too surprised actually,' Ozzie said, 'Julia always said she was curious about carpet munchin' and all. Now she's gettin' her share of it.'

Pete turned to look behind him after hearing the sound of a woman's voice mention something along the lines of; *there's the shabby gobshite who insulted my dog.*

'Ozzie, we need to seriously run for our lives and get to the car now…'

'Why, what's up?'

'That lady with the ugly do…that lady with the dog…and that must be her son, and he's a big bugger as well. Let's go, now!'

Pete tugged hard at Ozzie's arm but he remained steadfast. Ozzie was stubborn in those situations and by his own personal principle, never fled from a fight – regardless of whether he was right or wrong.

'Wait a second, he ain't gonna do nothin' to us…he's a big tosser full of hot air.'

'Ozzie, please mate…'

'Hoi you! You the geezer who's just said this lady's dog's fuckin' ugly!?'

'Yeah, I did. He must geddit from you! And what's with them Doctor Marten boots, ya big pussy!'

The tall and burly chap marched toward Ozzie with fists clenched and arms open, as if he wanted to embrace Ozzie, who immediately planted a well-placed front kick to the bald man's groin. He sank to the ground slowly, clutching his family jewels, and fell onto his side once his knees made contact with the ground. The elderly lady rushed to his aid, cradling his head in her arms, and by her words of comfort, she was clearly his grandmother.

'Poor, poor baby. Don't worry, nanna's here…them fuckers are gonna pay. BASTARDS!' she intoned whilst glaring in Pete and Ozzie's direction.

'Don't be such a fackin' tosser next time, dickie-poos!' Ozzie said, passionately but mockingly swivelling his hips, until Pete pulled him away from the nanna from hell.

'Come on, Ozzie,' Pete said, 'time to leave; quickly!'

The two pals rapidly made their way toward the exit and Pete was sure he could feel the nutty granny hot on their heels, and age and fitness didn't matter. She was in hot pursuit. 'Oi, you two…wankers,' she called out, 'somebody grab 'old of them two!'

Pete and Ozzie quickened their pace while trying their level best to not draw too much attention to themselves. It was usually a good thing in this day and age – although not at this particular time – that passers-by would undoubtedly rush to the aid of an old woman in need, especially if she mentioned grabbing hold of someone. For all anybody knew, Pete and Ozzie could have snatched her handbag. And talking of bags, the two pals had no choice but to broken-heartedly rid themselves of the rather weighty hessian ones they were carrying. Pete finally spotted his car among a group of youngsters sharing some cans of beer, and they both broke into a final sprint toward the vehicle. As they slammed shut the doors and locked themselves in, Ozzie turned round to look behind him and sure enough, they were being pursued by some six or seven men, a few of them armed with empty glass bottles and one fellow had a baseball bat. Pete didn't hesitate to reverse out of the gap he was in, spinning the back wheels and kicking up mud and grass. He quickly sped off toward the dry path just mere feet away from them, scattering the group of kids with beers, who immediately dove out of harm's way.

A loud thud shook the car as one of the burly men struck it hard with the baseball bat, while several glass bottles struck either side of the vehicle. Pete pounded on his horn, trying to shake up the amblers that had no sense of urgency whatsoever. Ozzie had rolled down his window and was shouting for everyone to; *get out the fackin' way!*

Pete snarled at him, ordering him to stop it, but Ozzie continued. They finally reached the main entrance gateway and once they hit the street, they were off. Pete accelerated quickly away from underneath Southall's iron bridge and drove toward Hanwell and then turned left into Greenford Avenue. After a short while, Pete turned right into a side street and pulled over just outside a parade of shops and turned round to face Ozzie, who was for the first time, taken aback by Pete's rather unhappy expression. In all the years they had been friends, he had never seen Pete look like a thunderstorm before. Pete got out of the car and circled it to inspect before getting in again, then resumed his glare in Ozzie's direction.

'Is the car okay?' asked Ozzie, sheepishly.

'There's a big dent across the back, on the right corner and my back light's smashed. There are also a couple of scratches and one little dent on both sides. Thanks a lot, Ozzie!'

'Why's it my ma fault?'

'You and your massive gob, that's what…'

'That big facker was comin' at us…I was protectin' us!'

'I don't mean just him! Ozzie, listen mate, you know I love your style…but sometimes, actually make that more than just sometimes…you have to just bite your tongue. And you certainly DON'T go insulting people's dogs…even if they *are* ugly!'

'Yeah, I guess…'

'That pain in the arse of an old woman started shouting and that's surely going to start off a revolt. Everyone's going to take the side of an old lady. We could've been seriously hurt if that mob had gotten hold of us!'

'She could really fackin' run, couldn't she…not bad for an old gal!'

'You're not taking this seriously at all,' Pete said, exasperatingly.

'Oh fackin' chill out!' Ozzie snapped, 'Look, that's just how I am, okay? Get over it!'

'No, it's not okay, Ozzie; it's not okay.'

'You just fink yer so fackin' high and mighty, don'tcha? Just 'cause you speak proper and you got some good education, that makes you better than anybody else…'

'That's not the case, and you know it. I'm just saying that it'll be best for all of us if you just controlled your tongue once in a while. Don't you see my point, Ozzie? My car's dented and scratched and it's going to cost me money to sort it and I'm telling you, we could have really got our heads kicked in because of you. Sorry, but I'm not backing down on this one. You were a total dickhead today!'

'Well, I'll tell ya what,' said Ozzie as he began getting out of the car, 'I'll fackin' walk home then. You can fack right off. I ain't changin' for anyone. I like meself just the way I am. You don't like me this way…your fackin' loss, ya posh twat!'

Ozzie slammed the car door hard, the impact rocking the vehicle like it were a boat on water, and then he disappeared somewhere into the cluster of houses that lay just beyond the end of the side street. Pete sighed deeply, started the car and drove off toward home. He'd had just about enough of Ozzie for today. The thought of Debbie holding hands with another girl passed through his mind. He didn't miss her, but he was definitely curious about what was going on.

Ozzie had traversed the green that cut down the middle of two roads leading down to the main road and up to Hanwell community centre and made his way up toward the latter. He knew that was where Charlie Chaplin went to school, as Pete told him a while ago. He also told him that that was where various social clubs were held, including a dating evening twice a week. He stopped to think for a moment, whether he wanted to go inside and find out a little more, but decided to pass this time, and proceeded to make his way toward the top of Browning Avenue, which led down to Drayton Bridge Road.

He turned left and began ascending the hill climb that led up to Drayton Green station on his right, and just as he'd reached the top of the hill, a large Jaguar drove by at a slow speed, its occupants staring out at him. Ozzie kept his eye on the vehicle just as he had reached the little gateway to the stone steps that led down to the station platform. The Jaguar slowed almost to a stop and the vehicles behind it began sounding their horns. Ozzie felt there was something wrong and prepared to make a run for it, down the flight of steps to the station.

The drivers in the cars behind the Jaguar rolled down their windows and began yelling their displeasure and the driver door of the Jaguar opened, revealing the leg of a suited male figure. The man stepped out of the vehicle and Ozzie's heart began racing as soon as he realised who it was; it was Kamal, with a face a little worse for wear, and soon after, Garry Peters emerged from the passenger side and looked toward Ozzie with a mocking sneer of satisfaction. Ozzie wasted no time and began running down the stone steps. He could hear more than one set of footsteps following behind him and panic began setting in. The car horns began sounding again, with more sustained blows and colourful language. Ozzie's heart jumped into his throat when he thought he heard a gunshot followed by a series of multiple screams.

He turned to look quickly behind him as he reached the bottom of the flight of steps. Kamal and Garry were still in pursuit, and Kamal had his hand inside the internal pocket of his grey jacket. Ozzie gulped and gasped as he saw the lightning fast blur that was his life flash before his eyes. He became paralysed on the spot for a brief moment as he took a couple of steps backwards, and hitting the brick wall of the small shelter on the platform, he froze on the spot. In an instant, Kamal lost his footing and fell forward onto the remaining steps just before reaching the bottom. The firearm he was clutching escaped his grip and slid across the ground, stopping just mere feet from where Ozzie was standing.

In a flash, Ozzie hurled himself onto the gun and snatched it up and pointed it toward Kamal, who was clutching his wrist in pain, while Garry Peters stopped in his tracks, skidding upon the last step and then falling on his backside, the sneer now vanished completely from his face. A gunshot came from the top of the flight of steps, but the bullet stopped just inches from Ozzie's face, as it hit the corner of the shelter, sending shards of brick dust into his face and eyes. Ozzie saw that it was the bulky frame of Raymond Franklin, silhouetted against the evening sky and orange streetlamps. He began descending the stone steps and Ozzie seized his chance and fled toward the end of the platform and onto the tracks. He immediately skipped over the rail and onto the centre of the track, where his pace would not be slowed by the white stones and he tried his utmost to place each running step upon the wooden sleepers, to keep up speed. Ozzie was a smoker and he feared his stamina wouldn't favour his escape, but he pressed onward. He now had Kamal's gun and was sure that Garry was unarmed, and Franklin appeared to be a crap shot. He could still hear their voices crying out for him but couldn't make out what they were saying, and surely didn't intend to hang around to find out.

Ozzie began to tire and his concentration was beginning to wane. It was growing dark fast and he could barely see his feet now and his steps were starting to be misplaced and no longer hitting the sleepers, but the stones instead, their loud crackle echoing around him, making him unsure if the echo was his own or the sounds of his pursuers hot on his heels. He looked behind him but saw only dark sky and shadowy buildings. He doubled himself over to catch his breath and then continued his desperate fugue, like a convict on the run from the law.

He made for a nearby building that resembled a large warehouse. A tall floodlight was ablaze just up ahead, some twenty or more yards away, beneath a railway bridge that led to a block of flats leading into West Ealing. The light from the lamp shone down onto a pathway that went from the building to a signal box near some sidings. Ozzie ran toward the wall and collapsed against it, drawing in as much breath as he could. He could hear not so distant crackles of railway stones underfoot, as his pursuers were getting nearer. Ozzie stood still just a few more seconds. The footsteps had slowed down to walking speed. They were tired as well, great, Ozzie thought. He moved away from where he was standing and walked around the back of the building to stay out of the floodlight's radiance.

He remained there for a few more precious seconds until the footsteps resumed. He was almost certain he could hear only two sets of footsteps now. Raymond had probably stayed behind with the Jaguar whilst the other two continued the search. That meant that he was still probably the only one with a firearm, unless Raymond gave Kamal his own. Ozzie kept his ear focused on the crackling footsteps. They were like a foul beast stalking him in the night, each second, getting closer and closer to where he was. He remained still until he had a better idea of how far and whereabouts they were coming from. He began moving slowly toward the furthermost corner of the edifice and unfortunately, into the floodlight's area of effect. The footsteps stopped. Had they seen him, or were they still searching? He hugged the wall tightly and moved round the corner. He had his back to the wall of the building and looking toward the bridge, the side nearest to him was lit by the floodlight. Beyond the bridge was just a vast sea of blackness and beyond that, some three hundred yards away, stood West Ealing station, its four platforms lit by just two streetlamps. Ozzie could see a few people waiting on the platform and pacing up and down whilst they waited for the train.

A strange and hollow howling sound began rising from the furthermost railway tracks. Ozzie sighed in disbelief as he realised what was coming. A high speed train was approaching from his right hand side and each second it drew nearer, his heart raced even faster. The Inter City 125 roared past as the front driving engine car screamed like a banshee. Ozzie's heart seemed like it had stopped while the seven carriages howled past followed by the rear engine car that appeared to shout back at him with angry clamour. Ozzie remained frozen on the spot, hoping that Kamal and Garry wouldn't have taken advantage of the train's noise to sneak up on him.

There was silence again. Ozzie stayed where he was and didn't dare make a sound. Not until he was sure that they were still looking for him. A long minute passed and then another. Ozzie heard nothing more for a good three minutes. Were they hiding somewhere and lying in wait until he emerged? Or were they still far enough for him to make a desperate run for it and dash toward the bridge, eventually to be swallowed by the large bank of blackness that lay ahead of him. He knew that just at the foot of the bridge on its furthest side, was the block of flats that stood in a cluster, therefore it would conceal him from his pursuers. All he needed to do was get there, but it involved a lengthy sprint from where he was, and over a large expanse of railway tracks.

That sound again, this time from the track that lay just mere feet away from him. It wasn't a high speed track. Fortunately, it was the railway that belonged to the local train that came from Southall and Hanwell. Ozzie looked to his right and saw the two white headlights approaching. All he had to do was time it. Just perfect timing and he would have a very good chance of getting away. The train was a three carriage diesel that didn't gather too much speed between Hanwell and West Ealing, which meant that he could make a run for it just before it got too close, and it would shield him from view long enough for him to sprint past the bridge and into the darkness beyond. The streets were just ahead of that, and he would be home free. The train drew nearer and nearer and Ozzie's heart raced faster and faster. Just a few metres more...the front of the train was around twenty yards from where he was standing and travelling at no more than about twenty five miles an hour. Ozzie pushed himself away from the wall and dashed forward, past the front of the train's bright headlights that for a few instants blinded his vision, and he ran for dear life toward the bridge. He was certain he heard a shout as he shot toward the darkness that was his best friend for those precious seconds.

He sailed past the bridge and felt the tenebrous shadow engulf him as he disappeared from view of Kamal and Garry. He clambered up a small embankment of grass and gravel and crawled through a small gap in the wire fence. He looked back for a few seconds and into the darkness that he'd left behind him. He'd done it. He discarded the gun into the nearby bushes over the fence and stood still for a few seconds. He heard the cries of two men in the distance. He recognised Garry's voice for sure. He didn't really know Kamal's voice. He never really said much. Ozzie turned and headed for West Ealing high street and would then cut through the park and near the back of Sainsbury's to get home. Kamal and Garry didn't know where he lived and he was sure to get home before they could return to the Jaguar and search for him.

Ozzie emerged from the road that ran behind the high street shops and onto West Ealing's main street. His heart rate slowed down to a more acceptable level, as he mingled with the hubbub of traffic and pedestrians that had engaged their after-work gear. Ozzie had a friend that worked just across the road from where he was standing and so he waited to cross the busy street once the little green man glowed. Ozzie walked quickly across the road once the urgent sounding bleeping chirped loudly above the town's noise, and headed for the bright red neon sign that read; MARGE'S CAFÉ.

After ordering a tomato soup and a toasted egg sandwich, he sat down at a little table by a window and waited for Marge to join him once she'd finished her shift and her employee arrived to take over from her. Ozzie watched every car that drifted along the high street, hoping that he wouldn't see the dreaded Jaguar. As he bit into his sandwich, he began to lose himself in mostly ugly thoughts. Not just on the events of the past few weeks and what happened earlier on, but he also dwelt on the altercation with his friend, Pete. Ozzie didn't exactly regret everything he said – it had been some time now that he had the distinct impression that Pete was a little bit up his own arse sometimes – but he thought perhaps he could have held back a little. Ozzie's hot head and incredibly loose tongue dropped him into trouble more often than not, but he had always been one to say it how it is, regardless of whom he hurt and how.

But the thought remained. He had Pete *and* Ralf to thank for saving his skin the first time around but at that precise moment, he felt he had no one. He hadn't heard from Ralf in quite a while and when he did try to phone him, there was never any reply.

'Hello stranger,' said Marge as she pulled up a chair and sat opposite Ozzie, 'how's my boy?'

Marge was in her fifties but didn't look it unless you looked closely. She wore plenty of make-up and preferred to wear her hair in a beehive style, as a tribute to her favourite pop star, Mari Wilson. She was often mistaken for her in the streets, much to her pleasure, until people saw her up close and realised that Marge was older than her idol.

'You don't look like you usually do,' said Marge.

'What do you mean?'

'You're usually happy... full of mischief, full of life, and full of shit. That's my Ozzie!'

'Stuff's been happening,' he said, as he sipped his tomato soup from the polystyrene cup.

'What stuff? Everything alright at home with your mum and sister and all...?'

'Can I come to your place tonight?' asked Ozzie, sheepishly lowering his head and peering over the rim of his cup, like a bashful toddler.

'Of course you can,' said Marge, smiling broadly but not baring teeth, 'you know you're always welcome.'

A few years ago, Ozzie and Marge met in a smoky night-lounge bar in London. Marge was a waitress there and Ozzie took a liking to her straight away while she waited at his table. He was taken by her kindly face and warm and smiley nature and when her shift had ended a couple of hours later, they were still in that same bar at the same table chatting over soft drinks and light cocktails. Ozzie felt remarkably comfortable around her and willingly opened up about so many things. Marge was the perfect listening ear and was not shocked or moved by anything Ozzie threw her way. Marge's relationship with the rocker was a cross between mystery and enigma – the mystery part was that no one knew of her existence, not even Pete and Ralf – the enigmatic part was the underlying question of what kind of relationship it was. Ozzie really liked her and felt compelled to be in her company at every given opportunity. Marge felt the same and always found it hard to end their evenings together. Despite their definitive chemistry, they never laid a hand upon each other, save for the odd fleeting kiss and caress here and there.

Marge turned the key in her front door and stepped inside, with Ozzie following close behind. As she flicked the light switch in the hall, Ozzie felt surprised by the lack of the usual clutter of clothes and various objects that would often be strewn about the place. Marge had being tidying up after herself. The place even smelled cleaner, although the musty odour of clothes and shoes didn't really bother him too much. His own bedroom was of a similar quality anyway, but with a worse smell. Marge lent upon the wall whilst she slid off her boots and headed into the kitchen and brought the kettle to life. She looked at Ozzie and smiled broadly. He reciprocated.

'I really like having you here, ya know,' she announced, with a wink of her big brown eyes.

'I like being here,' replied the rocker, 'really a lot…'

Marge walked over to him as the hissing of the kettle grew gradually louder. She took his hands in hers and kissed him on the lips, slowly and gently. Ozzie felt his legs begin to tremble and his loins tingled with excitement. Tonight, she looked more beautiful than ever, especially when she smiled. Ozzie placed a hand around her waist and drew her closer to him and pressed his lips tightly upon hers. He tickled her mouth with his tongue and she brought hers out to collide with his. The kettle clicked as Ozzie began raising her skirt and feeling the smooth skin of her shapely legs. He felt it was time to build a bridge that was a long time coming. They made love there and then, against the wall near the door, against the kitchen sink, on the floor, and once they were both totally naked, Ozzie hoisted Marge up and onto the worktop that was near the kitchen window. He yanked down the blind with one hand, and then continued to lose himself in the moment. And what a moment it was. He wished it would never end.

Printed in Great Britain
by Amazon